Also by Antoine Vanner:

The Dawlish Chronicles

Britannia's Innocent
February – May 1864

Britannia's Wolf
September 1877 - February 1878

Britannia's Reach
November 1879 - April 1880

Britannia's Shark
April – September 1881

Britannia's Spartan
June 1859 and April - August 1882

Britannia's Amazon
April – August 1882
(Includes bonus short story *Britannia's Eye*)

Britannia's Mission
August 1883 – February 1884

Britannia's Gamble
March 1884 – February 1885

Being incidents in the lives of:

Nicholas Dawlish R.N.
Born: Shrewsbury 16.12.1845
Died: Zeebrugge 23.04.1918

and

Florence Dawlish, née Morton
Born: Northampton 17.06.1855
Died: Portsmouth 12.05.1946

Britannia's Morass

The Dawlish Chronicles
September – December 1884

With bonus short story:

Britannia's Collector

By

Antoine Vanner

Old Salt Press

Library of Congress Cataloguing-in-Publication Data:

Antoine Vanner 1945 -

Britannia's Morass / Antoine Vanner.

Paperback: ISBN: 978-1-943404-31-5

E-Book: ISBN: 978-1-943404-32-2

(The Dawlish Chronicles Volume 9)

Cover design by Sara Lee Paterson

Published by Old Salt Press

Old Salt Press, LLC is based in Jersey City, New Jersey with an affiliate in New Zealand

For more information about our titles go to www.oldsaltpress.com

To learn more about the Dawlish Chronicles go to:
www.dawlishchronicles.com

Britannia's Morass

Prologue

Hampstead, London, February 1884

The dog was dead, poisoned two days before by meat thrown across the wall. There was no danger yet of a replacement for it was obvious, when they had watched her walk him on Hampstead Heath, that his owner had doted on him. They knew that widowed and childless women of middle years mourned lost pets with extravagant grief and did not replace them for months, or years, or ever.

The wall was no problem either. A section of hair mattress thrown across the spikes along the top allowed one to be heaved up to straddle it and drag the other up behind him. Once over, there were bushes and shadows enough to mask movement towards the villa. French windows at the rear gave on to the terrace and their rubber-soled tennis shoes hushed the sounds of their approach. Entry was easy, a circle of glass cut by diamond, a hand passed through, a key turned, the knob gently turned and a tug that told that there were no bolts. The door swung open and they were inside what must be the drawing room, air heavy with the scent of potpourri. Even after so many such intrusions, they still marvelled that so many wealthy houseowners took such scant precautions.

They moved with infinite caution, even though there was every indication that the villa's four occupants were sound asleep. Gaslight seeping around the edges of a blind on the first floor, just visible from the road outside, had identified what must be the mistress's bedroom. After it first came on, it had remained so for almost an hour before being extinguished. She might have been reading before sleep. Lights at windows on the smaller windows on the top floor had identified the rooms of the cook and her gardener husband and of the single maid. By now, those windows too had been dark for well over an hour.

They had watched the occupants' daily movements for over a week. One of them had struck up a conversation in a public house with the elderly gardener – his name was Fletcher. He had stood him a pint and given him a tip about the morrow's two-thirty at Doncaster. She was a good employer, Fletcher had said, more tolerant, more generous than her husband. He'd been a stockbroker who had died three years before and nobody missed him.

The door that led to the hallway creaked when opened a fraction. A drop of oil on each hinge cured that. It was precautions like this that distinguished the proud professional from the amateur driven by crass greed or destitution. Faint moonlight filtered through the stained glass of the front door at the hallway's end, enough to illuminate the stairs rising on the right, the outlines of a coat and umbrella stand, flowers in a vase on a table, other doors.

There was no need to light the dark lantern, not yet. They tried each door in turn – no haste, no hurry, the tiny oil can employed again when needed, for they knew nothing of the location of the individual rooms. Queries to the gardener about that, however roundabout, might have raised suspicion. They opened doors to the dining room, the library, a small parlour and a breakfast room before, at last, they found the study. They entered, locked the door – the key was on the inside – and drew the curtains. Only now did they light the dark lantern.

No word exchanged, they emptied the writing desk first, drawer by drawer, not pausing to examine the contents. They moved then to the glass-fronted book case. It contained what looked like ledgers on the upper shelves and loose portfolios of documents on those beneath. They might have been the widow's husband's, careful records of forgotten transactions, but they loaded them anyway into the two sacks they had brought. It was a relief that there was no safe, for that was what they had most feared. They checked behind the pictures on the wall and opened the frames of the two photographs on the desk. They showed the dear-departed himself, bewhiskered and glowering, and an old pair, dressed in the fashions of thirty years before, who might have been her parents. It was unlikely, but they had known of items secreted in such places. This time there were none. In ten minutes, every scrap of paper, and nothing else, was in the sacks.

It was time to go, to retrace their steps towards the drawing room's French window, to flit across the terrace and wait in the shadows at the wall. One produced a child's bird-shaped china waterpipe. He filled it from a small corked phial. Forethought and planning were essential in this profession. He put the tail to his mouth and began to blow. The sound from the gap beneath the beak was the trill of a nightingale. He blew only for a few seconds at a time, paused, blew again, varying the durations of the warbling. That a woodpigeon was cooing somewhere nearby made it sound all the more unexceptionable.

The clip-clop of unhurried hooves announced that the four-wheeler that had sheltered close by was on its way. Had the roadway been anything but deserted, it would have stopped and the driver would have dismounted and make as if to examine the horse for lameness. It took less than a minute to cross the wall again, pulling up the laden sacks, dropping them on the far side, and they were ready as the carriage approached. It did not slacken its speed. The rhythm of the hooves never faltered and they kept pace with it on their soft soles, opening the door, swinging the sacks inside, following themselves.

The sedate pace continued until Primrose Hill. Only then, with the grind of other wheels and clatter of other hooves around, did the driver urge the horse into a slow trot.

There was just one stop to make, an address in St. John's Wood. They would deposit the sacks behind the house and leave without knowing the name of the resident, or ever wanting to know it. Clients liked discretion and paid well for it.

Another job well done.

*

It was after nine o'clock when Mrs. Hodgson, the char who came in daily, entered the study to clean it, the last of her duties on the ground floor. She did not immediately notice that the desktop and its letter rack were clear of paper, nor that the book case had been emptied but, when she did, she thought nothing of it. There must be some reorganisation in hand that she had not been told of. It was only when she remarked about it to the house maid, Hannah, that concern was first aroused. Hannah went to the study, found the desk-drawers as empty as the book case, was alarmed. She brought the cook to survey the mystery, who in turn called in her husband. Nobody had said anything yet to Mrs. Chalmers-Bolger. Always a late riser, she liked to relax in the small parlour after breakfast with a novel and a cup of chocolate and did not want to be disturbed before eleven.

"Mr. Fletcher asks if he may have a word with you, ma'am." The cook was reluctant to face her mistress's irritation. Better to leave it to her husband.

"Is it about the gladioli again? I thought that he knew what I wanted. No? Then send him in. And make sure he takes off his boots this time."

He told what he had found, a rum business, it was, but, even before he finished, Mrs. Chalmers-Bolger was rushing towards the study. Hands trembling, she pulled out each drawer. She saw them empty but still turned them upside down and shook them as if the contents might somehow reappear.

"Somebody's been here!" She turned on Hannah, most recent of her employees, eight years' service. "You know about this, do you, you stupid girl? Tell me! Some follower of yours! Some young man who's been making sheep's eyes at you! Tell me!"

Hannah had thrown her apron over her face, was descending into hysterics and Mr. Fletcher was beginning to protest that she was an honest girl, honest as the day was long, none better.

Only then did the full force of the loss hit Mrs. Chalmers-Bolger. Frederick's — Lord Frederick's — letters, written on thick light-mauve paper, with matching envelopes addressed in the elegant Italic hand that she so loved, almost as much as his dear messages themselves. There had been four bundles, each tied with a ribbon, breathless and eternal love incarnate, treasures beyond price that she knew she would cherish to her dying day.

Anger was flooding in now to drown her sense of loss. There was no doubt as to what had happened. *How sharper than a serpent's tooth it is*

9

to have a thankless child,' Fredrick had once written so poetically. His scheming family, his dissolute sons, his avaricious daughters, their grasping spouses, were all intent, and with success so far, in making it impossible for him to declare his love openly, to make her his wife. Now, when his vast legal complications were close to resolution, the theft was the first step in some new and devilish plot to prevent her marriage to him.

She was beginning to weep and, weak at the knees, had to sit down. Ashamed to be seen like this by her servants, she waved them away. The cook and housemaid retreated but Mr. Fletcher stood his ground.

"It ain't nobody in this house, ma'am," he said. "Nor Mrs. Hodgson neither. We should send for the police. I can go and –"

"No!"

Her voice was almost a scream. Frederick would not want it, she knew. An image blazed in her mind of articles in the penny-press, of reporters descending gleefully on the house to bribe the staff, perhaps even lurid drawings in the Illustrated Police News. She had once come on Hannah reading the shocking publication and had confiscated it before studying it cover-to-cover herself with guilty pleasure. A peer of the realm could not afford such humiliation. It would break Frederick's noble heart.

She did not know afterwards how long she sat there, sometimes sobbing, sometimes quietly distraught, bereft of her treasure, the pain worse, far worse, than when her husband had died so suddenly.

But at last she realised that the triumph of Frederick's children, vipers and jackals though they be, was not complete. All was not lost. She left the study. Hannah was waiting outside, pity on her face, but she gestured to her to stand aside and ascended the stairs alone. She went to her bedroom and locked the door, then reached beneath her pillow.

There, as always, were the first three letters Frederick had ever written to her, his awkward excuses for the accident by which he had first seen her, his confession of love. It had been as hesitant and as touching as a schoolboy's first declaration, she thought. There too was his photograph, signed and dedicated to his darling Margaret, his features still resolute and handsome, those of a younger man, despite the burdens of high office that he had carried with such distinction for three decades.

And that was her consolation.

Take whatever else they might, they could not take him from her.

Her rock, her protector, her own.

Her Frederick.

Chapter 1

September 1884

Florence did not allow herself to weep after Nicholas left.

It had been a perfect day, she told herself, the best of this European tour that they had so long planned. She would be grateful for this day all her life, no matter how it had ended. They had been happy in each other as the paddle-steamer beat slowly up the vineyard-fringed Elbe valley from Dresden, each moment precious for the knowledge that he had survived so much in East Africa and on the Red Sea coast earlier in the year. Only when she had been to the naval hospital at Haslar with him, to visit the wounded he had brought back, did she realise how desperate the fighting at Tamai had been. He had made light of it to her. His term of command of HMS *Leonidas* had since ended and he was waiting for appointment to another ship.

When they had arrived back at the city's landing stage, the September evening's air was still warm. They had declined an offer from an expectant cabman and had walked instead back through the city's magnificent streets and squares to the Gasthof Alt Engelsdorf.

The telegram was waiting there. She knew that its content was serious when Nicholas went silent and took it to their bedroom to decipher it alone. He looked even more unhappy when he told her what it said, what he must now do.

Leave tonight, immediately, for Taranto, at the heel of Italy, join a Royal Navy vessel there.

What would come after that, the telegram had not said. She had speculated with Nicholas that it might have something to do with what now filled the British newspapers. A massive military expedition was to thrust up the Nile from Egypt to rescue General Charles Gordon, under siege by fanatic rebels in Khartoum. Nicholas had met him once, in Pekin, when he had been a boy, had remembered him fondly. Not that that counted. He would go anyway, wherever he was sent, do what whatever was asked of him, and more. She had known that since she had first met him and she had accepted it.

She had guessed who had sent that telegram. Even now she was not sure what exactly Topcliffe did or was, but he had called on Nicholas before. Each time he had obeyed, and each time it had almost killed him. And her too, in Cuba. The reminder was her scarred left arm, stiff and often aching. Later, when Nicholas had been in the Far East, she had had other dealings with the calculating old man – an admiral, she understood, though one never seen in uniform. Those were dealings that she had been instructed to keep secret even from Nicholas himself.

While he consulted train time tables, she packed for him. There was an express to Prague in less than two hours and from there he must find other connections to Italy. She saw that he was guilty about leaving her here. He gave her money, more than sufficient, to continue the tour if she wished. She might even telegraph her friend Agatha to join her, he said. She had nodded, but knew she wouldn't.

The final twenty minutes had been the worst. The realisation that this might be their last time together remained unspoken. Nicholas had mentioned that his will was lodged with Carlton and Bagshot, Solicitors, in Southsea, but she had hushed him. She had forced herself to laugh, and he tried to smile when she made him sit on his trunk to hold it closed while she tightened the straps.

"It's better that you don't come to the station," he said. "There's so little time anyway."

"It's better that way."

And then, for what seemed an eternity, they sat on the edge of the bed, holding each other in silence.

"It's time to go now, Nicholas," she said at last. "You'll need to have them fetch a cab for you."

"I love you, Florence."

"I love you, Nicholas."

And then he went.

*

She stayed in Dresden for three more days, as had been planned. A telegram arrived from Nicholas. He was at Florence itself, changing

13

trains, still heading south, and he made a lame joke that linked her name with the city's. She spent another day at the Semper Gallery in the Zwinger Palace, but the Old Masters there seemed to hold less delight now than when she had viewed them with Nicholas a few days before. She would have gone that evening to see *Der Freischütz* at the opera house – she had seen it before, in Munich, and it had delighted her – but at the last moment she could not bring herself to sit in an audience as a woman alone. It had been different with Nicholas, even though she suspected that the five operas they had attended in various cities in recent weeks might have bored him, despite all his protestations to the contrary. She loved him for that and for the touch of his hand on hers as the music had swelled, for the obvious pride he took in her as they had passed out through the lobby at the end. Baedeker in hand, she visited each of the baroque city's glories in the next two days but the joy she had felt in previous such expeditions was now gone. She sent coloured postcards to her cook and maid back at the villa in the Portsmouth suburb of Southsea, and to her parents and brothers. A full half-dozen, all different views, went to Nicholas's six-year old half-brother in Shrewsbury and as many again to his sister Susan's family in Preston. Over several days, she wrote a long letter to Agatha about the Elbe Valley, the Semper and the opera.

And all the while a sense of dread oppressed her, trying, and failing, to ignore it as she might. It drew her to the main railway station each early afternoon, for *The Times* of two-days past could be bought at the newsstand there shortly after midday. There was little new about Egypt, though the reports from there were still lengthy and verbose. The relief force was still gathering, eminent names were assuming command of its components, the first flotillas of transports had already set out upriver from Cairo. It would be a difficult campaign, the correspondent emphasised, control of the Nile critical for success. Nicholas had experience of river warfare, she knew. It had been in Paraguay, though he had always refused to tell her about what had happened there. With that experience, it would make sense if he were to have a role in the expedition. The names of other naval officers had been mentioned in *The Times*, but his was not She told herself that he would be safe, safe

14

enough at least, if he was on the river. It was in the barren desert wastes on either side that the greatest threat would come from the cruel and fanatic enemy. Yet however much she tried to convince herself, the dread remained.

The plan had been to move on to Weimar for three days. She debated with herself about going there now and anticipated little pleasure in it on her own. If she had even had her maid with her, it would be somehow better but she guessed that Nicholas would feel guiltier still about leaving her if she did not travel on. He had known how dear it was to her to expand her cultural horizon, and the city of Goethe and Schiller, its galleries and its opera house, were on her list. So she went, for his sake, not for hers.

It was a mistake.

The days there were even emptier than she had anticipated. She ticked off the sights in her Baedeker and dutifully commented on them in her diary each evening. She ate meals alone at hotel tables, subject to hostile glances from women and leers from their husbands. Britain was beckoning. Her routines there. Her regular oversight, as a trustee, of the management of the Sailor's Rest at Portsmouth. Her increasing acceptance by other naval wives despite her origins. Agatha's friendship. She would end the tour here, she decided, would forget Berlin, Hanover, Amsterdam and The Hague, and return directly to Britain.

There was no telegram from Nicholas before she left Weimar, even though the hotel had been booked in advance and he knew its address. She forced herself not to read significance into that.

*

The two-day journey had been continuous, one of comfortless sleep snatched in railway carriages, of food bolted in station restaurants, of a rough Channel crossing, but she was home at last in the villa at Albert Grove. Ten hours sleep refreshed her. She arose, filtered through the post that had arrived in her absence and found nothing of importance. Mrs. Singleton, who preferred to be addressed as Cook, a title she regarded, with good reason, as an honour, brought a light meal. Well packed, the cheap porcelain souvenirs Florence had brought for her and for Susan, the housemaid, had survived the journey, small milk jugs and sugar bowls decorated with pictures of Munich and of Dresden. Their delight in them touched her and she was sorry that she had not brought them more.

The house seemed very empty now. She had not felt it so keenly before, when Nicholas was overseas, but his duties in recent months had allowed him to live intermittently in Albert Grove. She had become accustomed to the comfortable companionship, the silences no less than the conversations, the walks together, the outings. Already she was regretting the loss. Awareness of her childlessness came back, as so often, but she thrust it away as she always did. There could never be any children, and there was no help for it, and it was better not to brood on it. She would immerse herself, as she had for three years now, in support of the Sailor's Rest.

The afternoon was warm and her walk took twenty minutes. The Rest, a converted public house, provided clean beds and baths and simple meals for seamen ashore and support and advice for families left behind. An indomitable spinster and temperance-advocate, Miss Agnes Weston, had previously set up such a hostel in Plymouth. When she had suggested a similar establishment in Portsmouth, Florence had been an active supporter and had helped supervise the building's conversion. It was well established by now and she devoted a few hours each week to overseeing contracts, accounts and maintenance.

There had been nothing of concern during her absence but she made it a point to inspect the kitchen anyway and to examine the last month's accounts. There had been one request to see her, from a seaman's wife.

"It's good you're back, ma'am," the superintendent, Mr. Selden, a retired bosun, said. "She's in a bad way, worried to death, she is. She wouldn't tell me about it. But somebody told her that she'd heard that you might listen."

"Have you her address? Good! Send somebody to her, tell her I'll see her here at eleven o'clock tomorrow."

Mrs Harvey was pale and thin, poorly dressed, twenty-five perhaps and looking forty, one child by the hand, a baby in her arms and her interesting condition all too obvious. Florence seated her, admired the children, sent for tea. It was five minutes before she learned that the lady's husband had been posted to the Mediterranean Fleet at Malta four months previously. She had heard nothing from him since.

"I wouldn't worry," Florence said. "You'll surely get a letter soon. If there had been an accident, you'd have been informed." She realised, even as she said it, that it was a stupid thing to say, for Mrs. Harvey began to weep.

"It ain't that ma'am. It ain't that. It's –" She was sobbing now, looking away in embarrassment.

Florence left her chair, went across, took the baby from her, held it. She wasn't sure if it was a boy or a girl. Its clothes were threadbare and smelling of urine but it still smiled at her as it settled against her shoulder.

"It can't be that bad, Mrs. Harvey. Whatever it is, we'll do something about it. Whatever it is, you don't need to be ashamed."

But she was, and it took ten minutes to wring the story from her word by word. The baby had been sick, had needed medicine. She lacked money. Her husband had often forgotten to remit part of his pay.

"Joe's a good man, he is. Took the pledge three times, he did, an' this time he promised me he'll keep it, no matter what. But I didn't have nothing and I was two months late on the rent and I'd pawned all I could an' the baby was sick again and –"

"You went to a moneylender." Florence had heard the same story several times before.

A nod. More tears.

"How much?"

"Ten bob, ma'am."

"And how much now?"

"Four pounds, he wants."

At a hundred percent a month, compound interest, it did not take long. And double again in another month, eight pounds, sixteen four weeks later.

"Did he suggest anything… anything you wouldn't like, Mrs. Harvey?" Many of such debts were cancelled that way, she had heard.

"No, ma'am. Not when I'm like this." She glanced down at the dress stretched tight over her swollen abdomen.

The older child, a little boy, was upset by his mother's distress and looked about to cry himself.

"Why don't you draw me a picture? I'd love that, I'd like to put it on my wall." Florence gave him a pencil and a sheet of paper. He seemed unsure what to do with it, so she drew a matchstick man herself. "Can you make one like that for me?"

He nodded, got busy.

His mother was silent, was looking out the window, desolate, aware probably, Florence thought, that she had said all she could, that she waited now for judgement.

It was beyond the Rest's remit.

I can afford it myself, would never miss it. Ending the tour had saved a lot. And Nicholas wouldn't begrudge it either. But…

She had heard tales just as heart-rending before but some had been mean deceptions. She had fallen for them, had felt a fool afterwards.

"Here's something to help you now." She opened her purse, gave Mrs. Harvey a half-crown and the little boy tuppence. "Somebody will be coming to talk to you about it. Maybe tonight. If not, then tomorrow."

The superintendent's wife, kindly but hard headed, well acquainted with the realities of Portsmouth's slums, would visit. If she was satisfied, her husband would see to it that two of his friends would visit the lender. They'd have four of Florence's sovereigns with them. The lender might indeed be induced to settle for less, how, she would not want to know. If so, then Mr. Selden's two messengers would be welcome to drink her health with the remainder.

"God bless you, ma'am."

The woman was standing up to go, pulling the little boy with her. His drawing had been a scribble but before he left Florence pinned on the wall behind her desk and told him it was beautiful.

The holiday had ended.

Friday, September nineteenth.

Life was back to normal.

*

Florence was practising piano four days later, her injured arm aching from the effort, striking occasional false notes, but still persisting, when she heard the electric door-bell shrilling. The maid looked sombre when she brought the telegram in on a silver tray. That was with good reason. They seldom brought good news.

"That will be all, Susan." Her hands were trembling, but did not want that seen.

She ripped the envelope open. The message was a long one, the longest telegram she had ever seen, the pasted printed strips covering almost an entire page. Her eyes ran immediately to the end, saw Nicholas's name. Relief coursed through her. He gave no explanation why he was sending it from Suez, not Cairo. He was well, but she should not expect to hear from him for at least four months. That surprised her. Newspaper correspondents seemed to have little trouble sending despatches, not yet at least, and he must surely be able to send her an occasional letter. He must have a good reason, she thought, though it did not comfort her. There was no need to worry about him, he said. She'd heard him say that too often before to believe it now. And the end he said he loved her. She put the message in the casket in which she kept every letter she had of him, from the very first. Her hand trembled as she closed the lid. She hoped that more, many more, would follow.

From now on she would take not just the *Morning Post* – Nicholas's favourite, solidly Tory – but the *Times* and *Telegraph* as well. All had reputable journalists with the troops. She bought a large cork board, a packet of coloured glass-headed pins and a map of Egypt. It was a disappointment that it showed only the northern part of the Sudan and the Nile's great loop there, with only scant details to either side. She hung the board on the study wall, pinned the map to it, and determined to follow progress as future reports indicated.

Yet, even so, the days dragged. She wrote to Agatha, told her she had returned early, hoped that she would come down to Southsea, as she so often did, to spend a weekend with her.

The reply was almost by return. It surprised her.

Come to London immediately, Agatha wrote. She needed Florence's help *'like two years ago'*.

The spiriting from the country of Agatha's errant brother, Oswald, had been the least of it then, had been the prelude to something far, far worse. Florence hoped that he had not been stupid enough to return in disguise and that the sordid business, kept secret from Nicholas for so long, was not rearing its head again.

Agatha had already reserved a room for her at the Charing Cross Hotel for two nights. The bill was already settled and she would be offended if Florence insisted in paying herself.

It was a sensitive gesture, one that spared Florence the embarrassment of coming to Agatha's father's Piccadilly Mansion. Her own father and her brother, Jack, still worked there as coachmen, the fourth generation to serve the Kegworth family.

And she had once been a housemaid there herself.

Agatha had rescued her from that.

She could not refuse her.

Chapter 2

A letter with an American stamp arrived just before Florence left for London. It was good news. Mrs. Mabel Bushwick, a friend valued almost as much as Agatha, and no less resolute, would be in England in two weeks' time. Representing the *Columbia Home Gazette*, she was coming to prepare a series of articles about women's education, *Our Sisters' Road to Freedom,* as she put it. She looked forward to visiting Southsea. There was no reference to the acid attack that had cost her so much pain during her previous visit. Mabel was not a woman who complained.

Florence arrived in London in early afternoon, registered at the Charing Cross Hotel, and unpacked. The hotel was built at the front of the railway station and when she looked down on the cobbled forecourt, where cabs and carriages came and went, she remembered nights there two years before when men who followed her had loitered there. It was a time best forgotten, one that had alerted her to a world of foul corruption which she had never known existed. Even now, bound by a promise to that cold old serpent, Topcliffe, she could never speak of it to Nicholas.

A page-boy from the hotel carried a message to the Piccadilly mansion, not to Agatha, but to Florence's own father. The lad was back a half-hour later. This evening would be convenient. She had another task for him now, to go to the public house half-way down Villiers Street, immediately next to the hotel and station, to reserve the private upstairs room she had booked there several times before. She spent two hours then in the National Gallery – Trafalgar Square was close – and the pictures there were some compensation for lost opportunities on the disrupted European tour. Two evening newspapers, purchased as she returned, had nothing new to tell about developments in Egypt or the Sudan. There was little else. A by-election in Aberdeenshire, a new board school in Streatham opened by Princess Helena, a train derailed in Norfolk but with minor injuries only. Two Russian nihilists, guilty of a bomb outrage in a crowded Paris theatre, had been guillotined in public. Wales had suffered flooding after torrential rain.

Her father was waiting for her in the upstairs room, overjoyed to see her, as always, but with the slight deference that always pained her when they met nowadays. He saw her as a lady now, she knew, an officer's wife, treated as an equal by the daughter of the household where she herself had once been in service. The Kegworths were generous employers but, however well paid and valued, her father was still a servant. He was wearing his private Sunday-best, not his livery. His services were not required that evening.

"His Lordship don't go out much into society anymore when he's in London," he said. "He wouldn't come here ever if it wasn't for Hyperion business, board meetings and suchlike. Never attends the House no more neither. Not since Lord Oswald... not since he went away. It broke his father's heart, nearly killed him, it did."

"And his mother?"

"Stays in Northamptonshire. The shame of it nearly killed her..."

Agatha had said as much before, that her parents, Lord and Lady Kegworth, had never recovered from their eldest son's public shaming and his ignominious flight ahead of an arrest warrant. Florence herself had arranged that flight with the aid of an American who called himself Henry Judson Raymond.

Food came, ordered from the chop-house next door.

Her father was avid for her stories of the tour, proud at mention of the operas and the galleries and the leisured progress from city to city.

"I never dreamed a daughter of mine would have a life like that –" He reached across the table and touched her hand. "And Captain Dawlish too. A good man, a very good man."

"You may call him 'Nicholas', Father," she said. "He'd prefer it if you did."

But he would never let himself call Nicholas that, she knew. They had met only twice, father-in-law and son-in-law, both times in this room. They had striven to be affable for her sake but neither had been at his ease. The gap had been too great.

"Called away to Egypt, is he, urgent like? Important work there, responsible, I'll wager. He'll be the right man, no doubt of it. You chose well, Florrie."

She knew that the gulf was widening with each year. Her life must seem impossibly remote, luxurious even. He could not imagine the economies required to rent that villa in Southsea, to fund that long-delayed tour, the need to maintain appearances on a modest naval salary. And, not either, the worries that haunted Nicholas each year when the revenues from his Shropshire farms once more disappointed.

"I imagine that Agatha's been very busy." Florence tried not to sound as if she was probing.

"Lady Agatha's always busy." Even in private he could never bring himself to drop the title. "What with her leaned friends, and her studies and her meetings, she's never still. And there's been the terrible business of Mrs. Chalmers-Bolger. You remember her?"

She did, though it took an effort. A frequent guest of the Kegworths, a school-friend of Agatha's mother. A plain, colourless and timorous woman who had once spoken kindly to Florence when she had tripped and spilled tea over her skirt when she was serving her. It could have happened anybody, she had told the trembling fifteen-year old maid, there was no need to be upset.

And now, some terrible business.

"What happened?"

"Drowned in Hampstead ponds, she was." He dropped his voice. "Of unsound mind, the coroner said. It had to be. Her cook and her gardener and her maid all said she hadn't been troubled for months. They didn't know why. She didn't sleep much, used to break down crying and didn't want nobody to see it. Lady Agatha spoke at the inquest too, said that the poor lady hadn't been herself since her husband died. An' afterwards she moved heaven and earth to find a vicar who'd give the poor woman Christian burial in consecrated ground. Her own vicar wouldn't, despite what the coroner said."

"Did Agatha's mother come to the funeral?"

23

"The only time she left the estate these two years. Fair upset she was too. She left it to Lady Agatha to help sort things out."

"What sort of things?"

"With the solicitor. An' we was up and down to the poor woman's house in Hampstead. Seeing to personal matters, like."

And that, Florence recognised, was as much as he would say. It was a matter of integrity for her father never to pry into the affairs of his employers. He knew his place, was loyal to the Kegworths and proud to serve them, was proud also of the respect and good remuneration he received in return. He was grateful that His Lordship had lent money to his elder son to allow him set up livery stables in Northampton. And Agatha, only a few years Florence's senior, had advanced her from maid to the status of paid companion when she had recognised her hunger for knowledge, had helped make her a lady, had made possible the meeting with the officer and gentleman who had married her.

Afterwards, her father walked her the two hundred yards back to the hotel and parted from her outside.

She back to her world, he to his.

A million miles apart.

*

They met at ten next morning, as they often had before, in the hotel's coffee-room. Agatha, large, clumsy, myopic, and as untidy as ever, beamed when she saw Florence. She in turn flushed with affection. And something more as well, though hard to define. The bond forged in that dreadful winter in Thrace six years before, when they had faced death and worse together. Pride that they had not broken, that they had stood by each other like sisters at the final, nightmare, climax. And more, the squalid scandal of two years before, discovery of an evil that reached into Agatha's own family. They had stood together then also.

There was news to be caught up on. Florence's tour, Nicholas's call to duty, return to normal life at Southsea. Shared delight about Mabel's forthcoming visit, for Agatha too had received notice of it. And she, first woman to have been elected a Fellow, had presented yet another paper to the Royal Society, something about mathematics that went beyond Florence's comprehension and, she suspected, most others' also. The affairs of the Rosewood House orphanage at Chigwell – a reminder, unremarked upon, of the past scandal – were demanding much of Agatha's time. Ill-health had forced Father and Mamma, to live quieter lives and darling Oswald was living in a villa on Corfu. He always asked to be remembered warmly to Florence when he wrote. It had not always been so.

Despite the urgency of Agatha's invitation, she had made no mention yet of needing help. Florence sensed that she was hesitating, was unsure how to raise the subject. She did so at last herself.

"Is there something that we'd better not talk about here?" There were perhaps a dozen people in the room, mainly ladies meeting in twos and threes, and the chance of being overheard was low. But confidences were never easy in public places.

"We should go to your room, Florence."

There were two wing-chairs there, a small table between.

"Do you remember Mrs. Chalmers-Bolger, Florence?"

She hoped she looked surprised, did not want to mention that her father had spoken of her.

"A friend of your mother's, wasn't she, Agatha? A kind woman. I remember her well."

"My godmother. She was always good to me. I used to call her Aunt Margaret, though she wasn't really." A pause, and then the words came in a rush. "She drowned herself. She'd planned it, she knew what she was doing. She put stones in her pockets and filled a bag with more and hung it around her neck. She did it at night, so nobody could see. She waded into one of the Hampstead ponds. They found her next day."

The details, and the determination needed, made it all the more poignant. She had always seemed a colourless but well-intentioned woman, diffident and retiring, in awe of her husband, in awe even of Agatha's mother. It was difficult to imagine her planning the mechanics of her own death, much less executing them.

25

"We can't judge, Agatha. Perhaps she was ill. Maybe it was something incurable and painful. Maybe cancer. She might have thought that it was better that way."

"No! The coroner demanded a post-mortem examination. There was nothing like that."

"When did you last see her?"

"Eighteen months, two years ago. There was little contact after Mamma stopped coming to London after... after Oswald left. But, when I saw her then, she looked happier than she'd ever seemed before. She seemed – it's hard to find the exact words. She seemed transformed, radiant, like a young girl. Her complexion, her hair, fashionable clothes, jewellery too. Things she'd never concerned herself much about that before. It was if she was ten years younger, even more."

"I'd heard that her husband had died."

"Two or three years before that."

"Did it affect her badly?"

"I think it was a relief. Mother told me that she thought that love had never grown between them. Her father made her marry him because he was a stockbroker, up and coming then, and wealthy later. But he was an unpleasant man, a tyrant. She had a lot to put up with. And there was talk too of other things."

"Women?"

Agatha nodded. "A lot of other women. He broke her heart."

"Did she have children?"

"None."

His death must have been a deliverance for her, Florence thought. She would have started to live again. It was not unusual for widows.

"But something must have changed since you last saw her, Agatha."

"I talked to her servants. It was over the last year, they said. worst in the last six months. Something was upsetting her. She didn't worry about her appearance any more, hardly ate, had broken sleep. For whole days she didn't get out of bed. They heard her sobbing behind closed doors. If only I'd have known, if only Mamma had known..."

"Did she leave a note?"

"No. Nothing. I was present when the house was searched."

"Were there relations?"

"Only a nephew. He's in Hong Kong. Some kind of official. Too far for him to come back."

"It might have been —" Florence hesitated. It was a delicate matter, normally unmentionable, hard to suggest even to Agatha. "It might have been the change of life."

"Not that, Florence. It was money. I only found out when I talked to her solicitor. A Mr. Brandon, he was her executor. Her husband had left her more than comfortable. And now she was penniless, everything gone in less than a year. She'd even mortgaged her house. If she'd have involved the solicitor, he'd have talked her out of it, but she didn't. What she'd received for the mortgage was gone also."

"Foolish investments? Speculation?" Florence said. Nicholas was always strong upon the subject. Better stick to Consols, he said, solid as the Bank of England, nothing could go wrong.

"That's what I thought too, Father also, Florence. But no, just payments, hundreds of pounds at a time, Mr. Brandon told me. All to different names and different accounts, people that neither he or her servants or my Mamma had ever heard of. There was nothing left, nothing for her nephew, not enough for the hundred pounds each she'd left her cook and gardener in her will, and fifty to her maid. She'd have been in the workhouse if she'd lived another month. Mamma paid the bequests to the servants. She paid for the funeral too. It would have been a pauper's grave if she hadn't."

Poverty was hard enough to bear for those who'd grown up with it, Florence knew. But for those who'd been bred to affluence, who assumed endless certainty and comfort and security, it could be immeasurably worse.

"It must have been shame that killed her," she said.

"It was worse than that, Florence. Shame murdered her."

Calm anger in Agatha's voice, all the more chilling from a woman who was naturally so benevolent, artless even.

"I want your help, Florence. To find out who drove to her death a simple, kind and well-meaning woman who never did harm to anybody. To know at the very least who did it, to bring them to account if I can and to …."

But Florence wasn't hearing the words. The moment was on her again, a moment such as she had known before three times in her life.

When she had joined Agatha to help those refugees in that caravanserai in Thrace.

When she had accompanied Nicholas to Cuba.

When she had brawled on a Portsmouth Street to try, without success, to save a wretched girl from abduction.

Decisions that had been unwise, even suicidal, as they almost proved. Decisions any sane woman would have shied away from but decisions, and commitments, that could not have been shirked if she was to maintain her self-respect.

"You're more practical than I am, Florence," Agatha was saying. "You understand people, and how to get things done and… and you have certain contacts."

Contacts that I don't want to renew if I can help it. But I remember too a gentle and caring woman making light of hot tea that I spilled over her.

Her decision was made.

"When do we begin, Agatha?"

"This afternoon. Two o'clock. We have an appointment with Mr. Brandon."

*

The offices of Dashwood, Dashwood, Willoughby and Brandon were in Chancery Lane, an easy walk from the hotel. Florence guessed that few private clients, and then only the most exalted, entered the opulent premises and that most of the business conducted there involved banking or commerce. Mr. Brandon had been a friend of Mr. Chalmers-Bolger, had managed his personal as well as his business affairs and could never have envisaged how those would end. When the worst had happened, he had contacted Agatha's father, a director of the Hyperion Consortium, for which he had acted on numerous occasions. Agatha had volunteered to deal with him in the aftermath of the tragedy.

"He was embarrassed about going through her private things," Agatha had said. "Clothing, personal items, anything of that sort. It wasn't usual for his firm. But there had to be an inventory. He asked if I might accompany his clerk when he made it. And because she might have left a letter the police were there too. It was horrible, but," the memory was clearly painful, "there was almost nothing. Not just no letter. Her jewellery was all gone, the better clothes also, even things like decent combs and hairbrushes. Just pawn tickets in her dressing table. I felt unclean just touching them."

Mr. Brandon was perhaps fifty and, though polite, gave the impression that he hoped to have no more to do with the matter. He looked at Florence's card with something like distaste.

"You're content to discuss the matter with this lady present, are you, Lady Agatha?"

"Mrs. Dawlish is my most valued confidante. You may raise anything, however sensitive, while she's present."

"If you're happy then, Lady Agatha." He pushed a thin file across the desk to her. "If anybody other than your father had requested this, we wouldn't have done it. I don't need to emphasise the need for discretion."

She flipped the file open. Just three or four sheets within. Four columns. Names, addresses, dates, amounts.

"These are the payments we could trace. The list's not complete. It's just a fraction of the total if we also consider what the house's mortgage brought." Brandon said. "There were few papers in her rooms. You remarked on that yourself, Lady Agatha, when you were present at the search. Not even household accounts and certainly no bank records going back further than a year. Heaven knows where the earlier ones have gone. And only the few letters found were recent ones from her nephew."

"Have you contacted these banks yourself, Mr. Brandon?" Agatha was peering at the list through her thick-lensed pince-nez.

"Only those who'd talk to us. Most banks are rightly uncooperative in such matters. But those with which we've good relations indicated that the accounts were opened by the lady providing solid references and making substantial deposits into them. Some were closed immediately after a single payment, often large enough to empty them. And the payee accounts seem to have been just as transitory."

Florence could see individual figures on the top page. Substantial sums, two hundred, two hundred and fifty, even four hundred pounds, round figures, no shillings and pence. There must be well over five thousand in total on that page alone.

"I'm surprised that any bank would permit her to behave like that," she said. The manager of the Hampshire and Dorset branch in Southsea had once asked her to come in to see him when Nicholas was overseas. She had overdrawn the account by just under five pounds. He had made it sound like a capital offence. "Surely any manager would have –"

"Tellson's manager would have intervened, had she stayed with Tellson's." Brandon cut her off. "But she closed her account there and transferred her funds to a dozen other banks, most not so solid or reputable either. She stood on her rights to do so. If I'd been informed –" He raised his hands as if helpless. "But I wasn't. Client confidentiality, you understand ma'am. Tellson's Bank has always placed high value on client confidentiality."

"The mortgage she took out, she must have needed a solicitor for that. Did you act for her?"

"No, Mrs. Dawlish. We knew nothing of it until we investigated after the… the unfortunate event. The mortgage was negotiated by an attorney in Bermondsey. Not an ornament to our profession, I fear, mostly concerned with small tradesmen's squabbles and petty criminal cases. Heaven knows how she could have found the fellow."

But she didn't find him, Florence thought. The woman she remembered would have shrunk from even entering such a poor district. Somebody had directed her to him.

"You must understand, ladies, that I only met Mrs. Chalmers-Bolger a few times myself," Brandon was saying. "We advised her on writing her will after her husband died. It was a courtesy to his memory. We don't normally take on such work. It was a simple testament. Everything to her nephew except for a few bequests to her servants. We had no other contact. I was as surprised by all these dreadful findings as you are now."

"And what do you advise, Mr. Brandon?" Agatha said.

"Nothing. No action. I apologise if that sounds brutal but I can't see that anything's recoverable. Somebody must have taken advantage of her, and she fell for it. It's not uncommon for widows of a certain age. But the decisions were hers. That's how the law would see it. She was a grown woman."

And he's washing his hands of it, Florence thought.

"Can't the police do something?"

"Dear Lady Agatha," he might have been talking to a backward child, "please believe me that they can do nothing in such cases, nor want to either. It may seem like a lot of money but, compared to other financial abuses in this city, it's a trifle."

"It's not just the money," Agatha said.

"That's correct. It's the lady's reputation even more so. She'd be a laughing stock if this matter was more widely known. She wouldn't want to be remembered like that. Nor would her husband have liked it either."

"So you won't be taking any further action?" Florence said.

"No, Mrs. –" He picked up her card, then dropped it. "Mrs. Dawlish. Nothing more. I hesitate to mention it, but my firm will scarcely cover the costs of proving probate after we've disposed of the jewellery we recovered from the pawnbrokers."

Florence stood. "I don't think that we should be taking up more of Mr. Brandon's valuable time, Agatha," she said.

If he had noticed, or resented, her sarcasm, he did not show it. He indeed looked relieved to see them go, even as he apologised again that he could do nothing more.

But at the door Florence turned to him and said, "Do you know the current addresses of Mrs. Chalmers-Bolger's servants?"

"I don't, ma'am. But perhaps my clerk may have them."

And he had.

Chapter 3

A ten-minute cab-ride brought them across the Thames to Lambeth's Roupell Street. The two-storey terrace houses opened directly on the pavements to either side but there was an air of conscious, if frugal, respectability about them. Well-scrubbed doorsteps, polished knockers, net curtains in the windows, the few children playing outside decently clad and shod. There was no indication of multiple occupation and many of the dwellings might well be owned by clerks or prosperous tradesmen.

The woman who opened the door of No. 64 was heavy, sixtyish, clad in black bombazine and with iron grey hair dragged back in a bun. She seemed suspicious when they asked for Mr. and Mrs. Fletcher.

"Who wants to know?" she said.

Agatha's card, more impressive, due to her title, than Florence's, brought an instant and obsequious invitation to enter from Mrs. Briggs, Mr. Fletcher's sister. He and his wife were staying with her temporarily. They were out at present, but she expected them back within the half-hour. She ushered Agatha and Florence into a small parlour packed with too much furniture and smelling of beeswax. Framed prints of Landseer stags and highland cattle crowded the walls. She would bring tea, she said, would not hear of a refusal. Before she disappeared, she mentioned with obvious pride that her husband, Mr. Briggs, owned this house, had his own plumbing business and employed four men.

The Fletchers arrived back ten minutes later and were surprised by the visit. Florence's heart went out to them. They were her parents' age, as neat in their best clothes as they too would be on an important occasion, the picture of modest propriety incarnate. But they were tired, beaten, their air of defeat unmistakable. They recognised Agatha, had seen her at the house in Hampstead when she had come with the solicitor's clerk. She hoped that she found them well.

"Well enough, ma'am." The husband looked towards his wife, as if for support, didn't get it. "But thank you for asking, ma'am."

Agatha urged them to sit and they looked unsure if they should do so. She introduced Mrs. Dawlish as her dear friend. Florence recognised discomfort that she knew that Agatha could not. It was the diffidence, often suspicion and fear too, of people bred to service who were suddenly confronted by forced familiarity with someone from the class that employed them. That usually happened only when something was wanted of them. Or, at worst, bad news. It was a feeling that she had known herself but it had taken that winter in Thrace to free her of it. She had become her own woman there, the woman who dared love an officer and a gentleman, the woman for whom he had risked career and social standing.

Mrs. Briggs had brought the tea, served in china cups that Florence guessed were used perhaps only once a year. She was hovering by the door now, her curiosity about the visit obvious. Only a direct approach would shift her and Agatha would not see that.

"Perhaps you might excuse us, Mrs. Briggs," Florence said. "There are some private matters to discuss with your brother."

She left, not pleased. The Fletchers looked more uncomfortable still, were glancing sideways at each other.

"Just some things that might have been overlooked," Agatha said. "Your mistress was my godmother, you know, and I'd –"

Mrs. Fletcher began to cry, deep sobs shaking her stout body, tears running down her round, kindly face. She pressed a handkerchief to her eyes. Her husband reached out, held her hand.

"There, there, Sally," he said. "There, there." He looked away, would not meet Agatha or Florence in the eye.

"It was a dreadful thing," Agatha said. "But the poor dear could not have been right in her mind at the time. We must remember that –"

Florence glanced to her, gave the slightest shake of her head.

Leave this to me. I understand it better.

And they knew each other long enough for Agatha to recognise it.

"It hasn't been easy, for you, Mr. Fletcher," Florence said. "For your wife either, has it?"

"No ma'am. Not at our age."

"No new situation yet?"

"None yet, ma'am."

"Tell her, Tom," his wife said.

"It ain't easy," he said. "But it'll come right. It surely will."

"Not without references, it won't, Tom!" Anger mixed with tears now. "Tell her ladyship that we've been to seven agencies already! Come back tomorrow, they say, an' we've been coming back, an' there's nothing doing. Not today neither. An' always the same story. No references!"

"We was eighteen years there in Hampstead, ma'am." His wife's vehemence had loosed his tongue. "Never a complaint, not the garden, not the cooking. Not even from her husband, an' he was no easy master. Good to us, she always was, told us we'd be looked after, that there'd be something for us when she went. An' we were glad of them bequests but they're not enough to live on forever. I don't blame her but –"

"I do!" Mrs. Fletcher's misery burst into fury. "It's not just money we got, ma'am, though God knows we're glad of it. It's the references! To have been eighteen years in a situation and no references! You know what every employer will make of that! Me an' Tom, we've been honest and loyal every day of them years, but who's to believe that without references? Would you ma'am? Or you, Your Ladyship?"

Florence spoke to Agatha.

"You told me several times that you heard the poor lady speaking so highly of Mr. and Mrs Fletcher? Treasures, she called them, I believe."

"Yes. Yes, Florence, I must have told you that." Agatha did not lie easily.

"I've no doubt you could provide references yourself for Mr. and Mrs. Fletcher, couldn't you? Just as Mrs. Chalmers-Bolger would have wished."

Do it, Agatha. We'll get nothing otherwise.

"Oh yes. Yes, Florence, I could. I'd be delighted."

"God bless you, Your Ladyship! And you, ma'am, Mrs. Dawlish!"

Tears from the wife, muffled thanks from the husband. Florence was moved by the humility of their gratitude, by their awareness of their own dependence.

I would have been like this too had not ...

35

She looked at her watch. "Heavens, Agatha! It's almost half-past three. We'll be late for that other appointment if we don't leave now!"

Agatha took the hint, though she looked surprised.

"Would it be convenient to bring the references tomorrow morning, Mr. Fletcher?" Florence said. "About ten o'clock, let's say? Good! And don't fret yourself any more, Mrs. Fletcher. You'll see that all will come well."

He wanted to send for a cab for them. There were boys enough outside who'd go.

"No need, Mr. Fletcher. And please thank your sister for her hospitality," Florence said. "We'll walk to the corner, and catch one there."

They had learned nothing.

Not yet.

Whatever the Fletchers could tell, the references would buy.

*

Florence came back alone next day. It was better that way, she convinced Agatha. She knew the Fletchers' world better. Her stay at the Charing Cross Hotel had been extended by two more nights and, when she walked across to Lambeth, she brought with her the two references Agatha had written and signed the evening before. On thick paper, letter-headed with the Kegworth crest and Piccadilly address, a red wax seal beneath the signatures. They looked impressive. Mrs. Fletcher began to cry when she saw hers and her husband was little less moved.

"I never knew the lady herself," Florence said. "A tragic business, I understand. Not at all herself before the end, I heard."

"Bad, ma'am. Very bad." Mrs Fletcher said.

Her husband nodded.

They were sitting, all three, sipping the tea that Mrs. Briggs had brought. She had once more left only with reluctance, was perhaps now listening outside the door.

36

"Lady Agatha said that the poor woman changed after her husband died," Florence said. "It must have been a blow. It must be hard to be a widow."

She saw a questioning look pass from Mrs. Fletcher to her husband, the slightest nod from him that said to go ahead, that she could talk. The references had been payment in advance. As decent people they knew there must be something in return.

"It wasn't then, like you'd think, ma'am. Not immediately after he died. Not that she didn't mourn him, because she must have. But a few months later she'd cheered up."

"Widows often do," Florence said.

"It was more than that, ma'am. Maybe, maybe not quite right for a woman of her age." Mrs. Fletcher shook her head.

"Clothes, perhaps? That's harmless enough," Florence said. "But yes, some of the modern fashions only suit younger women,"

"And she was off a lot," Mr. Fletcher said. The ice had indeed been broken. "Not gallivanting, mind you, ma'am, but off to London on her own, God knows where. But you had your suspicions, hadn't you, Sally?"

"I had, Tom. The first time, gone all the day she was, she came back with her hair dyed and her face painted. I'm not saying like a scarlet woman, nothing like that, but –"

"Just not the sort of thing for a woman of her age," Florence said.

"Exactly ma'am. And then the clothes. And the jewellery."

"An' the letters," Mr. Fletcher said. "Tell Mrs. Dawlish about the letters, Sally."

"But everybody gets letters," Florence felt a thrill. *Something at last.* "There's nothing strange in that. It's surely normal?"

"Not letters like these, it's not, ma'am. In purple envelopes they was. And with red sealing wax to close 'em and a crest on the back like on Lady Agatha's references."

"Surely not the same?"

"No ma'am, but like it. A little picture of a stag on it."

"And scented." Mr. Fletcher made it sound something unclean.

"Scented like lavender they was," his wife said. "Kept them locked in her writing desk, she did. And she was angry if Hannah, her maid, that is, came in when she was reading them. An' reading them she always was, again and again."

"And Hannah told us that there was all that writing too, Sally."

"She was scribbling night and day, Hannah said. But she didn't want anybody to know it. She took the letters to the pillar box herself. Pink, the envelopes were. Hannah saw them."

"There must have been some admirer," Florence said. "Some older gentleman, perhaps a widower. Maybe somebody she might have known when she was young. There're can't have been much harm in it. Did some gentleman perhaps make a call some time?"

"Never! If there was, then we never saw him. An' she didn't go out in society neither. Just stayed at home and wrote her letters and tittivated herself all day long, and all night too, for all I know!"

"But that's nothing like what Lady Agatha told me," Florence said. "That she'd let herself go before she died. That she seemed distraught."

"She was later, ma'am. She was like a madwoman then. Not the raving kind, but melancholy-like. Didn't eat nor sleep neither, an' always crying. Never combed her hair an' hardly washed her face. Food left on a tray outside her door and never touched. No more trips into town. She only went out to post her letters, and that never in daylight. Plain envelopes they used to be too, brown ones, not like the coloured ones before."

"Something must have happened," Florence said.

Mr. Fletcher looked at his wife, as if for approval.

"Tell the lady, Tom," she said. "Tell her about the burglary."

He told her.

About six months ago. If only the dog hadn't died just before. He'd have raised the alarm. Not a single document left. Nothing of value taken. The mistress had forbidden them to inform the police, or to talk to anybody about it. She had locked herself in her room for days afterwards, had emerged red-eyed, unkempt, and so she had remained. If they'd only known how it would end…

38

Agatha would have mentioned the burglary, had she known.
They could tell her nothing more.
It was little enough, but it was a start.

*

Hannah Moffat had not moved far. The address given for her, the Red Lion public house in Hampstead High Street, indicated to Florence that she had better approach her alone, rather than with Agatha. It was close enough to visit that afternoon. She usually avoided the underground Metropolitan Railway, because she loathed the coalsmoke in its tunnels that hung in her hair afterwards, but it brought her close to where she was going. She had another of Agatha's refences with her.

The Red Lion looked decorous, with an impressive façade, frosted window-glass, gleaming brass handles on its doors. She was relieved that it had a ladies' section, a snug, but even if it hadn't, the few men in the bar she had to pass though first looked elderly and respectable. The publican himself, a Mr. Baker, came to serve her. She explained that she had been a friend of Mrs. Chalmers-Bolger – it wasn't too much of a lie – and she had reasons to talk to Hannah. He said it had been a tragic business, very tragic, and Hannah had taken it badly. She took things to heart, she was like that, but she was over it now. A fine girl, he'd known her since a baby, and his son Matt would be a lucky man. They were to be wed at Easter.

"Is she here now, Mr. Baker?"

"She is ma'am. An' all above board too, my wife sees to that. Shares a room with our own daughter until she's married."

Florence liked her when she came. She was cheerful but not brash, confident enough to look her in the eye, respectful but not obsequious. It was easy to imagine her as a competent landlady in the future. Mr. Baker left them with a glass of sherry each and refused payment.

She corroborated everything the Fletchers had told before. She'd left service a month before her mistress's death. Matt had been pressing her to marry her for over a year. She was sorry for her mistress, didn't feel right about leaving her to a new maid who didn't know her. But there had been no new maid, she'd heard. Mrs. Chalmers-Bolger had not been herself but Hannah had thought that it would pass, that she might have been over the worst, and then…

It had been a shock, a terrible shock.

"You liked her, didn't you, Hannah?"

"She was good to me."

Perhaps this girl too might once have spilled hot tea.

"And she was still writing letters, was she, Hannah?"

"She didn't want me to see it, but she knew that I must have."

"Was she still getting them too? Scented ones maybe?"

"Not after the burglar broke in, ma'am. They stopped after that."

"It must have been an admirer, Hannah. From all I've heard, she was still an attractive woman. It would have been understandable. Some older gentleman maybe. All honourable, nothing amiss about it. Perhaps she used to meet him in town."

For the first time, the girl was not meeting her gaze.

"Have you any suspicions about that, Hannah?"

"Nothing really, ma'am, but…"

"Nothing, Hannah?"

"Well there was other letters after that, sometimes twice a day. In poor brown envelopes, an' different handwriting."

"You saw the postmarks?" Maids always made a point of looking. Florence had done so herself when she'd been one.

"Only from London, ma'am. Whatever was in them, she burned them. There was always ashes in her grate even when the weather was too warm to set a fire."

"There's nothing else you want to tell me, Hannah?"

A mute shake of the head.

There was more, even if she didn't want to tell. Time for another approach, an admission hard to make.

"Can you keep a secret, Hannah? You see me as a lady, don't you? But I wasn't always that. I too was in service once. A housemaid first, and then a lady's maid. I know what it's like. That a maid gets to know

40

more about her mistress than even her mother or her husband might. Somethings she mightn't want others to know. Not bad things, maybe just foolish. Things she might be afraid that others would laugh at if they knew."

No answer. The girl was looking up at the window's frosted glass. *She's hoping I'll go.*

"Somebody did something very cruel to her, Hannah. Somebody very wicked. They beggared her and drove her to madness. We can't put that right, but we can see them punished as much as possible, whoever they are."

It was the same feeling she had had in a morgue in Portsmouth two years before, another suicide, a young girl. She had wanted vengeance then and she had got it in the end, though it had involved her in more danger than she could ever have envisaged.

I want the same now.

"It's the last service you can do her, Hannah. Is there anything at all you want to tell me?"

A long pause before Hannah's words came in a flood.

"The week after the burglary. She cleared all the lotions and balms and rouge and powders from her dressing room."

"Rouge?" Florence was surprised. It was not something a respectable lady would use, certainly not one of Mrs. Chalmers-Bolger's age.

"Yes, she used rouge, ma'am. Not much, not much at all, but she did use it. A mountain of powders and bottles and jars, it was. She was always coming back from London with more, and there was others coming through the post too. A fortune's worth. An' it all went."

"Went where?"

"God knows, ma'am. She asked Mr. Fletcher for a sack and that's the last we knew. Tipped them in one of the Hampstead Ponds by herself, or something like that, I think. And from that moment she never put anything on her face again." The girl's eyes were filling. "Like an old woman she was, within a month. Pitiful it was to see."

"Was there anything at all she kept from that time… that time when she used to look after herself so well?"

Hesitation, then Hannah said, "There was some things under her pillow, ma'am. I'd known they was there a long time. I used to make her bed an' change the linen. She trusted me not to pry and, God is my judge, ma'am, I didn't. Just four envelopes."

"Purple? Scented?"

"More like mauve, ma'am. And scented yes, like lilacs."

"Like the ones she had locked in her writing desk?"

"Those ones was all stolen, ma'am, when the burglar came. Tied up with ribbon, they was. But the burglar missed them ones under her pillow. And I knew she kept reading them over and over again when things went bad with her. And crying something awful. Not loud. Sadder than that."

"You didn't tell the solicitor's man about those letters. Nor Lady Agatha either, when she came. You didn't even tell Mr. and Mrs. Fletcher, did you?"

The girl's underlip was quivering.

"You kept them, didn't you Hannah?"

She nodded.

"Tell me, Hannah."

"There was no harm in it, I swear that, ma'am. I knew there was something in them that embarrassed her and I didn't want nobody else to see them. But I never read them myself. I just wanted to remember her when she was happy. They was all that was left of her and that's why I didn't burn them."

"I need to see them, Hannah. Not just me, Lady Agatha too, the poor dead lady's goddaughter." She reached out and took the girl's hand. "I swear to you – bring your Bible if you doubt me and I'll lay this hand on it – I'll swear that we won't laugh or sneer, whatever they contain. There's only one thing we want. Justice. Punishment for whoever drove her to do what she did. Retribution."

Inside or outside the law. Thrace and Cuba and Rosewood House taught me. No compromise with evil, no mercy.

"I'll trust you, ma'am."

Not because I'm a lady. Because I admitted that once I wasn't.

Hannah stood. "I'll bring them."

She was back two minutes later.

It was a large manila envelope that she must have bought specially. A halfpenny had been pressed into the wax that sealed its flap. The contents made it bulge.

"I'll come back, Hannah. I'll tell you what happens, if anything does, and I'll bring this back."

Florence reached into her handbag and pulled out another envelope.

"There's something here for you to give your Matt on your wedding day, Hannah. He'll like it and he'll know it's true. Keep it until then."

The reference that Mrs. Chalmers-Bolger would have written.

A good one, well deserved.

Chapter 4

Florence resisted the temptation to open the envelope when she returned to the hotel. She knew that it had a telephone machine, and Agatha had told her that one had been installed at the Kegworth mansion on Piccadilly too only a few months previously. She had seen such an apparatus used once before but had never used one herself. Now, rather than send a messenger, she would attempt it.

It would cost a shilling, the clerk at the reception told her, and he sent a page with her to a glass-windowed wooden booth. Agatha had given her a telephone address, Piccadilly 26. The boy entered, listened into something like an ear-trumpet that was connected by a cord to a box with a bell on top and then wound a small metal crank. He waited until the bell rang – it was hardly audible through the glass – then spoke into another trumpet.

A half-minute passed, and then he nodded, came out and said, "There's a connection ma'am." He gestured for her to enter. "It's easy. Just sit there an' hold this to your ear and talk in there, loud like."

She gave him a thrupenny bit as he closed the door.

The voice she heard was faint, but unmistakable as that of Mr. Pollock, the Kegworth butler. She had once feared as well as respected him, but the fear was long gone and she had been touched by the pride he had taken since in her advancement. He could not hear her at first, and she had to shout, but yes, Lady Agatha would be brought to the machine. When she came, she too was hardly audible but she conveyed that she would be at the hotel within the hour.

Florence went to the railway station beneath the hotel and bought the week's *Illustrated London News*. Other than impressive drawings of paddle steamers and troops perched on camels, it didn't tell her any more about the Nile expedition than the *Times* and *Telegraph* had done that morning. The details didn't matter, just that the advance upriver was progressing. Correspondents and artists with the army seemed to have no problem getting their contributions back to London. It worried her that Nicholas had given her no address to write to. Letters must be

44

getting through with despatches, even if delayed. If he was with the forces on the river, then he would be reachable, and he would send letters. But he had warned that she should not expect to hear from him for at least four months. He could not be with the main force. She felt fear piling within her, determined that she would not brood on it, knew that it would nag her, no matter what.

Agatha came to her room. She was eager to hear the day's findings but she listened with patience, interjecting only an occasional query, growing paler, as more emerged. Only at the end did Florence take Hannah's manila envelope from her handbag.

"Do you think we should open it, Agatha?" She knew what she wanted herself. "She was your godmother, and you loved her. There might be things in this that you don't want to know."

"Open it."

Florence slit the flap with a nail file. Four mauve envelopes inside, still with the faint odour of lavender. The addresses, written in an elegant and flowing hand, were blotched. *With tears.* Each envelope had a small black crest on the back, a stag upon a shield. The fourth contained something thinner and stiffer than the others. It seemed best to look at its content first.

There was a photograph inside, a studio portrait in sepia, framed with card. A gentleman of perhaps sixty, still with his hair, white-bearded, handsome despite his age, hands grasping the lapels of his frock coat, right foot slightly in advance of the left, his stance indicative of confidence, wealth, power and arrogance. It might be the image of a banker or a politician. But the stance was in stark contrast to the sentiment of the handwriting below. *To my darling Margaret, mine forever.* And below it, a boldly flourished signature. *Your own Frederick.*

It could have been a prized memento had the eyes not been snipped out. Only a nail scissors could have done it so exactly. Florence felt revulsion at the depth of hatred that the mutilation had demanded.

"What is it? Show me." Agatha had seen that she was shocked.

She reached it across.

And Agatha was no less horrified. She sat in silence for a full minute, holding the photograph at one corner only, as if to avoid contamination.

"Who can he be? Do the letters say anything?"

"Let's look at them, Agatha."

The postmarks were dated and Florence selected the earliest. February the twenty-second, 1882. There was a single sheet, of the same stiff mauve paper as the envelope and the text was in the same flowing, Italic script. It had been unfolded and refolded again and again until it had nearly fallen into halves. Here too, the handwriting was blotched.

Florence scanned it in silence, began to feel sick, felt that she too was touching something tainted. She came to the end, went back to the beginning and began to read it aloud.

Dear Mrs. Chalmers-Bolger, he had addressed her, though he could only dare hope that a day might come when her own dear Christian name might pass his lips without offence. Then he was begging forgiveness for his forwardness in approaching her, but passion had overcome him, *that sweet but honourable desire that I had thought could come but once in a man's life, that which I believed, in those dread months after my own sweet Edith had passed to her reward, I would never taste again.*

A more intelligent woman would have thrown it in the fire without reading further, Florence thought. But Mrs. Chalmers-Bolger hadn't been very intelligent, just kind and trusting, a new widow who had been married young to a man she had never loved. At fifty-nine, that was what she'd been, she might still have had hope of something better.

One fleeting glimpse in Coptic Street yesterday has been enough, caught by accident though it was, a glimpse that has pierced me to my very heart. A glimpse which I cannot forget. A glimpse, short, oh too short, of beauty, serenity and grace.

It was ridiculous, the stuff of silver-fork novels fashionable in the wretched woman's girlhood. Had it not been for an image in her mind of a sodden body dragged from a pond, Florence would have laughed.

No words have passed between us and you may not indeed have taken any note of me, but happy chance has allowed me to learn your name. The pen trembles in my hand as I dare hope that we might indeed meet, that perhaps – But no! That would be to yearn for too high a prize! And yet! And yet! Might not I aspire at least for a reply, a few words in your own lovely hand that I might treasure even though it might dismiss with scorn an honourable heart that longs for — But no! I dare not write it!

But he did dare write an address.

338 King's Road, Chelsea.

And his signature.

Frederick, Lord Menston.

"Do you know the name, Agatha?"

"No. And I've never heard Father mention him either, though he knows so many in the House. But half the peers never bother to come to Westminster if they can help it, and then only when there's something that concerns their own direct interests. He might be one of them."

"Where's Coptic Street, Agatha?"

"I've never heard of it."

Florence picked up the photograph again. She turned it over. On the back was small ink stamp. Locatelli Photographic Studio, 157 Knightsbridge.

An expensive area, as was Chelsea, one where a peer of the realm might well patronise a photographer.

"Could she have replied to such nonsense?" Agatha said.

"She must have. This one's postmarked six days later. It refers to a reply."

He did not blame her that she had reproached him so gently. He had perhaps presumed too much and her admonition was well deserved. But hesitance was impossible when his life been had changed by that one chance encounter. *Until that moment, I saw the years stretching before me to the tomb as barren ones, made bitter by those who owe me most, for greed is worst when laced with ingratitude. I know that I am no more that hussar who rode so recklessly at Balaclava, nor yet the minister of the crown who bore the burdens of office, duty and honour so long, so willingly. Yet, I, a man not yet too far advanced in years, still hope to love.*

And then the plea.

To meet, however briefly. At Coptic Street perhaps, where discretion was assured, at a time that she herself would suggest.

Signed, *Your Frederick.*

47

"They must both have mutual friends in Coptic Street, wherever it is," Agatha said. "Some friends of her husband, maybe. He might have asked them to invite her for afternoon tea. They might have been pleased for him as a lonely widower and glad to help him through his bereavement."

"If they did, then he was making fools of them also. Let's see what the last letter says."

It had been joy, ecstasy beyond all expectation, to have met, he wrote, relief that neither scorn not rejection had greeted his humble suit.

Not did Dante's first sight of Beatrice, not Abelard's of Heloise, bring greater bliss. There is for me now but one goal, one thought that will haunt me night and day until it is attained. To make you, My Darling Margaret! – may I address you so, without offence? – make you my own dear Lady Menston and see you take your rightful place as mistress of Ferriby Park.

"So she did agree to meet him," Agatha said. "If only she's asked Mamma for advice! If only –"

"There's more, Agatha."

And it was worse.

Yet, discreet as our happy trysting place may be, it may not yet be safe enough from envious eyes! For, Dear Margaret, greed of my own children is yet an obstacle, a Damoclean Sword that hangs above our heads! I see it in their furtive eyes, the resentment, unspoken but fierce, that a new Mamma might reign in their own departed mother's place and lay hands upon the riches that they crave. My son – oh that it pains me now to call him such! – and his harpy wife, my daughters and their spendthrift spouses, none will hesitate to ridicule an aged parent's passion, nor to set their lackeys to spy upon his comings and his goings! Were it for myself alone I could bear it willingly, but that one who is the bright centre of my universe should so be slighted is too much to bear.

"The man's mad," Agatha said, but Florence kept reading.

And so, for now, my Darling Margaret, caution must rule us until I have cleared the way. For, fear not! It will happen, just as my younger self once plunged into the Crimean mouth of Hell towards the Russian guns. But for now, our meetings, joyous and face-to-face, must be but few, for serpents will be upon the watch. Only though letters — oh how precious will be those in your own gentle hand will be! — can we communicate.

He was no longer just *Your Frederick.* He was her devoted slave. And he panted for her reply.

They sat in silence for a minute after the last words.

"I don't think he's mad," Florence said. "I think he's a very cruel and very clever man."

His Darling Margaret had waded into that pond, she thought, her saturated skirts heavier with each step, her feet sinking into the ooze beneath. Terror might have overcome despair and resolution then and she might had tried to turn back, and then slip, fall, struggle up, choking, thrashing, going under again…

Her mind recoiled. Better not to dwell on that. Retribution demanded cunning, a cool head and merciless tenacity. She had learned that from Topcliffe.

"I don't think she'll have been the only one," Florence said. "There may be others at this very minute at the limits of their sanity." The phrase that Mabel Bushwick so often used came to mind. It had seemed so overblown, so amusing. But now it seemed appropriate.

Our Sisters.

"We've got to stop him, Agatha."

But first they'd have to find him.

*

Florence went down to the hotel's reception desk and asked to see the manager. He regretted that he had no copy of *Debrett's Peerage,* an omission he apologised for, and he thanked her for alerting him. There was however a copy of last year's *Who's Who,* a current *Kelly's Directory* and a detailed map of Central London.

There was such a man.

Menston, 6th Earl of, born 1823, Frederick Michael Richard Fitzhugh. He had succeeded to the title on his father's death in 1862. His mother, daughter of the 6th Baron Castleton, had died in 1867.

"Captain and Brevet Major, 11th Hussars," Florence said. "And he was in the Crimea, like he claimed, and he won a medal there. But nothing about those other burdens of office he mentioned."

"Was he married?"

"On August the fifth, 1857. To the Honourable Edith Maud Mary Aylmer, daughter of the second Baron Ashwood. She died in 1881. That would have made him a widower at the time of the first letter."

"His children? Is there a son and two daughters?"

"A son, Richard Beauchamp Frederick. He was born in 1858. And yes, two daughters, Hester Sarah Maud and Henrietta Georgina Selina, born in the following three years. They're all married."

"Just as in the letter, Florence."

"His residence is given as Ferriby Park, as in the letter too. It's in Yorkshire apparently. And in London his house is in St. James's Place. Nothing about King's Road in Chelsea. And he's a member of the Carlton Club."

"So is Father. He must know the name at least. But it's so hard to believe that such a man could have been so odious, so mean."

Poor deluded Margaret Chalmers-Bolger might have consulted *Who's Who,* Florence thought. It would have been in a bookshop perhaps, hoping that no acquaintance might see her, trepidation soaring to hope as she found confirmations of the details in the letters.

But anybody could buy *Who's Who,* and swindlers were not uncommon... and yet, and yet. Men who were as eminent and as respected as this Lord Menston appeared to be were often as ruthless in their exploitation of the weak as any heartless charlatan. Agatha's brother Oswald's disgrace, and all that it had led to, had shown Florence that.

Who's Who could tell no more, but *Kelly's* contained a surprise.

338 King's Road, Chelsea was a tobacconist's shop.

And the map revealed that Coptic Street lay just south of the British Museum. Not a cheap area.

All together, indications only, little better than hints.

But a start.

*

Florence travelled to King's Road by tram the following morning, the vehicle gliding smoothly over the rails as its two horses clip-clopped ahead. It was a cheaper than a cab. She would have to watch her expenditures and she already felt indebted to Agatha for the stay and meals in the hotel. She remained on board as the tram trundled past Number 338, Anderson and Son, Luxury Tobacconists. It looked as respectable, and as expensive, as the milliner's and the jeweller's to either side. She dismounted at the next halt and walked back, not out of place among the other women on the pavements. All were well dressed, affluent rather than wealthy, for this was the less fashionable part of Chelsea. Most might be wives of professional men, doctors or lawyers perhaps. Other than a few soberly dressed servants out with baskets to shop for fresh fruit or vegetables, nobody was hurried.

The smell inside the shop was rich and not unpleasant, hundreds of different tobacco mixtures stored in wooden drawers lining the walls behind the counters and in glass jars atop them. A sign proclaimed that cigarettes were made to order and cigars were a speciality, Havanas, Sumatras and Javas. Racks of briar and meerschaum pipes stood to the right of the entrance. An elderly customer, white-whiskered, was being served and he turned and glared at Florence as if she had entered some sacred precinct.

A youth in a brown shop coat came out to meet her and asked if he could assist.

"I'm looking for a present for my husband. It's his birthday soon and I want to surprise him. He's always set his heart upon a meerschaum but –" She dropped her voice, looked away as if embarrassed. "I couldn't afford anything too expensive."

He too lowered his voice. "I understand ma'am. I'm sure we can find you something."

She disliked him immediately for the hint of contempt beneath his unctuous, almost fawning, manner. He fetched a bentwood chair, seated her at a small table, spread a green cloth on it and laid out a succession

51

of Turks' heads, crowned monarchs, flower-wreathed maidens, raging lions and elegantly coiffured women. She lifted them, admired them, laid them down with something like a sigh when she learned the prices.

"Norbert would love these," she said. "He surely would. But is there perhaps … perhaps anything… a little, just a little, cheaper?"

And all the while she was studying not just the youth but the older man behind the counter, his father perhaps, his manner also obsequious as the irascible customer sniffed a succession of cigars and was satisfied with none of them.

The youth had gone to fetch more pipes and now he was back, less attentive now, looking out the window and stifling boredom as she turned over a few plainer pieces. *He knows I'm not going to make a purchase,* she thought, and still she dragged the process out, sighing softly, going back to ones she had rejected earlier.

Another customer entered, a fashionably dressed middle-aged man who stared at her with insolent curiosity before another assistant, previously unseen, emerged to serve him. She hoped that the customer might ask if there was a letter for him today, but he had just come for Black Latakia blend.

It was easy to imagine either customer, or both, receiving mail here that they did not want arriving at their home addresses. No fee involved, none asked for, but an unspoken understanding of continued patronage and acceptance of prices higher than the average. Given the large variety of tobaccos stocked, there would seem nothing unusual about customers coming here from elsewhere in London.

It was time to put an end to the charade. She had learned nothing certain but it was a credible possibility that Lord Menston might use this shop as an accommodation address. He didn't even need to visit in person. A trusted manservant could come in his place.

"Such a beautiful thing" She laid down the last, plainest, pipe with obvious regret. "I'll need to think about it." She didn't look the youth in the face, as if ashamed of her own genteel poverty. She thanked him, let him see her to the door and open it for her.

He must know that she would not be coming back, that she was just a wife with ideas beyond her means.

It was better so.

Chapter 5

Florence did not want to look again at the defaced photograph. The image was seared in her memory. It chilled her that a kindly and decent woman had sunk in such an abyss of resentment and despair as to have done this. And it made it impossible to show it at the photographic studio where it had apparently been taken.

Her walk from the tobacconist's to Knightsbridge took a half-hour. She was uncertain how she might manage her enquiry there. The Locatelli Studio had a double frontage, and the name-board above stated proudly that it had been founded in 1849. Portraits of various sizes were on display behind the plate-glass windows, some on easels, not just individuals and family groups but recognisable public figures, politicians, generals, writers and society beauties. The space beyond was furnished like a drawing room, elegant couches and wing chairs, large windows, what might be a real Landseer, periodicals on low tables, flower bouquets, potted palms. Nothing like a counter indicating vulgar commerce, nor any sight of photographic equipment.

A small discreet notice in one window proved an inspiration. Cabinet-card portraits were for sale of many of the most eminent, or notorious, figures in national life, all presumably persons who had given permission to be represented in the windows. It was common enough, for there always seemed to be an insatiable demand for such photographs, especially of admired women. Perhaps they received something from each sale. Tens of thousands had been sold of Mrs. Langtry alone. She wasn't represented here but Florence saw other faces that she recognised from illustrated papers.

She went in and instantly felt dowdy by comparison with the customers – referred to as patrons here, she guessed – waiting in comfort. An exquisite young man in a morning suit, a white carnation in his button hole, glided up to her. He had taken in her modest finery, had recognised her for what she was, she guessed, comfortable but not wealthy and out of place here. Even before she asked, he told her that Signor Locatelli's appointment book was full for weeks to come. If a sooner sitting was needed, then he could recommend Baxter and Sons in Fulham Road.

"It's not that, not this time." She forced herself to gush. "It's the wonderful cards in the window. Mrs. Cornwallis-West! So lovely! Lord Salisbury too. Such a distinguished man! My husband Norbert's a great admirer! And though I didn't see it, perhaps you have one of Lady Randolph Churchill too! Always so elegant!"

"Please step this way, ma'am."

He brought her to a smaller room, cabinet-cards stacked in a hundred or more pigeonholes behind a counter, and a separate door with a glass panel opening on the street that she probably should have entered through. He left her in the care of a young woman in a severe black dress.

She feigned interest in the photographs of dozen beauties, regretted that there was none of Lady Randolph, at last selected one of Mrs. Cornwallis-West and another of Miss Maud Branscombe, the actress. Dear Norbert would be delighted with the image of dear Sir Garnet Wolseley. He'd served with him in Zululand. She paid three shillings that she begrudged, saw them wrapped, put them in her handbag and moved toward the door. The assistant had made no move to help as she pulled it open. Then she turned back, closing it behind her.

"I don't know if you might help," she said. "My husband speaks so highly of one of his old commanding officers, such a fine man. He'd treasure a portrait of him. Old memories, you understand. Could you perhaps have one of him?"

"What was the name, ma'am?"

"Lord Menston."

The assistant showed no flicker of recognition but she referred to a list. No cabinet-card.

"Perhaps he might have come for a private sitting? Maybe there might be something in your records?"

"No, ma'am." Something of suspicion in the tone. "Signor Locatelli places high value on his patrons' privacy. Confidentiality's assured here ma'am."

It made no sense to tarry.

The photograph had been an expensive dead end.

*

Disappointed by the morning's work, she ate a light lunch at the hotel. Over coffee afterwards she read the newspapers. Nothing of note from Egypt, just continued slow progress up the Nile, vessels dragged up through cataracts with immense labour by men on shore. Nothing either that could indicate Nicholas's whereabouts. She had sworn that she would not allow herself to worry, but knew that she was failing, could only hope to mask her fears from others.

The last of the three addresses was the most unpromising of all. Margaret Chalmers-Bolger had met Lord Menston in Coptic Street. That was all she knew. She had no house number and since somebody else, perhaps a friend, must have owned it, she could think of no pretext for enquiring door to door. But she would go there nonetheless, though she expected only disappointment.

It was almost an hour's walk, not unpleasant in the autumn sunshine. She did not want to be seen consulting a map and so she had memorised the route. She entered the narrow Coptic Street where it led off from New Oxford Street. The far end provided a glimpse of part of the British Museum's stately grandeur. It was busy, but not thronged. She passed a few shops and business premises but thereafter narrow-fronted four-storey brick houses of the previous century lay on either side. All looked prosperous rather than wealthy, not ostentatious, easy to imagine as the homes of successful professional men rather than of more exalted levels of society. A cab had halted half-way up the street and a lady, clearly well-to-do, was stepping out, two neatly dressed young children with her, and a maid was already emerging from the house to carry in purchases. A little further on, another street opened to the right and just beyond was a branch of the Capital and Counties Bank. Only at the end of the street, where the Museum was just ahead, was it flanked by wider fronted houses of grander design, Georgian, not brick but Portland Stone, like the museum itself. If the unfortunate woman had met the real or purported Lord Menston in this street then it was likely to have been in one of these. Some senior administrator of the museum might live here, she thought, or some rich dilettante who wished to be close to its treasures.

She had not expected success, but the failure was disheartening nonetheless. The large curtained windows, the immaculate front doors with gleaming brass knockers told nothing. She turned and retreated down the street. For a moment the bank seemed a possibility. An initial accidental encounter, such has Menston had mentioned in his first letter, would be natural there. Then it dismissed itself. It was impossible to imagine it as the happy trysting place referred to in the third letter. She was almost back at the New Oxford Street intersection now. A brass plate on the right identified the offices of a wine merchant, with others indicating occupants of suites of rooms above. Now, to the left, a shop selling prints and, by it, an expensive-looking stationer.

And then, something, maybe nothing, but…

Number 9 had wide plate-glass windows that extended down almost to the pavement. Patterned net curtains, rich ivory white, barred view of the space within. Florence had to come closer to read the small brass plate beneath the number.

Temple de la Beauté.

No door knocker but, on the frame, the button of an electric bell. She glanced up. A large vase of flowers in each of the windows on the floor above, net curtains on the two above that again. She didn't stop, walked on to the corner, turned it and found a teashop a hundred yards or so beyond. The customers already seated were not unlike herself, respectable ladies of various ages resting in the middle of an afternoon's shopping. She ordered tea and a scone that she had no stomach for.

The name concerned her. It could be a house of assignation, she thought, though it was impossible to imagine the timid Margaret Chalmers-Bolger ever venturing, or blundering, in there if it was. The earliest of the letters had indicated that Lord Menston had seen her, as if by accident, at some location in this street, and she must have brought herself there in the first place. But a phrase that he had used was memorable because it was so overblown, so ludicrous.

A glimpse, short, oh too short, of beauty, serenity and grace.

There might be something innocent behind that brass plate, a provider of cosmetic services perhaps. There were many such, and frequently resorted to, she knew. They were seldom spoken of, even to family or friends. Women of a certain age did not want to admit to dyed hair or other rejuvenating assistance. And Hannah, Mrs. Chalmer-Bolger's maid, had mentioned a mountain of balms, lotions and rouge.

If Number 9 provided such services, then it seemed plausible that the silly woman might have ventured there on her own. She might have been alerted to its virtues and to its discretion by some friend of similar age. That Lord Menston might have been there at the same time seemed less innocent however. His wife was dead and if a sister of his resorted to the Temple, it was unlikely that she would have told him, or have asked him to collect her there.

Florence hesitated to go back and yet knew that, if she didn't, it would nag her through the night. She would have to investigate the place sooner or later. She finished her tea, paid her bill and returned to Coptic Street. Her resolution almost failed and her hand trembled as she pushed the electric bell, fearful that what lay beyond might be another of the whited sepulchres like those she had encountered two years before. She had discovered reserves of guile within herself then that she had never expected. They had served and saved her then. They must again.

A lady, smiling, well-spoken, thirtyish, dress fashionable but restrained, no jewellery, no trace of rouge, opened the door and welcomed her, enquired if she an appointment. That she hadn't was no matter. Madame Hortense was always honoured to accommodate new patrons.

She ushered Florence through the tiled hallway with flowers on a semi-circular table and a large gilded mirror above. Beyond was what looked like an elegantly furnished drawing room. It reminded her of Signor Locatelli's waiting area and was, if anything, yet more tastefully luxurious. A half-dozen women, ladies by dress and demeanour, were seated there, chatting, drinking tea, leafing through illustrated papers. She was the youngest here, she realised. The majority were middle-aged and one was positively wizened. All looked relaxed, as if familiar with this decorous ambiance. It was impossible to imagine this as – she shrunk from the word, but there was no avoiding it – a brothel.

The lady who had brought her in was stepping back as another, older, advanced to meet them. Her plum-coloured dress was severely elegant, of richer material than the first's and ornamented only by a gold-rimmed Wedgewood cameo brooch at her throat. She too was welcoming. She regretted that Madame Hortense was not here this afternoon but she herself – her name was Mrs. Bellamy – would be pleased to help. And might she enquire madame's name?

"Lacy. Mrs. Norbert Lacy." A name she had used before when she had not wanted to be identified as Mrs. Nicholas Dawlish.

"It's always better to have first consultations in my little office." Mrs. Bellamy lowered her cultured voice and smiled. "Absolute confidentiality is guaranteed within our Temple's walls."

It was more like a boudoir than an office. Here was the largest lady's dressing table that Florence had ever seen, glass-fronted cabinets to either side. A chaise longue, a chesterfield at right angles to it, a low table before them. The air heavy with the scent of hot-house flowers in half-a-dozen vases. Two large mirrors on the walls and a single painting, a languorous Roman lady, beautiful beyond dreams, reclining on a marble couch beside an ornamental pool and toying with a rose. The only concession to business was an expensive roll-top desk in one corner. A window gave on to a tiny walled garden, a fountain at its centre, the sort of hidden gem that lay behind so many austerely-fronted London houses.

Mrs Bellamy seated Florence on the chaise longue, then sat beside her, not too close, but as near as a friend might.

Had Mrs Lacy come far today?

From Hampshire, the village of Bentley, Florence said. It was the first name that came to her. She had been there only once, and she did not want to mention Southsea. The village was only an hour by rail from Waterloo Station, she said, and so convenient for shopping in London.

And how had she learned about Madame Hortense?

A dear friend, Florence said, a friend that – she hesitated – a friend whom she could talk to such things about.

"Ah!" Mrs. Bellamy smiled. "We all need such friends, don't we? And men, even the very kindest, never understand such things, do they?"

Florence hoped that she blushed. "My husband..." She looked away. "No! It's too hard to talk about it." She took a handkerchief from her reticule, dabbed at her eyes, wished that she had been less attentive to her appearance that morning.

"A lack of... let's say, ardour. It's not uncommon, dear. No lack of love, but –" gentle sympathy in Mrs. Bellamy's voice "the fire of passion damped just a little perhaps?"

A nod of dismal agreement.

"And yet the memories of past raptures linger, and longing that they might yet return. Is that not so, Mrs. Lacy?"

"Yes." Almost inaudible, face turned away.

"It's a story that we hear all too often here. Gentlemen, even the very best, poor dears, can be so blind to the grace and tranquil loveliness of their own dear spouses. And if they have a roving eye then –"

"No!" Florence said. "Not dear Norbert! He never would! Never!" She dabbed her eyes again. "It's just that..."

"Just that he needs a little encouragement? Is it that, perhaps, Mrs. Lacy? A reminder of the maiden beauty that first enchanted him and stole his heart?"

"I feel so ashamed," handkerchief in play again, "so ashamed that even a stranger can see it so plainly."

Mrs. Bellamy stretched out her hand, touched Florence's very gently.

"Not a stranger now. A friend, Mrs. Lacy. A friend who can help. A friend initiated into the secrets of feminine loveliness by Madame Hortense herself." She paused, then reverence in her tone as she continued. "Madame Hortense, once mentrix in the cosmetic arts to the

Empress Eugenie herself." She taken Florence's hand in hers now. "Stand up, dear Mrs. Lacy, bear with me a moment."

She led her to the dressing table, sat her down, pointed to the mirror.

"What do you see there, Mrs. Lacy?"

She saw what she always saw, a face that she marvelled Nicholas had ever found attractive, the cheek bones too prominent, she had always thought, the mouth too large. But he loved it most, found it irresistible, he always said, when she smiled. She said nothing now, only frowned.

"But what do I see?" Mrs. Bellamy said. "Features of classic grace, great liquid eyes. How their brown becomes you! Skin wanting but just a little help to restore a glorious bloom. And yes, a wrinkle here, but still just a tiny one," touching to corner of the right eye, "not yet a crow's foot, easy to make disappear. And here, Mrs. Lacy, at the sides of your mouth, the same concern, but easily remedied. And your hair! Rich, splendidly golden! It needs just a little attention to keep it so for years to come."

Florence made herself try to smile while seeming unconvinced.

"And sometimes after children, Mrs. Lacy, sometimes —"

"No. No children."

"Ahh," said Mrs. Bellamy.

She reached out to the bottles and containers marshalled in neat rows on the table. Her hand hovered above them for a moment, as if in indecision, then selected a blue and white-patterned porcelain jar. She opened it, peered inside, looked closely at Florence's cheek, then put it back and picked out another.

"This one might be right," she said. "Please allow me, Mrs. Lacy."

She dipped her middle finger in the jar, used it to dab a tiny white globule on Florence's left cheek and began to rub it gently in. It had a pleasant floral scent, strong enough to prevail over that of the flowers in the vases. The area covered was no larger than a halfpenny.

"We must wait a moment for the balm to do its work, Mrs. Lacy."

"What is it?"

"Cream of gazelle milk, infused with nectars of the blossoms of the northern slopes of the Pamir mountains. And a certain rare ingredient that Madame Hortense keeps secret to herself."

She reached for a small silver-handled magnifying glass on the table and began to study Florence's cheek.

"Not quite satisfactory," she was frowning, scanning the jars and bottles. "Your skin is so delicate, Mrs. Lacy. Something yet more subtle is needed…" Her hand was hovering again, reaching to another jar, touching, opening, shaking her head and thinking better of it, at last selecting another.

"Perhaps the other cheek, Mrs. Lacy, just a small trial."

Another dab. The scent no less agreeable than before but somewhat stronger. The lightest of touches as she rubbed, and then it was time to wait once more.

"Gazelle cream too, Mrs Bellamy?" A tone of hushed admiration.

"No, Mrs. Lacy. Rarer still. Butter churned from the milk of the grey oryx of the Kyrgyz plains." She had picked up the magnifying glass again, was studying the small circle of moist skin.

"Yes! Just right! I think that this is what your skin demands, Mrs. Lacy. An application over the whole countenance, night and morning. Just for a week, no more, enough to prepare the epidermis for something yet more subtle thereafter."

"But, but…" Fluster and embarrassment. "But…" And then a rush. "Is it not very expensive? I'm not sure…"

Mrs. Bellamy was touching Florence's hand. "No need for concern! You will have this oryx butter as a gift. No, don't refuse! I insist! A lady who ventures within these portals must never leave emptyhanded, whether or not she intends to return. It's Madame Hortense's golden rule." She went to one of the cabinets and took out a decorated jar, the size of a mustard pot, its lid sealed with red wax. "For you, Mrs Lacy. Use it well."

She had a booklet in her hand now also, the paper glossy, six or eight pages perhaps, an engraving of the Botticelli's Venus on the cover. Florence took it, saw the title. *Woman's Mystery, Woman's Heritage.*

"By Madame Hortense herself, wisdom valued by so many consorts of the crowned heads of Europe and beyond. And suggestions too for other assistance should you decide to return yourself."

"I must think about it. If it costs too much…"

Mrs. Bellamy had Florence by the elbow now, was patting her hand as she guided her to the door

"Don't trouble yourself over matters pecuniary, dear Mrs. Lacy," she said. "Madame Hortense regards her work here as a sacred trust. Rest assured that there are no absolute prices here. Beggar-maid or duchess, any woman who enters here is treated just the same and the charge is adjusted to circumstances."

Mrs. Bellamy conducted her to the street door herself and hoped that she would return as a friend.

Florence had seen that the wizened lady was no longer in the waiting room, but two more ladies had arrived, one very stout.

But no beggar-maid.

Chapter 6

Agatha came to the hotel that evening.

With bad news.

"Father knew Lord Menston," she said. "Not well, because he seldom came to the House unless the party needed his vote for something critical. He was happy shooting and fishing on his Yorkshire estate and hardly ever left it. But now, Florence, it's a terrible thing! That he can't leave it anymore and hasn't for six or eight years. It's horrible."

"Why?"

"He was thrown from his horse in the hunting field. He's totally paralysed."

The sort of detail that *Who's Who* never recorded. A living death. It had been merciful that Nicholas's older brother had been killed instantly in a similar accident.

"What about his London house?"

"Rented out to Sir George Berkley of the Board of Trade. Father knows him well, he's been there. Lord Menston's son, Richard, has cared for him ever since his wife died. Poor woman, the accident broke her heart and she'd worn herself out looking after him."

"So he didn't write those letters. He couldn't have."

On the walk back to the hotel, Florence had found the possibility of a titled roué finding foolish women in the *Temple de la Beauté* plausible. That was no longer the case. Whoever wrote the letters was now an even greater mystery than before.

"He wouldn't have written them, even if he could," Agatha said. "He wasn't, no, he isn't, that kind of man. It was a cruel and wicked trick to use his name."

And yet it had been so easy. The details were so readily available in *Who's Who* that Mrs. Chalmers-Bolger could have checked to allay any doubts she might have had. Whoever the man was, a single visit to the Locatelli Studio would have been enough to have that photograph taken. There might have been other copies made too. At this moment there could be other women flattered to have received one. The effusive

64

correspondence would follow. Then the fortune spent on cosmetic treatments and the temptation of a noble marriage. And at last the threat of ridicule, the reality of blackmail.

There was little to tell about the visit to the photographic studio but, when she had arrived back at the hotel, Florence had noted down every detail she could remember of the *Temple de la Beauté* in Coptic Street. Agatha listened without interrupting while she told the full story. Here, coldly recounted, there seemed something ludicrous about it, and yet it was plain that insecure and gullible women, with more money than sense, could find the place attractive.

When Florence finished, Agatha said, "I don't believe that there are gazelles in the Pamirs. No, I'm sure of it. Nor grey oryx on the Kyrgyz plains either."

But there were yet more exotic beasts to be found in the lists of creams and balms and lotions in the later pages of Madame Hortense's *Woman's Mystery, Woman's Heritage*. The Nubian Ocelot yielded a perfume more subtle than any civet. A secretion of the Golden Wapiti of the wild Canadian north had been valued for long ages past by the native maidens of those frigid regions. Inca princesses had bathed in the milk of Snow-White Llamas, thought until recently to be extinct, but now established in a small herd at a remote estate in Scotland. From secret Gobi oases, tireless Bactrian Camels plodded with orchid petals along the fabled Silk Road. The mightiest Leviathans of the oceans gave up their ambergris and even the lard of the long-haired yaks of the Tibetan Plateau had been prized for centuries by Indian ranees. And delicate blooms from the deep forests of Borneo, saps of hardy shrubs on Andean slopes, herbs gathered on the banks of the Oxus, resins pressed from rare barks in Karelian woods.

Agatha was beginning to laugh. "Listen to this, Florence. *Soluble minerals, but lately discovered by intrepid men of science in the remotest valleys of Tartary, have —*"

"No! It isn't funny!" Florence was remembering that wizened old lady in the waiting room. She must have fallen for this, was probably paying through the nose for it.

"Nobody could believe this nonsense, Florence."

"You wouldn't, Agatha. But you're a Fellow of the Royal Society. You're not a lonely ageing widow or a plain wife whose husband's showing undue interest in the governess."

Florence was suddenly sorry that she'd said it. For Agatha, brilliant and learned though she might be, was not just plain but large and clumsy too. For all the generous dowry that Kegworth wealth would bestow, she had never attracted any man, and knew she never would. Despite friendship and shared mortal danger, it was impossible to guess what longings lay beneath the placid surface. Had she been less intelligent, she too might have been thrilled by Mrs. Bellamy's blandishments.

"If your poor godmother had read this, do you think she might have been impressed?"

A pause, then Agatha said, "I think she would. She wasn't very clever. I only realised that when I grew older. But it didn't matter. She was always good."

Madame Hortense's wisdom filled the booklet's front pages. Beauty was *Woman's Hallowed Birthright*, the *Eternal Fountain* from which *Love So Freely Flowed*, the *Foundation of the Future*, the *Inspiration of the Noblest Deeds and Noblest Thoughts in the Long Ages of Human Endeavour*. It was the *Secret Mystery* shared by *All Womankind, Maiden and Wife and Mother Alike*. And yet it brought *A Duty to Tend its Sacred Flame,* for it alone could *Bind the Hearts of Men with Sweet Flowerlike Chains* and guide them gently to those *Paths of Marital Bliss* that lead to *True Happiness.*

And Madame Hortense's grandmother, her mentrix, once perfumier to Marie-Antoinette, had asked her upon her deathbed that she pledge her life to *Beauty*. That vow had brought her to the *Ends of the Earth*, to its *Remotest Wilds*, to palaces and seraglios, to *Hidden Shrines where Priestesses Guard Cosmetic Lore of Lost Ages*. And now, in her own golden years, Madame Hortense was dedicated to sharing those secrets with *Humanity's Great Sisterhood.*

"Whoever wrote this, wrote those letters also," Florence said. "There can't be two people in all England who can write like this."

"And there's no mention of money anywhere," Agatha was leafing through the lists again. "Not for a single pot of Nubian Balm or jar of Lotion of Samarra or an Empyrean Bath or a Celestial Laving."

"But Mrs. Bellamy mentioned money. No prices, but a charge adjusted to circumstances, she said. I've no doubt that she was gauging what I'm worth, and how stupid I might be, from the moment that she saw me."

Florence paused, sensed that Agatha was as bewildered and disappointed as she was herself.

"We don't really know much more, do we, Agatha? Just where your poor godmother probably spent a fortune on rubbish and where she met some scoundrel who defrauded and blackmailed her."

"What can we do next? We can't do nothing, Florence."

A flush of affection, a memory of setting out together through a savage winter to that caravanserai in Thrace to aid the refugees. Incapable, both of them, of imaging the horrors that lay ahead, yet sustaining each other through the nightmare that followed. Nothing had been impossible then, nothing was impossible now.

"We don't know enough," Florence said. "I'm going to have to go back to the Temple and play the ninny there, see where it brings me."

She reached for the jar that Mrs. Bellamy had given her. On close inspection it was a cheap thing, the sort of dragon-decorated Chinese ware imported in quantity but, like many gifts, it implied an obligation. She broke its seal and extended it to Agatha, who dipped her forefinger in it and massaged the white blob into her cheek.

"It's no different to what my hairdresser sells me, Florence. No better, no worse, and she makes no claims about Kyrgyz oryxes either."

"I'm to use it for a week and it'll work miracles, no doubt. I could go back then, see what more I'm offered. And after that, I don't know."

"Are you sure you want to go there on your own?"

Florence had been thinking about that ever since she'd left Coptic Street. Though she would like to have somebody with her, she didn't want to bring Agatha there. Agatha lacked the sort of guile that she knew that she herself possessed.

"It's best alone. Mrs. Lacy of Bentley would never confide such a matter with even her own sister. She'd be too embarrassed. And she knows that women talk. She'd be afraid above all that word of it might get back to Darling Norbert."

"Perhaps you'd favour an Empyrean Bath?" Agatha was smiling. "Even dear Norbert's passion might be enflamed by its results."

"A bath like that may need the milk of llamas. Even poor dim Mrs. Lacy would guess that it could not be instantly available, that notice would be needed if it's to come from some secret estate in the Outer Hebrides or some such."

"Nothing like that, Florence. Let's go step by step.".

Something could be booked tomorrow before returning to Southsea.

∗

Florence waited until half-past ten before taking a hansom up to Coptic Street, arriving at a time that made her story of coming up by train from Bentley convincing. Mrs. Bellamy was engaged but the lady who had first admitted her yesterday, now identified as Mrs. Mobray, was glad to help. She brought Florence to a smaller consulting room than before, disregarding several ladies in the waiting area, and sat her down.

And Florence, well-prepared, well-rehearsed, slightly dishevelled, a strong scent of Kyrgyz Oryx wafting from her face, was flustered. Madame Hortense's words had given her hope and she would welcome her assistance, but – the words trailed off in embarrassment, and she looked away – she'd heard what Mrs. Bellamy had said but she still feared that it might cost too much. Dear Norbert was not a mean man, no, quite the opposite, the allowance he gave her generous, but if he knew... If he hadn't been away in Ireland it would have been hard to find a reason for coming up to London like this. But he'd be away at least another month and …

"He'll find his lovely bride again when he returns," Mrs. Mobray said. She lowered her voice, tone confidential. "Not just the

68

countenance, but the whole body as beautiful as any loving husband might desire. No gentleman would grudge the cost of that."

Florence was looking away and had her handkerchief out, dabbing her eyes. "That' what I dream of," she said. "It's not sinful to think like that, is it? Like Madame Hortense says. Every woman's birthright."

"Why not make an appointment now?" Mrs. Mobray said. "A first rejuvenation. A week, let's say, from now, when the balm that Mrs. Bellamy has given you has done the initial work. And no! No price. Just a small donation."

"A donation?"

"Let's say two guineas." Mrs. Mobray smiled. "And perhaps a small token of appreciation for the maid who'll assist. That would be more than enough."

Cheaper than I ever could have expected. Too cheap.

The appointment was for Tuesday the following week, eleven-thirty, time enough to get from Portsmouth and back again within in the day, even more comfortable for a journey from Bentley if it was ever queried. Mrs. Mobray asked for Mrs. Lacy's address. If there was any problem about the appointment she would be informed by letter. Crooksgrove Lodge, a name thought up the night before, sounded plausible. It was duly noted. But no, Florence said, better no communication. There were rumours that the postmistress in Bentley was inquisitive, that she steamed letters open before they were delivered, that she knew everybody's business. Mrs. Mobray smiled and said yes, she understood, that was all too often the case. A sentence of hard-labour, a long one, was too good for such people when they were exposed.

As Florence passed out through the waiting area, she saw an old gentleman seated by an equally old lady, sitting companionably close, one reading *The Times*, the other a magazine. They looked as if they might have been together for a half a century. None of the other ladies waiting showed any sign that his presence disturbed them. But it was significant nonetheless. It might not be unusual for gentlemen to come here to wait for wives.

69

She hailed a hansom to bring her back to the hotel. It waited while she collected her portmanteau from the hall porter, then took her on to Waterloo Station. She had not discussed with Agatha what she now intended. The train back to Portsmouth stopped at Clapham Junction and she dismounted there. She entrusted her baggage to the ticket-collector. She promised him a shilling, then began her walk towards Clapham Common. It was two years since she had last seen Western Lodge, the mansion of Mr. Henry Judson Raymond that fronted on to it, but its air of solid wealth and propriety still impressed. Society, including his friend, the Prince of Wales, knew him as a rich American expatriate sportsman who preferred the British social scene to that of his native country.

But she knew him as something else.

She had almost died in his company in Cuba and, without his help, Agatha's brother Oswald could never have been spirited from the country with a warrant for gross indecency outstanding against him. It was Raymond's steam-yacht, the *Shamrock*, that had carried Oswald to France and the start of unending exile.

And he did things for Topcliffe.

If any man could advise her now, and perhaps help, it would be Raymond.

She recognised the footman who opened the door. His manner was impeccable, his face impassive but he had the build of a prize-fighter. She suspected that he remembered her too, though he did not indicate it. And no, Mr. Raymond was not at home.

"May I see the lady of the house then?"

She had never been sure if there was one. Raymond never mentioned a wife or other woman but she had suspected that there was one when she had been here before. There was an indefinable quality about the décor that indicated a woman's touch. Mistresses were not uncommon in the Prince of Wales's circle.

"I'm sorry ma'am, there must be some mistake. I suggest that –"

"I'm not leaving! I want to see her. She probably knows my name anyway! Give her this!"

70

Mrs. Nicholas Dawlish, her own card, her own identity.

Her knees were weakening and she dared not make any more of a scene. He was about to close the door in her face, then thought better of it. She thought she saw a flicker of recognition.

"Please step this way, ma'am."

The parlour that she waited in was as elegant as she had remembered, the furnishings, the carpets, the four portraits on the walls, Georgian beauties. Knowing Raymond, they might well be genuine Gainsboroughs or Reynolds.

The woman who entered five minutes later did not introduce herself, nor did she ask Florence to sit again after she had risen to greet her. She might be forty, not beautiful, but handsome, superbly dressed and coiffured. And with an air of hardness and calculation.

"Mrs. Dawlish, I understand." The slightest American intonation. No smile, no welcome. "I've heard the name. What brings you here?"

"I want to discuss something with Mr. Raymond."

"What something?"

"A private matter."

"Mr. Raymond will be informed. He's not in the county at present."

"When is he coming back?"

"It's impossible to say." She moved to the bell-pull and tugged it.

A maid appeared, so soon that she must have been waiting outside. Florence recognised her. Raymond had sent her on an errand during that affair of Oswald's.

"This lady is leaving. Kindly show her out."

Without another word, she turned on her heel and left the room.

It was only when Florence was on the train again – it was a straight run from Clapham to Portsmouth – that she accepted she had hoped for so much, that she was so disappointed. Raymond could have been the ideal ally.

We're on our own now, Agatha and I.

And then a flash of comfort.

Mabel Bushwick must already be somewhere in mid-Atlantic.

*

Southsea's and Portsmouth's routines again, the concerns of the Sailor's Rest, piano practice, reading — nothing would be enough to mask Florence's nagging concern about Nicholas. There was another worry too, stronger now that she was away from Agatha and could not discuss it face to face. She had no doubt now that the *Temple de la Beauté* had been instrumental in beggaring Margaret Chalmers-Bolger and driving her into despair and suicide. It was just possible that she might have been the only victim, or at least the only one driven to such an end, the subject of a single opportunistic fraud. But Florence doubted it, suspected that something far larger was involved, something akin to the evil that she had encountered two years before. Something that she could not get involved with without risk to herself.

And yet... and yet... She could not turn her back on it.

There was no concrete action she could take just now. None, except to go to the local printer that supplied Nicholas's and hers headed notepaper and cards. Her friend, Mrs. Norbert Lacy of Crooksgrove Lodge, Bentley, Hampshire, had admired the cards, Florence told the printer, and had asked if she could procure similar ones for her. There were no street numbers in such a rural area and the actuality of the address was virtually impossible to trace.

They looked innocent, when she picked up the hundred that she had ordered, and might be of minimal value in whatever lay ahead. But they were a reminder that she was committed.

Chapter 7

Florence went to the Sailor's Rest two days after she returned. She was in her office, glancing over the suppliers' bills for the week – she and one other of the trustees had to sign each payment cheque – when Mr. Selden, the superintendent, knocked, entered and stood before her desk. When he had greeted her on arrival, he had seemed less than his usual cheerful self. Now he looked downright uncomfortable. She gestured to the chair before her desk and he sat down.

"I've seldom seen it look so spick and span here, Mr. Selden." She smiled. "Maybe I should stay away more often."

"There's something you should know about, ma'am." He was shifting in the chair. "Nothing too serious, no, not too serious at all. But I thought you should know."

"It can't be too bad, Mr. Selden. Not with you here to keep things in order. Now just tell me what it is."

"It's that Mrs. Harvey, ma'am. The woman who came her with her kids. The woman who owed money."

"So Mrs. Selden went to see her?" Florence felt disappointed already. She had liked as well as pitied the woman. It would be bitter to learn if she was a fraud.

"The missus went, well enough. An' 'twas like the woman said, worse even. One room and hardly a bite of food or a stick of furniture in it. Pitiful, it was."

"So, did the moneylender's debt got settled, Mr. Selden?" Florence was already thinking that she should send her maid with a basket of food.

"It got settled alright, ma'am, but –" A tremor in his voice, his tongue darting over his lips. "It got a bit out of hand, ma'am. Nothing too bad, the police didn't hear about it. But I knew you wouldn't like it, that it might come back to you and –"

Florence felt a hollowness in her stomach. Mr. Selden's hesitation indicated worse to come.

"Just start at the beginning" she said. "I left four pounds to clear the debt. And two of your friends were to visit the moneylender. What happened then?"

"I thought of Bert Haskins, He served with me on the old *Majestic*. Works in a warehouse now. An' Matt Wheatley - we was in the Baltic together in *Cornwallis* in '54. Foreman in a chandler's now. Steady chaps, no nonsense about 'em and they'd take none either an' –"

"So, they took none, did they, Mr. Selden?" She was feeling sick now.

"It'd have been alright if they'd both been there. Just a few words to the wise when they called around at Barney Chadband's, that's him as lends the money. Nothing more, definitely nothing more, just let him know that there were folks around who didn't hold with him gouging seamen's wives and children. That's what we agreed, all three of us. Just like you wanted, Mrs. Dawlish, nothing …"

She was hardly hearing the words. She had been stupid to have suggested it. No, worse, stupid to have authorised it.

"You said that your friends weren't both there, Mr. Selden."

"It was bad luck. When Bert went around to collect Matt Wheatley that night, Matt had just been taken poorly. Something he'd eaten. He couldn't move more than ten feet from the … from the closet, beggin' your pardon, ma'am. He couldn't leave the house. He felt bad about it, didn't want to let Bert down, me neither."

"So Bert went on his own?"

Mr. Selden shook his head. "Matt's son was there, having his supper. Bill's his name. Not a bad lad, a good son, works in the same place as his dad. He said he'd go with Bert instead of Matt."

"They went to the moneylender together. What did you call him? Yes, Chadband. They had the four pounds with them, did they?"

Misery in the nod.

"Where does this Chadband live?"

"He's got an old-clothes shop in Crasswell Street. It's a small one, off Commercial Road. It don't get much custom but he don't care. Lending money's the real business there."

"Was anybody else in the shop?"

"Just him."

"How much did they offer?"

"Two quid. He just laughed at them. Said it was four. Not a penny more, not a penny less."

"Did they offer more than two?"

"Two-ten. Two-fifteen. Then three. Nothing doing. He told them to get out and then..." Mr. Selden paused before the words came in a rush. "Then this Chadband went too far, said things about Mrs. Harvey, poor woman that she is, called her something that ain't decent, ma'am. And Bill, he's a good son, like I said. Worships his own mother, wouldn't hear of any other woman spoken of like that. But he's a bit hot headed and –"

"And he hit Chadband?"

"Yes, ma'am."

"Hard?"

"Gave him a black eye and a thick lip before Bert pulled him off. Bert calmed Chadband down. Gave him the full four quid."

"Did Chadband call the police?"

"No. He wouldn't want them around his place." Mr. Selden paused. "That should be the end of it. ma'am. Me and Bert and Matt, we all had a word with young Bill. He'll keep his mouth shut about it all."

"Have you heard anything about it since?"

"Nothing. There were no witnesses." Mr. Selden tried to smile and failed. "An' Barney Chadband'll be more careful in future who he'll lend to at his top rate."

Florence felt chilled. It could have been so much worse. An item in the *Portsmouth Argus*. Police enquiries leading back to the Sailor's Rest. Her name. Nicholas's would be mentioned too. She had been stupid, she knew, had had a narrow escape, should have thought enough beforehand to foresee this possibility.

"We've learned our lesson, Mr. Selden," she said. "Don't reproach yourself. The fault's mine, not yours. There won't be anything like this again."

"Thank you, ma'am." He seemed to be relieved when he left. Unlike her.

*

It haunted her in the coming days, on Sunday most of all, when she was most left to her own devices. At St. Jude's that morning it struck her that she was not like the other women singing in the pews around her, comfortable ladies with comfortable lives bounded by care for husband, home and children. She had come through more than they could in a dozen lifetimes. And she had survived, had saved others too. But observance of legal niceties had counted for nothing when she had faced evils here in Britain. Power and strength and guile alone had been all that mattered in Thrace and Cuba. Such – she sought the word – such hardness, she had to admit, had become second nature to her, waiting for something to arouse it. Something as petty as that moneylender. Thoughtless, foolhardy, driven by overconfidence, she had overstepped the mark. Only the Grace of God had saved her and she thanked him for it.

But still it nagged, as she walked that afternoon along the Esplanade, as she crossed back over Southsea Common, as she tried to immerse herself in Mrs. Braddon's latest novel, as she wrote a long letter to Agatha about the second visit to Coptic Street. She mentioned the appointment there on the coming Thursday and suggested that they meet afterwards before she returned to Southsea.

She lay awake half of Sunday night, tortured by thought of what would have followed had Chadband fallen against a sharp edge, had cracked his skull, had been taken to hospital, had died. Bert and Bill on a charge of murder, or maybe manslaughter. She wasn't sure of the legal distinction, or which was worse. Mr. Selden and herself as accessories before the fact and probably gaol for both. Shame for her family. The Sailor's Rest in disrepute, heartbreak for its inspirer, Miss Agnes Weston. And, most dreadful of all, Nicholas's career in ruins She could imagine the newspaper headlines, *Respected Naval Captain's wife found guilty of ...*

76

In the end she got up, put on a dressing gown, and went down to the study to read. But another fear was growing now. She had no idea where the visits to Coptic Street might lead. She had committed far too readily, too unthinkingly, to getting justice for Margaret Chalmers-Bolger, had been too confident in her own strength. Whoever was involved in driving that poor woman to her death was likely to be far more dangerous, far more clever, far more vengeful than any backstreet moneylender. With Henry Judson Raymond's advice and aid it might have been safe to continue. She was sure he would not have refused her, but he was absent. It wasn't too late to withdraw, a small internal voice reminded her. She had done her best, could not be expected to go beyond a certain point.

But she had committed.

To Agatha, to her best friend.

If she were to withdraw from that commitment it could only be when she knew more about what the real dangers were.

Mind made-up to keep the *Temple de la Beauté* appointment on Thursday, she went back to bed.

And slept.

*

Florence travelled up to London on Thursday morning by the seven-fifteen and arrived in Waterloo Station in ample time to reach Coptic Street a half-hour before her appointment. She wanted to spend time in the waiting area, to see its comings and goings and – she wasn't sure whether she hoped for, or dreaded, the prospect – perhaps inspire the interest of some fake-titled gentleman. She took her seat to wait, declined the offer of tea or elderflower cordial and began to leaf through a ladies' fashion magazine, glancing up occasionally to observe the five other customers. She was the youngest here, the least richly and least fashionably dressed also. One lady might be five years her elder, three were in their forties, maybe fifties, and one would never see sixty again. At intervals, young and beautiful women in well-cut but practical nurse-

77

style uniforms came to led them away. They seemed to know them well, were respectfully familiar. It would be Florence's own turn soon.

Two more customers now, both accompanied by maids who were led off to wait in some less opulent surroundings. One lady looked exactly as Florence had imagined Mrs. Chalmers-Bolger. She had not seen her for fifteen years, would probably not have recognised her as she was before she died. This lady was not less than fifty, but dressed as a women twenty years younger might, one addicted to bright colours and ostentatious costume jewellery. Her body was large, rather than heavy, her face soft from self-indulgence, and the overall impression was of benign foolishness. Mutton dressed as lamb, that horrible expression, flashed in Florence's mind and she was ashamed of it. But she was impressed when this lady's maid dropped her mistress's Paisley shawl when she relieved her of it. The girl was flustered as she picked it up and folded it, was apologetic, but the lady reassured her. It was nothing, nothing at all, my dear, and she hoped she'd have a good cup of tea with the other maids while she was waiting. She caught Florence looking towards her and smiled and nodded, the first there who had taken any notice of her.

Another customer had arrived, a striking woman, Florence's own age, comparable in looks and elegance with the beauties sighted in the Locatelli Studio's window. The dark-haired, moustachioed man with her, no less elegant in his black frock coat, striped trousers, a white gardenia in his buttonhole, was perhaps five years older. He handed the attendant his silk hat and cane, then waved her away and conducted the lady himself to a chaise longue, sat by her, then beckoned to the girl again. He did not request, he demanded. His wife would like elderberry cordial. And coffee for himself. Florence saw him glance towards her for a moment. Brief as that moment was, she felt herself weighed and found wanting, and then he passed on to survey the others there.

"Mrs. Lacy, if you'll step this way, please? Mrs. Mobray will see you now." An attendant, smiling. "My name's Claudette, madam." The slightest trace of Cockney undermined the French intonation.

She led Florence from the room, up the staircase to the next floor, along a landing off which four separate doors opened. Another flight of stairs led to the floor above. Carpets underfoot, vases of flowers on small tables, oil paintings of half-clad nymphs in glades.

Mrs. Mobray was waiting in the treatment room, a spotless white apron over her silk dress, no less spotless armbands to protect its sleeves. Two dressing tables, wash basins, a reclining chair like a dentist's, two low beds covered with linen sheets, a small table piled with white towels, a screen in one corner, glass-fronted cabinets filled with jars and bottles. And, here too, hothouse blooms in vases.

Welcome, and small talk. The journey up from Hampshire had been easy. Mrs. Lacy had so looked forward to this session but she was, she confessed, a little apprehensive. That was normal, Mrs. Mobray said. All that was needed was to relax. On this first treatment it was best to begin with the face, shoulders and arms. They were so open to admiration and, she laughed, to gentlemen's scrutiny on formal occasions! Perhaps there was some such event coming up? A ball perhaps? A reception? Mrs. Lacy shook her head sadly.

Claudette led her behind the screen and helped her remove her jacket and blouse, drew up her hair and bound it in a silk scarf, then brought her back. She helped her on to one of the beds and cushioned her head with a pillow.

Mrs. Mobray watched in admiration.

"I'm reminded of some lines of Coleridge," she said. "From his sweet poem, Christabel. *'Her gentle limbs did she undress, and lay down in her loveliness.'* No, Mrs. Lacy, no false modesty! Appropriate, I assure you."

Now, with a magnifying glass, she began to examine Florence's skin, pursing her lips, nodding, shaking her head once, going back to examine the corners of the eyes and the edges of the mouth more intently, making notes in a small book with a silver pencil. She frowned at the sight of the long scar on Florence's left arm but made no comment. She could not suspect that it had been inflicted by a Spanish sabre. The wound had been inexpertly stitched in Cuba and Florence would never bare her arms in public again.

At last Mrs. Mobray said, "Mrs. Bellamy chose well. The oryx butter was just right. But now perhaps something gentler still. Claudette! The attar unguent, please."

Now it began, the girl gently messaging the substance into Florence's face, moving down to her neck, back up again to her cheeks, temples and forehead, rubbing lightly along the sides of her nose and mouth. The sensation was comforting, almost soporific. Mrs. Mobray's only part was to gesture Claudette away at intervals and examine the skin though her lens. At last it was time to pause, to let the unguent do its work.

"Something gentler for the hands now," Mrs. Mobray said. "They look so delicate. Claudette, bring the... No! It's better that I attend to it myself." She went to a cabinet, stood for a moment as if in deep thought, then took out a jar. "Sap of Erythrina," she said, "best, I think, for you, Mrs. Lacy."

"The scent's so delightful," Florence said. Mrs. Mobray was rubbing the yellowish cream into her hand. "It must be so rare."

"Madame Hortense says she's lucky if she can secure twenty ounces in the year, sometimes even less."

"And... and expensive?" Unease in her tone.

"No need for you to worry about that, Mrs. Lacy."

Time now to move to the chair, tilted back, white towels on the head and arm rests. Claudette began to massage Florence's shoulders and arms with another cream, its origin kept secret by Madame Hortense even from Mrs. Bellamy much less Mrs. Mobray.

And all the while Florence felt herself enjoying the treatment Her skin did feel better, she thought, softer, more supple, and the underlying muscles felt more relaxed than she had ever known them. Even if the creams had humbler origins than claimed, they were still effective. These women knew their business.

"How does it feel, Mrs. Lacy?"

"Like a girl again." It wasn't wholly untrue.

"Ahh," said Mrs. Mobray. "Mr. Lacy will be pleased when he returns from the Emerald Isle! No, Mrs. Lacy! No need to blush! We're both married ladies! Have you heard from him? He's well I trust?"

It was the moment that Florence had half-foreseen, was wholly prepared for. She had worked out the details, refined the story in the previous days.

"He's well," she said, "but, but..."

"A wife cannot but be concerned, Mrs. Lacy. Ireland's such an unsettled place. On the brink of anarchy, I understand."

"Yes!" said Florence. "Dreadful! Such ungrateful people! Fenians and Land Leaguers and Home Rulers and that appalling Mr. Parnell! Assassins the lot of them! They should all be shot, Dear Norbert says. Shoot them, or ship them to America. There's no other way for it."

"I hope that Mr. Lacy is not in danger himself? Maybe his responsibilities..."

"Private business but –" A catch in Florence's voice. "But such a disappointment. Norbert had been so hopeful." She looked away as if embarrassed to have said too much.

"Life can be so cruel," Mrs. Mobray said. "And all too often to the very best, to those who least deserve it."

"Norbert had expected so much. He'd been promised the estate in County Mayo since he was a boy." Florence injected bitter resentment into her voice. "His Uncle Walter had never married and there was no other heir. Norbert was heartbroken, of course, when he heard he'd died. He went across for the funeral. He didn't take me with him. It wasn't a place to bring a woman, he said, not with all the agitation there."

"So thoughtful, Mrs. Lacy. I can understand why you love him so. And then there was to be a disappointment?" A pause. "A surprise, I suppose? The will, perhaps? It happens so often, some kind old man and some scheming young woman taking advantage of him."

"Worse than that!" Florence let her anger grow. "Norbert got the estate. But there were debts we'd never known of! Gambling! Women too! Drink! And mortgages! It all came out! Uncle Walter had left the estate's management to an agent, and the agent cheated him, and the

81

tenants haven't paid rent these last three years. The Land League and the Fenians saw to that!"

"Dreadful, Mrs. Lacy!" Mrs. Mobray was shaking her head. "Dreadful!"

Florence had jerked up to a full sitting position, was grasping an arm rest so tightly that her knuckles whitened. Her voice sounded on the verge of hysteria and Claudette drew back and stopped massaging.

"It's driving poor Norbert to distraction, Mrs. Mobray! He's trying to sell the estate. There's no other option if the debts are to be cleared! And with Ireland in such chaos, nobody wants to buy. We're content with our little place in Hampshire but we'd hoped for just a little more."

"Cruel, Mrs. Lacy. So cruel. But troubles always pass, don't they Mrs. Lacy? Where there's love, where there's a happy marriage, that's golden above all else, isn't it?" Mrs. Mobray turned to Claudette. "We might take a little break here. And, Mrs. Lacy, tea perhaps? Camomile maybe? So very soothing. And so good for the skin and hair."

While Claudette was gone to fetch it, the magnifying glass was again brought into play. Florence leaned back, tried to look embarrassed by her outburst and Mrs. Mobray seemed too diplomatic to refer to it while she made more notes in her little book.

"I'll need Mrs. Bellamy's opinion on what to apply next," she said at last. "Your skin is so fine, Mrs. Lacy, so exceptionally fine. It's better that I have a second opinion."

She waited until Claudette returned with the tea, then left. Florence chatted with the girl. Had she been here long? Almost two years, and two in Paris before that. She loved the work. There could be few better employers than Madame Hortense. She hoped to have a business like this for herself one day.

"It was as I thought, but I wanted confirmation," Mrs. Mobray said when she returned. "Better to take no chances. Oil of Mahameru is ideal. Claudette! Fetch a bottle."

Only the lightest of applications, dabbed on and wiped with cotton. And then the treatment was finished. Claudette helped Florence to her feet, brought her behind the screen and assisted her to dress.

"The donation…" Florence looked embarrassed when she emerged, brown envelope in hand.

Mrs. Mobray smiled. "Just leave it on the table, Mrs. Lacy."

And a half-crown pressed into Claudette's palm.

"Progress, Mrs. Lacy, significant progress today," Mrs. Mobray was holding up a hand mirror. "Younger, almost a girl again! But there is more needed, something yet more ambitious next time. I'll discuss it with Mrs. Bellamy. She's seen my notes. She'll know what's best."

And the something more ambitious was an Empyrean Bath, Mrs. Bellamy said, when Florence was ushered into her office. It was not easily arranged, for the llamas did not yield large quantities of milk and priority must be given to older clients.

"The donation, would it be…"

"For you, Mrs. Lacy, just twenty-five guineas," Mrs. Bellamy said.

No reference to beggar-maids, and Florence didn't raise them.

"It is a lot," she said. "I'm not sure… could there be some way to spread the donation over time?"

Mrs. Bellamy's brows knit in concentration. Then her face lightened.

"There is an arrangement that Madame Hortense has approved a few times. A very few times. I'd have to put it to her. I can't promise that she'd agree."

"Oh, Mrs. Bellamy! What could it be?"

"A reduction. Madame Hortense has even consented to complete remission once or twice for ladies who introduce friends who'd appreciate the Temple's services. Older ladies perhaps, in more need of greater rejuvenation than you are, Mrs. Lacy. If you know such persons, I've no doubt they'd be eternally grateful for the introduction."

And Mrs. Lacy, relieved, said that she'd have to think about it. She might know one or two such ladies. It would need a delicate approach if offence was not to be taken. Madame Hortense's *Woman's Mystery, Woman's Heritage* might help. Could she have a few copies?

She could, and Mrs. Bellamy give her a jar of Samarkand Balm also. Gratis, and to be applied liberally, before and after sleep.

Chapter 8

Florence felt pleased when she emerged from the Temple. She had carried it off well, she told herself, had identified herself as a member of the class that hovered just above the level of shabby gentility but had aspirations far higher. Hopes of greater affluence had been dashed and Dear Norbert would be unlikely to be sympathetic to expenditures at the *Temple de la Beauté*. She had not overdone it and she'd played the role of a vain woman well, short of money but eager for what it would buy, anxious about her social position and her hold upon her husband. She had done it well enough that Mrs. Bellamy and Mrs. Mobray, both hard-headed women who knew the world, had accepted it, had recognised her cupidity and had set out to exploit it.

"It must have been how Mrs. Chalmers-Bolger was drawn in," she told Agatha when they met for tea at the Charing Cross Hotel that afternoon. "Somebody she knew told her about the Temple. Some friend she trusted, somebody like Mrs. Lacy, some greedy person who was paid in nothing more than treatments and baths, and lotions and creams bought at a street-corner chemist's shop and ladled into fancy jars."

"It's horrible to think of," Agatha said. "Such betrayal, such wickedness."

"Whoever that friend was, she'd have been too stupid to think of it like that. Just as Mrs. Lacy wouldn't."

"Aunt Margaret's servants, that cook you spoke to, Florence, that maid, Hannah, they must know who her friends were. It can't be hard to identify that false one among them, bring home to her what she'd done."

It was tempting and it would be easy.

But futile.

"It's that place in Coptic Street that matters," Florence said. "Lord knows how many other naïve women are being beggared or blackmailed there like poor dead Mrs. Chalmers-Bolger. We can't help her, but we could help them."

"How?"

"I don't know. Not yet. I'll have to think about it."

But she had thought about it already, had the vague outline of a plan, one not yet ready to discuss. And it would depend on so much...

She looked at her watch. "I'll have to go soon, Agatha, I want to catch the five forty-five back home."

"When can we talk again?"

"Doesn't Mabel arrive in the next few days? She said she'd contact me when she did. You too? Good. Let's arrange something then. Lunch perhaps, or tea here."

The first step.

*

She was not best pleased after she had made a surprise inspection at the Sailor's Rest next morning. Nicholas was emphatic about thorough inspections, best not pre-announced, being essential to the health and efficiency of a ship. She had taken the advice to heart and applied it on occasion to the Rest, donning white gloves to run a finger over cooking surfaces and inside cold ovens, tasting food herself and checking linen. In Nicholas's absence, the ritual felt something like a tribute. And on this occasion, as nearly always, there was almost nothing to complain of, only satisfaction to be expressed.

It was Mr. Selden's news that disturbed her.

"There's been another woman here, ma'am. With kids. Marshall's her name. Hasn't been here before. She wanted to see you."

"Did she say why?"

"No, ma'am. Just that she wanted to see you."

Please God, not another Mrs. Harvey, not more moneylender trouble.

"Did she say where she lives?"

She had. It wasn't far.

"Send somebody to fetch her. I'll be here for the next hour."

Florence went to her office, opened her mail. Three quotes for repairing a crumbling chimney, one significantly more than for the last such job and the two others wildly so. It indicated collusion between the contractors. She had decided to call in a fourth, one who hadn't worked at the Rest before, and offer a fair price, take it or leave it, when Mr. Selden knocked. Mrs. Marshall had arrived.

She had a little girl by the hand, just old enough to be able to walk, and a baby wrapped in a shawl. All adequately, if poorly, dressed. Florence had her sit down and asked Mr. Selden to have tea brought.

"God bless you, ma'am," the woman said as soon as the door was closed. "God bless you!" She started up, leaned across the table, caught Florence's hand and held it to her face. "God bless you, ma'am for what you done." She was weeping now.

Florence did not draw the hand away, laid her own on it. "It's alright, Mrs. Marshall," she said. "It's alright." She could think of nothing else.

The woman sat back at last, was brushing tears from her eyes. The baby had started to cry.

"I don't think we've met before," Florence said.

"No, ma'am."

"Is your husband a seaman?" A safe guess.

He was in HMS *Netley*, at Bermuda. He had been gone six months. She'd heard little from him.

Tea arrived, a plate of biscuits with it, and as it was poured Florence admired the baby, took it herself and rocked it, refrained from questioning. The little girl, named Judy, wolfed down a biscuit, took another, devoured it, then another.

She's never seen or tasted one before.

When they were alone again, Mrs. Marshall said, "It ain't just me, ma'am. Other women too, but they dursn't come. We're thankful, ma'am. We truly are."

Florence said, "You're thanking me for something, Mrs. Marshal, but I don't know what I've done for you."

"Barney Chadband, ma'am. Him you had beaten."

Florence felt her heart almost stop. She had hoped never to hear that name again.

"I think there's a misunderstanding…" Her mouth was dry, her hands trembling.

"Taught a good lesson, he was," Mrs. Marshall's tears had dried. "Learned it too, ma'am. Changed his tune, he has."

"You'd borrowed money from him?"

"Five bob, two months ago. I'd paid six back but he wanted another four, an' more again next month. Go to the pawn, he said, get it any way you damn-well like, pardon the language ma'am. An' then –"

"He let you off?" It seemed inevitable.

"Sent one of his people round, he did. Jem Rowley it was, an' he said I'd paid enough an' that it was the end of it. Barney wouldn't come himself, ma'am, not with two black eyes, they say, an' he don't want to be seen outside his shop. An' if it hadn't been for you, ma'am, he'd be sucking me and God knows how any others dry. That's why I came to thank you, ma'am."

Florence realised that one of the two callers on Barney Chadband, most likely Bill, the younger one, had not held his tongue. A single drunken boast in a public house would have been enough. Delivering a well-deserved hiding, enough to deter the moneylender from preying on absent seamen's wives, was something to be proud of. It was impossible to know how far the story had spread.

Florence eased her hair from the baby's grasp and handed it back.

"I know nothing about any of this, Mrs. Marshall. You mustn't repeat any of it either. Gossip does nobody any good." Florence knew that nothing more she said now could make it any better. The only hope was to ask Mr. Seldon to have a severe talk with Bill and hope that the matter be soon forgotten. By others, maybe, but not by herself.

She conducted Mrs. Marshall to the door and gave her two shillings. "For the children."

Doing even that much made her feel ill.

It seemed like a bribe.

*

The coming days were misery, dominated by fear that her fame as avenger of exploited debtors had already spread. It was little comfort that Bill Wheatley had accepted the ire of his father and of Bert Haskins, or that Mr. Selden had carried a verbal apology from him to Florence. It would be bad enough if it stopped here, but her imagination troubled her with a dozen further possible outcomes, none pleasant. When she attended a tea party at the residence of the port admiral's wife, a woman who liked and respected her, as she did her in turn, she realised that half the naval wives present would take shocked delight in any such events. It was only Lady Adelaide de Courcey's friendship with her, built, no others knew, on tragedy two years before, that earned her a degree of acceptance. Her husband might be seen as up and coming officer but many still delighted in the stories that she had once been a servant. Association with moneylenders, brawls and intimidation would confirm the opinions they'd held of her since first acquaintance. And for Nicholas – No! She must not think of it. Madness lay that way.

Mabel Bushwick's letter arrived a day later. She had posted it at Liverpool after the *Oregon* docked and was on her way to London, where she'd stay at the Rutland Hotel in Queen Square, Bloomsbury. She suggested meeting Florence and Agatha in two days' time. Would that be convenient? It would, Florence wrote back, two-thirty at the coffee room in the Charing Cross Hotel. She's let Agatha know that also.

Better there than at Mabel's hotel.

That was too close to Coptic Street.

*

Mabel had always been impressive, her not unhandsome face, so often set in a frown of concentration and earnestness, radiating courage and determination. Now there was something more, a confidence and pride in accomplishment. The late, always unmentioned, and probably unmentionable, Mr. Bushwick had left her penniless. Only a resort to journalism had saved her from destitution and bought educations for her two sons. Events in England two years before, when she had come to write about wealthy American heiresses marrying British aristocracy, had proved her a loyal and compassionate friend. Her high collar hid the scars she carried since that time, the burns of the vitriol meant for Florence that had fallen on her instead. She had suffered agony then, and probably discomfort since, but pride would never allow her to complain of it.

"Not here for Dollar Princesses this time?" Florence said.

Mabel smiled. "A much more worthy topic. But the princesses more than paid the rent. They brought calls for articles from other journals too. And newspapers. And work on the West Coast. But it's still the *Columbia Home Gazette* that occupies most of my time."

"And you're still in the vanguard of the march towards female suffrage?" Florence said. It was a phrase that Mabel so often used herself. It might sound sententious in other mouths than hers, but her conviction lent it dignity.

"It'll come, Florence. Someday there'll be victory."

"Have you already many visits arranged here?" Agatha said.

Mabel had. Everything from young ladies' expensive boarding schools to orphanages, city missions, reformatories, over a dozen, all over England.

"I've an appointment with the new editor of the *St. James Fortnightly Review*," Mabel said. "He's interested in articles by me. And it was such a tragedy about his predecessor. That man who built it up. He was so tireless." She dropped her voice. "Could it have been suicide?"

"No," Florence said. "An accident with his gaslight. But yes, a tragedy indeed." No need to dwell on it. The coroner had believed it.

"And you won't forget Rosewood House, will you, dear Mabel?" Agatha said. "You'll see such changes! The girls there are so happy now!"

Mabel would be in England for over two months, time enough for her working and travelling schedule not to be too exhausting. Time enough also to take up the standing invitation Agatha had offered to the Kegworth Estate in Northamptonshire and to stay with Florence at Southsea.

There should be time enough also for what I have in mind. But first let Mabel talk. Come to it gradually.

"Is Count Livitski still in London? Still at the Russian Embassy?" Mabel said. "I never had the opportunity to thank him after … after the accident."

His intervention had saved Mabel from yet worse scarring that night. What had followed for the perpetrator had been brutal, but essential. Neither Mabel nor Agatha, knew anything of that, but Florence would never forget it.

"The count went back to St. Petersburg," Florence said. "Some other government posting, I'd imagine."

A very dangerous man, Topcliffe had called him. A suggestion to the Russian ambassador that Livitski's activities were not compatible with his diplomatic role had caused him to leave London. And there were others reasons why Florence preferred not to talk of him. She turned the conversation back to Mabel's own activities since she had last been here.

Mabel had been busy and was proud of it, writing of experiences no woman ever had written of before. Three weeks of twelve-hour days working in a New York laundry, two of washing dishes in a respected restaurant near Wall Street, two more of making cardboard boxes in a loft workshop, had identified inhuman work conditions, filthy kitchens, starvation pay, lack of the most basic of sanitary provisions. Her articles had evoked brief outrage, quickly forgotten, though little more than that. But it was a start, a new type of journalism, she said, and she was becoming known for it.

"You mentioned the West Coast too, Mabel? In California, was it?"

Six weeks there had yielded material for a series of articles in *Appleton's,* apparently a prestigious magazine, and later collected and published as a book. It had sold well. Mabel had found and interviewed nineteen Forty-Niner women who had come west during the Gold Rush. They had crossed prairies, deserts and mountains and a few had lost children on the way and one had borne one. Now in late middle-age, most had raised families, some had run stores or boarding houses or laundries. One, a millionairess, or close to it, owned orange groves, another a sawmill. And one operated a profitable establishment of ill-fame.

"A gentlemen's sporting house, she called it," Mabel said. "She was proud of it too It was patronised, she claimed, by some of San Francisco's most eminent men of business and commerce. Even gentlemen from the California Legislature."

"You surely couldn't write about that!" Agatha said.

"Only with good taste. These things do need to be confronted. Only when our sisters recognise the full extent of such evils can they, and decent men, put an end to them."

"Thank God that Rosewood House saves so many girls from such dreadful fates," Florence said. "It's gone from strength to strength since you were here last, Mabel. And all due to Agatha's direction. No, dear, don't be modest! You must tell Mabel about all you've achieved there!"

Agatha, heading the Board of Trustees, provided no direct supervision. There was a salaried lady-superintendent for that. But connections through her family, and her own through the Royal Society, ensured steady funding from wealthy benefactors. And mention of the Royal Society led on to her latest paper to it. The title alone left Florence as mystified as Mabel, but that didn't matter.

The conversation turned to Nicholas. Florence told what she could, and made light of her concerns for him. She was grateful that they recognised that it was better not to dwell on the subject and to talk instead about how the Sailor's Rest must occupy so much of her time.

It was Agatha, unprompted, unaware of what Florence had hoped for, who mentioned Mrs. Chalmers-Bolger's tragedy. She said nothing of the causes, spoke only of the lonely death, the despair, the unwillingness to appeal to those who loved her.

"There must have been a reason," Mabel said. She mentioned the same as Florence had, something incurable maybe, something painful.

"No!" Florence paused, then used the word she knew would rivet Mabel's interest. "She was murdered."

"Is that what the police thought?" A journalist's question.

"No. But she was murdered just the same as if she'd been held under the water by force."

Mabel looked towards Agatha. "Do you think this too?"

"I don't just think it. I believe it."

"She was beggared," Florence said. "She was taken advantage of, bled dry, blackmailed too. We're sure of that. She was at the end of her tether and –"

"Stop," Mabel said. "Tell it from the beginning."

And Florence did.

She paused only to ask Agatha to confirm or add details. Mabel let her finish before asking any questions.

"You hadn't seen her for a few years, had you, Agatha?"

"No." A hint of shame. "I should have. But no. I didn't."

"So you can't really know anything about her mental state, do you?"

"No."

"But the servants saw it. They were sure of it," Florence said. "Servants see such things more clearly than anybody else."

I Know. I was one once.

Mabel had taken a notebook and pencil from her reticule, had put on her pince-nez.

"Let's start again."

It was a different Mabel now, not the warm friend but a thorough, passionless interrogator, question after question, teasing out what was fact from what was speculation, going back to earlier answers when she spotted inconsistencies and contradictions. Florence realised now how superficial, how naïve, had been her own investigations, how many opportunities to delve deeper she had missed. But there was one consolation. Mabel was interested.

"You're not going to give this up, are you, Florence?" she said at last. "Or you either, Agatha?"

No, not now, they said. Not with knowing what they did.

"You know it could be dangerous, don't you?" Mabel must be remembering that acid attack two years before. "So what are you going to do? Florence? Agatha?"

They didn't know.

Mabel didn't know either, could not advise anything.

But she said she'd think about it.

As Florence had hoped.

*

Another lonely weekend, church, piano practice, walks on the Southsea Esplanade. More Mrs. Braddon, more newspapers that told little, more pins stuck on the map of Egypt marking slow British progress up the Nile. If she could write to Nicholas it would have made it easier. She longed for more than the Sailor's Rest, even with its problems, to divert her fears, but not her love, from him.

Mabel's letter arrived on the Monday morning, written on stationary of the Grand Hotel in Birmingham. She wanted to talk some more about the tragedy. A reply by post should reach her before midday on Wednesday, when she was coming back to London, would be lodging again at the Rutland Hotel for three nights and leaving for Edinburgh thereafter. Could they meet that Wednesday evening and could Florence perhaps extend her stay by one more night at least?

She's tempted.

Florence went to the post office, found a copy of *Kelly's Directory* there, sought for a hotel in Bayswater, a respectable but not overly expensive area. She found four, chose the Mercer Hotel in Inverness Terrace. It was likely to be comfortable and within her budget.

And far from Coptic Street.

She went back home, wrote a letter to the Mercer, booking rooms for herself for two nights and for Mrs. Mabel Bushwick for three. Then she wrote another to Mabel, telling her what she'd done, and asking her to cancel her reservation at the Rutland. She felt better when she'd posted them.

Chapter 9

Mabel's answering letter from Birmingham was a good sign, confirming agreement to the change of hotels. Florence travelled to London on Wednesday morning and took a cab from Waterloo Station to the Mercer Hotel. She mulled over whether to invite Agatha to the meeting with Mabel that evening, decided against it. Agatha was clever, brilliant indeed, but not wise in the ways of the world and had no guile. Better to talk to her tomorrow, after meeting Mabel.

"You've something in mind. Tell me about it. I'll tell you my own thoughts after," Mabel said. She had arrived at around six o'clock. They had dined together in the hotel and had, by agreement, talked only of other matters until they had moved to Florence's bedroom. Mabel listened without comment.

"This could lead to a whole new series of articles for you, Mabel," Florence said. Not just in America, journals here would reprint them too. I'm sure there's an appetite for things like that nowadays."

"Do you think I haven't thought of that already? Go on."

"Let's say you're not a lady journalist, Mabel. Imagine you're a widow, Mrs. Daley, Mrs. Emily Daley." She'd been constructing that new woman in recent days. Memories of her time in the United States with Nicholas helped. "You're rich. Comfortably rich, well-heeled let's say, but no mansions on Broadway or cottages in Newport. Your husband made money in soap or candles or floor-polish or something like that. In one of the smaller cities, less known here. You helped him build the business, scrimped and saved for it. And when it prospered, he disappointed you. Other women, maybe even another family. You're not sorry he's dead."

"You're striking close to home, Florence." Mabel wasn't smiling.

Florence felt mortified by her own thoughtlessness. "She's nobody like you, Mabel," she said. "She's had little education and she's embarrassed by it."

"Go on."

"She has an only child, a son. We'll call him Franklin. He's grown up and he's running the business. He worships her – worships you rather – and he knows how you worked, knows what his father did and he despises him for it. So he indulges you and you let him."

"And I'm looking for another husband, am I? I'm not a dollar princess but maybe a dollar dowager?"

"No. You aren't looking, not actively. But you're susceptible. And you'd be flattered if some noble British widower showed interest."

"And I'm not beautiful, am I, Florence?" Mabel was smiling now.

"No more than I am. That's why you'd benefit from some treatment at Madame Hortense's *Temple de la Beauté*."

"Why am I in England?"

"At the start of a European tour. Your second. You loved the first, saw places and sights you'd dreamed of, never imagined seeing. You've wanted to come back. You have the time for it and you have the money too. Another wealthy American tourist. Europe's swarming with them."

"How have I come to know Mrs. Lacy? She's from outside London somewhere. It doesn't sound likely that I'd have encountered her."

"We met in Dresden last year. You were tremendously impressed by Darling Norbert's manners, thought him something more lordly than the impoverished squire he is. All three of us made an excursion up the Elbe one day by steamer and you loved it You're keen to renew the acquaintance and it's such a pity that Dear Norbert is at present in Ireland. And Mrs Lacy, not to put too fine a point on it, won't hesitate to sponge off you."

"I've never been in Europe, Florence. Only in England. I don't know enough to sound convincing."

"But I've been. Up the Rhine and down the Danube. Vienna, Prague, Dresden, Weimar. And another time to Venice and to Fiume too. I can tell you about them."

"Where's Fiume?"

"On the Adriatic. An ideal place to spend a winter. As you did, Mrs. Daley, on Norbert's and my recommendation. It did you a world of good."

"But this Hortense woman seems to have travelled, maybe that Mrs. Bellamy also. They may know many of these places, details that I won't. They could catch me out."

"Not if I've schooled you, Mabel. And not if you spend all tomorrow in your room with these." Florence had brought four Baedeker guidebooks. They were stacked on the bedside table, two dozen or more paper strips jutting from between each's pages. "I've marked what you need to learn. I'll quiz you about them tomorrow evening and then we'll make a coherent story about your previous tour."

"Where will Mrs. Daley be staying? I've commitments already, appointments around this country. Even two in Scotland. I won't be in London all the time."

"You didn't meet only Mr. and Mrs. Lacy on your tour," Florence said. "You've had invitations from a half-dozen other acquaintances you made. We'll make up a convincing list of them, real names, from *Who's Who* maybe, in case Mrs Bellamy checks, as I'm sure she will. But for now, you're staying with Mrs. Lacy in Hampshire, and you may be coming back to her place again at intervals."

"And the first step would be a treatment at the Temple?"

"Maybe two or three of them. You'd have to fit them in between your other travelling obligations. A very greedy Mrs. Lacy will go to Coptic Street tomorrow to arrange one for the day after."

"You're assuming I'm saying 'Yes', Florence."

"Tell me yes or no at breakfast. In the meantime, let's put more flesh on Mrs. Daley."

*

"May I share this table with you, ma'am?"

Florence looked up from her copy of the *Morning Post* propped against the toast rack on the breakfast table to see Mabel. Her accent had changed, ever so little, since the previous evening.

"Of course." Florence gestured to the place opposite. "My name is Lacy, by the way. And you are?"

Mabel reached out her hand. "Mrs. Emily Daley, ma'am. Of Indianapolis, Indiana."

She had made her decision.

*

Florence left Mabel to her study of the Baedekers and waited until half-past-ten, time enough to have reached London by rail from Bentley, before taking a hansom to Coptic Street. She had it halt outside the Temple's front door, paid the cabby through the hatch in the roof, and dismounted. Nobody looking out could suspect that she had come from anywhere else than Waterloo Station.

The attendant who opened the door recognised her, addressed her by name. Florence tried to appear flustered, apologetic.

"I don't have an appointment… I know it must be an inconvenience but I was hoping that …"

"No need for concern, Mrs. Lacy. No need at all. We'll see what can be done. Just follow me."

Five ladies waiting, two of them in pairs. No gentlemen.

Florence hesitated before taking a seat. She dropped her voice.

"If I could speak to Mrs. Bellamy? I know she isn't expecting me but if she has time…"

The attendant was back five minutes later. Mrs Bellamy was always glad to see Mrs. Lacy.

In the office that looked like a boudoir, Mrs Bellamy welcomed Florence, seated her on the chaise longue and sat opposite her on the chesterfield.

"Now, Mrs. Lacy. What can I do for you?"

No compliments about Florence's rejuvenated skin, no mention of Gazelle Cream of the Pamirs or Oil of Mahameru.

"I had a surprise, a very pleasant surprise, Mrs. Bellamy!" Florence's words were gushing out. "Out of the blue. An American lady whom Dear Norbert and I met in Dresden last year. Mrs. Daley, so nice a woman! She's just arrived from New York and she'll be making another

European tour. She dropped me a line to say she was in England, that she'd be staying a few weeks here and visiting other friends."

"And you invited her to stay with you, Mrs. Lacy?"

"Yes! She arrived at my house yesterday and she's staying until Sunday. So good to see her! And... and she mentioned that she'd noticed an improvement in my complexion. These Americans, even the best of them, are so direct! I admitted that I did have a little help. She was worried that the sea winds and airs on the crossing had done her skin no good and so she asked if I could let her into my secret."

"And you gave her a copy of *Woman's Mystery, Woman's Heritage,* did you, Mrs. Lacy?" Amusement in Mrs. Bellamy's tone. "It was lucky you had one, wasn't it?"

"She was entranced. And I gave her that jar of Samarkand Balm you let me have and she tried it and she was so impressed."

"Was her husband impressed too, Mrs. Lacy?"

"She doesn't have a husband. She was widowed three years ago, poor woman, and her son is grown up."

"Perhaps a consultation here might undo the ravages of the Atlantic air." Mrs. Bellamy was smiling. *I understand you, and you understand me,* that smile said.

"That's what I thought too, Mrs. Bellamy. That's what I said to her."

"Did this friend of yours, this Mrs. Daley, come with you to London today?"

"No, not today. I asked a neighbour, Mrs. Cobb, the doctor's wife, to bring her to Winchester to see the cathedral. But I could bring her tomorrow if –"

"If the terms were right, Mrs. Lacy?"

"Well, if ... It's not really that... But if you could..."

And as her words trailed off Florence thought, *Somebody else sat here like this, some friend of Margaret Chalmers-Bolger, forging the first link of the chain that dragged her into that pond on Hampstead Heath.* Necessary as it was, she felt degraded by the pretence.

Mrs. Bellamy ignored her, rose, walked to her desk and consulted a large business-diary.

98

"Tomorrow at two o'clock, you can be here? Good. I can see to her myself. And Claudette can see to you." Again that look. *I understand you.* "And no need for a donation. Just give Claudette a shilling if you're satisfied. That'll be enough."

No offer of a free Empyrean Bath. When Florence stood on the street again, it was with a free jar of scented yak-lard. She felt soiled, wanted to bathe. Just with plain soap and water.

That would have to wait. She took a hansom back to Waterloo Station, ordered lunch there in the dining room, dawdled over coffee and a magazine afterwards. The possibility of being followed was minimal, but she wouldn't take the chance. Hard experience, two-years before, had taught that lesson. Only when she was satisfied that she was not, did she take another cab back to the Mercer Hotel.

*

Mabel had been assiduous in her study and could, all but verbatim, repeat entire paragraphs of the Baedekers. She knew the itinerary of her previous, imagined, European tour in detail. It was the same route that Florence had taken with Nicholas so recently, with the addition of two mild Adriatic-winter months spent at the Hotel Tersatica in Fiume. The gardens there had especially pleased her. Mabel remembered which stages she had travelled by train and which by river-steamer, in which hotel, all of them luxurious, she had stayed in at each place.

If Florence suggested a city, Basel, Munich, Vienna, Prague, Dresden or any of another dozen, Mabel could reel off the names of the cathedrals, palaces and museums and other sights. She had a few favourite paintings in each of the main art-galleries. She knew what food she liked, and what she didn't like. She admired the Germans, found the Austrians charming, and thought the Swiss mercenary. She remembered the names of other tourists she had met, American, British, even Russian, none of them aristocratic, but comfortable financially, often through business, as she was herself. She was the personification of a woman, intelligent but uneducated, who had been given a chance in middle years

99

to expand beyond the boundaries of a life dominated by moneymaking and by a husband, and was now exulting in that freedom.

"I won't need a tenth, not a hundredth, of any of this," she told Florence. "But I don't know what the tenth will be. And it's important for me to feel the role. Not to be caught off guard either."

"Was it like this when you went into that laundry?"

"That was difficult. Much more difficult."

"Now tell me more about Mrs. Daley, Mabel."

She did. Of the poverty of her orphaned youth. Of her husband and her son. Of years of scraping and saving and the long battle for success in the floor-polish business, of the fire that had all but devastated their first home and how they had escaped, scarred but with their lives.

"We're missing something, Florence. Who's Mrs. Lacy?"

And Florence was no less detailed, her own story brooded on and improved during the last week. She remembered the details of Bentley village and surroundings from her single visit there, when she had met a splendid old lady. And Dear Norbert, unlucky in the management of his small estate and the frustration of his inheritance hopes, was not a happy man nowadays. Until things improved there would be no more European tours.

"Now let's say you're Mrs. Bellamy, Florence," Mabel said, "and I've just walked in to your Temple boudoir. Let's play the first meeting out."

They went on past midnight and, when they ended, they both felt confident that they could not be better prepared.

*

They took a cab to Coptic Street next day at half-past twelve, arriving as if from Waterloo Station. Mabel had dressed her best. The clothes were high-quality and fashionable, Florence recognised. Journalism was proving profitable. She herself had dressed to look more shabby.

Mrs. Mobray met them at the door and ushered them into the waiting area, saw them seated and served with tea. Mabel made no attempt to hide her curiosity, scrutinising other customers, not looking away when they glared back, going over to inspect the paintings on the wall more closely, sniffing at the flowers in vases, coming back to tell Florence in a loud whisper how impressed she was.

Mrs. Bellamy herself came to collect Mabel. She apologised that Madame Hortense's expertise had been called upon today by a certain illustrious personage, whom she was not allowed to name. She hoped that she could fill her place, however inadequately. Mabel looked suitably impressed as she was led away.

Florence had hardly been acknowledged. She should have been grateful for it, she knew, confirmation that she was convincing in the role of Mrs. Lacy, but it hurt nonetheless. She leafed through a magazine for twenty minutes. Customers who had entered later than her were ushered away. And then the elegant lady and gentleman she had seen previously came in. As before, he sat her down himself, demanded tea for her this time and coffee for himself. He had a swagger and a brutal confidence about him that Florence knew so many women seemed to admire. She loathed it. In her days as a servant she had seen too many like him. The lady was whisked away for treatment within five minutes and he sat back and opened a newspaper, scanned it for a few minutes, looking up the while to stare briefly at the other women waiting. He met Florence's gaze for a moment. She saw that he had remembered her, but even before she turned her head away, she saw that he had once more dismissed her. Shortly afterwards he rose, walked over to another lady sitting alone, fortyish, plain and stout, but expensively dressed. He asked if he could take one of the magazines on the table before her. Soon they were in conversation.

He could be another faux Lord Menston. Or the approach might be as innocent as anything ever could be with husbands like that. Florence smiled. It was easy to imagine Nicholas's contempt.

"Mrs. Lacy. Please follow me." Claudette again.

The treatment room to which she brought Florence was smaller, and on a higher floor than on the previous occasion.

Claudette was not unfriendly, but little interested either, confining herself to a few remarks about travelling by train and the current weather.

She massaged cream – from Bahia Blanca, no further details volunteered – into Florence's face, neck and arms. It looked and smelled no different to what Florence had on her dressing table at home, bought in a Southsea chemist's shop. No magnifying-glass examination of the skin afterwards, but a small jar of the same cream offered and accepted. The whole treatment took fifteen minutes and Florence didn't leave half-a-crown. A shilling was more than was deserved.

When she got back to the waiting area, Mabel had not yet returned. The gentleman was on his own again, for his target had been taken away for treatment. Florence had a growing suspicion that he was here for the day, for he soon struck up a conversation with a new customer. She wondered if he might in time be a smitten admirer of Mabel.

A tedious hour passed before Mrs. Bellamy brought Mabel back. And she did look better, no doubt of it. She was effusively thankful and was looking forward to her next appointment, Thursday next week, after she had returned from back from Edinburgh. No suggestion by Mrs. Bellamy that Florence might return at the same time. An attendant was sent to fetch a cab, and when it arrived, Mrs. Bellamy saw them off at the front door. It took them to Waterloo, and there they sat, with tea, in the first-class dining room. The station had a telephone machine and Florence, proud to know how to use it, called Agatha. She arrived twenty minutes later.

"That Bellamy's no fool," Mabel said. "And, by the way, I don't think there's any such person as Madame Hortense. Mrs. B's more than enough on her own. She would have made an excellent journalist and she dug every detail out of me that she could. Not directly, but guiding the conversation, allowing me to boast a little, asking little probing questions. And she has travelled. I've no doubt she picked up her skills in several places in Europe. It was best that we'd prepared, Florence. She'd have caught me out about Vienna and Prague otherwise."

"I couldn't have done it," Agatha said "I really couldn't."

"She was very sympathetic when I hinted that I'd been so lonely on the tour, much as I enjoyed it. To have seen so many happy married couples, and me without anybody to share such wonders with. Only a hint, and I didn't labour it."

"Do you think, Mabel, that she's considering hooking you?" Florence said.

"I think she's tempted. The treatment was free today and I'm to have an Empyrean Bath on Thursday."

"Would they see…" Florence was reluctant to mention the word. She remembered Mabel's agony when the vitriol had burned into her neck and shoulders. Even now, the injured flesh must look appalling.

"The scars?" Mabel said. "Mrs. Daley would regard them a cheap price for having saved baby Franklin when our house was burned down. She wouldn't be shy about them, not to another woman."

"Is the bath to be expensive?"

"Like the plain, blunt Hoosier that Mrs. Daley is, I asked about the price. Perhaps a donation of fifteen guineas, Mrs. Bellamy said. And I was so happy with my rejuvenation already – I hope you're impressed by my face – that I said that I though it reasonable. *Woman's Mystery, Woman's Heritage* had awakened me to my duty to myself."

"What will happen after Wednesday?" Agatha said.

"Maybe nothing. It'll depend on Mrs. Bellamy's assessment of Mrs. Daley's gullibility. She's already convinced that she's rich."

They broke up.

Florence took the train back to Portsmouth, arrived home in Southsea near ten o'clock.

She gave the Bahia Blanca cream to Susan.

Chapter 10

Florence slept late, had a leisurely breakfast, and read through the newspapers delivered to the house. The correspondents moving up the Nile with the British expedition had little new to report and she suspected, and feared, that, if they had, they would have nothing to say about Nicholas. He was somewhere in those vast vacant spaces on the map, and not on the river. She was sure of that now. The fear that she might never see him again was with her always, however much she tried to ignore it.

The other news was no less depressing. Agrarian unrest in Ireland, two Grimsby fishing boats lost with all hands in the North Sea, a mother and two children in Hartlepool slaughtered by a drunken father. A solemn editorial in the *Morning Post* warned that Britain was nursing a viper in its bosom by permitting so many political exiles, nihilists among them, to settle here. And Mr. Gladstone – how she loathed that old humbug! – had been pontificating about electoral reform.

She had left the weekly *Portsmouth Argus,* published the day before, for last. Its concerns were local, even parochial – social occasions, arrivals and departures of naval ships, community events, advertisements, births, marriages and deaths. A quick leaf-through would be enough, for the sun outside was beckoning for a walk on the Esplanade. Nothing held her interest until, in a column on the fourth page near the top, she saw a heading.

Murderous Attack on Portsmouth Shopkeeper

Below it, in smaller font: *Victim brought to Royal Hospital*

And below that: *Police seek Perpetrator*

It could be a coincidence, it might not be the same shopkeeper, but she was frightened now, and without reading in detail she scanned the lines below.

The name was there.

Chadband.

Hands trembling, heart thumping, she went back to the top and read the full item.

At ten o'clock on Thursday evening, Mr. Barnabas Chadband, dealer in second-hand clothing, was assaulted in his shop in Crasswell Street. His assistant was in a back room at the time and, alerted by Mr. Chadband's cries, found him dragged across the counter, already bleeding and being pummelled by a large man of middle years. Scorning his own safety, the assistant had attempted to save his employer but was himself knocked to the ground before the unknown assailant rushed from the shop. Mr. Chadband had sustained injuries enough to detain him in hospital, to where had had been brought on a handcart. No arrest had yet been made but Inspector Towton of the Portsmouth City Police had confirmed to the *Argus's* reporter that the case was under investigation. Crimes of this type would not be tolerated in Portsmouth, he had stated.

Florence read it a second and a third time. Moneylenders must have many enemies, the chances that the assailant might have any link to the Sailor's Rest must be remote.

But…

It made it worse still that she recognised another name. Towton, the police-inspector. She remembered him from two years before, when she had approached him about a girl's abduction. He had treated her like a nuisance, had been insolently contemptuous of her. Naval officers' wives were not expected to involve themselves in such matters, he had told her, especially when their husbands were away at sea. Any link of her name to the Chadband assault would delight him. He wouldn't hesitate to make the *Argus* reporter aware of it, or to mention her once using her umbrella in a street brawl, an incident that had never appeared in the newspaper at the time.

She sat still for a long time, almost on the point of nausea. The fears that had tortured her after Bill Wheatley's thrashing of Chadband, and Mrs. Marshall's visit afterwards, had almost faded. Now they were back in a raging flood, far stronger than before. Uncertainty was going to make them worse still, would drive her to madness. Bad as the news might be, she had to know more.

Her knees were weak when she stood up and she must have looked pale when she summoned Susan, who asked her if she was unwell. She denied it and sent her to fetch a cab. Feeling as she did, she did not trust herself to walk to the Seaman's Rest.

Mr. Selden was not there when she arrived, but he was expected. She went to her office, tried to busy herself with bills and a new builder's estimate but could not concentrate.

When he arrived, she saw from his face that he knew why she was here, saw too that he looked worried. She had brought the *Argus* with her, had laid it on the desk, and now she pointed in silence to the article. She didn't want him to hear a quaver in her voice.

"I was afraid of the same, ma'am," he said. "It wasn't Bill Wheatley, though. He was at Southampton, his employer sent him the day before. Didn't get back until last night."

Thank God! Relief surged through her.

He wasn't finished. "But it was a seaman, ma'am. They arrested him last night. I've just heard the news."

"Did he ever come here? Did his wife?"

"No, ma'am. Neither of 'em. But…"

"But what, Mr. Selden?" She could see that he was searching for words to break something unpalatable gently.

"His name's Atwell, ma'am. Dave Atwell."

The name was vaguely familiar.

"Should I know him, Mr. Selden?"

"He was one of the wounded men that Captain Dawlish brought from *Leonidas*. An' the captain arranged a good post for him in HMS *Vernon* after he'd recovered. Something that'd keep him at home for a bit."

She felt ashamed. She should have remembered. He must have been one of the men she had seen when she had gone with Nicholas to visit *Leonidas's* wounded in the Royal Navy Hospital at Haslar. She'd heard the names, had forgotten all but that of Purdon, the gunnery lieutenant. She remembered that because his injury had appalled her.

106

"How had this man, what's his name? Yes, Atwell. How had he been wounded at Tamai?"

"His leg. And he was beaten round the head. Badly."

She could visualise him now, a heavy man, slow of speech. His leg had been in plaster. As well as being broken, it had been ripped open by a Beja warrior's spear, Nicholas said. His head had been bandaged also. He had been movingly thankful that his captain had come to visit, and that she had accompanied him.

"They're sure it's him?"

"There are witnesses."

"Where is he now?"

"In the police cells. They'll bring him before the magistrate on Monday."

One thought only.

What would Nicholas do?

One answer only.

He'd stand by this man.

And she must do it in his place.

*

The next step would be dangerous. She sat thinking about it for a long time. The longer she did, the more she realised that she knew little or nothing of legal processes. She needed advice, knew only one place to get it. This was Saturday and most offices closed at one o'clock. There was time to get to those of Carlton and Bagshot, Solicitors, before then. Palmerston Road was only a quarter-hour walk away. Mr. Carlton had died years before but Mr. Bagshot, old but vigorous, ran the business without any younger partner. For all that his experience had been limited to family and property matters, he had proved remarkably supportive at the time of the abduction case. She could trust him.

He came to the outer office to meet her after his clerk had announced her arrival. Concern, perhaps even pity, on his face. She realised that he feared that she had bad news of Nicholas and she was touched to see he was relieved to hear that there was none. He ushered her into his office, sat her down, hoped he could assist.

It was better to make no mention of her own, remote, association with the moneylender, to present the case purely in terms of concern for a man who had stood beside her husband in battle and had been seriously wounded. It was what Captain Dawlish would have wanted. Mr. Bagshot made notes and heard her out.

"That's all you know, Mrs. Dawlish. No other details?"

Nothing more than she had read in the *Argus* and what she'd heard from Mr. Selden. It sounded very insubstantial.

"And you met this man Atwell just that once, ma'am?"

She nodded. She knew nothing about him other than that he had been wounded.

"But my husband spoke well of him. He'd been in the thick of the battle. He was lucky not to have had his leg amputated and he was badly concussed too. He was one of the wounded men from HMS *Leonidas* whom Nicholas arranged to be brought to hospital here from Malta when he gave up command of the ship."

"You said this Atwell is assigned to HMS *Vernon* now?"

Vernon was well known here, a ship that never went to sea, an old wooden vessel moored in the harbour. Most of her crew and officers lived ashore. She was the navy's torpedo school, not only instructing in use of this new weapon, but extending and testing its capabilities. Nicholas had served as deputy to the Senior Instructor for almost two years and had been responsible for designing improvements of the weapon. It would have been easy for him to use his contacts and arrange a posting there for Atwell. It would be less demanding than service at sea and allow him to live with his family until his health was fully restored. Nicholas hadn't mentioned it to her, but that was typical of him. He never spoke of acts of charity he did. Those she knew about, she had learned of by accident.

"I've been told he's in *Vernon*," she said. "It may not be the case. I'll need to check."

"It's a serious offence, Mrs. Dawlish. It's only by the mercy of Providence that it's not a case of murder. And you don't really know the man, do you? It's admirable that you want to help but, if you do, I'd advise that it's from a distance."

"He's coming before the magistrate on Monday. What'll happen then? Could he be convicted?"

"It's serious enough to be beyond a magistrate's remit. He'll be remanded and sent for trial at a Crown Court. But it's better that he has a solicitor on Monday. He must know what he shouldn't say if the magistrate presses him. It's better he says nothing, that he just enters a plea of guilty or not guilty."

"Could you help, Mr. Bagshot?"

"I can see him. Today if possible. And, if necessary, I could be in court on Monday."

"Will it... will it be expensive?" She hated to say it, but she had to be careful about money. Recent travel to and from London had been costly. And there was more in the offing.

"I wouldn't worry about that, Mrs. Dawlish. I'm an old man. I have all I need, and more. Now, to business. Where's this Atwell held at present?"

At the central police station, she assumed. He'd start there, he said. If not, he'd get further directions there. And would Mrs. Dawlish be at home about six o'clock? He hoped he'd have news by then.

*

Mr. Bagshot was punctual to the minute. He accepted a small glass of sherry when Florence seated him in the drawing room. He waited until Susan had left to speak.

"It's a bad business, Mrs. Dawlish. Very serious. He didn't want to talk and I had to spend a long time drawing him out. All he would say in the end was that he'd done no wrong in the sight of Almighty God. Nothing more."

"Where is he?"

"In the second place I visited. The Blackwell Street station."

Florence had dreaded that he would be there.

"Inspector Towton's?"

Mr. Bagshot nodded. He had dealt with him before on her behalf.

"The inspector was present when I visited. He remembered you and asked if you'd sent me. He must have guessed that you had, since there was a seaman involved."

"Did you tell him?"

"I pleaded legal confidentiality. That a friend had commissioned me to act for Mr. Atwell and that I needed to see him. The inspector couldn't refuse that, insolent as he ever was. I talked to Atwell in a cell. He's being held alone."

"Did you tell him that I'd asked you to see him?"

"I didn't mention your name. I only said that it was a well-wisher associated with HMS *Leonidas*."

This can't last, she thought. Towton was already suspicious. It was only a matter of time before her interest became widely known. And with rumours abounding about her inspiration of an earlier attack on Chadband ...

You crossed the Rubicon when you sent Mr. Bagshot. No option now but to play this out. With guile, by any means necessary.

"Did Atwell admit anything to Towton?"

"Not a word. He wouldn't be drawn. Not even after witnesses had identified him. He kept refusing to answer questions and he wouldn't make a statement. That will go badly against him in court, Inspector Towton told me."

"Do you think he's sane, Mr. Bagshot? He was beaten around the head at Tamai. He was senseless for a day or so besides his leg wound."

"I'm not a doctor. But he seems sane to me. Angry, very angry, but as sane as you or me. I think he knew exactly what he was doing. He went to that shop with intent, I've no doubt of it. That's what would have hanged him had the Chadband fellow died. It's hardly better for Atwell that he didn't. He's facing penal servitude for fifteen, eighteen years at worst. The law doesn't allow the judge much leeway in sentencing."

"And Atwell knows that?"

"I told him and he said he didn't care."

"Not either for what it means for his wife? Or for his children?" Florence didn't know if he had any.

"He refused to talk about them. They were his own affair, he said. He was adamant about that. I didn't persist and just concentrated on explaining how essential it was that he only confirm his name on Monday, plead 'Not Guilty' when asked, and say not a word more. It took time but, in the end, he agreed that I should represent him."

Florence thanked him before he left.

"No thanks, Mrs. Dawlish. At my time of life, anything outside the day's routine is welcome."

She would come to his office on Monday afternoon to hear what had happened in court. The proxy encounter with Atwell had not reassured her and she felt even more frightened than before.

*

A question that she should have thought of asking Mr. Bagshot nagged Florence through the evening and spoiled her sleep afterwards. The report in the *Argus* had implied that the assailant had made a successful escape from the shop. Witnesses had not been mentioned, but that Atwell had been arrested so soon indicated that at least one person had recognised him. That was most likely Chadband's assistant, perhaps even the moneylender himself. If so, it implied earlier contact and that in turn almost certainly involved money. Was Atwell's wife another who'd become indebted while her husband was away on service? But it was five months since he had returned from *Leonidas*, and if it were such debt, then he must surely have known of it before now. If he was as reliable a man as Nicholas thought him, Atwell would have been unlikely not to share his worries with a trusted leading hand on *Vernon*, who in turn would have raised it with an officer. That was how it was in happy ships,

111

even in ones that never went to sea. Some solution would have been found, something other than a savage attack that could have brought him to the gallows.

She was already thinking beyond the magistrate's hearing. The real trial, that in a Crown Court, was yet to come. Defence would cost money. How much, she didn't know, but probably far beyond the resources of Atwell and his family. She could make a contribution, but much more might well be needed. In newspaper accounts of trials, she had read of character witnesses. They might help but – it was a distasteful possibility, but could not be ignored – Atwell might be a brutal thug who well deserved punishment. Even moneylenders had a right to life and men who fought bravely in battle were not necessarily saints in peacetime. It might be possible to find officers to testify in favour of his character. Purdon, *Leonidas's* gunnery lieutenant could be one. But what if Atwell's character was not one that they could praise under oath?

She had to find out more about him.

Cautiously.

*

She knew only one officer who was at present serving on *Vernon*. Lieutenant Henry Jackson had succeeded Nicholas as Senior Instructor.

"As much a scientist as a sailor," he'd said of him, "and he's good as both. He knows more about electricity than anyone else in the navy. He's a coming man."

Florence had met him only twice, each time at social events. They had exchanged little more than pleasantries, but it was enough to facilitate contact now. He was unmarried, she remembered, and most likely lived ashore, as Nicholas had done during his own tenure, rather than on the old ship itself. She'd have to find him.

After church, she went directly to the Sailor's Rest, found Mr. Selden there in his Sunday best, stopping by only briefly, he said, to satisfy himself that all was shipshape. He knew Lieutenant Jackson only by repute but he'd make enquiries. Lots of seamen would be dropping

112

in to the Rest that day. He'd ask someone to bring a message to her house as soon as an address was known. She went back to the villa, spent the rest of the morning practicing piano.

A boy arrived just before lunch with a note from Mr. Selden. Lieutenant Jackson lived in lodgings not too far distant. Florence had Susan take the boy to the kitchen for a sandwich while she herself sat down to pen a note to Jackson on headed paper. She did not know if he'd be at home this Sunday afternoon, but it was worth a try. It would not be seemly to invite a personable young man alone to her house but she suggested meeting in the coffee room of the huge Queen's Hotel on the north side of Southsea Common at four o'clock. It was close enough for her to walk to, public enough not to invite scandal. She mentioned Atwell's name, referred to Nicholas's interest in him, and said she would like to discuss an urgent matter regarding him as soon as possible. She sealed the envelope, had the boy called back, gave him sixpence and sent him off.

He was back a half-hour later. Lieutenant Jackson sent his compliments and would be pleased to meet her at four.

Chapter 11

Jackson was punctual to the minute. Florence had arrived before him and was still uncomfortable about the propriety of meeting a man not her husband like this. She did not have to worry. He was a stiff and correct young man, and he approached her as he might an aged maiden-aunt. He was not one for small talk and after a few pleasantries, he said, "I understand you want to talk about the Atwell affair, ma'am."

"You know about it already, lieutenant?"

He did, all HMS *Vernon* did, and it had come as a surprise.

"A very steady man," he said. "Reliable. He'll never make a petty officer but he's the sort of AB that's the bedrock of any crew. Your husband thought the same when he recommended him. 'A good man in a tight corner', he said. I think he'd be happy to see you take an interest in the case, Mrs. Dawlish."

"He'd had a head wound. Could that perhaps have caused momentary lapses into insanity?"

"It's possible, it's always possible, but I never noticed it. And I would have. He's been helmsman on a fast craft I'm using for torpedo-launching trials. It needs coolness as well as skill. His shipmates like him too, even though I understand they joke about his preaching."

"Preaching?"

"He's apparently very strong on temperance and he urges others to take the pledge. He's involved with some Non-Conformist chapel."

"Has he a clean service record?"

"Immaculate. I've checked it. He's been exemplary through his whole eleven years. If he's religious, it isn't because of a conversion after previous debauchery. He was always like that. That's why it was hard to believe when the police came to tell us that he'd been arrested, and the more so since he'd seemed no different in the previous days to what he always was."

"Would you swear as to his character, Lieutenant Jackson? Not tomorrow, it won't be needed then. But later. In a higher court."

Jackson was silent for a moment, then said. "Yes. I'd swear to it. I wouldn't hesitate, if it would help."

Vernon's captain was on leave, the executive officer was on business at Devonport and Jackson was in temporary command. When he heard of the arrest, he'd sent a young sub-lieutenant to the police station to make enquiries. He had found Atwell crouched in a corner of a cell, a blanket clutched around him, unwilling to talk. Inspector Towton had ordered his belt removed, his shirt too, lest he twist it into a rope. Suicide was always a possibility with cases like this, he'd said.

Florence told about her meetings with Mr. Bagshot and his visit to the prisoner. Jackson knew about them already and thanked her. He'd asked a chaplain to visit Atwell that morning. A good practical man, no sanctimony about him, crews liked him. Atwell was more communicative by then, though sullen, and he'd been grateful for the Bible the chaplain had brought him. He had even overcome his stout Non-Conformist distrust of the Church of England enough to pray with the chaplain. But he was still unwilling to discuss his case. He said again that he'd done no wrong in the sight of Almighty God. It was that, rather than Mr. Bagshot's advice, that had convinced him to plead Not Guilty on the morrow. The chaplain had promised to be in the courtroom but could do no more than assure Atwell that he was not abandoned.

"Did he say anything about his family?" The concern that tormented Florence.

"He refused. And when the chaplain offered to go to see the family this afternoon, he asked him not to. He got quite agitated about it. It would do no good, he said, his wife wouldn't want to talk to him."

The woman must be distraught, Florence thought. Not just the present nightmare but the spectre of future destitution. Mrs. Atwell must know that her husband was facing long imprisonment and that his scant naval pay would end. Florence remembered Nicholas telling her that an able-seaman was paid twenty-seven pounds a year, just over ten shillings a week. It seemed a miracle that anyone could maintain a family on so little. She herself paid Susan twelve pounds a year, and she had free food and board in addition.

"Are there children, Lieutenant Jackson?"

"Three. All little."

Her immediate reaction was to envisage going herself to see the woman. She'd had sufficient experience of dealing with welfare cases before and her manner was such that women confided in her.

But that was the danger.

If Mrs. Atwell had indeed been in in debt to Chadband, and if she had known of Florence's rumoured involvement in his beating by Bill Wheatley, and of the debt-relief that had followed for several women, then a thread of guilt could well be traced back to herself.

But if I don't know more, it will hang over me, drive me mad. If I know the danger's real, then I can do something about it. I don't know what, but there must be something. Better to meet the problem head-on than to wait like a passive victim. But I shouldn't be seen to be taking the lead.

"Perhaps Mrs. Atwell wouldn't refuse a visit by one of the *Vernon* officers' wives," she said. "An older lady perhaps. Somebody motherly, who'd be trusted, who could judge what help is needed, and perhaps organise a collection."

Jackson was biting. "Maybe Mrs. Enderby, the executive officer's wife. She's a kindly woman. She's a lot involved with church fetes, that kind of thing, but —" He was frowning.

"But perhaps not familiar with the city's poorer areas?" Florence remembered seeing her at one of Lady de Courcey's tea parties. A shy woman, with a grown-up family, who said little. "Where does Mrs. Atwell live?"

"Clingford Lane, off Tudor Street, I'm told. And yes, poor."

"I've been shocked myself by some of the things I've seen in such places. It's not wise for a lady to venture into them alone."

"Exactly, Mrs. Dawlish. But if you could perhaps accompany her? And Mrs. Atwell will know about your husband. She'd might well welcome seeing you."

It was settled. Jackson would contact Mrs. Enderby with the suggestion. He'd let Florence know if she was willing and, if so, a meeting would follow.

*

116

Mr. Bagshot came to Albert Grove after the magistrate's court session the following morning. Atwell's case had been dealt with in two minutes. His identity had been confirmed, he had entered a plea of 'not guilty' to the charge of inflicting grievous bodily harm and he had been remanded in custody in Portsmouth's Kingston Prison. His case would be heard in the Crown Court, no date yet available but likely to be about three weeks from now. He had shown no emotion, either in the court or when he was being led away.

"It'll go badly for him," Mr. Bagshot said. "Unless there's some mitigating factor, he'll get the full term. We've no idea of his motive. It's clear that it wasn't robbery, though a prosecutor might imply it. Unless we know why a steady Godfearing man almost committed murder, there's no hope of putting up a credible defence."

"Are you still prepared to help?" Florence said.

"I can prepare the case, whatever it is, but there's little, almost nothing, to build on yet. But I'm a solicitor, Mrs. Dawlish. I can't plead in court. We'd need a good barrister for that."

"Would he be expensive?"

"Yes, I fear. And I know nobody here who'd take it on *pro bono.*"

Even if payment was possible, it was unlikely that a barrister of the calibre needed would be found in Portsmouth, Florence thought. If Atwell was not to break stones for the next eighteen years, he needed somebody at the pinnacle of his profession. Somebody expensive.

*

A seaman, young, strapping and handsome, to Susan's delight, arrived with a message from Jackson just before lunch the next day. Mrs. Enderby had welcomed the suggestion and would call on Mrs. Dawlish at three that afternoon. Florence was embarrassed by the offer. Mrs. Enderby was twenty years older than her at the least, but her husband was a commander and Florence was a captain's wife. She would have had no hesitation going to the older lady's house but Mrs. Enderby had assumed that she would not. Differences of rank counted for as much here as when she herself had been a member of the servants' hall in the

Kegworth household. The gulf between scullery maid and butler was perhaps wider than that between seaman and admiral.

"I'm not sure what we can do for the poor woman," Mrs. Enderby said after Florence had seated her in the parlour. "A collection maybe, Lieutenant Jackson said."

"That may be the easy part," Florence said. This woman has never been through the fire, she thought. Economies to maintain respectability on a naval salary, yes, but not the want that drove desperate mothers to moneylenders or yet worse measures.

"Perhaps with Lady de Courcey's support …"

"We must talk to Mrs. Atwell first," Florence said. "She may need more than money. Advice, support, comfort."

"But I heard that she wouldn't see anybody, not even a chaplain."

"She'll see us though," Florence said. "And there's no time like the present, Mrs. Enderby. Have you got time? Yes? Good!" She went to the bell pull and tugged. When Susan answered the call, she was sent to fetch a cab.

Tudor Street, when they reached it, looked as if it seldom saw many such vehicles. Lines of washing hung over it between the three-and four storied houses on either side. Open front doors signalled multiple occupancy and the women chatting at scrubbed doorsteps looked at the cab with interest rather than suspicion. Children released by now from school played on the pavements, none barefoot, girls playing hopscotch, boys swinging on a rope around a lamp-post. Pots of geraniums stood on window ledges, the glass behind them clean, and, in some cases, white net curtains shielding the interiors. The area was poor, but there was no squalor. There was dignity here, even a sense of hope, maybe of aspiration, though entire families might live here in one or two or, at best, three rooms.

Clingford Lane was too narrow for the cab to enter, so they dismounted at the entrance. The poverty did not look absolute here either. Florence declined the cabby's offer to wait. Every movement that she and her companion would make would be noted and discussed for days by the residents. She did not want to give the impression of the visit being for form's sake only or that she and her companion felt unsafe and in need of the protection of the cabby, scant though it could be. The sight of well-dressed ladies must be a novelty here and several children clustered about them. Florence had brought a bag of boiled sweets and she gave one to each, to the smallest first. Mrs Enderby was suddenly a different woman. She admired a baby carried by an older sister, then asked if she could hold it herself. It snuggled against her and grasped and pulled her hair and she laughed.

"Are you looking for Mrs. Atwell, ma'am?" A grey-haired woman, who had what must be her grandchild by the hand, approached. The question was an obvious one. Nothing else would have brought two such strangers here.

"We'd be grateful if you would help us find her," Florence said.

"She's gone, poor soul. Her and the children. On Saturday."

"Where to?"

"Don't know where exactly, ma'am They say her sister came to take her. I didn't see it meself. But her neighbours will know."

She led them down the lane, the troop of children following, Mrs. Enderby still with the baby in her arms. The house was small, two storeys, a single window and a hall-door opening on the street, another window on the floor above. The Atwells lived up there, the woman said. That might mean three rooms, Florence thought. That would count as luxury around here.

A knock on a closed door opening off the hall brought out a toothless and bald old man. He was hard of hearing and could not understand even when the woman shouted in his ear that the ladies were here about Mrs. Atwell. The noise brought out a younger woman from some inner room, two children following.

Florence introduced herself and Mrs. Enderby, explained that they were here to help if they could.

"What's that? What's that? Mrs Atwell is it?" The old man had understood at last. "Damn good riddance! You tell 'em, Maggie!"

"Go out, dad." His daughter had caught him by the elbow. "You go out there now, get a bit of air." He might not hear her but he allowed her to propel him to the hall-door and out on to the street. He looked bewildered and trudged away.

"Don't mind him, ladies," she said. "He don't mean no harm. It was just he didn't like her, nor the husband neither. Always telling him to steer clear of the pub, he was, an' pestering him to take the pledge."

"Could we come in please, ma'am?" Florence said. "Just for a few minutes?"

They could. Mrs. Enderby handed the baby back to its sister, the woman with her grandchild looked aggrieved that she was not included, and Maggie sent her own two children out to play.

The room was spotless, though Maggie, Mrs. Mitchell, apologised for its unreadiness for visitors. A made-up iron bedstead, probably the old man's, occupied one corner. For the rest it was both living room and kitchen, a coal fire in the grate, an iron crane above on which to hang cooking pots, a grid also, battered and unmatched armchairs on either side, a large cupboard, a table, two upright chairs. No gaslight but an ornate kerosene lamp, its brass gleaming, a pair of china dogs and several small framed photographs on the mantlepiece, a mirror above and to one side a lithograph portrait of the Queen. A closed door probably led to the family's sleeping room. There was a dignity about the place and Florence suspected that the Atwells' accommodation above might have something of the same.

Mrs. Mitchell seated her visitors in the armchairs and sat at the table herself. She'd guessed already why they were here and she knew that Atwell had been removed to Kingston Prison because a curious neighbour had gone to the magistrate's court that morning.

"We knew there was something up when we heard the shouting and crying and banging up above!" The memory was half-horrifying, half-thrilling her. "Thursday night it was. My Jim was just back from his work an' sitting down to his supper. We'd never heard the like. Right quiet the Atwells always was, her an' the kids so neat and clean, an' Tom Atwell hisself always so godly when he was home from sea, an' handing out tracts and inviting us to chapel. Never raised his voice he did, not to her or anybody else we knew of."

"He was away for a long time on my husband's ship," Florence said. "Did you know him before he left?"

"They was here for seven years, ma'am, ever since they was wee. He weren't here much. He was at sea, as you know. But when he came back he was as good a husband an' as good a father as any woman might wish. Adored his kids, he did, an' always willing to help a neighbour in need. A hero too in foreign parts, I'm told, though he never bragged of it. That's how he was wounded, but I expect you know that."

"I saw Mr. Atwell in the hospital in Haslar when my husband brought me to visit him and his ship's other injured." The memory of the half-dozen bed-ridden men sitting up stiffly in freshly laundered nightshirts, and grateful that their captain had come to see them, was poignant. "He was making a good recovery then," Florence said. "But, tell me, Mrs. Mitchell, did he seem any different when he was released from hospital?"

"No different, ma'am. Just that he had to walk with a stick for a few weeks, but he made light of it. That's why we was so shocked when we heard the shouting. Nobody had never heard him raise his voice before, nor Joan Atwell screaming neither."

"On Thursday evening, you said?"

When Chadband had been all but killed.

"Thursday it was, ma'am, about nine o'clock. My Jim went out to see what was up but Tom Atwell almost knocked him down, running down the stairs and out the door. Like a madman, he was, Jim said. An' I went upstairs to see if I could help but his wife, she'd bolted the door and wouldn't let me in, an' I could hear her crying an' sobbing, and the children howling too, behind it. Jim came up too an' begged her to let us in but she wouldn't."

It was a story like many that Florence had heard several times before from women, sometimes bruised, asking her for help at the Rest. But Mrs. Enderby hadn't and was looking shocked.

"Could you not have sent for the police?" she said.

Mrs. Mitchell all but laughed. "D'ye think they'd bother themselves with things like that, ma'am? Not when no murder's done?"

"So what did you do?" Florence said.

"We was still outside her door, an' Jim wondering if he should break it down. The Mullards from next door had come too an' the Shaws from across the way – they was chapel also – and then Tom Atwell was back, face and fists all bloody an' he wouldn't say where he had been an' then he too was pounding on the door an' still she was sobbing and crying within and she wouldn't open. Then, after a while, he went all calm and began to cry himself and after that he went out, wandering the streets he must have been, poor soul, an' we didn't see him again until the next night."

"Did Mrs. Atwell come out when he'd left?"

"Later than that, ma'am. She'd only let me in so I could see that the kids was all right, and they was, poor dears. Right broke up it was in there though, things smashed and thrown around."

"Had she been hurt?" Florence had seen women enough with black eyes and bruisers. And often protesting afterwards that their husbands were good at heart, and always giving them one last chance.

"No, nothing like that, ma'am. I'm not surprised neither. Tom Atwell wouldn't have it in him to hurt her, no matter what else they're accusing him of. She'd tell me nothing, only say that she wanted to be gone an' I asked her how. 'Send a telegram for me to me sister Kate,' says she. 'She'll come for me, she's over Southampton-way.' She gave me the address and wanted to give me the money too, but I said no, an' my Jim sent it for her the next morning. She kept herself locked in until her sister came that afternoon an' took her and the kids away. An' that's all I can tell you. Tragic it is, tragic, ma'am."

"But Mr Atwell did come back?"

"Not until after the family was gone. Friday night, that was. He let himself in, and we could hear him sobbing something awful. Then the constables arrived, three of 'em, with a sergeant, an' at the sight of them there was no more fight in poor Tom. He went with them like a lamb."

"So his wife is in Southampton now?" Mrs. Enderby was dabbing her eyes with a lace handkerchief. "I trust her sister's able to care for her and the children?"

"I can't say, ma'am, but I kept the address. You can have it."

Mrs. Enderby was hesitating.

"I'll take it," Florence stood. "You've been so very helpful, Mrs. Mitchell. You, and your husband too, you both behaved very well. And

122

now we have to go and not take up more of your time. And no, there's no need to send somebody for a cab."

At the door, Florence turned back to Mrs Mitchell.

"Did you like Mrs. Atwell?" she asked.

The question took the woman by surprise, as was intended.

"Thought a lot of herself an' her family she did –" Mrs Mitchell stopped herself. "She was a nice woman. I couldn't say otherwise, ma'am."

Florence pressed two shillings into her hand.

"That's for the telegram," she said.

Chapter 12

Florence had expected to find out more and only by speaking to Mrs. Atwell could any coherent defence be found for her husband. That she had been in debt to Chadband seemed a near certainty, but her neighbour on the floor below had made no mention of any moneylender. Mrs. Mitchell seemed indeed to delight in others' business and if she'd known about loans, she would have said it. Southampton, to where Mrs. Atwell's sister had taken her, was close, a half-hour by rail, but visiting her would have to wait. Florence was already committed to going to London next day. When she parted from Mrs. Enderby, they agreed to travel together to Southampton on Saturday. Ineffectual as the older lady was, her presence would still be valuable, her shocked concern making Florence's probing seem less obvious.

When she got back home, Florence had just enough time to pen a note for Agatha and send Susan with it to catch the evening post. She was already booked to stay two nights at the Mercer Hotel. Mabel would arrive there from Edinburgh in the late afternoon and they would, all three, dine together later. Now Florence asked Agatha to come earlier, to meet her there at two o'clock. There was something important to discuss.

The newspapers occupied her on the train next morning, the correspondents with little new to say about the Nile campaign but saying it anyway, and at length. She searched, as she did every day, for some hint of what Nicholas might be doing and, as always, found nothing. All she could do to help him was to endure in hope.

Agatha arrived late at the Mercer. She had been in the British Museum's reading room, had lost count of time. Florence invited her to her room, since what she wanted to say had best be said in private. She asked for tea to be sent up and, until it arrived, confined herself to pleasantries.

"I've been very stupid, Agatha," she said when the maid had left. She felt a tremor in her voice, feared that the pent-up worries of recent days would overwhelm her.

"You're never stupid, Florence." Agatha came over and embraced her. "We'd have died in Thrace together if it hadn't been for you. You're the practical one of us, not me."

Florence told it all, starting with the first appeal from a desperate indebted wife and the suggestion she herself had made that the moneylender be warned. With the benefit of hindsight, she felt ashamed that she had been so foolish, that she had not foreseen how things could have gone so awry.

"It's Nicholas whom I've betrayed most of all. I don't know where he is or what he's doing, except that he's doing it well and that his life's most certainly in danger." She was fighting back the urge to weep. "If what I've done comes out in court, if I'm linked to Chadband, then I'll have wrecked Nicholas's career and disgraced him, no matter what he achieves in Egypt or the Sudan or whatever god-forsaken place he's in."

"Do you think this Mr. Atwell's guilty?"

"I don't think there can be much doubt about it."

"But you're not abandoning him, are you, Florence?"

"I don't want to. But —"

"Would Nicholas turn his back on him? No, Florence, you know he wouldn't, not even if it cost him his career. Whatever the outcome, he'll love and honour you regardless."

They sat in silence for a minute until Florence recovered her composure. It embarrassed her to be seen like this, even by Agatha.

At last she said, "I can't save this man on my own. From all I've heard from my solicitor, the case against him will be all but indefensible." She had rehearsed these words in her mind a dozen times. "Unless he has a good barrister, one of the very best, he'll go to penal servitude for years. He can't afford such a lawyer, and I don't know if I can raise contributions enough to pay for one. I don't know if —"

Agatha caught her hand and held it. "You didn't hesitate to help when my brother was in . . . in disgrace. Not even though he'd always treated you with such contempt. Oswald would be breaking stone and sewing mailbags now, were it not for you, Florence. My father knows that too. He's thankful for it."

125

"In this, I've nobody else to turn to than you, Agatha."

"I'll speak to Father. I won't tell him everything, just that we need an advocate. He'll know what to do. He knows everybody. He'll help you, Florence." Agatha rose. "And now, we've got two hours still before Mabel arrives. There's time to take a stroll together and we'll talk no more of this for now."

"Just one thing, Agatha. No word of this to Mabel."

It made sense.

Best to keep the two concerns separate.

*

Seated with Agatha in the hotel lounge, chatting about trivialities only, Florence could see through the open doors to the hotel's reception desk. There were other guests in the room. A married couple, what might be two spinster sisters, a white-haired clergyman leafing through the *Illustrated London News*. Mabel was due soon, for the train from Edinburgh should have arrived at King's Cross a half-hour before. New guests arrived, were welcomed, were conducted to their rooms.

And then Mabel, tired-looking from her journey. She glanced towards the lounge only after she had signed the register. Florence saw her from the corner of her eye for she had looked away. Agatha's back was turned to the reception. Only when Mabel's valises had been carried away by a page did she move towards the lounge, pleasure of recognition on her face. Florence stood to meet her.

"Mrs. Daley! What a delight to see you! A pleasant journey I trust?"

"Exhausting, Mrs. Lacy. Positively exhausting." Mabel looked towards the still-seated Agatha. "And this lady must be the friend you mentioned?"

Agatha lurched to her feet and blinked through her pince-nez. Florence introduced Mrs. Daley of Indianapolis to Mrs. Yardley of Cheriton, Hampshire, a dear friend from schooldays on.

It was all as agreed the week before, not a three-sided charade but a preparation for Mabel's Empyrean Bath on the morrow. They would carry it on through the evening, through dinner, on until Florence's brother, Jack, would arrive with a clarence at eleven o'clock to carry Agatha back to her father's Piccadilly mansion.

Mrs. Yardley, the new acquaintance of Mrs. Lacy's American friend, would be curious about every detail of her background, her family, her source of wealth, of her previous European tour, of her present activities in Britain. An inquisitive busybody, prompted when necessary by her friend Mrs. Lacy, Mrs. Yardley would wring from Mrs. Daley sad admissions of loneliness, regrets about life with her dead husband, wistful memories of a young man whom she had once loved and who had died on the battlefield of Shiloh.

Florence attacked during dinner, contesting memories, pouncing on contradictions, probing for any inconsistencies with what had been told to Mrs. Bellamy during Mrs. Daley's treatment the previous week. The time since then had been well spent. Five decades of life and struggle and success and disappointment in Indianapolis had been enriched in detail in Mabel's mind. While in Edinburgh she had not been there to visit an industrial school but, as Mrs. Daley, to visit Dr. and Mrs. Hector Lennox. whom she had met on a steamer on the Danube the previous year. Her visit to them was fictitious but the names were real, the address real too, found in *Kelly's Directory*. Mrs. Bellamy was welcome to check.

Mabel returned only once to her own identity, the journalist of the *Columbia Home Gazette*.

"I'm leaving for Coventry the day after tomorrow. Two days there and another two in Manchester after that. It's all arranged. Visits to orphanages, a home for fallen women, a hospital for incurables. If some Lothario from the *Temple de la Beauté* wants to contact me in that time, how can he?"

Florence had given it prior thought. "Mrs. Daley will be a guest of several other acquaintances in the north. You know the names and addresses, don't you? But it'll never for longer than two nights, so she'll be using the poste restante at Manchester's main post office."

127

And so it went on, steady and relentless. Mabel's few lapses during the evening were minor ones and when Florence, as Mrs. Lacy, queried them, they were convincingly explained away by faulty memory.

The American lady who retired to bed that night was not Mabel. She was Mrs. Emily Daley.

*

Mrs. Daley went alone to the *Temple de la Beauté* in mid-morning. It was raining heavily and Florence stayed in the hotel, frustrated that she could do nothing but wait, peruse the newspapers and read a novel. The hours seemed endless and it was past three o'clock then Mrs. Daley returned. Had she been fully rejuvenated, it did not show but, as Mabel, she laughed it off.

"Was it real milk?" The idea of the Empyrean Bath had aroused Florence's curiosity no less than her amusement.

"Cows', I'd guess, though I wouldn't recognise llamas' if it had been," Mabel said. "A hip bath, several gallons, well-watered, and with a lot of heavy scent and flower petals. The feminine constitution needs a full two hours to absorb the full strength from the revivifying immersion, Mrs Bellamy told me, and another gallon or two of heated milk was added."

"Were you –" Florence hesitated. The question bordered on the indecent. "Were you naked?"

"Mrs. Bellamy's too good a judge of character to suggest anything like that to a plain Hoosier woman, even if she' a little silly since being widowed. But I don't think she'd hesitate with others."

"What did you wear then, Mabel?" There was a certain fascination about it, easy to see how others could be drawn in.

"A girl called Claudette helped me disrobe – that's the word she used. She was shocked when she saw my scars but she covered it up well and made no remark as she helped me change into a silk chemise to bathe in."

"Was Mrs. Bellamy reminded of Coleridge, the poet?"

128

"Some nonsense about a woman undressing her gentle limbs? Yes, she quoted it. How did you guess, Florence?"

"Because she and Mrs. Mobray probably use it on every woman who enters the place."

Mabel laughed. "Not only there, I'd guess. She probably used it when she was summoned to St. Petersburg to administer a course of baths for a certain personage whose identity she was sworn not to identify. She told me that was the crowning moment of her career."

"I daren't even speculate about that!" Florence said.

"Claudette dried me when I emerged, all very decorous, believe me. She said that the towels were of Arabian wool. After that, I had a soft robe of Scythian samite to rest in until the massages could begin, over an hour of them. Oh, and also a glass of nectar of Andalusian peach to refresh me."

And all the time, Mrs. Bellamy had been present, coaxing information, sympathising about life's setbacks, phrasing in different terms the same questions she had asked before to seek inconsistencies. She confided that the loss of her own beloved husband in a railway accident, nine years before, had brought her to the edge of suicide. Only finding love, unexpected at her time of life, had saved her. Her second husband, a banker, had pressed her to retire after their marriage. But loyalty to Madame Hortense, and dedication to the cause of beauty, had made it impossible to step back from her duties at the Temple. Yet always she returned to the business in Indianapolis. She was fascinated by how it had grown and probed gently what it now was worth. But she never asked the question directly.

"She examined my skin three times," Mabel said. "Before and after the bath, then after the final massage, then the same nonsense as before with her magnifying lens. The woman's a genius, I'll give her that, hesitating over choices of perfumes, knitting her brows in concentration, nodding to herself when she makes a decision. I can see many women being impressed. She'd make a fortune if she set up in New York."

"She's making one here already, Mabel. And can I guess that she wasn't wholly satisfied by how it all turned out?"

129

"Progress had been made, she said, but only a start. But a lady of my age – she was discreet about alluding to it – will need further baths. Different perfumes, even different flower petals, if today's gains are to be consolidated. So I've made another appointment. Thursday, a week from today when I'm back from Manchester. I told Mrs. B that I could be contacted by poste restante if there was any need for her to change arrangements."

But it was what happened before being led away to the bath that was perhaps most important. Two men had been in the waiting area. One was the same dark-haired, swaggering gentleman with the white gardenia accompanying the same elegant lady with whom he had been there previously. The other was an older man.

"Like Mr. Chester Arthur," Mabel said. "Our president."

Florence had seen pictures of him, a solid, beefy man with a shaven chin, a full head of hair and sideburns curving up to meet his thick moustache. A look that exuded prosperity.

"I'd judge him fifty or fifty-five, Florence. He had a lady with him, somewhat older, I'd say, and well past any hope of rejuvenation. He told the assistant who came out to fetch her to take good care of his sister. Loud enough for me and anybody else near to hear. His sister, not his wife. They had already left when I came out again."

Another faux-lord and widower?

Possibly.

*

Agatha came to dine with them that evening but the atmosphere was subdued. Successful as the bath had been in confirming that Mrs. Daley was a rich and possibly susceptible widow, there was nothing more that could be done for now but hope that Mrs. Bellamy might bite. If she did not, the quest for retribution for Mrs. Chalmers-Bolger would be at an end, the only result an article in the *Columbia Home Gazette* about beauty treatments for the rich and fashionable in London.

When Agatha was leaving, she took Florence to one side and spoke to her alone.

"I've talked with Father about a barrister," she said. "He's sympathetic. He's thought of somebody and he's contacting him this evening. And he said not to worry about anything. Not after what you did for Oswald."

Some hope at last for Tom Atwell.

Florence slept the better for it.

*

"Mrs. Dawlish? A letter for you ma'am, hand delivered."

A page had approached the table where Florence was sharing an early breakfast with Mabel, who was leaving shortly. The spindly handwriting on the envelope was unmistakable. There was a single sheet within. Agatha would come by at nine o'clock. A meeting had been arranged at Lincoln's Inn at ten. And a name, vaguely familiar.

Neville Eversham.

Florence said nothing about it to Mabel but, after she had seen her leave, she learned at the reception that the hotel nursed enough social ambition to possess a copy of *Who's Who*.

In the string of letters after the name only two really counted.

Q and C.

Queen's Counsel A recognition of competence and experience, a sure path to wealth by pleading at the bar, a prerequisite for reaching the highest levels of the judiciary. The most brilliant QCs were public figures, renowned for success in hopeless cases, whether in prosecution or defence, famed for eloquence, for discovery of ingenious legal loopholes, for wresting admissions from unwilling witnesses and driving them to contradict themselves.

And it was that last skill that stirred in Florence's memory. A case two years before, one that involved an opium-addled Lascar seaman accused of murdering a woman of the streets in Limehouse. She could not remember the details, only that an eminent lawyer had taken it up,

131

had saved the wretched man from the gallows by unmasking a web of police corruption and false witness. She was almost sure that the lawyer's name had been Eversham.

She read the *Who's Who* details again. M.A. (Oxon), Barrister at Lincoln's Inn, sometime counsel to the Attorney General and junior counsel to the Treasury. His pedigree looked no less impressive, nor his wife's either, daughter of the Master of the Rolls. This man was legal aristocracy, on a different plane than that of Nicholas's country-town solicitor father. It was hard to understand why a penniless foreign seaman could have afforded his services or could have attracted the interest of such a man.

Agatha, sensitive and unwilling, as always, to inviting Florence to travel in a vehicle driven by her father or her brother, arrived in a hansom. The traffic was slow as ever, but it gave time to talk.

Florence's memory had been correct. Eversham had been the Lascar's defender.

"He's a cousin," Agatha said. "a distant one, third or fourth on Father's side."

"Have you met him?"

"No, but Father has. He says the party is trying to prevail on him to stand for a seat in Parliament. He could have a safe one. It's thought he'd be a likely Lord Chancellor in the future if he did."

"And he's not interested?" Florence found it inconceivable that any man could turn away from such a glittering prize if it were in his reach. She had always felt ambition herself and she knew, and admired, how it drove Nicholas.

"Half of that family are lawyers and the other half are clergy," Agatha said. "Each half wants to be what the other is, Father says, and this Neville is seemingly no different. Sometimes he volunteers to help, *pro bono,* in criminal cases. He makes a fortune in the courts and maybe he fears that he's a camel contemplating a needle's eye. I think that's why he saved that poor man whom the police had lied about. He might do as much now for Mr. Atwell."

The hansom had passed through Bloomsbury and had turned on to Newman's Row, a blank brick wall on the left separating it from the ornate and soaring buildings of Lincoln's Inn beyond. It halted at an arched gateway and they dismounted there, asked directions of a porter, then passed into the great quadrangle beyond. Florence was struck by the change. In a few steps she had moved from the bustle of the London streets to a different world. Ancient buildings looking inwards on tree-shaded lawns. A great dining hall. A chapel larger than most parish churches. Barristers in their gown and wigs, some standing about to smoke and confer, others rushing to the nearby courts of justice, trailed by their harassed clerks. Name boards announced the occupants of each four or five storey building, whether of Tudor or Jacobean brick exuberance or of severe Georgian elegance. Hundreds of lawyers had their chambers here, as thousands had for centuries past. It was a man's world, she thought, an alien one where women were tolerated as clients only. She didn't want to admit that it felt intimidating, but it did.

They asked twice for directions, for Agatha had not been here before either, but at last they found the sign, Eversham, Eversham and Capel, 2 Stone Buildings, one of a half-dozen chambers there.

At the entrance Florence stopped and turned to Agatha.

"Do you think he'll want to take this case?"

"Only you can convince him, Florence."

"How?"

"Just tell him as you told me. Tell him everything."

"Even that I had a moneylender threatened? That he was thrashed afterwards?"

"That too, Florence."

She had no choice if Tom Atwell was to escape servitude.

The die was cast.

Chapter 13

Florence was glad to find an empty compartment in the 'Ladies Only' carriage of the train that carried her back to Portsmouth that afternoon. She felt exhausted by the ordeal at Lincoln's Inn. It had not been that Neville Eversham had been discourteous, cruel or unpleasant in any way. That was not within his nature, she recognised. But he was thorough, even more so than Mabel.

Tall, thin, almost ascetic-looking, perhaps forty-five, eyes friendly behind gold-rimmed pince-nez, voice never rising, sometimes mildly humorous, she liked him from first introduction. He joked with Agatha that, as cousins, they were remiss in not meeting long before. He complimented Florence on Nicholas's service in East Africa the previous year – the papers had been full of it for a while. His office was as immaculately neat and ordered as he was himself. It was easy to lapse into conversation while a junior clerk was despatched to fetch tea.

He waved away their thanks for meeting at such short notice. This day's business in court could well be handled by a junior.

"A criminal case, Mr. Eversham?" Florence imagined something complicated, the shadow of the gallows hanging over it.

Eversham laughed. "I've been involved with only a few criminal cases ever. The newspapers made too much of that business in Limehouse that you may have heard of it. So no! It's a much more mundane case today, a chancery matter. That's my speciality. Probate, wills, trusts, bankruptcy, property disputes. Dull, Mrs. Dawlish, dull but necessary."

"But I'm not here for anything like that." Florence felt alarm. Evesham's defence of the Lascar seaman, that spontaneous act of charity, might have succeeded only by a fluke. "It's a criminal case and," she paused, "and the man's guilty as sin."

"Only twelve good men and true can decide that, Mrs. Dawlish. The man's innocent, for now at least. So start at the beginning, please. Tell me why you're interested."

She had prepared for this. "Because this man, Tom Atwell, stood beside my husband in battle," she said. "Because he was wounded, badly wounded. Because he has a wife and three young children and because they and others like them are the prey of moneylenders. Because if my husband was in Britain now – he's somewhere in the Sudan this moment – he'd want to be here today and making the same plea that I do now."

Evesham didn't comment. He drew up a writing pad, took a pencil in his hand.

"Start at the beginning, Mrs. Dawlish. Leave nothing out. Nothing."

She wasn't sure where the beginning was, but she began with the visit to the wounded seamen in the hospital at Haslar. She had lain awake worrying whether and how to explain her own unwitting inspiration of the first assault on Chadband. Now she forced herself to do so, as if speaking of some other person, looking past Eversham towards the autumnal trees outside the window.

"You only did it for the best, Florence." Agatha had seen how difficult the admission was. "You never expected that –"

Eversham waved for her silence, though with no sense of angry impatience. He nodded for Florence to continue. He had filled two pages with notes already.

She was honest about her growing fears when she had heard of debts being cancelled, of rumours going about that she had had a role in it. And then the shock of opening the *Portsmouth Argus* and reading of the moneylender's near-fatal beating. Her immediate response, her instant decision to assist the accused man, her recourse to Mr. Bagshot, her appeal to him to visit Atwell in custody and represent him in the magistrate's court, her contacting Lieutenant Jackson, her attempt to speak to Mrs. Atwell. All seemed, as she summarised them, to be the actions of someone else, of an unthinking, panicked woman, floundering in a morass of her own making. Told like this, the story had huge gaps within it, not least that she still had no idea of Atwell's motivation.

At no point did Eversham interrupt, nor pose any question when Florence paused, searching for a word or phrase, willing herself to imagine again, and feel, each moment she described. He waited in silence as she collected herself, made no attempt to prompt, gestured several times to Agatha to refrain when she was about to intervene.

And at last it was over and Florence felt drained by it, fearful too that she had left out or incorrectly represented some detail.

"Now tell me, Mrs. Dawlish, how you have come to know Lady Agatha?"

His question was the last she could have expected. It was the most embarrassing to answer in these surroundings.

"I was her maid once." The admission was still hard to make after all these years, but she guessed that Eversham would have elicited it anyway. "She saw that I hungered to be more. She helped me with books and learning and made me her companion and –"

"Let me tell it, Florence," Agatha leaned across to hold her hand. "She became my sister. In Turkey, in the war there, when there was murder and violation and hunger and massacre, Florence never faltered, not even in the face of death or worse. She brought me and two hundred and more refugees to safety through snow and mud and ice with Cossacks tracking us each step, and swooping on us like wolves when they could." Tears were running down her cheeks and her voice was faltering. "That's when we met Nicholas Dawlish, and Florence proved herself as worthy of him as he was as her, and as they've proved it again and again since."

Florence was looking away, embarrassed, her eyes filling.

"And not just that, Cousin Neville," Agatha's voice firmer now and she had steeled herself for an admission of her own. "You must know already about our family disgrace. Half of society does. Nobody ever mentions it to our faces, but they still talk and laugh about it nonetheless. That Oswald had to flee, that he's living abroad and can't return, that the stories about him are… are so shaming. But it was Florence who helped him leave, not for any love of him but for loyalty to our family."

"You understood the risks, Mrs. Dawlish?" Eversham showed neither surprise nor shock. "Not just for yourself? For your husband's career also?"

She nodded. There had been sleepless nights then too.

136

"Does Captain Dawlish know what you did?"

"No. He was in Korea then. There were reasons for not telling him when he returned." She paused. "Honourable reasons."

Ones that Admiral Sir Richard Topcliffe, that figure who held sway over Nicholas's career, had bound her never to speak of.

Raison d'état. Topcliffe's own words. And he'd added that some concerns are stronger even than justice.

"You know that it can be worse for you now, Mrs. Dawlish, immeasurably worse, if this Tom Atwell case is to be defended as it demands?" Sympathy, maybe respect, in Eversham's eyes but cold logic in his words. "Do you understand that the prosecution might see fit to call you as a witness? Are you aware of what the mere act of doing so, much less any admissions under oath, could mean for your husband and yourself?"

Misery in her nod. The knowledge had tormented her for days.

He turned to Agatha. "It's better that you leave us, cousin. The Inn's chapel and the hall might interest you. I'll ask a clerk to guide you. If you might return at …" He flicked his watch open. "At let's say one o'clock."

Over two hours away.

And then interrogation began.

There seemed no order to the questions, none until some later one exposed a point of ignorance or uncertainty or unsupported assumption. Nothing was direct in this man's approach, she realised. Determined though she was not to appear intimidated, her fear grew with each minute. He dissected her story half-a-dozen times, always from a different perspective. Even if all the gaps could have been filled – Atwell's motivation most of all – each question, each answer, drew her closer to the conclusion that the case was hopeless.

She could hear a small, cold, logical, tempting, and shaming, voice inside her brain. Better to accept the inevitable, to let the court dispose of the case in twenty minutes. Questioning of witnesses with the quiet efficiency she was enduring at this moment and impassioned appeal to a jury, would not change the outcome, would rather wake sleeping dogs to no avail.

And threaten me, maybe destroy me. And Nicholas too.

At last she could bear it no longer.

"He'll be convicted, no matter what, won't he, Mr. Eversham?"

"We don't know enough to say that yet."

"Are you willing to take on the case if you think he will be?"

"I've made no decision one way or the other, Mrs. Dawlish. I haven't seen or spoken to the man. You haven't either, and you should not. You said he had a head injury. Perhaps I'll call for a medical opinion. I'll decide after I've seen him. And the witnesses who identified him to the police, who could they be? The moneylender's own associates or honest bystanders, or maybe both? And Atwell's wife? She can't be put on the stand to testify for or against him but she must know something."

"I've arranged with Mrs. Enderby to visit her in Southampton tomorrow," Florence said.

"Does she know you're coming?"

"No."

"All to the good. But be careful"

She had feared that he would have advised against it. That he didn't, gave some hope.

"You mentioned that Lieutenant Jackson was willing to stand as a character witness. Could there be other officers? From HMS *Leonidas*? Wounded in the same action perhaps?"

"A Lieutenant Purdon. The ship's gunnery lieutenant. Nicholas regarded him very highly. I can ask him."

Eversham pushed a button on his desk. An electric bell sounded in the adjoining office. An old man earlier identified as the chief clerk entered.

"Be so kind as to rearrange my calendar for Tuesday," Eversham said. "I won't be here. Mr. Granger can handle the Winchelsea case that day and Mr. Larkin the Grafton-Hume. There's nothing momentous due in either yet. I'll talk to them later about it."

He turned to Florence.

"I'll come to Portsmouth on Tuesday morning. I'll telegraph you details of my arrival. Please talk to your Mr. Bagshot as soon as possible.

I must see him and you together. You may have something to tell of Mrs. Atwell by then. Ask him too to arrange for me to visit the prisoner with him. I'll need to talk to Lieutenant Jackson also. Could you can arrange it, please? Good. And we might dine with Mr. Bagshot before I return to London, see what we have."

"Will you have decided by then, Mr. Eversham?"

"I'll have decided," he said.

*

Florence and Mrs. Enderby were in Southampton next morning by eleven. A hansom carried them to Hatton Street, north of the docks, the closed hall-doors of the little brick houses and the curtains in the windows indicating single-family occupancy and treasured respectability. The address to which Mrs. Atwell's sister Kate had swept her and her children was a shop there on a corner with an intersecting street. It sold groceries and looked modestly prosperous. The name on the board above was Deacon.

The bell on the door tinkled as they entered. A small, bald middle-aged man in a brown shop-coat, a large white apron over it, was serving a customer. He must have seen the cab outside, and Florence and Mrs. Enderby descending, but other than a quick glance, with something like venom in it, he made no acknowledgement of their presence. He was measuring sugar in a scale, dropping tiny additions from a scoop into the pan, removing a little, adding again until at last he could say to the customer, "That's exactly four ounces, ma'am," and tipped it in a paper bag. She wanted baking soda then, and flour, and arrowroot. They too were doled out and measured with the same slow and deliberate exactitude, followed by six rashers sliced from a side of smoked bacon and weighed with no less precision. Another customer, a shabby woman with two children entered. He greeted her as Mrs. Carpenter and said he be with her directly he was finished with Mrs. Prichard's order. Florence guessed that he knew who she and her companion must be and that he was enjoying ignoring them. She sensed that Mrs. Enderby was embarrassed by it but, determined not to give him satisfaction, Florence began a trivial conversation with her in an undertone.

He served the second customer too, no more hurriedly, and he would have served a third too, had one entered, before he at last made as if to notice his visitors.

"How can I serve you, ladies?" Venom now in his tone as well as in his glance.

A foul little man, Florence thought, but she was polite when she asked if Mrs. Atwell was staying here.

"Who wants to know?" he said.

Florence handed him her card.

"Her husband served on my husband's ship. He's been serving lately on this lady's husband's too. He's in trouble. We're here to see if we can give Mrs. Atwell any assistance."

"Two ladies bountiful, is it?" His face was reddening. "Coming to talk down to us? Coming to stick their noses where they're not wanted?"

"We only –" The conciliation in Mrs. Enderby's tone didn't save her from being cut off.

"Don't concern yourself with us, ma'am." His voice was rising. "We keep our own business to ourselves round here, thank you very much!"

"I asked for Mrs. Atwell," Florence was restraining her own anger now. "If she's here, she can decide herself if she wants to talk to us."

"Well, she don't want, an' you can take that from me. An' if you don't like it, an' if you're not out of here in two minutes I'll call –"

"What's all this shouting I hear, Harry?" A door from the interior had opened and a red-headed woman stuck her head out.

"These two women was just going, Kate," his bluster was already evaporating. "They was just here to –"

"To talk to Mrs. Atwell," Florence said. "To help her any way we can. We know that she might need it."

"You hear that, Harry Deacon?" The woman too had recognised what they were. "Two ladies, an' you can't talk civil to them. You're a disgrace, you are, Harry". Her voice softened. "If you'll step this way, ladies, we can talk quiet like." She ushered them through the door.

140

There was a living room within. A well-polished mahogany dining table, three chairs on either side, a dresser laden with willow-pattern china, a few pieces of silver on a sideboard, framed photographs, a lithograph of highland cattle, armchairs either side of an ornate and laden mantelpiece, a gilt-framed mirror above it and a glowing coal fire beneath even though the autumn was not far advanced. All immaculate. The shop was providing a comfortable living.

"Don't you take no notice of Harry." The woman, forty, gaunt, a forceful air about her, was seating them at either side of the fire. "Took all this business bad, he did, afraid we'd never be able to hold up our heads again. There was never nothing like it in either family, he said."

"You're Mrs. Henry Deacon, Mrs. Atwell's sister, aren't you?"

She was, and her sister Joan was younger by four years. Florence introduced herself and Mrs. Enderby. Their cards impressed Mrs. Deacon enough for her to prop them against a Staffordshire china figurine of Garibaldi on the mantelpiece. She had prevailed on her husband to go across to Portsmouth to be present in the magistrate's court, she said. She knew that Tom Atwell was now on remand, that he would be tried soon and what sentence was hanging over him.

"Could we perhaps speak to Mrs. Atwell?" Florence said.

"I can barely talk to her myself, ma'am. Hardly opens her door when I bring a tray up to her. She won't come down because she knows that Harry don't want her here. She don't leave her room all day, sobbing something awful a lot of the time."

"But what about her children?" Mrs. Enderby was moved.

"She keeps the youngest with her all the time, poor little lamb. An' the older ones don't quite know what's going on except that it's bad. My own two bring them out to play. They're out now. But they're never happy."

"Nor could they be! Oh, the pity of it!" Mrs. Enderby was shaking her head.

There must be thousands of children suffering like this every day, Florence thought, yet this woman had never been confronted by the reality before. But compassion on its own was never enough.

141

"You went to collect your sister after you received a telegram, didn't you, Mrs. Deacon?" Florence said. It was easy to imagine this woman speeding without hesitation to the rescue. "That was a good Christian thing to do."

"I couldn't do no less, ma'am, not for my own flesh and blood, no matter what Harry said."

"When you got there – it was the morning after, wasn't it? – did your sister tell you what had happened?"

"She was only crying, ma'am, too upset to talk. Only from the Mitchells on the floor below did I hear the story. And it shocked me, it really did. I couldn't have believed it of Tom Atwell, I couldn't, even if my Harry never had much time for him."

It was the first critical opinion of the man that Florence had heard. Better let it pass for now, come back to it later.

"I understand there was damage in the rooms?" she said. "Furniture upset maybe, things thrown about?"

Mrs. Deacon nodded. "That was the worst of it, ma'am. Neat as a new pin, Joan's place always was, and a lot of lovely stuff there too and now it was broke up something awful. And the kids were terrified by seeing their dad like that. The littlest hasn't spoken since."

"Had your sister been injured?" Florence knew the answer already.

"Tom wouldn't have done that, no matter what. Joan told me that herself. 'Didn't lay a finger on me,' she said 'and poor Tom'll never want to lay one on me ever again neither.' And then she started crying something worse."

"It was a nice place they had, was it?" Florence said. "Like this? It's like a new pin here, Mrs. Deacon, quite lovely. It must run in your family."

"We was brought up comfortable-like and decent. Our dad had a shop, like this one, in Fareham. Our brother has it still. So we expected the best when we married."

"I think you chose well, Mrs. Deacon." Florence nodded towards the door to the shop. "Your husband's bark is worse than his bite, I think. A good provider, I can see."

142

"Harry's a good husband and father, ma'am." Said with satisfaction.

"It's what we heard about Tom Atwell too. Also a good provider, was he?"

"He did his best, ma'am." The tone now guarded.

A lot of lovely stuff. An Able Seaman's pay. Twenty-seven pounds a year.

"You're sure that Mrs. Atwell wouldn't want to speak to us?" It was frustrating to know that she was on a floor above, that she must have heard the hansom, might have seen them dismount, have guessed who they were. "Or maybe she might talk to Mrs. Enderby alone? Or just to me? I've things to tell her about the trial. That we've arranged for a solicitor. How she might be able to help her husband's defence."

"If Joan don't talk to me then she won't talk to you neither, ma'am," Mrs. Deacon said. "She was always a headstrong girl. She wouldn't have married Tom Atwell otherwise but she wouldn't listen. Marrying beneath her, she was, my Harry told her. And he was right. For all that Tom was chapel and teetotal, he was still just a seaman. I won't say a word against him, but he'll never be anything else."

There was nothing more to be learned, Florence realised. Not for now at least. She nodded to her companion, a prearranged signal.

"You must be put to a lot of extra expense," Mrs. Enderby said. "Your travel and your sister's. Her food. And the children's too."

"I don't begrudge it, ma'am."

"Some of Mr. Atwell's shipmates made a small collection, the officers too. You won't be offended, will you?" She handed her a purse.

Mrs. Deacon was not offended.

"It's important that your sister tells what happened," Florence said as they moved to the door. "Not to us perhaps, but maybe to the solicitor. It might save her husband, or reduce the sentence at the very least. Tell her about this visit, what we're trying to do. You have my card. Drop me a line if she changes her mind. I'll come immediately."

The shop outside was thronged. Business was good. Mrs. Deacon slipped behind the counter to help her husband as they left.

It was essential now to get back to Portsmouth.

Florence wanted to see Mr. Bagshot as soon as possible.

143

Chapter 14

Eversham travelled to Portsmouth by the earliest train on Tuesday morning. Florence, accompanied by Mr. Bagshot, met him at the station. Dressed now in country tweeds, he looked a different man to the dapper advocate of Lincoln's Inn. There was time only for a brief meeting in the coffee-lounge of the nearby Anchor Hotel before the two gentlemen must leave for a visit to Tom Atwell at Kingston Prison.

Mr. Bagshot had been active since Florence had met him on Saturday afternoon. He had been half-delighted, half-intimidated, by the possibility of working with an eminent QC for the first time in his life. Since then he had been to see Atwell again – who would still say nothing, though he consented to representation – and had arranged the interview for this morning. He had done more, had spoken to Inspector Towton and discovered the names of the witnesses, two only, who had identified Atwell.

Florence had been no less busy She had seen Lieutenant Jackson again, had arranged that he'd meet Eversham at Mr. Bagshot's office. Through Jackson she had learned that Edward Purdon, HMS *Leonidas's* erstwhile gunnery lieutenant, was still recuperating at his parents' house near Winchester. It was close enough to visit easily and she did so on the Monday. Nicholas had always spoken highly of him but she had only met him twice, at HMS *Leonidas's* first commissioning and later in the hospital at Haslar. The wound Purdon had received at Tamai was still unhealed then and he had been swathed in bandages. She had telegraphed ahead that she wanted to speak to him. Now he was fit for duty again, he told her when he met at the station in a dog cart. He bore her home to lunch. His father, a doctor, and his mother were welcoming. Afterwards she talked with him in the garden. He made no complaint about his injury. She admired him for that. He was hoping for appointment to a new ship soon, perhaps with Captain Dawlish again, if possible.

If there's ever another ship for Nicholas, or Nicholas for a ship.

144

Purdon remembered Atwell with praise and gratitude. He would be glad to appear at his trial, speak up for his character.

But that was as much as was positive to report to Eversham. Florence's attempt at meeting Mrs. Atwell had proved futile. She told what she had heard about her but held back from mentioning the suspicion that had been growing in her own mind ever since. Raising it seemed unfair. The woman might be innocent.

"It's good that you didn't press her sister." Eversham had noted all she told him. "Now the door's open and you parted amicably. It may be necessary to return."

He left for the prison with Mr. Bagshot. They would be conferring in his office later and would be meeting Lieutenant Jackson there. Florence could do nothing until they would meet again that evening.

She went to the Seaman's Rest and busied herself with double-checking accounts she knew already were correct and inspecting rooms and kitchens she knew already to be clean. Work alone diverted her from her concern for Nicholas, her worry about her link to Chadband, her uncertainty as to where the *Temple de la Beauté* charade might lead. Part of her hoped, unworthily, she recognised, that Eversham might state that evening that he was not prepared to pursue Atwell's case, that justice must take its course without him. She had done enough, a wheedling, cowardly little inner voice told her. A perfunctory trial would end the matter without threat to her. She tried to close her mind to it, but still it returned. The investigation of the Coptic Street affair seemed almost trivial by comparison. She should not have got involved in that either, that same voice told her. She was out of her depth, still floundering. She should have stayed in Europe after Nicholas had left, should have travelled for another month or more, travelling from gallery to gallery and opera house to opera house.

At last she could bear it no longer and she went out to walk back and forth twice along the Esplanade. She had little comfort from the dull autumn day. The sky was leaden, the wind chill, white horses on the grey sea stretching out beyond the Spithead forts, harbingers of winter. It

145

matched her mood too well. Back at the villa she found no solace either, her arm aching painfully when she forced herself into her piano practice.

She had reserved a private dining room at the Anchor Hotel and they met there at seven. Both men were smiling when they entered.

"You're taking the case, aren't you?" It was spontaneous. She had risen to her feet, blurted it out, though she had sworn to herself that she would wait for Mr. Eversham to announce his decision.

"Patience, Mrs. Dawlish! Patience!" He held his hand up in mock reprimand. "Would you deny an advocate the right to choose his moment of dramatic timing?" And then the smile was gone and his tone was serious. "Yes. I'll defend that man. I can't guarantee acquittal, but there's a chance of reducing the tariff if he's convicted."

The meal was hurried. Florence did not notice what she ate, if indeed she did at all. The two men seemed to have worked easily together. Atwell had been surprised that Mr. Bagshot had brought a barrister and, even though he did not know his eminence, he had been alarmed at the cost. He had wept when told that unknown friends would see to that.

But he had still refused to say what had happened on the night of the assault.

"The nearest was when he admitted that he'd snapped," Eversham said. "He said there were things no man could bear, and the Lord would not judge him. He said it twice or three times in different ways but he wouldn't elaborate. It wasn't pleasant to see."

A lot of lovely stuff. An Able Seaman's pay. Twenty-seven pounds a year.

Eversham noticed Florence's unease.

"You've some suspicion, haven't you, Mrs. Dawlish?"

She nodded.

"Something distasteful?"

"That moneylender. Chadband. He might not have been guilty of it, but others like him are." It was embarrassing to mention the subject to two men. "Some of them … they don't want just money. They demand other things as well." She was blushing. So too was Mr. Bagshot, and he

146

was looking away. "From women whose husbands are away. Women who're desperate, who have children to feed."

"We're not here to cast first stones," Eversham met her gaze. "But we can't ignore the possibility that this appalling Chadband might have made such demands. Mrs. Atwell's unwillingness to see you hints at it."

Florence nodded.

"Could you find any evidence about it, Mrs. Dawlish? Perhaps not involving her, but other women prepared to testify?"

"No woman would take the stand on such a matter." Mr. Bagshot was shaking his head.

"We'll cross that bridge later," Eversham said. He turned again to Florence. "Could you find women who're prepared to talk about it? Maybe not even the worst, the act itself, but demands refused. And no mention of testifying. Just information."

The question took her aback. The dawning reality of what it would involve was terrifying. Identifying women who'd taken loans, prying, in as roundabout a way as possible, into their experiences, eliciting confessions of things they wanted to forget. All too soon the word would get about that the warning-off of Chadband had been a first step only, that she was now embarked on a crusade against all of Portsmouth's moneylenders.

But it might save Atwell, save him some years at least.

"It would be difficult." She could not bring herself to say 'No'.

"I might be able to assist." Naïve goodwill in Mr. Bagshot's tone.

It was inconceivable to imagine him understanding, much less venturing into, the world in question, or doing anything but unintended harm.

"Have you told Mr. Bagshot everything you told me, Mrs. Dawlish?" Eversham said. "About yourself? Your own ... your own error of judgement?"

"No." She had felt ashamed to admit it to the old man.

"Please tell him now, Mrs. Dawlish."

When she did, she saw that he was shocked. He knew Nicholas, had managed his affairs for years, could see the implications for him. But when he spoke it was in sorrow.

"You should have come to me, Mrs. Dawlish, not send those men. I could have…" His voice trailed off in recognition that there were things beyond the reach, or interest, of the law.

Regret stabbed her. Even if he could have done nothing, she should have trusted him.

"Difficult, you said, Mrs Dawlish," Eversham said, "and dangerous for you too. But it's been so since your first step to help Atwell. You knew that, but you still went ahead." He paused, let the appeal to her honour sink in. "Can there be others you could work through. Others you can trust?"

"There might be." Her brain was racing. An idea had struck, improbable, a forlorn hope perhaps.

And even that would have its dangers.

"Just consider it, Mrs. Dawlish. And if there is a way, please let Mr. Bagshot know. Will you do that?"

"It will take a few days before I can know if it's possible. But by the end of the week I will."

That would leave almost three weeks. A date in November was set for the trial at the assizes in Winchester.

Eversham did not press her further, went on to say how impressed he was by Lieutenant Jackson. A character reference from a man like that would count for much, he said. And he was looking forward to meeting Lieutenant Purdon, who had told Florence that he was willing to travel to Lincoln's Inn for consultations.

Dinner had finished and they were taking coffee now. Eversham must leave soon for the station. There was a comforting sense of a link created, one welcomed by all three, unity in a common purpose.

"What made you decide to help, Mr. Eversham?" His decision intrigued Florence.

He sat back, paused, then said. "He moved me. Whatever it was, it drove him to despair. A decent man. I couldn't turn my back."

"You did it before, didn't you? Like that man in Limehouse. A seaman also. Did he move you also?"

"He had scarcely a word of English. That was what struck me when I first read about the murder in a newspaper. He had nobody, no Mrs. Dawlish, no Cousin Agatha. It troubled me. I've had so much. He had nothing but his life and he was about to lose it. Unjustly, as it proved."

He seemed almost embarrassed to speak of it, hesitant to boast of virtue.

"There wasn't much credit due to me. The most inexperienced young barrister could have saved him once he'd examined the police reports. An inspector keen to maintain a record of success and two constables ready to perjure themselves to satisfy him. What's beaten from a man isn't always the truth."

"But he was innocent, wasn't he? And Atwell isn't."

"You're not deserting him because you think that, are you, Mrs. Dawlish? And I'm not judging him. I'm leaving that to the jury."

He looked at his watch.

It was time to leave.

*

A telegram had arrived a half-hour before Florence reached home. She opened it with trembling hands.

Not from or about Nicholas.

A single strip of printed text pasted to the page.

SUITOR CONTACTED STOP YOU BOOKED MERCER TWO NIGHTS WEDNESDAY STOP MABEL.

Mrs. Bellamy had bitten.

*

Florence arrived in London in early afternoon next day and went directly to the Mercer Hotel. She knew that Mabel was returning from Manchester that day, in time for her second Empyrean Bath on the

149

morrow, but she did not know when. She, Agatha and Florence had agreed to meet only if something significant resulted from the session at the Temple. Now, ahead of it, something significant had indeed happened and what had gone before now seemed little more than a game. The telegram presaged a raising of the stakes. There was still time to withdraw. The decision, she told herself, must be Mabel's, not Agatha's or hers. And still . . . They had come so far.

The afternoon passed slowly. Rain outside discouraged a stroll and she stayed, trying to read, in her room. She had left a note for Mabel at the reception, announcing that she had arrived. It was not until after seven o'clock that the expected knock sounded on her door.

Mabel was still in her travelling clothes, her face flushed with what might be either fear or excitement. They embraced and Florence sat her down.

"Here." Mabel had fished an envelope from her reticule. It was of thick cream paper, the address in an elegant Italic hand.

Mrs. Emily Daley, Poste Restante, Manchester.

The postmark indicated that it had left London two days before. The crest on the rear closing-flap was identical in size to that on the envelopes received by Mrs. Chalmers-Bolger but it bore a lion rampant, not a stag.

The letter within, cream also, no scent, was crested too, and written in the same graceful script, but it was less eloquent, more matter of fact in tone and content, than the first sent to poor silly Mrs Chalmers-Bolger. Whoever had written it had recognised Mrs. Daley as an astute woman of business, if a lonely and lovelorn one.

The writer begged pardon for his forwardness. He had escorted his widowed sister to the *Temple de la Beauté* a few days since and had glimpsed Mrs. Daley there. He had overheard her speak and had recognised her accent as American. It had intrigued him, for he had spent two years at the embassy in Washington. He had been so bold as to enquire as to her identity and learned that she was to return to the Temple on the same day as his sister. The coincidence seemed a happy one. Knowing the frank and open manners of her compatriots, he hoped that she might not be offended if he engaged her in conversation. The progress of the Great Republic fascinated him. He would be at the Temple ahead of her but would understand if she was unwilling to converse. A single nod to him would be enough for him to remain silent. He ended by asking that no blame be attached to the staff at the Temple for divulging her contact address.

The signature, no scrawl, was easily read.

Clifford Belton (KCB)

"What does KCB mean?" Mabel asked.

"Knight Commander of the Bath. It's an order of Chivalry."

"Like the Round Table?"

"Nothing so romantic. It's a reward for service, the sort of recognition that a diplomat might gain. Some men would sell their souls for it. Some wives would sell themselves to get one for their husbands. It makes him Sir Clifford to you and me."

"Grander than President Arthur then." Mabel was smiling.

"He's got a grand address too. Sloane Street, Chelsea. Very fashionable and very expensive."

"Do you think there's really such a person, Florence?"

"*Who's Who* will know," she said.

She rang for a page and, when he came, asked for the volume to be brought up. The print was small and, to read it, she had to put on the spectacles that she did not want Nicholas to know about.

And Sir Clifford Belton was indeed there, not just KCB alone but a string of other letters, starting with his MA (Oxon) in 1848. He had attended Eton, and Oxford's Lincoln College afterwards, had spent a year at Heidelberg, had served positions of increasing seniority in the embassies at St. Petersburg, Madrid and Copenhagen before Washington. His career had peaked with appointment as ambassador to the Kingdom of the Netherlands 1878 – 1883.

"A widower too," Florence said. "Married Matilda Emmeline, daughter of the Hon. Augustus Netherington in 1853. She died in 1877. Four children, a son and three daughters."

"And the address?"

"Sloane Street. Just as in the letter."

"Is there any mention of what he might have done in the year since he came back from the Netherlands?"

"Nothing," Florence said. "I wouldn't be surprised if he's paralysed, catatonic or locked in an asylum. Whoever wrote this nonsense, it wasn't the real Sir Clifford. It was the same person who sent those letters to Mrs. Chalmers-Bolger."

"But that person didn't look like a bit like Mr. Chester Arthur," Mabel said. "We saw his photograph. And the poor woman met him in the flesh at least once. They're two different men."

"Mrs. Bellamy might have half-a-dozen like them at her beck and call," Florence said. "Out-of-work actors probably. She may keep that scrivener of hers in permanent employ, though. He writes a splendid hand. But we need to know more about the actual Sir Clifford. Agatha's father must. He knows everybody that matters. I'll send her a message this evening. She could meet us tomorrow afternoon, after you've met your admirer. She may know more about the real man by then."

She stopped, realised that she was assuming much. Mrs. Bellamy and her people were dangerous, had not hesitated to bleed Mrs. Chalmers-Bolger white and drive her to her death.

"Are going to meet this man, Mabel?"

"No. I'm not. But Mrs. Daley is."

"On her own? Might it not be safer, too and more proper for a respectable widow, if she had a friend with her? Mrs. Lacy would be glad to accompany her."

"Mrs. Daley wouldn't want that. She'd already be feeling foolish, even if she's flattered by Sir Clifford's approach. If nothing comes of it, she wouldn't want anybody else to know, least of all that venal gossip, Mrs. Lacy."

They would dine together and Mabel went to change. Florence rang down again for a page and, when he came, asked him to bring paper and ink. She wrote a short note to Agatha, asked her to determine Sir Clifford Belton's current status There was no time to explain why, only to say it was important. Agatha should meet Mabel and herself at this hotel at two o'clock tomorrow.

She asked for something else also. Her own brother's services.

At the cost of a shilling, the page would have the note in Agatha's hands within the hour. There was nothing more to do for now.

For she had determined not to raise the other matter on her mind until after Mabel's Empyrean Bath and encounter with her admirer.

Only then.

And she feared refusal.

Chapter 15

Florence was glad that a light drizzle was falling when she watched Mabel set out in a hansom for the *Temple de la Beauté*. Her brother Jack would be at Coptic Street by now, passing up and down at intervals, to observe Mabel's arrival and ensure a safe departure. In normal street clothes, not his coachman's livery, the rain would make it look normal for him to be muffled, a scarf high around his face, his hat pulled down, recognition difficult. It was possibly a fool's errand, and in this weather a miserable one too, but Florence wanted assurance that when Mabel left the Temple, she would do so in safety and alone. She knew Jack from before – he had helped save her on that dreadful night of the vitriol – but Florence did not want her to know that he hovered close. The more insecure she felt, the more convincingly she would carry herself. So too would Mrs. Daley feel as she steeled herself to for a flattering but perhaps unwise encounter.

The forenoon passed slowly. The newspapers had nothing new to tell about the Sudan. Mrs. Braddon's novel did not grip, and the rain outside precluded strolling. Mabel's bath was scheduled for eleven but she would arrive almost an hour early to give her admirer his opportunity. If queried, she could claim to be mistaken over the timing. It was unlikely that she would be back at the hotel before two. Jack would be saturated, and cold, long before she emerged from the Temple.

Agatha arrived at two o'clock. Mabel didn't.

"I can't remember meeting Sir Clifford Belton, though I probably did," Agatha said. "Father said he's been several times at receptions in our home, but then, there've been so many. And dear Oswald must know him too. All those diplomatic people know each other. But why are asking about him, Florence?"

She told her. Agatha had already guessed. She began to laugh.

"Father must have been wondering why I asked. 'You're not thinking of marrying him, are you?' he said. You know he's never given up hope of seeing me settled. 'Belton's the dullest man in England', he said, 'dull but clever, very clever. That's why he was sent to Roscal'."

"Where's Roscal?" Florence had heard the name sometime, remembered nothing more.

"An island in the West Indies. Half is British, that's Roscal, and the other half's independent. It was divided between Britain and France in a peace treaty, years and years ago, but the slaves rose up and threw out the French and set up their own republic and called it Guimbi. So there are all sorts of sensitivities about administration and that's why Sir Clifford's been appointed governor of the British part. He'll offend nobody, though he might bore them to death, Father says, but he'll be patient and ingenious enough to reduce tensions."

"When did he go there?"

"Six or eight months ago."

Florence was impressed by Mrs. Bellamy's thoroughness in selecting him. "No time for the latest issue of *Who's Who* to record the appointment," she said. "If Mrs. Daley was astute enough to consult it before deciding to meet him, she'd expect him to be in Britain still."

It was another hour before Mabel returned.

"He's smitten!" She was sweeping off her hat and laughing. "He's smitten by Mrs. Daley! Not only Sir Clifford, but his sister too!"

It had gone better than hoped. He had been in the waiting area already, sitting on a settee with the woman he had been with before and facing the entrance.

"When I was brought in, he looked up with great soulful, pleading eyes. The man's an actor, no doubt of it. I didn't nod, just smiled demurely and looked away. The maid sat me down and not two minutes later he came across. All very correct. He introduced himself, I smiled, then looked away and tried to seem pleased as well as embarrassed, and he suggested that I might join him and his sister. She'd heard so much from him about America and she'd be fascinated to chat with an American lady. I hesitated a little, then went across with him."

"Was she pleased to see you?"

"Not at first. They'd arranged it splendidly. He played it as if his sister knew nothing of him having written to me. He'd mistaken me for a lady he'd met in Washington. That was why he came across to me, he

155

said. Though I wasn't that lady, it was still a pleasure to meet an American. He thought that his sister would too. So he introduced her. Mrs. Lucinda Cavendish, widow of Professor Edwin Cavendish. Then he looked a mite confused and apologised for not asking me my name before. He left me with her while he went off to ask an attendant to bring a separate chair for him. She didn't seem pleased at all to see me. I guess she'd have been a protective older sister when they were young. But after I gushed a while about how different London was to Indianapolis, and how much superior, she began to thaw."

"What was he doing all the while?"

"Fussing, arranging for tea or coffee or elderflower cordial. He said very little. That was the genius of it. She did almost all the talking. How she and her own dear departed Edwin had enjoyed their visits to Clifford in the European capitals he'd served in, but they'd never been to America. She couldn't face the Atlantic crossing. Dover to Calais was enough for her. And how glad she'd been that their mother had lived to see him knighted. He was trying to make little of that, to be modest, when she mentioned it."

"Would Mrs Daley have believed her?" Florence said.

"Without a doubt. And Mrs. Bushwick might have believed her too if she hadn't known." Mabel hesitated. "You're really sure they're fakes, are you?"

Agatha told her about the real Sir Clifford's assignment to Roscal. Well as brother and sister played it, there was no doubt. Fakes.

"I think she's the smarter of the two," Mabel said. "She was clever about it when she started probing me, she didn't rush and let me talk with hardly an interruption. I trotted out my poor dead husband, told how empty life was without him but how great a comfort my son Franklin had been. Only one widow could understand another's loss, she said, and the pain of bereavement was sometimes even worse for men. She had seen it in her own brother – by that stage he'd gone off again to ask for more elderflower – and he'd never quite got over the loss of his Matilda, whom he'd worshipped. Oh, how she worried about him!"

Mrs. Mobray had come with an apology to both ladies from Mrs. Bellamy. She would have come herself but she was busy with another client. There had been an unavoidable delay in arrival of the llama's milk for the Empyrean Baths for which each lady was here.

"Sir Clifford looked delighted. 'It's no inconvenience if the time's to be spent in such charming company,' he said, and he looked at me and I looked away and tried to blush."

"I couldn't have managed it, Mabel," Florence said. "I'd have started to laugh."

"But Mrs. Daley loved it. The first man in decades to flatter her and a drunken and philandering husband in his grave. Then Sir Clifford took the lead. In Washington he'd been charged with study of American trade and industry. Coal, iron, copper, canneries, textiles, grain and railways. Never the furniture or floor-polish industry though. But he was entranced to hear about it, even more by how my husband and I had started our business in a rented cellar and had grown it to one of the largest in Indianapolis. They both looked impressed. 'That's the American spirit, Lucinda,' he said to his sister. 'Boundless ambition and hard work.' And in my frank and independent Hoosier way I said it was."

"You didn't underplay it, did you, Mabel?" Florence was smiling.

"No. I could see that I was telling them what they hoped to hear. I let slip that the business was incorporated now, and that I held half the shares. We Americans aren't shy about our wealth. And that Franklin, my son, had already acquired similar firms in Cleveland and Cincinnati, and a boot-polish factory in Columbus, and was at present negotiating to buy another in Pittsburgh. When I left for Europe, I'd told him, 'You'll be the Polish King of the United States!' but he replied 'No, Mother, not that. I'd far prefer to see you the Polish Queen and reigning from a mansion on Fifth Avenue. I owe you so much, Mother!' The recollection so moved me that I had to dab my eyes."

"I nearly am myself," Florence said. "I'm moved, I really am!"

"There was a long silence then and at last Clifford turned to his sister. He looked grave enough to weep and said to her what a joy it must be to have a grateful child. And she reached out and took his hand and

157

patted it and I looked away, embarrassed. Then I began babbling about my coming tour of Europe and what advice they'd have for me. It was then I knew I had them."

"How?"

"'He brightened, as if he'd just had an idea. 'My dinner party next week,' he said to his sister. 'You'll be there, Lucinda, and Lord and Lady Exmoor too and Sir Joseph Carver. Seasoned travellers all! Would it not be a splendid opportunity for Mrs. Daley to learn more about the Continent?' Then he said to me, 'Would you do the honour of being my guest on Wednesday evening?' But before I could answer Lucinda said to him, 'Your son George will be present too. Remember that, Clifford! And his ghastly wife will be there as well.' He tried to looked taken aback by that. It was the first time he didn't manage to be convincing but he made the best of it. 'Let me look after that, Lucinda,' he said and asked me where he might send the formal invitation."

"Poste restante, Plymouth?" Florence remembered Mabel's professional itinerary.

"Exactly. I'm leaving tomorrow to visit a refuge for the deaf and dumb near there. I'll be back in London on Tuesday."

A silence, shared awareness of yet another threshold to be passed. And retreat still possible.

"You're sure you'd want to dine with them, Mabel?" Florence said at last. "They're dangerous people."

"As little as I wanted to go into a laundry or make carboard boxes in an attic. But I went anyway. Most certainly I'll dine with them."

Jack's protection will be needed again, but there will be time to arrange that with Agatha.

When Mabel had emerged into the waiting area again two hours later, refreshed if not yet completely rejuvenated, they had already left. Mrs. Bellamy had decreed that another bath was desirable. The offering suggested had shrunk to ten guineas in recognition of client loyalty and Mabel had left with a large ornate bottle of Lotion of Samarra. There was only one time available in the bookings ledger that Mrs. Bellamy had perused. A week from today.

And, by coincidence, the day after Sir Clifford's planned dinner.

*

Florence, Mabel and Agatha dined together in the hotel. They had agreed not to discuss the *Temple de la Beauté* and Mabel told about her recent days in Manchester. She had viewed the institutions that she had visited there with a critical eye, had teased out information and insights that another might have overlooked, had identified strengths and weaknesses, recognised what might be applicable in the United States and what not. She had the makings of a powerful series of articles in the *Columbia Home Gazette*.

And all the time that Mabel talked, Florence was impressed by her memory of detail and her willingness to ask questions that others would have avoided from politeness. That she was serious, largely devoid of humour, and what she had was ironic, was no less important than that she was driven. Anger at exploitation, contempt for meagre and smug benevolence, outrage that so much more could be done for so little extra, all drove her more than pity for any individual. Circumstance alone, the threat of destitution, had forced her into journalism. In it she had found more than a livelihood. A vocation. That her articles and revelations chipped at, rather than tore down, the abuses she despised, or advanced in such infant steps the causes she espoused, did not deter her. Mabel might not know it herself yet, Florence recognised, but she would go from strength to strength, carrying others with her.

And it was that recognition that decided Florence to ask that for which she had feared refusal. Her forlorn hope.

"There's another matter, Mabel," she said just as they were about to stand up. "Agatha knows about it, but I didn't want to ask more of you. You're already doing so much."

"Some other institution deserving a visit, Florence?"

"Something much more difficult. And it would have to happen very quickly. It would demand a lot of you. It could be asking too much."

"I can't say worse than 'No'."

159

"If you do, I'll understand," Florence said. "It's better to discuss it in my room."

*

It developed into an interrogation as thorough as that to which Eversham had submitted Florence. She had started with the visit of the indebted wife to the Sailor's Rest on the morning after her own return to Britain, told of Chadband's first beating, the unwanted respect it had gained her among other women, the alarm and fear it had caused her.

"Do you object if I take notes?" Mabel had listened in silence but was now putting on her pince-nez and producing her notebook.

It was a hopeful sign and Florence didn't object. Only then did she move on to the Atwell case and tell about each meeting. She didn't disguise her fear of the implications for Nicholas or herself.

"I wouldn't have gone on, have were it not for Agatha." She felt her eyes brimming. "Without her, and without her cousin – he's a good man, a noble one – I'd have given up."

Agatha reached out and held her hand, the pressure comforting.

Mabel didn't comment, just said, "Go on."

Now the kernel of the matter, the visit to Mrs. Atwell's sister, the refusal of the woman herself to appear, Florence's growing suspicion that the moneylender's demands had been more than financial alone. *A lot of lovely stuff. An Able Seaman's pay.* The possibility that the wretched woman might have yielded to those demands, that she had confessed to her husband.

Agatha was hearing this for the first time, and looking horrified, but Mabel showed no surprise.

"She can't be called to testify, not for or not against her husband," Florence said. "But Mr. Eversham thinks that, if other women were ready to speak about Chadband, about the sort of man he is, it could help. Not to go in the witness box, just give information about how this horrible man treats women. Mr. Eversham's a skilled lawyer, he'll find

160

some way of using it. If, if you Mabel…" Her voice trailed off. She didn't not know what more to say or to suggest.

"If I could gather that information, Florence?" Mabel said. "Why do you think that?"

"Because you're good at getting people to talk. Women especially. And you listen and you sort the wheat from the chaff. You find causes, don't just see effects. As when you found why so many of those poor women were working in that laundry, even if half of them spoke hardly a word of English. And…" Florence paused, concerned that what she would say would sound sententious. "Because you believe in Justice. The spirit, not the letter."

"When is the trial?"

Florence told her. Under three weeks.

"When I might be busy fighting off the amorous advances of Sir Clifford Belton and when I'll certainly be searching for material for my *Columbia Home Gazette* articles. They're what puts food on the table."

"I said I might be asking too much."

"And how would I do it, Florence?"

She had thought about it, was sure it could be done, even in the time available. "You could stay with me in Southsea," she said. "I'd introduce you to Mr. Seldon, the superintendent of the Sailor's Rest and tell him you're studying British charities. Just as you are. You'd like to include the Rest, and he'd believe it. I'd step back then, let you get contacts from him and –"

"Stop, Florence! That wouldn't work."

"So you won't help?"

"I didn't say that." Mabel's tone was gentler now. "It wouldn't work like you suggest. I care too much for you to do it like that, Florence. I could not be seen to know you. You think your reputation is at risk now? It'll be a hundred times worse if you're associated with an American woman-journalist delving into sordid matters you're associated with already."

"In what other way could it be done?"

161

Mabel ignored the question and turned to Agatha. "Did you mention me to your lawyer cousin?"

"No."

"That's good. You didn't either, Florence? No? Even better."

"You may want time to think about it." Florence saw that this was not the time to press further.

"Let's talk at breakfast," Mabel said, "And Agatha, can you join us too? Get here by eight? Good"

She had not refused.

*

It would be on Mabel's own terms, no discussion, no questions of her answered. And conditional on her demands being met. To the letter.

"You're to leave home, Florence. It doesn't matter where you go as long as you're not seen in Southsea before the trial. Go back there now, pack your things and leave. All I want from you are addresses I can reach you at."

"And for replies?"

"No replies. We'll meet again only after the trial."

"What can I tell Mr. Bagshot?"

"Nothing. See him when you get back to Southsea today, have some story about sick relatives or the like. A beloved aunt or a consumptive niece. Some appeal that you can't refuse. And you'll have every confidence in him preparing the defence with Agatha's cousin. If they want to try to get Mrs. Atwell to talk, that'll be their choice. From what you've told me, she won't."

"Can I explain to Mr. Eversham?"

"No. He isn't to know that I exist. And Agatha, keep in contact with your cousin, show curiosity about preparations, but tell nothing other than that Florence has been called away on family matters. If you're needed to do anything more, I'll write to you. But I do need your cousin's address, and Mr. Bagshot's too. Just in case."

"Am I to do nothing, Mabel?" Florence was uncomfortable. "What are you going to do?"

"You won't know. It's better that you don't."

"What about the *Temple de la Beauté*? And Sir Clifford?"

"Leave that to me too."

"And it's all or nothing, Mabel? Take it or leave it?"

"Trust me, Florence. I haven't starved since I took up journalism."

It was a gamble, but it could make Atwell's predicament no worse.

"I trust you, Mabel"

Time now to get back home to Southsea.

For one night only.

Chapter 16

Florence had placed her trust in Mabel's skills and judgement, had pledged not to interfere between now and Atwell's trial. She would be absent from the Portsmouth area in that time and she decided that the absence must be mental no less than physical. She would force herself not even to think of the case, or come home, until after the assizes in Winchester. She made her travel plans accordingly.

She arrived back in Southsea in late afternoon and went directly to Mr. Bagshot's house. He was surprised to see her, even more to learn that she had to depart the following day for Preston and had no idea of when she could return. Nicholas's sister, Susan, was unexpectedly ill there and needed assistance with her brood. Florence was apologetic but Mr. Bagshot assured her that she needn't be. He felt honoured to be working with Mr. Eversham. He had been to Lincoln's Inn himself the day before, for further discussions of Atwell's defence, and had arranged a meeting with him in the prison, and with Lieutenants Jackson and Purdon too in the coming week. Mrs. Dawlish could put her mind at rest. With all due modesty, Mr. Bagshot said, the matter was in capable hands.

In the villa in Albert Grove, Florence told Cook and Susan that from the next day they could take successive weeks free. One was to be present at all times to housekeep, make excuses to callers and forward mail. She suspected that the handsome young seaman who had brought a message from Lieutenant Jackson might well be visiting during the weeks of Susan's tenure and she warned her accordingly. Susan blushed, assured her that no such thing would happen. She wasn't that sort of girl, though the fervency of her denial hinted otherwise. She was sent out to send a telegram to Preston and, when she returned, packed two trunks of clothing and necessities under Florence's supervision.

The urge to write a note to Mr. Selden at the Sailor's Rest, to ask for his cooperation with any journalist who might visit, was very strong.

"Don't even tell me the place's address," Mabel had said. "If I need to make contacts through it, I'll find it in my own way."

There would be no note but, on Monday morning, Cook would visit the Rest, explain Florence's unexpected departure and no doubt enjoy the superintendent's hospitality.

She set out for London by the earliest train in the morning. It was a Sunday and the services were restricted. Unexpected expenditure had been high recently, and now there was to be yet more, so at the station she hesitated about travelling first-class. She promised herself other economies and did so anyway. It was almost midday before she reached Waterloo. The trunks were too bulky for a hansom, so a four-wheel growler carried her across London to Euston station. The city was an empty and depressing place on the Sabbath. There was none of the usual bustle, the shops were closed and a sense of gloom hung about the family groups trudging to the parks for bleak recreation on their one day free of labour. The onward journey northwards towards Lancashire was little more inspiring, green fields ever more frequently interspersed by vast swathes of smoke-blackened industrial landscape, oceans of slate roofs, glimpses of squalid yards backing on to the track, grim vistas of small brick houses lining narrow streets. There were just two stops on this express and she had a ladies' compartment all to herself for most of the way, allowing her to read in comfort.

She was touched when she arrived at Preston to find Nicholas's brother-in-law, Adolphus Harkness, waiting on the platform. Unsure of the time of her arrival, he had been there to meet two earlier trains but he made no complaint. She had not liked the man on the few occasions she had met him, for he was often the worse for drink, and Nicholas liked him even less. But now there was genuine concern on his face when he asked, in a rush, "Is it Nicholas? Is it something bad?" and his relief was genuine too when he said, "Thank God! Oh, thank God! We were so worried when we received your telegram!"

Florence felt a surge of guilt. Her own concern for Nicholas had taken too little account of others. Of his sister Susan, of his father in Shrewsbury, of the six-year old half-brother there who idolised him, even of this boorish brother-in-law. She would not have been the only one following the news from the expedition up the Nile. What little reassurance she could have given, she had not. She had seen war, knew how Nicholas conducted himself, how equipped he was to prevail, and she had not shared that bleak reassurance with them.

Adolphus's carriage, a clarence, was waiting outside. Whatever failings he might have, he was a good provider, a cotton-mill owner who had built on his father's success. In three generations, a Harkness had advanced from hand-weaver to local magnate.

The day was drawing in now, rain falling, as the vehicle sped through the cobbled streets, where even on a Sunday the smell of coal-smoke was strong, and towards the open countryside. Florence learned that Susan was yet again in an interesting condition. She was uncertain how many children there now were but by circumlocutions she eased from Adolphus that there were nine. The eldest, a boy, had been in Hamburg for eighteen months, working for a business contact there and learning German. Another was to follow in a year's time. The remainder were still in school.

The family was a matter at last disposed of and Adolphus reverted to his favourite topics. The ingratitude and lethargy of his workers, the rising threat of socialism and the militancy of the trade-unions. Nobody in government took such concerns seriously, nor understood how money must be made. He had picked up the word *Communard* somewhere and he used it freely

The house, a small mansion, lay in a rural setting outside the city, near Whittingham. The grounds were small, but they boasted their own gate lodge, a statement of aspiration to something grander still. In one more generation, Florence thought, the transformation would be complete, The Harkness family would be by then embarrassed by the source of its wealth – trade, not land – and with a son in parliament perhaps and daughters courted by scions of the financially-straitened lower aristocracy.

The sight of Susan shocked her. It was impossible to imagine that this bloated and exhausted woman, moving her bulk so ponderously, could have been the vivacious and beautiful girl whom Nicholas had remembered from his youth. It was she who had brought laughter into

166

the motherless household, he had said. She who had taken him in her arms and comforted him when he had sobbed at night in the misery of hazy recollection of a woman he had scarcely known. It was to her he had written monthly since he had joined the navy at thirteen, and sometimes week by week, numbered letters accumulating until he could post them at the next port of call. She still fretted over him, for Florence had written previously to say that he was somewhere in Egypt. She was his elder by four years. It had seemed a vast difference at the time. Now, at forty-three, she was an old woman, frightened, she told Florence on the second day of her visit, that she might not survive what was likely in any case to be her last confinement. Her mother, Nicholas's mother, had died in childbirth.

The week that Florence had allowed herself here was so pleasant that she felt guilty she had come here only once before. The company of the children, the younger ones most of all, was a pleasure and there was a dog-cart at the stables in which she could take them out herself. A coachman's daughter, accustomed to horses since childhood, it was a delight to tell the groom to stand aside, to amaze the children by tackling up the cob herself and putting him between the shafts, to drive with an assured hand at a spanking pace along the country lanes. Only the sad look of longing on Susan's face as they departed on each expedition cast a cloud.

To her own surprise, she found herself warming to Adolphus. He was terrified for Susan, he confessed in confidence. He had reduced his drinking, though not enough not to be maudlin when he recalled first meeting her during a holiday on the Isle of Man. It was at once both ludicrous and moving to hear this balding red-faced man speak of the most beautiful girl he'd ever known, of the happiness they had shared, of his near-despair at the thought of maybe losing her. What broke the ice with him was the fun that Florence had brought the children, the hide and seek, the guessing games, the stories read from books, the bowlderised memories of her adventures in Turkey that evoked such horrified delight. Susan had once been like that with the children too, he said, but those days would not return. He might never have spoken like this to anybody else, Florence realised, certainly not to any other man, and never in a millennium to Nicholas.

And so the fun continued, and she was grateful for it, even though, each time she took the youngest child, a girl, on her lap she felt a pang. She would never have, could never have, a child of her own. She had only Nicholas, and he might never return.

"Will Uncle Nicholas be coming back?"

Martin, thirteen, had a tremor in his voice. He'd seen Nicholas only a handful of times, knew him through his mother's stories as a romantic Nelsonic hero rather than as the serious, austere and steadfast man whom Florence loved.

"He'll come back." She drew the boy to her, hugged him. "He'll come back and he'll come to see you all."

Could he join the navy himself, Martin asked? He loved the steam engines in his father's mills, thought that must be an advantage. He should discuss it with Nicholas himself, Florence said, must come to visit Southsea, be brought to visit warships in harbour. Nicholas would like this boy. She remembered the warmth with which he recalled his own uncle, the consumptive naval officer who had died young and had bequeathed him six farms in Shropshire.

And it was to those farms that the coming week would bring her. Managed by an agent, the accounts might merit similar scrutiny to that which she subjected those of the Sailor's Rest. She had no suspicion of the man, but she would welcome the task, proud of the proficiency she had gained. The reply to a letter she sent to Nicholas's father, a solicitor in Shrewsbury, surprised her. He himself had never ben unfriendly to her, but his wife, his second wife, had never disguised her dislike.

Florence had visited only once before, and then with Nicholas. He had refused to come without her. Now she had cast her proposed visit as one of business. She would stay at a hotel but she wrote that she hoped to come by for tea. But the reply was from Mrs. Rowena Dawlish and it chided her for considering staying elsewhere but in Nicholas's old home. And her son Edgar, Ted to the family, was entranced at the idea of seeing his Aunt Florence again. She must never be a stranger. Welcome as it was, the letter was somehow disconcerting.

The days passed and Florence forced herself to ignore their significance. On Wednesday Mabel would have dined with Sir Clifford Belton, on Thursday would have yet another Empyrean Bath. On one day or another other Mr. Bagshot would be attempting to draw admissions from a sullen prisoner and the next, be proud to be at Lincoln's Inn, flattered to be in consultation with a Queen's Council. Without her, these affairs would roll on, as in some uncertain time the whole world would too forever. As they would without Nicholas if... She thrust the thought away.

*

Mabel's bombshell arrived with Friday's last postal delivery.

Sir Clifford's letter had reached her, via the Plymouth poste restante, on Tuesday afternoon. His apologies were profuse. He had to be open, in all honesty, he felt, about the reasons for withdrawing the invitation to Wednesday night's dinner. His son George so treasured his late mother's memory that he regarded his father meeting a charming lady, and introducing her at such a gathering, as a defilement.

Bitter words had been exchanged, made worse by George's wife. Alerted by her, Sir Clifford's daughters had also expressed hostile concern. It was too early, he now recognised, to make the introduction but his son would come round in time, his daughters also. They would see that an honest friendship and, dared he hope, perhaps even more in time, could mean no betrayal of their mother. Mrs Daley already had an admirer in his sister, Mrs. Cavendish. She would pour oil on the troubled family waters. He had closed by saying that an enquiry at the *Temple de la Beauté* had indicated that Mrs Daley had an appointment there on Thursday. He hoped he might see her then. And if this letter had presumed too much, he would understand if she did not wish to speak to him.

"I had half-expected it," Mabel had written, "but Mrs. Daley would not have. The cancelled invitation wouldn't matter to her. She'd read only the admission of admiration and of hope. Nothing would keep her from the Temple on Thursday."

They had been there, brother and sister, when she arrived, a half-hour earlier than her appointment, and they had invited her to sit with them. Sir Clifford looked uncomfortable. "Like a schoolboy who had done something that he shouldn't have, but was glad he did." Mabel had blushed and stammered while they discussed the weather.

Once again, there had been a delay of the full delivery of llama's milk. Mrs. Mobray had apologised that one of the two churns that had arrived from Scotland had been delivered to a wrong address. It had now been located, should be here within the hour. But in the meantime, there was enough for one Empyrean bath only. And Mrs. Daley had insisted that Mrs. Cavendish avail of it. She herself could wait. She had glanced at Sir Clifford and smiled when she said that time always passed easily in pleasant company. She had recorded the conversation as soon as she had returned to her hotel.

Had she been offended by his letter? he had asked.

She had tried to look embarrassed. No, not offended.

Older men, widowers especially, often felt the pangs of loneliness, he said.

Mrs. Daley understood. Older ladies, widows, often felt the same.

Might he address her as Emily?

Only if she might... she had hesitated, was a little breathless. Only if she might call him Clifford.

That would delight him. He saw nothing unseemly, and she agreed, about friendships between older gentlemen and ladies. Especially if in the future – but no! He had stopped himself, said he was afraid he might have said too much already.

She had not been shocked. She too had hoped to find such friendship but it had been difficult in the limited society of Indianapolis. Innocent friendships could be so cruelly ridiculed by wagging tongues.

And grown-up children often did not understand, Clifford had said.

Neither would her son Franklin, though he was the best that any mother could ever have. She thought it would break his heart if any other man were to take her from him. He had placed her on too high a pedestal.

Clifford was envious. His son and even his daughters – no! Better to keep that sorrow to himself.

She had reached out to touch his hand as he turned his head away, then withdrew it immediately.

Perhaps he had tested his children too soon, he said. Their mother's memory was still so dear them. But when the right time came for them to meet her, after his sister had helped prepare the way, they would be won over instantly.

Mabel had been wondering by now how long she could maintain the charade. It was a relief when Mrs. Mobray appeared to confirm arrival of the missing churn. The Empyrean Bath was in preparation. Only five minutes more.

Time's winged chariot moved all too quickly, Clifford said. These moments had been golden. Perhaps…

Yes? A hesitation. Yes, Clifford?

Perhaps here, a week from now? His sister would be glad to come again…

She would make the appointment before she left today.

Might he write again?

She would be visiting friends in Hampshire and on the Isle of Wight, acquaintances she'd made on her previous tour in Europe, never longer than a night or two. Best to write to her by the poste restante at Portsmouth.

The only indication in the whole letter that she was going there.

And he would long for a letter in her own dear hand.

She had smiled, and nodded.

But perhaps not to his address in Sloane Street lest his children hear mention of it from a curious servant, he said. Better to an old friend's address, he suggested.

338 King's Road, Chelsea.

171

He did not mention that it was a tobacconist's shop.

Florence read the letter through once more, felt a glow of satisfaction that Mrs. Bellamy and her associates were bring drawn in. And Mabel was enjoying herself. There could be no risk for her as long as the meetings were at the *Temple de la Beauté*, for Agatha was ensuring that Jack was keeping discreet watch. Mabel would have run greater risks when she had worked in that laundry.

It was in Portsmouth that the danger would lie.

There she would have no protection

*

Florence yielded to Susan's and the children's, and even Adolphus's, pleading and stayed two days longer than intended, leaving for Shrewsbury on the following Monday morning. Susan's confinement was expected within a month, and Florence would return for that.

Nicholas's father, Andrew Dawlish, had Ted with him when he met her at the station. The boy broke free, ran to her and threw his arms about her. She was no less joyed. Mr. Dawlish, as she had always addressed him, was half-relieved, half-concerned, that there was still no news of his Nicholas. But he was delighted that she had come and he had already arranged meetings with the agent and visits to the farms. It would be a busy five days, longer he hoped, and she must think of Rowena as her own stepmother no less than Nicholas's.

Florence was apprehensive about meeting her, despite the apparent warmth of the letter received from her. Daughter of a local squire, only a decade older than Florence herself, this other Mrs. Dawlish had regarded the younger's origins as a disgrace to the family, and had not hesitated to hint at them. But now, at the house, her welcome seemed genuine and she was perhaps as anxious as Florence herself. She must have Nicholas's old room, she said, it would make her feel close to him.

And it did.

It was unchanged for almost thirty years. The books he had devoured still lay on the shelves – she would read from them to Ted –

and the patchwork quilt that he remembered still covered the bed and the mezzotint of Trafalgar still hung on the wall. It was hard to imagine the bereaved child who had once wept here in his sister's arms being now a leader of men somewhere in the wastes of the Sudan, facing – what? Pride, love and fear washed through her at the thought.

Rowena insisted on Florence calling her by her name and brought her to see relations in the following days. The stable-boy drove the family trap on the first occasion only and Florence took the reins herself each subsequent time, much to Ted's delight. She was introduced as the wife of Captain Dawlish, Rowena's step-son, a man who had been granted an audience with Her Majesty herself at Windsor. There might have been something of calculation, of social aggrandisement, in her step-mother-in-law's advertisement of the relationship, but as the days passed, there was something else too, a desire for genuine friendship.

The farms were all but a liability. During his earlier career Nicholas had been grateful for them paying the cost of his uniform, though little more. He had kept them for sentimental reasons only as a last link to his uncle. A day spent with the agent, and perusal of the accounts, confirmed that this year would be little more profitable. It was no surprise. Agricultural prices had been low for years now. Florence saw that it was worse still for the tenants when she visited the properties. Life and labour were hard, comfort meagre. Grown-up children had left for better-paid work in the factories in the cities further east, and some had even gone to America and Australia.

When Nicholas came back – if he came back, a small cold internal voice reminded her – she should advise him to sell. Should, but wouldn't. He would never admit it, even to her, for he despised open display of virtue, but a sense of duty to the tenants would prevent him. Another landlord might be less understanding.

She heard nothing more from Mabel but a brief letter from Agatha suggested that they meet in Winchester the night before the trial. Mr. Eversham had indicated that there was no reason they should not attend.

It was a summons back to another, more dangerous world.

And no mention of Mabel's activities, whatever they might be.

*

The night before she was to set off south again, Rowena took her aside after dinner.

"Has Andrew said anything to you about his health?"

"He looks hale and hearty," Florence said "He's like a man of fifty" It wasn't quite true but he did look younger than his seventy-one years.

"There's a problem with his heart. He could go at any time, the doctors say. Without warning."

"Does he know?"

"He knows but he won't admit it. He works like he always did."

As Nicholas too would behave. If... if he ever gets to that age.

"It could be years yet," Florence said. "He may bury the rest of us. He might live to see Ted married."

"It's Ted I want to talk about. You know he adores you?"

She knew. And she him. The week spent with him had been a joy.

"My sister Jane died two years ago. My sister Mary's ill now. Cancer, like our mother died of. None older than fifty. I know that it'll take me before then too, Florence."

She tried to make light of it. "You can't be sure of that. It's pure coincidence. It doesn't run in families." And then she recognised the look on Rowena's face. Regret. Infinite regret. "Is everything all right now?" she asked. "Is it..."

"It may be nothing. But if it is, then... then would you and Nicholas take Ted in?" She was starting to weep. "Would you raise him as your own?"

Florence went across, embraced her.

No need for any other answer.

Chapter 17

Agatha was already at the Black Swan Inn, close to Winchester railway station, when Florence arrived on Wednesday evening. Mr. Eversham had suggested to his cousin that it would be better to book three nights since he did not expect the trial to finish on Thursday. He and Mr. Bagshot would be staying elsewhere in town. It would be better not to be seen together before the trial but Mr. Bagshot's clerk was arranging for both ladies to have reserved seats in the public gallery. They should dress as inconspicuously as possible. Agatha had heard nothing more from Mabel than Florence had. She had gone to Portsmouth, but what she had done there, or had not done, was unknown. And both were satisfied with her progress against Mrs. Bellamy.

"There are letters already signed in the name of Sir Clifford Belton," Florence said. "He's using the same accommodation address that Mrs. Chalmers-Bolger's admirer wrote to." It was easy to imagine that young assistant, perhaps indeed the son in Anderson and Son, Luxury Tobacconists, yielding easily under questioning. "Even if Mabel hasn't enough for magazine articles, the real Sir Clifford's family will be up in arms once they're informed. He's a man of influence and they won't tolerate it. I can foresee police raids and prosecutions and the *Temple de la Beauté* closed and shuttered."

They talked inconsequentially through dinner about Florence's family visits and Agatha's latest studies, but both skirted what would happen on the morrow. Florence was frightened, feared that in some way her own involvement might be revealed. She had never been in a courtroom, knew them only from novels as scenes of drama. The possibility of the prosecuting counsel, or some confederate of Chadband's, acting as a prosecution witness, swinging around to point an accusing finger haunted her. She had debated with herself again and again whether she should attend this trial at all, or whether it was better to keep aloof, trust to Mr. Eversham, be satisfied that she had done all she could for Atwell's defence.

But always the same thought returned, not comforting, but challenging. Nicholas would have been here to testify. Even if his man was to be led away to long years of hard labour, Nicholas would have held his eye to the last, silent confirmation that, convict or not, he still had his trust and his respect. And she would be there in his place.

*

The Court was within walking distance and they were present, and seated at the front of the public gallery, before the first case opened. The benches were half-empty and Florence recognised nobody among the shabby men and women on them, relatives, she surmised, of defendants or victims. Most looked sombre, others were quietly weeping and a few seemed angry. The jury took their places. In their Sunday best, all had the look of prosperous shop-owners or successful tradesmen. They took their oaths. The Court rose for the entry of Mr. Justice Cadman, resplendent in black robe and bob-wig, his dignity spoiled by a pinched face and thick-lensed round spectacles. He glared around the courtroom and took his seat. Atwell's case was third on the list and the first two were disposed of within thirty minutes each.

Four witnesses, one a public-house landlord, testified to a drunken labourer thrusting a broken bottle into the face of another drinker. The victim, still in hospital, had lost an eye and would be scarred for life. It was hard to imagine the defendant capable of it. He was a small man, pale and bald, aged before his time. He looked defeated, and probably always had been. His eyes never lifted from the spikes around the dock in which he stood. He had no defence counsel and Florence saw that it didn't matter. She wondered why he had pleaded innocent. The evidence was clear and the defendant, by a shake of his head, declined the invitation to speak.

The judge summed up by saying that the facts were undisputed. The jury huddled in their box for perhaps three minutes before the foreman announced a guilty verdict. An older woman, close to Florence, grey, worn with the marks of long poverty, began to sob and a younger, her daughter perhaps, tried to quieten her. An usher appeared and led them outside. Any more such conduct, Mr Justice Cadman said, and he would have the courtroom cleared. As for the current case, he had seen too much of this sort of crime recently. He had no hesitation in sentencing the prisoner to ten years' penal servitude. His order to the warders, "Take him down", had a chilling finality about it. The condemned man still did not raise his head as he descended the steps towards the holding cells below.

The second case involved a nineteen-year old assistant in a draper's shop, accused of the theft of a five-pound note. He too had pleaded innocent. The owner's daughter testified that she had seen him take it from the till and put it in his pocket. His employer claimed that, when he confronted him, he had confessed that he intended to bet it on a horse. Like the former defendant, he had no defence counsel but when given the opportunity to speak for himself he broke down and blubbered that he had every intention of paying it back from his winnings but the horse had never finished. The judge reminded the jury that their verdict must reflect the facts of the case. The theft had occurred and, though the prisoner had pleaded innocent, he had admitted the theft in their presence. Again, no need to leave the jury-box. Guilty. The youth was weeping as Mr. Justice Cadman emphasised that the breach of duties of good faith and trust must be taken into account and he sentenced him to four years' penal servitude.

Impossible as Florence found it to sympathise with either defendant, she was still horrified by the cold impersonality and the relentless finality of the process. She sensed the same in Agatha and both remained silent as they sat where they were during the fifteen-minute break that followed. Somewhere in a cell below, Atwell must be sitting in numb misery, awaiting the moment when he too must ascend the stairway into the dock. He had not flinched before Beja spears at Tamai, but he had comrades around him then, excitement to sustain him. The solitary waiting now must be even more dreadful.

The courtroom was filling again. Mr. Eversham and Mr. Bagshot had entered and were shaking hands and exchanging pleasantries with the prosecution counsel, a Mr. Boyd. The shimmer of Mr Eversham's silk gown proclaimed him a Queen's Counsel, unexpected and unusual in such a court. Both he and Mr. Bagshot had looked up and had seen Florence and Agatha, but neither gave any sign of acknowledgement.

The public gallery was filling now, almost to capacity. Florence scanned the faces, seeking those of Atwell's in-laws or neighbours. An old couple, poorly but decently dressed, was seated near the front. The woman was holding a handkerchief to her eyes and weeping, the man pale, dazed, pressing her hand. They must be Atwell's parents. Other family members might be outside, Florence hoped, and Mr. Bagshot might have recommended calling some as character witnesses, but they could not be seated in the public gallery until after they had testified. Many of the new entrants were strong-looking and muscular men, mostly young, uncomfortable in suits and neckties, shipmates of Atwell's perhaps. Her surmise was proven correct when one greeted her, with respect, by name. She didn't recognise him but she thought that he might have been one of the men she had visited with Nicholas in the hospital at Haslar.

Mr. Justice Cadman returned, glared once more around the courtroom, seemed displeased to see that the public gallery was full and even less so when here were a few low calls of encouragement from it when Atwell was led up into the dock. Further such behaviour would not be tolerated, he warned, and Contempt of Court was a charge that merited severe penalties. He reminded the jury that it was still bound by oath.

Florence hardly heard him. She was seeing Atwell now not as a wounded hero of Tamai but as a broken man, shoulders slumped, head bowed, a face that had glimpsed the desolation that lies beyond despair. He looked up only when he was asked how he was pleading.

"Not Guilty."

There was the slightest hint of defiant pride in those words.

And perhaps of hope also.

*

178

Florence had brought a lined notebook, several pencils and a sharpener. She would take notes, for she wanted to tell Nicholas about it when he returned, to let him know how she had stood by the man who had stood by him at Tamai.

The prosecution case was simple, little different to that made against the two previous defendants. Florence suspected that no different approach than bare presentation of the facts was needed for hundreds of trials in courts like this. The prosecution counsel, Mr. Boyd, a stooped and greying man of fifty, gave an impression of weary dedication to a task that bored him.

Sergeant Herbert Barlow delivered his brief testimony in stilted language. Pursuant to a complaint received at the Blackwell Street Police Station at ten minutes past eleven on the evening of Thursday October the ninth he had proceeded with two constables and the complainant, a Mr. James Rowley, to the premises of Mr. Barnaby Chadband in Crasswell Street. He had found the gentleman lying on a mattress that had been brought down into the shop. His face was bruised and bleeding, and both eyes were blackening.

Had Mr Chadband been able to identify his attacker?

He was in no state to speak. He was having pain breathing and the doctor already in attendance feared that his ribs might have been broken. A handcart had been located to bring him to the Royal Hospital. Mr Rowley had indicated that he had pursued the assailant but was unable to catch him. He had stated that, due to the nature of the scuffle and the chase, he was unable to recognise him. Mr. Rowley had been tripped up by accident by a witness in Commercial Street, from whom a statement had subsequently been taken.

Mr. Boyd thanked the sergeant and said that Mr. Rowley and the other witness would be called to testify. They could speak for themselves.

Mr. Eversham had no questions for Sergeant Barlow.

Florence felt a thrill of fear when Inspector Towton appeared as next witness. The memory of his insolent callousness two years before still rankled. She hoped that he would not look up and see her here.

Towton had gone to the Royal Hospital himself, the afternoon following the attack, to take a statement from Mr. Chadband. He had found the gentleman in pain, though well enough to talk. Asked if he had recognised his assailant, Mr. Chadband replied that he thought that it could have been a Mr. Atwell, a seaman who had once come his shop to dispute a bill incurred by his wife. Enquiries by constables had ascertained that Atwell was resident in Clingford Lane. He was found at that address by constables whom Inspector Towton sent that evening.

And Atwell had been brought to Blackwell Street station?

Yes. Inspector Towton had questioned him immediately. Atwell had been sullen and uncooperative. The victim's assistant, who had chased the assailant, and a witness who had tried to stop him, had both been brought to the station. When confronted with Atwell, they had identified him as the man they had seen. Atwell had refused to answer any questions and he was charged on the basis of recognition by the witnesses.

It was a polished performance, Florence recognised, a coherent account delivered with assurance and without hesitation. Inspector Towton's face was stern and gave the impression of a dedicated man doing a distasteful job. He must have testified hundreds of times like this, must have impressed many other juries as he did this one.

The prosecution had no further questions but, when invited, Mr Eversham had.

Smiling, even a little diffident, Mr. Eversham approached the witness box. The inspector's testimony had been very clear, he said, and he only wished to clarify a few minor points.

Was it necessary for a senior officer to go personally to a hospital to take a statement?

In this case, yes. Due to the nature of the injuries, this might well have become a case of murder. Inspector Towton looked towards the jury, solid citizens all. Honest businessmen in their own premises were entitled to the full protection of the law, he said. Two jurymen were nodding.

And the witness knew Mr. Chadband as an honest businessman?

Towton hesitated, started to answer, was cut off as the prosecutor rose to his feet and objected. The witness's opinion of the victim was not relevant. The judge concurred and Mr. Eversham apologised. But he was not finished.

Had there been any previous incidents at Mr. Chadband's shop?

Again, a hesitation.

Not recently.

When then, and how often?

Mr Boyd objected again. This trial was concerned only with the events on the ninth of October. Before the judge could comment, Mr. Eversham had withdrawn his question. He had only one more.

Had the accused's name ever come to the attention of the police previously.

No, not to Inspector Towton's knowledge.

Mr. Eversham said that he understood that, on occasion, witnesses were required to identify suspects from among innocent parties called in off the street and of a generally similar appearance. He had forgotten the term.

An identification parade, Inspector Towton volunteered.

Ahh. That was it. An identification parade. Were the two witnesses asked to identify the prisoner in this way?

No.

Just face to face? Individually?

Yes.

Had the accused said anything about being present at Mr. Chadband's shop?

He had refused to answer any questions whatsoever.

And the incident had occurred at around ten o'clock in the evening?

It had.

Mr. Evesham thanked him. He had no further questions. The prosecution had none either and the witness was released. Florence felt as if a weight was lifted from her as he left. He had not seen her.

It was just past noon. Mr. Justice Cadman enquired if the testimony of the next witness might be lengthy. That was probable, Mr. Boyd said. The judge saw it as an appropriate time then to break for lunch. The trial would resume at half-past one. The jury was to remain sequestered and would be provided with refreshment.

Florence and Agatha waited until after the gallery had emptied before they left. Lieutenant Jackson was talking to another gentleman outside, an officer, from his bearing, though Florence did not know him. Jackson caught Florence's eye, smiled and nodded, but did not approach. Wherever he lunched, it was not at the Black Swan, where Florence and Mabel did. Neither said much during the meal but Florence glanced at the notes she had taken, pages of them already, and found it difficult to read her own frenzied handwriting. It was impossible to judge how well, or how badly, progress so far should be interpreted.

Recollection of that silent, desolate, figure in the dock hovered over them and spoiled their appetites

*

A cold wet drizzle from a leaden sky did nothing to lighten their mood when Florence and Agatha walked back from the hotel to the courthouse.

When the afternoon session opened, Mr. Boyd began by saying that an important witness who should be here today was unable to attend. Still suffering from the injuries sustained in the brutal assault in his own shop, Mr. Barnaby Chadband, though at home again, had sent a doctor's certificate. It confirmed that he was not yet sufficiently recovered to leave his house. Mr. Chadband had however sworn an affidavit as to the events on October the ninth. He was confident that he had recognised Atwell as the attacker since he had met him once previously. The affidavit had been made available to the defence.

182

Mr. James Rowley was now called.

He was of medium build, red-faced and broken-nosed, portly, bursting from a too-tight blue suit, with the look of a bruiser. Florence had seen many civilians like him in Portsmouth, the sort who had a reputation for holding their own in bar-room battles with naval personnel. He seemed familiar with court procedures and he took the oath with an expression of forced sincerity on his face.

Was he in Mr. Chadband's employ? Mr. Boyd asked.

He had been his assistant for upwards of fifteen years.

Was Mr. Chadband a good employer?

Nobody could hope for a better.

What was the nature of Mr. Chadband's business?

He bought and sold clothing.

Was Mr Rowley at Mr. Chadband's shop on the ninth of October?

He had been there all evening, mostly sorting garments in a back room. Mr. Chadband had been in the shop, behind the counter.

Was the connecting door open or closed?

Closed.

Could he tell the court what had happened?

It was almost ten o'clock, just before closing time, when he heard shouts from the shop. He dashed out and saw that Mr. Chadband had been dragged halfway across the counter. He was being beaten and his face was already bleeding and one eye was closed.

Could he identify the attacker?

He could. He pointed to the dock.

Did he know the man's name at the time?

Not then. He had never seen him before. He knew it now.

What had he done then?

What any good employee would have done when he saw his employer being assaulted. He went to his aid.

Was he frightened to do so?

Yes, he was. He thought that the assailant was a madman but he managed to get behind him and drag him away from the counter. The prisoner had struggled free and made for the door. He followed him down Crasswell Street – he was running fast – and around the corner into Commercial Road. He shouted 'Stop thief!' as he ran.

Why had he shouted that?

He had assumed that Mr. Chadband had been robbed.

Were there many people around?

Not many. It was late on a Thursday. People had to get up early for work next day.

Had anybody tried to assist?

One man tried to block the prisoner's path. He was a barber, putting up his shutters. The prisoner dodged past but he himself had collided with the barber and both went down on the pavement. By the time he rose there was no sign of the fugitive.

And then?

He returned to the shop, found Mr. Chadband almost unconscious and asked a neighbour to go for a doctor. After leaving his employer in the doctor's care he had gone to the police station in Blackwell Street to report the incident.

The prosecution had no further questions.

Now Mr Eversham's turn. He was again diffident, almost apologetic, soft spoken. He had only a few questions, he said.

Were Mr. Rowley's duties confined to sorting clothes?

No. He bought and collected them as well sometimes.

Old-clothes?

Yes.

Collected in the poorer areas of Portsmouth?

Mainly.

It was an honourable trade, Mr. Eversham said. He must be a familiar face in some areas.

He supposed he must be.

And was he generally known as James Rowley? Or as something more familiar perhaps? Jem or Jim or Jimmy?

A lot of people called him Jem.

Mr. Boyd rose an asked if this line of questioning was relevant.

Mr. Eversham craved the court's indulgence. He wished to build up a picture in his mind of what had happened. Mr. Justice Cadman said that he would allow only a few more such questions.

Did Mr. Rowley sometimes collect more than clothes? Rents perhaps?

Mr. Chadband had no rental properties.

Repayment of loans perhaps?

Hesitation by the witness.

Mr. Boyd rose to his feet, as if to object, then thought better of it, and sat down again. The judge was showing more interest now than any time earlier in the day. The defence could continue questioning, he said.

Mr. Eversham reminded the witness that he was on oath. Did he ever collect loan repayments on Mr. Chadband's behalf?

On occasion, yes. There was nothing wrong about that.

What sort of loans?

Assistance to people who had money trouble.

Wives of seamen who were serving overseas, perhaps?

Now and again. Other cases too. Mr. Chadband liked to help people if he could. He was a charitable man.

Mr Eversham smiled and moved across to the table at which he had sat with Mr. Bagshot. It was regrettable that there were not more charitable men like Mr. Chadband, he said. He was not himself familiar with Portsmouth but he had been disturbed by an article about conditions there which he had read last evening. He paused at the table and Mr. Bagshot took something from a manila folder and handed it to him. Mr. Eversham held it up.

Florence recognised it from its cover even before he spoke. She looked at the jury. Several members were leaning forward to scrutinise it. At least one seemed to have recognised it. Its exposures of scandals and abuses, usually salacious, had secured it a high circulation countrywide.

Did Mr. Rowley sometimes read this estimable publication, the *St. James Fortnightly Review*? Mr. Eversham asked. Yesterday's edition perhaps?

The witness looked surprised. No. He didn't read often.

A pity, Mr. Eversham said. He might otherwise have been able to comment on disturbing issues raised in an article by an American lady journalist who had recently visited the city. Matters related to moneylending, demands of a sordid nature made on poor women, even on wives of seaman serving on foreign stations. It was sad that an American visitor should see Britain in such a light.

Mr. Boyd was on his feet again. The article was of no relevance to the case now on trial. It was one of assault and battery only.

Mr. Justice Cadman concurred and directed Mr. Eversham to put away the magazine. Any further questions must be directly relevant to the charge itself.

Mr. Eversham apologised. He had no more questions for the witness.

Florence looked towards the dock. Atwell's face was covered by his hands and his shoulders were heaving as he wept. Pity on the faces of the two warders flanking him.

It was almost three o'clock.

The judge ordered a quarter-hour break.

There was one more prosecution witness to be heard thereafter and the defence had not yet begun its case.

The trial would extend into the next day.

*

Mr. Joseph Payne confirmed that he was a barber with a shop in Commercial Street. That his hair had been dyed raven-black did nothing to disguise his age. He was sixty-five at the least, stooped and hunched like so many in his profession. It was probable that he had never been in a court before, for he seemed over-awed and nervous, even when taking the oath, as if he himself were on trial.

Could he tell what happened on the evening of October the ninth?

His last customer had just left and he had been putting up the shutters. It was a heavy job for one man, but his assistant was ill and he

186

had to do it alone. He had just secured the last shutter when he heard the cry of 'Stop thief!'

The witness, less anxious by now, launched into the story that he must have told customers dozens of times since and would tell even more often in the future.

He had looked up to see two men running towards him, one only a few yards ahead of the other. From the cry of 'Stop Thief!' he understood immediately what was happening. He moved to the centre of the pavement, held his arms out to block the man running towards him.

Was he frightened to do so?

He had no time to think, he just did it. But he was too late. The running man skirted around him but the second crashed into him and they both fell to the ground. By the time they were on their feet again the fugitive had disappeared. The other man had called him a foul name for interfering, had said that he'd have caught the fugitive but for him. The witness had felt insulted, the more so since he had suffered a bruised knee, and standing long hours was essential for his business.

What had he done then?

He had gone home directly and knew nothing further until a police constable had come to his shop next day to bring him to Blackwell Street station to make an identification.

Was the person he was asked to identify present in the court today?

He was. Over there, in the dock.

Had he recognised him as the man who had run past him outside his shop on the evening of October the ninth?

He believed he was.

Mr Boyd had no further questions.

And now the turn of the defence.

Mr. Eversham, smiling, complimented the witness on his courage in confronting a fugitive, especially since he was no longer a young man. Had he been long in business at the same address?

He had, and his father and grandfather, before him.

Over a hundred years in all?

At the very least.

A century of service in the home of the Royal Navy, Mr. Eversham said. A Portsmouth institution. Perhaps the witness's grandfather might have shaved the chin of the great Lord Nelson himself?

He didn't doubt it. He'd have been proud if he had.

Approving laughter and some clapping from the gallery. Even Mr. Justice Cadman was smiling, even though he rapped his gavel and called for order.

Did the witness previously know the gentleman who had knocked into him?

He'd seen him before. He believed his name was Jem Rowley but he only knew him by repute.

Ahh, Mr. Eversham said. By repute. Only by repute. The faintest shake of his head. He paused before his next question.

About what time did the incident occur?

Shortly after ten. That was when he normally closed on week nights, though later on Saturdays.

And he was absolutely sure that the prisoner in the dock was the man he had seen running towards him?

He was.

Was there a lamp-post close to the shop?

There was. At the corner.

At the corner of Commercial Street and Clingford Lane?

Yes.

So the fugitive's back was to the light? Surely his face would have been dark?

Well . . . Yes. But there were lights in some windows in the street.

Lights showing through blinds?

Yes.

More like a glow rather than direct light?

Yes.

And he was fully confident of the identification?

He was.

Would the witness look up into the public gallery please? There, on the front row, third from the left.

The man there half rose. One of the seamen, Florence realised, not unlike Atwell in build and hair colour and weathered look.

Could the witness be sure – and he must remember that he was under oath – that he would not confuse the accused with that man, were he confronted by him? Or there, with that gentleman in the row behind him, two further to the right? Another seaman, generally similar.

The witness opened his mouth to speak, then hesitated, was silent.

It was difficult to be sure in this courtroom's gloom, wasn't it? Mr. Eversham said. It was darkening outside and almost time for the courtroom lamps to be lit.

The barber nodded.

Mr. Eversham picked up a book from his table. A reputable almanac, he said, a publication of the Royal Observatory at Greenwich. He flipped it open at a page marked with a quill, ran his finger down, found a place. It indicated that sunset on October the ninth was at half-past five. So it would have been very dark, had it not been for the streetlamp and the dim light from several windows, just after ten on the night of the incident?

Yes.

For how long had the witness seen the face of the running man? Three, four seconds? Five? More?

Not more. Maybe five. The barber's tongue darted out to wet his lips and he was glancing towards the judge.

Who else was present when the witness had identified the prisoner in Blackwell Street station?

Just himself. And a police inspector and a sergeant, and the constable who had summoned him.

If those two gentlemen in the gallery, against whom no aspersions were being cast, had been present at the station with the man now standing in the dock, would he have identified him without hesitation?

Silence. The barber was shifting in his seat.

Mr. Eversham reminded him again that he was under oath, that he had called on Almighty God to vouch for the truth of what he would testify.

Still silence.

The witness must answer the question, Mr. Justice Cadman said.

And he did. The answer was that he could not be sure.

Mr. Eversham thanked him and had no further questions.

Proceedings were finished for the day, the judge said. There were no facilities for overnight sequestration of the jury but he trusted that its members would not talk or speculate about the case with family or friends. They should not leave their houses even – he smiled – for a welcome pint at a local hostelry.

And as soon as she could get from the building, Florence would be heading straight to the newsstand at the railway station to buy the *Fortnightly*. She would have to hurry. Once the jurymen reached home, some at least would be sending wives, children or servants scurrying to buy it too. Half the copies in Winchester were likely to be snapped up within the hour.

Mabel had not disappointed.

Chapter 18

Florence was too impatient to read the *St. James Fortnightly* to wait until she returned to the Black Swan. She went instead into the ladies' waiting room at the station. The light was dim, and she had to wear her spectacles, but her heart soared when she saw the list of contents on the front cover.

The Shame of Portsmouth – an American perspective. By Mrs. M. Bushwick of the Columbia Home Gazette.

It was the issue's premier article, introduced by a paragraph from the editor. Mrs. Bushwick was the most-respected lady journalist in the United States, he wrote, renowned for her fearless investigations of social abuses. He had felt privileged to meet her on a previous visit to our shores. Now she was back and he was pleased that she had agreed to contribute an article, though he was ashamed for Britain that the plight of the poor here shocked such a distinguished visitor.

Mrs Bushwick began her article by saying that she had not intended to write on this topic. She had crossed the ocean this time to study women's education in Britain in all its forms, from young ladies' seminaries to refuges for the fallen and succour for the handicapped. Interest in St. Winifred's Home for the Blind, Deaf and Dumb had brought her to Portsmouth. Its successes, brought about by its enlightened regime and progressive methods, were famed even across the Atlantic.

The visit to St. Winifred's had not disappointed. There were lessons to be learned from it by similar establishments in the United States. But what did disappoint were tales of poverty she heard there from mothers who had entrusted children to it. Mrs Bushwick had thereafter visited some of these women in their own homes, often just single rooms occupied by six or eight people. The squalor was no different to what she had encountered in the slums of New York and Boston. The problems were the same too. Drink, indebtedness, overcrowding, poor sanitation, inadequate incomes, or none at all. Mrs Bushwick quoted some of the women, under the promise of anonymity.

191

Mrs. W, a widow whose work as a casual house-cleaner brought in seven shillings a week, if she was lucky, supported five children. A sixth, a blind daughter, was at St. Winifred's.

Mrs X, whose husband was a drunkard, in and out of jail for years, fed her five children with scraps picked from refuse at the city's meat and vegetable markets. Her last baby had died of diphtheria. She admitted that on occasion she had begged at prosperous houses.

Mrs. Y's husband was a naval seaman, absent for long periods, who made inadequate provision for remittance of his pay. She had pawned anything of value she possessed and could not afford to redeem them. Washing glasses in a public-house brought a few shillings but without support of her relatives her children would go hungry, as she herself often did to spare them.

Another widow, Mrs. Z, whose husband, a carter, had been killed by a runaway horse, and was herself in bad health, survived with four other children on the earnings of her sixteen-year old son and his one-year younger sister. She was thankful to St. Winifred's for relieving her of the care of a deaf and dumb daughter.

A common feature of the many stories that Mrs Bushwick had heard, and she had quoted just a few, was frequent dependence on borrowing. Not just from relations, but from lenders who advanced small sums at usurious rates. Such people operated under cover of some legitimate business, sometimes rag and bone men, or dealers in old-clothes. Debts grew at a rate that made repayment impossible, yet their unrelenting demands made the collectors feared and hated figures. Worst of all was that some lenders, or their agents, were often willing to cancel debt in return for favours of an immoral nature. One of the women quoted had admitted, in shame, that she herself had yielded in this way and another could name a woman who had drowned herself rather than submit. And the police, all of the women claimed, had no interest in the problem. Rumour abounded that some constables, and even sergeants, were complicit.

Such stories could be heard in any great city on either side of the Atlantic but Mrs Bushwick was shocked to hear them in the home of the

192

Royal Navy, Britain's pride, mistress of the oceans and guarantor of an empire's greatness. It was in sadness rather than reproof that she reported them. She hoped that this article would stir outrage in Portsmouth, if no other city, to face the evil of petty usury.

The remainder was what Florence would have expected of Mabel, italics emphasising the sacredness of her causes, the keys to reform. Recognition of the *Rights of Woman* and granting of *Women's Suffrage* – the wild frontier states of Wyoming, Utah and Washington had shown the way. *Female Solidarity* was essential across all boundaries of class, wealth, race and creed. Decent men, who loved their mothers, wives and daughters, must see this.

No mention of the Sailor's Rest.

No way in which Florence could be linked to any of the stories, or could even identify the women quoted.

Mabel had indeed not disappointed.

*

Florence arrived early in court with Agatha next morning and again they were seated at the front of the gallery. A little further along the row, she saw that the old couple whom she had assumed were Atwell's parents had returned and were sitting in quiet desolation. Mrs. Deacon, their son's sister-in-law, was sitting with them today. She was rather too gaudily dressed for such an austere occasion but she drew admiring looks from the seamen. There were more of them today in the benches behind.

Mr. Eversham opened his defence next morning by calling the Reverend Mr. Samuel Teale. A Methodist minister, white-haired and frail, he moved with arthritic slowness and took his seat in the witness box with self-conscious dignity. He looked across towards Atwell in the dock and smiled. He had brought his own bible, an old friend and comfort, he said, and he asked if he might take his oath on it. Mr. Justice Cadman consented.

Mr. Eversham began his questioning. Mr. Teale had served thirty-two years in the chapel in Sudbury Street, Portsmouth had he not?

Thirty-three in mid-December. And eleven before that in other chapels in the city.

An impressive record of service, Mr. Eversham said, one to be proud of. And had the witness been acquainted with the prisoner at any time during those years?

For almost all of them. Mr. Teale had baptised David Atwell. He had married his parents also. And their parents before them had been chapel-folk too.

Had the prisoner attended Sunday School as a boy?

Without fail. He had won prizes for his knowledge of Scripture.

Life in the Royal Navy might include temptations, drink, and worse, that many young men fell prey to. Had it concerned Mr Teale that the prisoner had chosen that way of life?

No. He knew that David was strong in his faith, pure in mind and body, and had already taken the temperance pledge. He expected him to be an example to his fellow seamen.

Had anything caused Mr. Teale in the years since to alter that opinion?

No. David had remained a steadfast member of the chapel and had brought his own children there for baptism. When home from service at sea he had been active in promoting temperance.

Would he describe the prisoner as a violent man?

No. Decidedly not.

Mr. Eversham thanked the witness. He had no further questions. Neither had Mr. Boyd for the prosecution. Mr. Justice Cadman announced a fifteen-minute break. During it, the Reverend Mr. Teale, now allowed, after giving his evidence, to sit as a spectator, was brought in by an usher and seated, next to the Atwells and Mrs. Deacon.

Lieutenant Henry Jackson was the next witness called. He was in full uniform. When asked by Mr. Eversham, he identified himself as deputy to the senior instructor in HMS *Vernon*.

Had he seen active service?

Yes. In Zululand, in '79, with HMS *Active's* naval brigade.

Did he think that made him a good judge of men?

With all due modesty, yes. All officers had to be.

Was HMS *Vernon* a seagoing warship?

No. It was moored at Portsmouth, the navy's mine and torpedo school. Personnel based there were also frequently involved in testing of new weapons and techniques.

Did the prisoner serve directly under the witness?

On occasion, yes. He was a respected helmsman and skilled in handling small, fast craft. Steering accuracy was essential in torpedo-launching trials.

Was there danger involved in such work?

There could be. It needed a cool head and a sure hand.

And Able Seaman Atwell had those?

Yes.

Was he popular among his shipmates?

Popular and respected. Though sometimes they joked about his over-addiction to temperance and his efforts to remind them of its value.

Laughter in the gallery resulted in three raps of the judge's gavel.

Service in a ship permanently moored at a man's home city, close to friends and family, must be sought after. How had the prisoner come to be posted to HMS *Vernon*?

On the recommendation of Captain Dawlish of HMS *Leonidas*. Able Seaman Atwell had been a member of her crew, part of the naval brigade that participated in the Battle of Tamai in March this year.

Where the prisoner had been wounded?

Yes, seriously enough to be returned to Britain to recuperate. Captain Dawlish, now overseas again, had once served in the same capacity on *Vernon* as the witness did now. Captain Dawlish regarded Able Seaman Atwell as well suited to service on *Vernon* and viewed a year or two of such as appropriate reward for the prisoner's behaviour at that battle. Other senior officers had concurred.

Would Lieutenant Jackson wish to have Abel Seaman Atwell serve under him again, should circumstances allow?

Without hesitation.

195

The defence had no more questions. Neither had the prosecution. Lieutenant Jackson was dismissed.

The next witness was called, the last, Mr. Eversham said, for the defence.

Florence saw shock, a mixture of revulsion, pity and surprise, on the faces of the jury, and others on that side of the court, when Lieutenant Edward Purdon entered. She had felt the same herself, and hoped that she had managed to conceal it, when she had visited him some weeks before. Only when he turned was the full horror of his face revealed to the entire court. He had been a handsome man, and seen from the left he still was, but on the right cheek was one long livid scar that dragged his features over in a savage, leering grin. His diction was slurred as he took the oath, for the unseen tongue and gums had also been mangled. Florence felt pity change to admiration, as it had before. She sensed that others around her did also. He had accepted his injury, would not be defeated by it, would meet the world undaunted, with his face as it now was.

Was Lieutenant Purdon assigned to a ship at present? Mr. Eversham asked.

Not at present. He was convalescing at his parent's home nearby. He was hoping for a new ship in the near future.

How had he come to know the prisoner?

When he had served as HMS *Leonidas's* gunnery officer. Able-Seaman Atwell was a member of the crew.

How was he regarded?

Highly. He had had a clean charge sheet since joining the navy over a decade before. Many on the lower deck were all but illiterate and AB Atwell was known for his willingness to write letters for them at their dictation. His advocacy of temperance was frequently joked about, but never with malice, and he took it in good heart.

Had HMS *Leonidas* seen active service in that time?

Yes. Off the coast of Korea. And later, in the Indian Ocean, action ashore and afloat against a large slave-raiding enterprise. When returning to Britain she had supported action ashore on the Red Sea Coast of the Sudan.

How long had that last commission been?

About six months.

And Able Seaman Atwell's wife and three children had been left behind in Portsmouth all that time, missing the support of a loving husband and father?

That was inevitable.

Separation must be hard for all parties, Mr. Eversham said. It was hard for civilians to understand just what demands the Navy made on families as well as on officers and seamen. He paused before his next question.

Had not HMS *Leonidas's* service climaxed with her crew's participation in the Battle of Tamai?

She had provided a naval brigade. Several other ships had provided similar units. They had come ashore at Suakin to support General Graham's advance against Beja forces.

Beja? Those tribesmen known in the popular press as Fuzzie-Wuzzies?

Yes. Dervish adherents. Allies of the fanatics now threatening General Gordon in Khartoum.

Had the prisoner been present at the battle?

Yes, he was one of half-dozen guarding the Gatling gun under the witness's own command. It has been placed at the front left corner of the square formed by General Graham's forces when attacked.

A square that broke under enemy assault?

Yes. The Beja had come on like a solid wall, disregarding casualties. It was necessary to abandon the Gatling and fall back.

The situation was desperate?

Yes. Hand to hand fighting. Spears, swords, cutlasses, bayonets, no time to reload personal firearms. The witness had seen a spear driving at his face, had twisted his head in time and the blade had ripped through his cheek. He had learned later than it had knocked out teeth also. He stumbled back, dazed, to join Captain Dawlish and others making a stand He had not yet begun to feel the pain.

A nightmare? Mr. Eversham suggested.

Worse. It was confused, a melee. The witness had been knocked down by a blow to his chest. He could not say how, since he was already dazed. He had looked up to see a Beja warrior standing above him with a raised sword. He remembered that it was smeared scarlet. He had known that Death was imminent.

And then?

A bayonet had burst through the Beja's chest, driven in from behind He dropped the spear and fell across the witness's legs.

Whose bayonet?

Lieutenant Purdon pointed to the dock. Able Seaman Atwell's.

And then?

More Beja crowding on, slashing and thrusting. The witness had tried to rise himself but was unable to do so. He tried to push rounds into the cylinder of his emptied revolver but his hands were shaking too much. But Able-Seaman Atwell had stood over him, holding back assailants with his bayonet until he too was beaten down by a blow to his head. He had collapsed across the witness, had received a spear wound in the leg as he lay there, would no doubt have been killed if the tide of battle had not turned at that instant.

It had been worse than Florence had imagined. Nicholas had shielded her from the full reality when he had told her of the battle. She saw something of the same horror on the faces of the jury. Some would have read of the clash in newspapers, but correspondents used more exalted and less graphic phrases.

So Able Seaman Atwell had saved the witness's life?

Yes. And saved it with no thought of the risk of his own. He could have retreated further and left him. But he didn't.

Would Lieutenant Purdon wish to have Able Seaman Atwell serve under him again, should circumstances allow?

Without a doubt. So too would Captain Dawlish.

Mr. Boyd objected. The witness could not speak on behalf of that gallant officer.

Lieutenant Purdon apologised.

Mr. Eversham thanked him for his service, no less than for the clarity of his testimony. He had no further questions and, once again, neither had Mr. Boyd.

The accused had waived his right to testify in his own defence.

Time now for the prosecution's closing speech.

A brutal assault on a businessman in his own premises had left him badly injured, Mr. Boyd said. That was the kernel of the matter. Was the prisoner in the dock guilty of that, Yes or No? He had been identified by the victim in his sworn affidavit and by the victim's rescuer in this very courtroom. The evidence of Inspector Towton, an experienced and respected officer, had cast no doubt on the validity of the identifications. The defendant might well have been of good character but he was a man trained to practice violence of the most extreme type. He had declined to take the stand himself to offer one word in his own defence. There was only one conclusion that a reasonable man could draw. Guilty.

It was not an impressive performance, poorly expressed and even more poorly delivered. Florence guessed that this prosecutor seldom had difficulty in obtaining convictions if most of his cases were anything like the two others heard the previous day. But it chilled her nonetheless.

Because it was true.

The trial was about one thing only, whether Atwell as guilty of assaulting the moneylender. She had known that when she had first talked of the matter to Mr. Eversham.

Guilty as sin, she had said then.

And if she were sitting in that jury now, that was the only verdict that she could in all conscience deliver.

And yet, and yet…

Mr. Eversham was on his feet now, summarising the defence case in a low, calm tone, with none of the arrogant confidence that Florence would have expected from a Queen's Counsel. His sympathy was with Mr. Chadband, as that of everybody in this court must be. He deplored the idea that any reputable businessman, one indeed renowned, according to the testimony of his own employee and rescuer, for his benevolent assistance to any poor person in a state of financial embarrassment, should be attacked within the haven of his own premises.

But the identification of the prisoner as the perpetrator was suspect. The prosecution witness, Mr. Joseph Payne, had been confronted with the prisoner face-to-face in the Blackwell Street police station and had not been asked to choose him from a line of others. When challenged by the defence, Mr. Payne had withdrawn his identification in full view of the court. The other witness called, Mr. Chadband's employee, could only have seen the assailant's face for brief seconds when he dragged him from his master. It strained credibility that in the heat of that desperate moment he could have registered every feature of that face before the chase began.

Mr. Eversham shook his head. Slowly, with sadness.

Was it on such grounds that a man, a man whose integrity and courage had been attested to by three witnesses of irreproachable character, could be condemned to years of hard labour? Could his wife and children be so deprived of his loving kindness, just as Her Majesty herself would lose the service of a loyal seaman? It would be a sad day for British justice if such a man were convicted on such flimsy grounds.

Mr Eversham rested his case.

Florence had been moved, so too was Agatha, dabbing her eyes with a lace-edged handkerchief. Atwell's mother was weeping uncontrollably and the seamen behind, if not calling out, were shuffling on their benches and about to do so.

But he's still guilty of the charge, Florence thought. *Guilty as sin.*

Time to adjourn for lunch. Mr. Justice Cadman would sum up thereafter. Then it would be the jury's turn to go to work.

*

200

The judge's summing-up was a disappointment, little more than a reiteration of the prosecution's closing speech. The jury members must ask themselves one question only. Had the prisoner, beyond all reasonable doubt, assaulted Mr. Barnaby Chadband?

The jury huddled, as they had after the previous day's cases. Shaking of heads, whispers, nods, one member's signs of exasperation. Two long minutes passed. Then the foreman rose, corpulent, red-faced, be-whiskered, easy to imagine as the owner of a large drapery or hardware emporium. He had an air of vast self-importance about him when he said that the jury wished to withdraw for discussion. Permission was given and the courtroom was cleared.

Mr. Bagshot's clerk brought a message to Florence and Agatha as they left. They should wait at the Black Swan and they'd be warned when the jury was returning.

"How long could that be?" Florence had heard of juries discussing verdicts for days. She wasn't sure if they were still detained and supplied only with bread and water until they'd reached one.

"It's Friday, ma'am," the clerk said. "They've all got shops or businesses of some sort. They'll want to be back to them tomorrow for closing out the week. They'll want an end to it this afternoon. That's always the way of it."

"Would that be –" She feared the answer.

"Good or bad, ma'am? Good. If even a few of 'em hold out for not guilty, an' Mr. Eversham and Mr. Bagshot think they will, then the rest will give in."

He was correct.

Florence and Agatha had just seated themselves in the coffee room of the Black Swan when he was back.

The jury had taken twenty minutes and the verdict had already been delivered.

Not Guilty.

Chapter 19

Mr. Eversham and Mr. Bagshot dined with them at the Black Swan early that evening. Florence had resisted the urge to go across to the court to thank and congratulate them there. It was better not to be recognised by Mrs. Deacon, who would most surely have dragged Atwell and his parents over to thank her for her interest. Better too not to be seen with Lieutenants Jackson and Purdon either, though she would write them notes of thanks next week. But she found herself on the verge of tears, unsure whether her gratitude was for Atwell's deliverance or for removal of the risk of her own association coming to light. Only now, released, did she realise just how heavy had been her fear of disgrace.

"What decided the jury, cousin?" Agatha would never say it, but she too was rightly proud of her role.

"Who knows?" Mr. Eversham said. "It's never one thing alone, not even the same thing for every juryman. Doubt maybe, genuine conscientious doubt. For a few, the need to be finished with it quickly and get back to business – those will agree with any opinion that would cut the deliberations short. And also pity sometimes. Men who fulminate among friends about the need to hang and flog more, and bring back transportation, can be remarkably compassionate when confronted by the actual defendant and his circumstances. And recognition, by some, that the strict letter of the law doesn't guarantee justice. That's when they disregard the judge's direction. Like today."

"So Atwell wasn't guilty of the crime?" Florence remembered her own words. *Guilty as Sin.*

"That's what twelve good men and true decided, Mrs. Dawlish. And maybe they thought too that Mr. Chadband had got what he deserved. Would you disagree with them?"

"No," she said.

"Atwell's in the bosom of his family tonight, thank God." Mr Bagshot had taken too much wine, was flushed with pride. "I'm sorry you did not see it, Mrs. Dawlish. His wife was waiting outside with her sister and brother-in-law. She hung back when her husband emerged, hid her face in her shawl and tried to turn away, but he reached for her and took her in his arms, and I turned away myself. We did a good thing. A very good thing."

"That American lady did a very good thing too," Mr. Eversham had caught Florence's gaze and held it.

"How did you learn of that article, cousin?" Agatha said.

"A messenger from the *Fortnightly Review* hand-delivered it to Lincoln's Inn. Hot from the press and with the editor's compliments, he said, but he could tell me nothing more. When I got home, I found that another copy had been delivered there."

"It was fortuitous," Mr. Bagshot said, "that the lady should have been in England at this time and investigating charitable institutions. And that she would be in Portsmouth too, and at this time." Unfeigned innocence in his voice. "God moves in mysterious ways."

"And miracles do sometimes happen." Florence said. She held Mr. Eversham's gaze and saw him smile.

It was time to break up and head for the railway station. Mr. Eversham was returning to London and Mr. Bagshot would escort Florence and Agatha to Southsea.

The ordeal was over.

*

They breakfasted late next morning, Saturday, and Florence sent the maid to the post-office. Agatha had an address for Mabel, now in Newcastle, and they sent her a telegram, suggesting meeting in London at the Mercer Hotel.

And two other words.

Not Guilty.

Afterwards they walked along the Esplanade. The grey skies and grey white-capped waters stretching towards the Channel did nothing to diminish the continuing sense of elation. An ironclad was heading out to sea. From her bizarre profile, and from what Nicholas had told her, Florence recognised her as either *Colossus* or *Edinburgh*, latest additions to the fleet. He had hankered after command of one of them. He would never say it, but she knew that he had been disappointed.

The sight brought him close to her. She was resigned now to having no news. Correspondents with the Nile expedition had reported that it had passed the First and Second Cataracts and would soon be past the Third. Progress was inexorable. The relief force would be in Khartoum within weeks, they predicted, Gordon saved, honour preserved. The commanders' names were household words by now, their stern images sketched by the illustrated papers' artists. They produced drawings too of the naval contingent, working wonders with blocks and tackles to haul laden craft through rapids. But still no mention of Nicholas, though his contemporary in age and rank, Captain Lord Charles Beresford, was the darling of the press. Florence had met him once and had disliked his brashness. All she could do was hope. And long for Nicholas.

Agatha was keen to see the latest improvements at the Sailor's Rest but Florence was resolved to stay away. Mr. Selden was strict and honest. Under his supervision, it could run well for a month without her inspections. She wanted no thanks, no meetings with seamen's wives, no unthinking goodwill. She had learned her lesson, had escaped from the morass of her own making.

Two days of relaxation, reading, piano practice, church, walks, notes of thanks, afternoon tea at the Queen's Hotel, and, most relaxing of all, an agreement not to talk about the *Temple de la Beauté* until meeting Mabel. She had confirmed by wire that she would be in London on Monday evening. Her time in Britain was to end soon and the affair must be brought to resolution. And to justice. It would be another battle.

But not yet.

Time now to gather strength for it.

*

They had returned from another morning walk along the Esplanade, enjoyable despite cold and an overcast sky and rain threatening. They were sitting, taking tea and reading newspapers in Florence's study, when they heard the door-bell. The maid, entered a minute later.

"There's people at the door wants to see you, ma'am. A whole family."

Florence guessed who they were. She had hoped that they would not come here, but was touched now that they had.

"Show them into the parlour, Susan, bring tea, and biscuits for the children."

Agatha joined her. Atwell and his wife and three children were standing in the centre of the room, uncertain about the protocol. He was in a blue suit, uncomfortable in collar and tie, turning his billy-cock hat in his hands. His wife was more demurely dressed than Florence suspected she would usually like. Her eyes had been darting around, hungry for the furnishing and ornaments and the modest luxury, but she paled when Florence greeted her. The children, a girl of two or three, a boy of four and an older sister, were well scrubbed, their clothes starched and spotless. They must have been warned to behave themselves, for they shrunk behind their mother.

Atwell began to stammer his thanks, but Florence said that she was glad to see them all together, a happy family. She introduced Agatha and asked them to sit. They perched on the edges of the chairs. Mrs. Atwell's eyes were cast down, her lip quivering. She was clearly frightened. Agatha had taken possession of the children, was sitting on the chaise-longue, the smallest on her lap and the others drawn close against her either side.

Atwell thanked Florence again. He had not expected such help, would never forget it. She made light of what she had done. It was the two legal gentlemen who deserved thanks.

"Mr Eversham is Lady Agatha's cousin. I told her about the case and she asked him. He was glad to help."

"We didn't get no chance to thank him," Atwell said. "Him and Mr. Bagshot was gone before we knew it. They left us to ourselves when… when they let me out. And we didn't see you neither, ma'am. An' we didn't know about this lady, nor how she'd helped."

His wife was nodding, had still not looked up. Agatha waved away his thanks. There was no need, it was enough to see the family reunited.

The wife was beginning to weep now, but she rose, came across, took Florence's hand and held it to her cheek, might have knelt had she not been prevented.

She knows that I know. About Chadband. Or it could have been Rowley. Or even both.

Florence thrust the thought away. Pity filled her.

"You came to me sister's place and I didn't want to come down to see you, ma'am. I didn't mean no disrespect but I was ash –" Mrs. Atwell stopped. "I was frightened ma'am, didn't know where to turn. An' then you did all this, an' this other lady too –"

It was embarrassing, might have got worse, had Susan not arrived with a tray.

"Leave it here please," Florence said. She looked to the children. "Maybe you can help me? Can you carry this plate around and offer everybody a biscuit? And then you can have one for yourselves."

"Not one," Agatha pushed them to their feet. "Two or three or four for such good children."

Florence poured the tea, enquired about sugar and milk and dispensed it. Agatha handed the cups to Atwell and his wife. He had lifted her up, had brought her back to her chair, was red and speechless with embarrassment. She was sniffling.

Fifteen excruciating minutes. Florence's attempts to start conversation met with monosyllabic answers, nervous smiles. Shared consciousness that all were longing for it to end but awareness that courtesy demanded some indeterminate minimum duration. Yes, Atwell was well recovered since Florence had seen him in the hospital at Haslar and yes, he was returning to service in HMS *Vernon* and yes, the boy would be starting school next year and yes, his parents and his wife's were in good health, though her mother suffered something awful from rheumatism in damp weather. Only the children, whom Agatha was leading around the room and making laugh as she explained the pictures on the wall, were oblivious of the tension.

It was time at last to ask if they would like another cup of tea, but no, as Florence had expected, they must leave now, were going to visit Mr. Bagshot to thank him also. Agatha gave Atwell one of Mr. Eversham's cards and yes, he would be glad of a letter from them. And yes, Lieutenant Purdon would be grateful too. Florence gave his address.

At the door Florence gave each child a shilling and Agatha the same also, despite their parents' protests. They passed out into the street beyond.

Florence wondered if Mabel had spoken to Mrs. Atwell. She wouldn't ask. It was better not to know.

*

Florence went directly to the Mercer Hotel after she and Agatha travelled to London on Monday morning. Agatha went home but came to the hotel in early evening. Mabel, when she arrived, was fatigued by her train journey, but eager to know about the trial. She listened in silence until Florence finished.

"The *Fortnightly* article helped?" Satisfaction in her voice, grim pride in a task well accomplished.

"It may have been the most important thing," Florence said. "I've no doubt that many of the jurymen spent the evening perusing it. They could read between the lines, especially after Mr. Eversham's questioning of Jem Rowley, the moneylender's creature."

"The *Fortnightly's* editor suspected nothing," Mabel said. "I went to see him and he remembered me from when I was in London before. He'd heard about my laundry and restaurant-kitchen and cardboard box articles. Yes! A few copies of the *Gazette* reach this far. He hoped to find some English lady-journalist who'd do something similar, but he hasn't yet. So I told him why I was visiting Britain this time, about the schools and institutions, and I offered him an article. He bit. And what I gave him was better than he he'd expected, more lurid too and just in time for his next edition."

She had come to Portsmouth under her own name, had made no secret of her presence, had stayed at the Queen's Hotel, had made no contact with the Sailor's Rest. The few tales of misery she had heard from mothers of children at St. Winifred's Home had furnished leads enough, a few seamen's wives among them. Even here in this London hotel, she mentioned no names. Sources' identities must always be sacrosanct, she said. In a single week she had gathered enough for a half-dozen more articles, and the *Columbia Home Gazette* would carry them. They could be a prelude to an investigation of moneylending in a large American city, Boston maybe, or Chicago. The public had an insatiable appetite for outrage, even though it had less for difficult remedies.

"Did the editor see anything strange about asking to have those two copies sent to Mr. Eversham?" Florence had no good memory of him.

"No. I said I'd met Mr. Eversham at a reception and had spoken briefly to him. That he seemed interested in my work. That he might value contacts with the *Fortnightly*. That was enough."

And Mabel's other news. She had enjoyed one more Empyrean Bath since they had last met. Dear lovesick Clifford had been in the Temple's waiting area again with his sister.

"The same nonsense as before," Mabel said. "Loneliness, longing, inability of adult children to understand. I told him I'd be leaving for Europe soon but was undecided on what sights to see. He was full of suggestions. The chateaux of the Loire, the glories of Venice, the majesty of Rome, the Bay of Naples. That man could write a guidebook! His sister was having her bath by then and —" She began to laugh, shoulders shaking.

"Tell us, Mabel!"

She took half a minute to recover. "He took my hand and looked in my eyes. His were so tearful that I'd wager he'd dropped glycerine in them. Then he said —" She began to laugh again. "You won't believe this. 'Emily, Emily my dearest,' he said, 'how I would like to see such sights again myself. But only with a companion, a loving companion, by my side.' And then he let go my hand and he brushed his own across his eyes, and turned away as if he'd said too much. That was the moment when Claudette came to bring me to my own bath. It was perfectly timed."

"And you just left the poor man in desolate misery?" Florence said.

"I couldn't be so heartless. When I stood up, I reached for his hand. Claudette looked away. She plays it well too. I pressed it for a moment and said 'Dear, dear Clifford.' He held my hand against his cheek and then I left him."

"Was he still there when you came back?"

"No. But I wrote to him that afternoon, care of that tobacconist. I've kept a copy. I've kept copies of all of mine We'll need them. It was a serious letter too. Concern about the step that I was contemplating. Longing for happiness as I did, I feared that my beloved son Franklin might regard it differently. It haunted me that he might see me as foolish, that he might think that I was deserting him. It was that, and that only, that made me hesitate to commit to the love of a noble man. Could Dear Clifford understand? Could he write to tell me?"

"I've no doubt he could."

"Of course. To poste restante in Portsmouth. When it came it was even more full of protestations than before. I sent a reply. I felt like a young girl again, still dreamed, and could he forgive my hesitations? Etcetera and etcetera."

"Did he write back after that?"

"To poste restante, Newcastle. The longest of all. Here, you can read it for yourself."

Florence laughed when she did and she passed it to Agatha, who found it no less ridiculous.

And suddenly Florence realised that Mabel was silent, triumph and humour gone, and her own amusement died.

"What is it, Mabel?"

"It must stop now."

"Stop?"

"It's getting too dangerous, Florence. They have letters from me. No, letters from Mrs. Daley. Foolish, silly letters. He'll have kept copies of his own to me for Mrs. Bellamy. There's enough in them to show how

Mrs. Daley was first enticed, and then herself enticing. All letters, from her or from him, for which she'd pay a fortune rather than have her son see."

"But Dear Clifford can't suspect anything," Agatha said. "Not even that wicked Mrs. Bellamy could suspect it."

Mabel shook her head. "It's only a matter of time before they start checking about Indianapolis. They'll want her son's address to hold over her. And when they'll find there's none then —" She stopped, was pale.

Florence sensed her fear. She had seen acid burn Mabel's shoulders and barely miss her face two years before. Under the elegantly severe clothing, the scars must be hideous. Florence herself had underestimated evil's capacity for revenge at that time but it was Mabel who had paid the price. And she had never reproached her for it.

"It's just a feeling," Mabel said. "Maybe I'm too cautious. But I had the same feeling at the laundry. The boss there wasn't a man to cross. I wanted to be gone before he found out what I was. So I gave no notice, just didn't come one morning."

She's right. It's been too successful to last indefinitely.

"I haven't written back to Dear Clifford," Mabel said. "And he's got no Poste Restante address to write to."

"When are you going back to America?" Florence said.

"It was to be two weeks from now. I'd arranged visits to schools and whatnot in Norwich and Leeds and Sheffield. And then sail from Liverpool on the *Pavonia*. I'm booked on her. But now perhaps —"

"Go now! As soon as you can, Mabel. Cancel the Norwich and Leeds appointments. There must be a sooner ship. We already have as much as we need to destroy Mrs. Bellamy and her gang."

"You wouldn't think the worse of me?"

"No! And you, Agatha, you won't either, will you? Of course not."

"And when I'm gone," Mabel said. "What then?"

"We can discuss that in the morning," Florence said. "You're tired. We'll do it after breakfast. And then we'll go to Thomas Cook's agency and get you booked. For this week, if possible."

It should have struck her before, she realised, that they had given too little thought to what must follow.

Time now to grasp that nettle.

Chapter 20

The letters, Dear Clifford's originals and copies of Mabel's replies, were lodged for now in Agatha's father's safe. He had not queried her request to put a sealed file there. Florence, Agatha and Mabel had discussed at length how best to use the letters. The most obvious way was to put the material in the hands of the real Sir Clifford Belton's son. Contact with the police would follow, and a court case for fraud and impersonation.

And yet…

"Your father told you, Agatha, that the actual Sir Clifford Belton was the dullest man in England," Florence said. "Would he want his name in the courts? Wouldn't he be afraid of others saying that there must no smoke without fire? Many people always like to think the worst. Would his children like to see him ridiculed? He hasn't been injured personally, has he? Why should he or his family press the matter? If he's as clever as he's purported to be, wouldn't he just ignore it?"

"Perhaps." Agatha did not sound convinced.

"Even if he did," Florence said, "would the whole scandal of the luxurious baths and lotions and salves for stupid women be exposed? Even if Mrs. Bellamy went to gaol, the Temple would most likely continue to run under Mrs. Mobray's management and there'll be no dearth of new Mrs. Chalmers-Bolgers for her to beggar." She turned to Mabel "Do you think the *Fortnightly Review* would carry an article by you?"

"Not with this present editor. And I don't blame him. Your law of defamation's strong here, libel you call it, and Mrs. Bellamy can well afford an attorney as skilled as Agatha's cousin."

"What about the law in the United States?"

"Nothing like so strong. If Mrs. B tried to sue the *Home Gazette* in New York she'd be laughed out of court, even if she got there in the first place. I could name her in my articles there."

"What would be in them, Mabel?"

"We'd first run the series, five or six pieces, about the schools and asylums. My own investigations."

"And the shame of a great British city?" Florence said.

"That too. Readers like to be shocked."

"What next?"

"Intrepid lady journalist hears about the Chalmers-Bolger case. No need to use the poor woman's name. Mrs. X will do. Intrepid lady's outraged and decides to expose the *Temple de la Beauté*, address supplied, in all its ugliness. She'll investigate, just as she did the laundries and hotel kitchens. The *Gazette's* circulation soared with those. She knows the risks of the investigation, but solid American common sense will see her through. She'll impersonate a respectable Indianapolis widow, Mrs. Emily Daley. Half the readers will see themselves in her, and all of them with drunken husbands will want to be her. She'll be embarrassed by the Temple's treatments, the sinful luxury, gentle limbs undressed, silk chemises, llama's milk, the French bath attendant, but she'll grit her teeth and endure. Then the tempting serpent will make his overture. You could write the rest yourselves."

"Would you quote the letters?"

"Maybe even some in full. But I'll see. Selective quoting's often best. All the names. Except yours, Florence and yours, Agatha. Details of the real Sir Clifford too and sympathy for his besmirched name. The price list for those ludicrous cosmetics. The tobacconist's address. Concern that other ladies are probably still being beggared or blackmailed. And are the British authorities concerned? Are they turning a blind eye? And could similar abuses be happening in our own Great Republic?"

"But it'll be published in America, not in Britain," Florence said. "Nobody will see it here."

"But when it's on the printed page there, newspapers and journals here can report that it's been published. And they will, because the story will sell. They can quote. They can send reporters to the Temple and the tobacconist to ask for refutations. Even if they won't risk naming names, they can say enough to make identities easily discoverable. They'll report it, and it'll sell their papers."

"The real Sir Clifford and his family would be in a good position then to sue." Florence turned to Agatha. "Perhaps your father would have a word with the Home Secretary to suggest that the police investigate. At the very least the Temple's a house of assignation."

It would take time, two months or more before publication. They debated the merits and disadvantages, agreed at last that it would be for the best. Mrs. Bellamy and the faux Sir Clifford would be complacent by then, would have moved on to other quarries, might well have dismissed Mrs. Daley as a real person whose nerve had failed when she contemplated her son's disapproval. Retribution would be a bolt from a clear sky, and when it came it would be devastating.

It was time then to book Mabel's ticket for New York.

*

Mabel left from Liverpool on the fast Cunarder *Servia*. Dear besotted Clifford must long in vain now. Mrs. Daley of Indianapolis had vanished at the Liverpool quayside.

Florence went with Mabel to see her off. She felt a pang at parting, hoped she would see her again. And, more than that, she hoped that they might work together again sometime. Driven by necessity, Mabel was creating a profession, was forging a path that other women could follow.

If I were to lose Nicholas, then perhaps I too would...

She thrust the thought aside.

She would not allow herself to consider it.

He would return.

*

She went on to Preston, an hour by rail from Liverpool. Susan's time was near and she would need support. It was good that Florence did. The time came earlier than expected, the birth easier than expected too, mother spared and infant whole and healthy. Joy in the family, joy in new life, joy in Susan's recovery, joy in the dog-cart rides with the other children despite the November rains, joy in the sight of Adolphus sober, joy in the bond forming with Nephew Martin and his questions about

214

his uncle and the navy, joy in the intimacy of memories of Nicholas shared with Susan, each knowing him in a different way

And joy that the new child would be called Florence. Compensation for that loss that had brought her and Nicholas even closer together through shared grief, regret for what might have been, acceptance that they could never now have children of their own.

I'll know and cherish her for — how long? Thirty, maybe forty, years, perhaps with children herself. She'll live far on into the new century, will see wonders I cannot dream of, may live on to remember me, with love, I hope, in the unimaginable decade beginning in 1960.

The second Florence was shawl-wrapped in her mother's arms on the Preston station platform, brothers and sisters about, Adolphus gruffly thankful, when Florence left a week later. She leaned from the window, waving her handkerchief to them, as the train drew out and they waved back and the younger ones wept for her going.

The routine of life in Southsea was attractive again. Piano practice, Esplanade walks, early darkness that somehow felt welcome in this season, fireside reading as the rain fell and the wind moaned outside, accounts and mundane concerns of the Sailor's Rest.

She was looking forward to it all.

*

Florence arrived home late on Saturday, November the twenty-second, and spent the next day settling into her familiar life again. She was not unhappy. When she scanned the newspapers, she sensed however that, despite boldly confident assertions, all was not well on the Nile. Progress seemed slow, very slow. And that might not bode well for Nicholas, wherever he was.

She was reading bills and writing cheques in her study on Monday morning. A light rain was falling outside, and her walk must wait. She heard the doorbell. Susan, the house maid, appeared and looked flustered

"There's a lady wants to see you, ma'am."

215

Dear Lord! Not another seaman's wife in trouble!

"Has she come here before?"

"No, ma'am. An' she pushed past me, rough she was, and she's waiting in the hall. Said that she's staying there 'til you see her."

"Did she give her name, Susan?"

"No, ma'am. Just that she was a friend of Mrs. Lacy. Of Mrs. Norbert Lacy of Bentley, she said, an' you'd know then who she was."

An aeon passed, cold, sickening dread, spirit crying out that this could not be real.

And then accepting.

Mrs. Bellamy.

"Ask the lady to wait in the drawing room," Florence said. "I'll join her presently."

No option.

Chapter 21

"You're a bad hostess, Mrs. Dawlish," Mrs. Bellamy said. "I haven't been offered tea."

She had not risen when Florence entered, remaining seated in regal assurance in the armchair Nicholas favoured. Her travelling dress was severe but fashionable, her hat no less so, the same cameo brooch as before her only ornamentation. She might have been the middle-aged wife of an admiral, courted and feared by less senior officers' wives.

"Was that a whiff of Bahia Blanca Cream that I detected from that girl who let me in? Does she know that it costs five guineas a jar? You're being rather generous at Madame Hortense's expense, aren't you Mrs. Dawlish?"

"What do you want?" Florence's knees were weak, her stomach hollow and she knew her lower lip was quivering. She tried not to show her fear but knew that blood must be draining from her face.

"What do I want? Just to do a little business, Mrs. Dawlish. Or may I call you Florence?"

"Mrs. Dawlish will do."

Mrs. Bellamy shrugged. "It's a business matter, so maybe it's better that way. No need for false pretences. I know you, and you know me, but, like each other or not, there's business to be done. It's in your interest, and in your husband's interest too, as well as mine, that we manage it with a minimum of unpleasantness."

"How did you guess?" Florence despised the tremor in her own voice. The reference to Nicholas terrified her.

"Who Mrs. Lacy really is? I didn't guess. I never guess. I need certainty in my business. I found you later in the game than I'd have liked, but I did find you."

There was no gloating triumph or hostility in her voice or manner. A businesswoman about her business That was what chilled Florence most.

"You had me followed?"

217

"You, only later. Your American friend first. You played it well, very well, both of you, all plausible, all credible, but you kept it going too long."

As Mabel had feared. But had feared too late. And I should have feared it too.

"What gave us away?"

Florence was trying to maintain the same calm, the same lack of outward hostility. With every word, this woman was claiming dominance. She would not let her have it.

"Your Mrs. Daley gave you away. She'd done very well up to then, I grant you that. Sir Clifford was actually smitten and it wasn't pretence either. He used to be an actor, by the way, but what he does now is much more profitable."

"And that hag with him is no doubt his wife, not his sister?"

"She is, and she was jealous enough to have murdered Mrs. Daley if she'd had the chance. But I was taken in too. I admit that. I thought the Daley woman ideal for what I need. A rich widow longing for love but knowing that the sands are running out. A fear of mockery haunts all women like her. I've seen it again and again. And a devoted son she's afraid of disappointing. Women like that pay up. They always do. They have to."

"But you saw through her in the end?"

"I had enough material to start the less-romantic part of the process. But before I did, I had to be sure that she really had the money. It's not hard to find out things like that nowadays. A helpful consul with American trade directories. And there was nothing in them about any polish industry in Indianapolis. I telegraphed to a friend in Philadelphia who sent an agent west to make enquiries. A hundred dollars, or so, well spent. And no Mrs. Emily Daley, no loving son Franklin, no growing Hoosier business empire. It wasn't hard after that to find out who she really is. She's a journalist, isn't she?"

"Yes." No sense denying it.

"Once I knew that she was a fraud, I had somebody go to the poste restante office in Newcastle. He had to hang about there for two days but he'd paid a clerk to tip him the wink when a woman claimed the letter for Mrs. Daley. So he followed her to where she was staying. A shilling or two will buy a look at most hotel registers in England. He saw that she was actually Mrs Mabel Bushwick. It was easy then to follow her to London, to see you and your friend, Lord Kegworth's daughter, meeting her in the Mercer Hotel."

It could have been any one of a dozen other guests in the hotel's dining room, solid, respectable looking people…

"You'd registered as Mrs. Dawlish. You gave your address also, thank you. There's been time enough since then to find out all I need to know about Mrs. Bushwick of the *Columbia Home Gazette*. She's well respected over there, my friend in Philadelphia tells me. And all too that I needed to know about the wife of Captain Nicholas Dawlish." She paused. "Of the Royal Navy."

It stung. Florence had been proud of how she had conceived the campaign, how she had guided it, how she had covered her movements. Now it had fallen apart.

"You still haven't asked if I'd like tea." Mrs. Bellamy rose, walked across to the bell rope and rang it as if she were in her own home. "You can tell the girl also that you'll have a late lunch and that I won't stay for it. We've a great deal to discuss and I need to get back to London."

Susan came and Florence gave the instructions. She needed to know more of this woman, needed time to absorb this horror, time to think.

"I still can't understand why you became involved," Mrs. Bellamy said. "What was in it for you?"

"Retribution."

"Retribution?"

"For Margaret Chalmers-Bolger."

A moment of incomprehension on Mrs. Bellamy's features and then, remembering, she said, "That woman who drowned herself in the Hampstead ponds?"

"That woman. She was Agatha's godmother."

"A very foolish woman. Too afraid of the opinion of a nephew in China who came to see her once every five years. Nobody twisted her

219

arm to come to the Temple. Nobody's arm is ever twisted. They come by their own choice."

Florence had despised her before. Now she hated her, wanted to fly at her, rake her fingernails across her face, drag her by the hair across the room, pound her head again the wall. But it would profit her nothing, a small internal voice told her, and she listened to it.

"But the late-lamented Margaret served her purpose," Mrs. Bellamy said. "She showed me that some of my people were less thorough than I'd thought." Still the businesswoman's tone. "You'd never have found about her involvement with the Temple otherwise. We'll be much more thorough in future."

Susan appeared with the tea tray, sensed the tension while she poured. She looked to Florence, asking silently if she could help. Getting no response, she looked frightened when she left. There would be shocked speculation in the kitchen.

"I asked what you want," Florence said. "You haven't told me."

"You can tell Mrs. Mabel Bushwick that I'll destroy you if she writes or publishes a word, whether here or in America. That's first."

Destroy.

"And more afterwards?"

"A lot more, Mrs. Dawlish."

"What more? Money?"

"What money have you and your husband between you? Almost nothing. You were all but a pauper when you married him. Yes, I know that you were a servant once. And him, just an officer's salary, and a lot of it gone just renting this house and keeping up appearances, I'd wager. And those few miserable farms he has in Shropshire. I know about them also. If I wanted money from you, Mrs. Dawlish, you could never afford even the first payment."

"What then?"

"Information, Mrs. Dawlish. Rather specific information, worth a great deal to certain people."

It could only be one type.

"Something to do with my husband?"

"A great deal to do with your husband."

"I'll never –"

Mrs. Bellamy cut her off. "Spare me the talk about loyalty and honour and what you'd die before doing, Mrs. Dawlish. I've heard so much of it before, but women, and men too, always see sense in the end. Let's spare ourselves that little ritual."

"You said you'd destroy me."

"Not just you, Mrs. Dawlish. That gallant captain of yours too. He'll go down with you. Not to gaol, as you well might yourself, but down no less. Do you think his beloved navy will keep him if the popular press seizes on some truths that will come out about you?"

"What truths?" Mouth dry, voice trembling. Easy to guess.

"Abetting the escape of a pederast for whose arrest a warrant is still live. That brother of Lady Agatha's. Her name will come into it too."

It wasn't like that! An inner voice screamed. *I'd no reason to like Oswald but he was innocent of what they charged. He was a scapegoat for others, a victim himself. And at that moment he'd behaved with more honour than I'd ever expected.*

And then another voice, colder. *None of that matters.*

"You know you're a heroine, Mrs. Dawlish, for many gentlemen with certain, let's say unusual, inclinations. Like Lord Oswald's friends. You remember Lord Arthur Kidderminster and the Honourable Gabriel Foster, don't you? I'm broadminded myself about their tastes, but the law isn't. The word has got about in their circle that you were very helpful to one of their own. But some of those gentlemen could be very indiscreet if approached in the right way, and a few could be very voluble if they had to choose between you and hard labour for themselves."

Nicholas knew none of this. He was in Korea at the time. But that wouldn't save his name.

"You're a heroine too for others closer to home, Mrs. Dawlish. For some seamen's wives and, yes, they can be very indiscreet too. How a moneylender, a Mr. Chadband, became less exiguous in his demands after he'd had a beating at your suggestion. That was by a young man called Bill Wheatley, wasn't it? You've no idea how much admired you were for that. A captain's wife too."

I didn't intend ... but no, that doesn't matter either.

"And that wasn't the end of it, was it, Mrs. Dawlish? It's quite remarkable what things can happen when your husband's far from home. The honest Mr. Chadband all but killed in his own shop in a second attack. The seaman who did it defended by your precious Agatha's cousin, *pro bono* too, I hear, and there wasn't a word in court about that first assault. It's the sort of story that the editor of some crusading rag like the *Fortnightly Review* would give his eye-teeth for."

Florence hardly heard her.

I've faced as bad before. In Thrace. In Cuba. Not just reputation then, but life itself. Agatha's, Nicholas's, mine. I was not beaten then and I will not be beaten by this foul woman now.

"Let's talk about the information you want, Mrs. Bellamy."

They did.

And it was very specific.

*

After Mrs. Bellamy had left — she had given Susan a shilling for calling a cab for her — Florence had no appetite for lunch. She sat alone in her study for a long time, her mind numb, the enormity of what that woman had demanded far beyond anything she had ever feared.

Information not just once, Mrs. Bellamy had said. It could last for years and when Florence had conquered her first repulsion for it, she would settle down to the arrangement, find it profitable indeed. Men as well as women, many with secrets more shocking that Florence's, helped Mrs Bellamy in similar ways. Distinguished people had found their way to the *Temple de la Beauté*'s door. Politicians, even ministers, and wives of politicians, diplomats and wives of diplomats, ecclesiastics and wives of ecclesiastics, giants of industry and commerce and wives of giants of industry and commerce, all had once felt as resentful towards Mrs. Bellamy as Florence did now. But they had accustomed themselves to giving her something when they could. And she was not ungenerous to them if that something was valuable to others. A few had come to regard her as a friend.

She could have had this house burgled, Mrs. Bellamy said, ransacked for Captain Dawlish's papers, notebooks, drawings, anything that dated from the time when he had been attached to HMS *Vernon*. Or any time later. But there would be no need for criminal entry that might alarm the neighbours. Mrs. Dawlish could make her own search and arrange delivery. As soon as possible, not later than Saturday. A business arrangement only.

And a last suggestion before Mrs. Bellamy left.

That Florence would go to the post office in Albert Road, ten minutes' walk distant, and telegraph Mrs. Bushwick in New York to call her off. The premises were being watched and ten shillings to a clerk would determine if the message had been sent.

It was half-past two before Florence bestirred herself. She drafted the telegram. It would be the most expensive she ever sent. Her hand was shaking as she did, as much from the fury rising in her as from fear. Writing a letter to Agatha was no less painful. The activities they, all three, had been involved in – she was not specific – must be suspended. There were good reasons. Agatha should not contact her until further notice, not by any means. She must not be offended and Florence knew that she would not be. In time, there would be explanations. Susan, the maid, would be sent out later to post that letter in the nearest pillar-box. But first, the telegram.

Heavy rain was falling outside. Nicholas's heavy civilian mackintosh hung on the hallstand and she threw it over her own coat and took a large umbrella. The mackintosh's weight was comforting, brought recollection of Nicholas's embrace, but even so, her skirt hem and her boots were sodden when she reached to post office. Six people there. Only one seemed to have come for business, a half-deaf old lady, arguing over the postage demanded for a parcel. The others had come in to shelter from the downpour, another woman, men who looked like clerks, a saturated tramp hovering near the counter to catch some warmth from the stove beyond it. Any, or none, of them could be Mrs. Bellamy's

223

lackey. It didn't matter. The uncertainty was enough to enforce obedience.

Florence sent the telegram, went out into the wet cold misery again and felt tears running down her cheeks. It had all started so well and it had come to this.

But she was not beaten.

*

Florence left the villa again at half-past four next morning, through the rear entrance. She was wearing an old dress borrowed from Cook, a soiled apron over it, a battered hat of hers too, half of the wax fruit that adorned it long lost. Over it all Florence drew a threadbare Turkish-Army greatcoat, its insignia removed. It was dear to her, would hang in her attic all her life. She had been wearing it when Nicholas had arrived at that caravanserai in Thrace when all seemed lost, and she had worn it on the dreadful retreat that had followed, when he had lain delirious in a jolting cart and she had saved him.

A cab could have alerted attention, if the villa was being watched. She had to assume that it was, but her emergence from the shadows in the lane behind might not be expected. She waited until absolutely sure that the street was deserted before she slipped out. Soft rain, almost a mist, chilled her at once. She slumped as she headed westwards along wet pavements, the weary plod of a drudge old before her time. The hessian shopping bag she carried, used daily by Susan for fetching groceries, and its contents, grew heavier with each step. The glow of street lamps revealed others like her, charwomen, the lowliest of household helps, despised and patronised by regular servants, trudging towards squalid labour in scullery or in privy. She, like they, was invisible, meriting no notice even from policemen sneaking furtive cigarettes in shop doorways. She would arouse no greater interest on the train.

She reached the station a half-hour before the earliest service to London. She asked if it would it stop at Clapham Junction. It would, and she bought a third-class ticket. The refreshment room was already open but it was beyond the means of the poorest, the role she now was playing. There was a coffee-stall outside, cabmen stamping their feet, delivery men awaiting newspapers from London, a few shivering wretches who had spent the night in any available shelter, now grateful for the warmth of the mugs they clasped. Florence paid a penny for one for herself, and another for a slice of bread and dripping. She had not got it in her heart to refuse to buy the same for two derelicts who begged from her. Before the train left, she would go into the ladies' lavatory and remove her apron and put it in the bag. Then she would find a corner in a compartment and try to sleep.

She was almost certain that she had not been followed.

*

Florence jolted into wakefulness when the train stopped at Woking. It would not be far now. It was dismal grey daylight and when she cleared the fogged window with her sleeve, the drifting rain outside depressed her. A day that promised little, seemed made for disappointment.

She left the train at Clapham Junction, following on foot the same route she had taken before to the Common. Her anxiety was greatest now, for she was banking on Raymond having returned to Britain. The elegance of Western Lodge mocked her own poor bedraggled state when she stood before it. This was how the poor must always feel, she thought. She hesitated to go up the steps to the front door, for it was too easy to have it slammed in her face, and decided instead to go around the side to find the kitchen door. It might be difficult if Raymond's French chef was there, but she guessed that his work would start later than this, when he would prepare lunch. She knocked and the door was opened by a woman such as she herself impersonated. A char. The blast of warm air from within was welcome.

"What do you want?"

"To speak to Mr. Raymond."

"Who is it, Martha?" Voice of an unseen woman, cook or kitchen maid perhaps.

225

"She says she wants to see Mr. Raymond."

"I'm not leaving." Florence planted her foot on the doorstep.

"She says she ain't leaving."

"I'm coming, Martha."

It was the cook, apron and cap snow-white and starched, monarch of this domain, but with a kindly face. She took in Florence's sodden clothes, her features raw with damp and cold.

"Are you hungry, ma'am?" She said.

It happens at my own kitchen door too, people begging for food. It never struck me that the humiliation could be so great.

"No. Thank you, no. But I want to see Mr. Raymond. Is he at home?"

"He ain't up yet, won't have his breakfast for another hour. But he don't see nobody just like that. Just sit by the range a while, ma'am, an' warm up before you go. And you can have a cup of tea, an' Martha will give you bread and butter. Jam too. You'd like that, wouldn't you?"

Florence reached inside her dress and found a card. Wet and limp, it looked as if she'd picked it up from the gutter.

"That's mine," she said. "I'm Mrs. Nicholas Dawlish. It's really me. He knows me. He'll see me if you give him this."

"You've seen terrible trouble then, ma'am," Pity in the cook's eyes. "Just sit by the stove for a while. Look, Martha's pulling a chair over for you."

Questions unasked in those eyes too. Was it drink or widowing or another woman or bankruptcy that had reduced her to this?

"I'm not leaving," Florence said again. "I'm not leaving until he's seen it." She said it several times more.

Until at last the cook called for a housemaid and sent the card up and steam rose from Florence's clothes as she sat close to the range.

There was hope.

226

Chapter 22

Florence was brought to what must be Raymond's study. A welcome coal fire was glowing there. She was there less than three minutes when he appeared in a silk dressing gown. He could not have been long back in England, for he was deeply tanned. The dark, clever eyes above the moustache that curved up to meet the side-whiskers on his otherwise clean-shaven face showed what might or might not be genuine pleasure. She knew him well enough to be unsure.

"Mrs. Dawlish! What a wonderful surprise!" He took both her hands in his, led her to a chair.

She wondered if the American woman who had turned her away, when she was last here, had ever mentioned her to him. Even if she had, he might find it convenient to behave as if she hadn't.

He can be trusted only up to a point, Nicholas had once said, though he was uncertain what that point might be. But it had not been reached in Cuba, where Florence had played the role of Raymond's wife, as chastely as if he had been her brother, or when he assisted Oswald's flight from Britain on his steam yacht *Shamrock*. And there had been even yet more sensitive matters later. A good ally, if it suited him, and a dangerous and calculating enemy. He was clever, audacious and cunning, with contacts in high places who found him useful, and probably he them.

He had taken in her poor and sodden clothing, was looking at the hessian bag she held on her lap.

"There's trouble, Mrs. Dawlish?" Only when she had been seen in public with him in Cuba had he ever addressed by her Christian name.

"Bad," she said. "Very bad."

"Complicated?"

"Very complicated." She turned away, did not want to see her weak when he had known her strong.

"And Captain Dawlish isn't in Britain?"

"No." He probably guessed that already, she thought.

"Don't tell me about it yet. You must have dry clothes first"

The maid he called for brought her up to a bedroom that she recognised. She had rested there one afternoon before setting out on a subterfuge to conduct Oswald to the coast, her fear of recognition and arrest as great as his. Now the maid brought her hot water, towels, a lady's day dress made for a slightly larger woman, perhaps for that American, of whom there seemed no sign today. Underwear and stockings also, new items, folded in tissue paper in decorated cardboard boxes closed with ribbons. Expensive, like everything here. When she was brought to Raymond's study afterwards, she found him immaculately dressed. As he always was.

She knew something of what he did but suspected that nobody knew all. Nothing she could say would shock him. Nor would he betray anything she said. She was sure of that. No, almost sure.

"Now tell me all about it," he said.

When she had last come here, and been turned away, she would have told everything. It had seemed so straightforward then, the exposure of the *Temple de la Beauté*'s exploitation and blackmail of guileless women. She had wanted Raymond's advice, for he knew the world in which Mrs. Bellamy and her like prospered, and indeed prospered himself. There had been a sense of adventure about it then. She had enjoyed the initial investigations, had indeed been proud of them, had no great sense of risk. But there was more at stake now, infinitely more, and she could take no chances.

"I can't tell you," she said.

"Why are you here then?"

"Because I want to talk to Topcliffe. You probably know where to find him. I don't."

She had met Admiral Sir Richard Topcliffe twice only, frightened and impressed by what he must be. She was not sure exactly what, other than that he had power, not just power over Nicholas's career, but infinitely more. On the second occasion, when Topcliffe had asked to see her, it was Raymond who had arranged the meeting. It had not been at the Admiralty and she doubted if he would welcome her making enquiries there.

"Why do you think he will be interested?" Raymond did not sound offended by her refusal to confide in himself.

"He'll be very interested. He'll thank you for alerting him."

"You're not going to say anything more, are you, Mrs. Dawlish? I know you well enough." He laughed, moved to a writing desk, scribbled on a paper, then pulled the bell-rope.

The footman who came was the bruiser who had answered the door when she was here before. Raymond thrust the paper towards him. "Call that number for me."

There must be a telephone machine here, she realised, and indeed, a minute later, she could hear faint ringing. Raymond filled the waiting with small talk but made no further enquiries. Five minutes passed, more ringing, then the same again ten minutes later. Topcliffe, Florence suspected, was not easy to locate. She had all but exhausted the topic of her European tour, when the footman came back. Raymond scanned the note he handed him.

"The clarence," he told the man, "have it ready in half-an-hour." He turned to Florence. "Our friend will see us at half-past twelve".

*

It was the same gleaming black carriage and the same two beautiful matched bays that had carried her with Oswald on the first stage of his flight. She even remembered the name of the coachman, Staunton. He took them north at a smart clip across Battersea Bridge, then turned east along Cheyne Walk. There was wealth here, must be wealth also in the four-storey house of the last century – white-painted brick, black door and window frames – before which they halted.

"Is it his house?" It was not where Florence had met Topcliffe previously.

"No. A friend's."

As on the last occasion, it was the same thickset and grizzled figure, with the look of an old seaman about him, who opened the door. What furniture there was in the hallway was covered with dust sheets, so too, most of that in the drawing room where Topcliffe waited. He was in tweeds, not uniform.

He stood up, greeted Florence, invited her to sit. For all his smiles, despite his handsome bearded face and polished manner, she sensed the reptilian coldness that she had before. A man who used others without scruple, a man who delighted in power.

"Are you concerned about your husband, Mrs. Dawlish?"

Topcliffe must know that she was, for he had probably sent that telegram to Dresden, but would not admit it.

"It's not about him, Sir Richard." *Though, God knows, I'm concerned for him night and day.* "It's something else. Something I want to discuss with you alone."

"I'll leave Mrs. Dawlish in your care, sir," Raymond said. "I'll wait outside."

When he had left, Topcliffe said, "Now tell me about it, ma'am."

Difficult and shaming as it was, she left nothing out.

He looked towards the ceiling as she talked, hands folded pyramid-fashion before him and not interrupting. She sensed that mention of Mrs. Bellamy's name did not surprise him. His silence felt like a reproach, contempt for her naivety and ill-judgement, for the morass into which she had brought herself. But, when she finished, he offered no reproof.

"So Mrs. Bellamy wants more than just papers from *Vernon*?"

"That if – no – that when my husband returns he might on occasion carry documents home and maybe leave them about. She'd want copies, was confident that I'd find a way to transcribe them. Any papers, no matter how mundane they might seem to me."

"You've brought something like that here today, Mrs. Dawlish?" He nodded towards her hessian bag.

"It's all I could find was in a small sea-chest in the attic. There's not much." She reached inside the bag but he held up a hand to stop her.

"Did Bellamy mention anything specific?" He spoke the name with what might have been familiarity, even a hint of admiration.

"She said she wanted me to bring her anything I could about something called the Dawlish Cam. The same name as my husband's, but I've never heard of it."

"He's an honourable man," Topcliffe said. "He wouldn't mention it to you. There were fewer than a hundred in the entire navy who knew about it and they were sworn not to speak of it."

"Mrs Bellamy didn't know what it was. Only the name. She knew though that certain people value it very highly." She saw that he was smiling. Satisfaction rather than amusement. "She didn't want the thing itself, Mrs. Bellamy said. But drawings, calculations, anything about the design. The people she talked of would pay for them."

"Your husband designed it at *Vernon*, Mrs. Dawlish. It failed at first but he persevered. He machined the original himself and he tested it in all weathers and perfected it. But, and it's no discredit to him, we have something even better than it now. Others don't know that however."

"What is it? Is it something to do with torpedoes?" She remembered him coming home, saturated, half frozen, after endless firing tests during a stormy autumn five years before.

"It controls the depth they run at, Mrs. Dawlish. It was superb in its time but we've got something even more effective now, not that others are aware of that. You don't need to know the details. You'll be more convincing that way. And yes, at least two parties would pay well for it."

She hardly heard the final words. Only a few words mattered.

You'll be more convincing.

It wasn't going to end as easily as she had hoped.

"Please show me the documents you found." He motioned to a large sheet-covered table.

She had found nothing other than private letters and old bills in Nicholas's writing desk. In the attic, the old chest that he had brought to sea as a midshipman was unlocked, an indication that it was unlikely to contain anything confidential. There were letters in ribbon-tied bundles inside, some postmarked a quarter-century before. She recognised the spiky scrawl of his father and Susan's more graceful hand in the addresses. An unfamiliar script, bold and confident, must be that of

James, the elder brother whom he still mourned. A few yellowing Spanish-language newspapers from February 1866. They must have had some significance then for Nicholas but she had no time now to peruse them. Everything else she found she had brought.

"There isn't much, Sir Richard."

She had wrapped it all in an oil-cloth table cover from the kitchen. Now she unfolded it and laid the contents on the table.

A half-dozen navigational charts opened to show stains and pencil-marks. Topcliffe scanned them, pushed them aside without a word.

He was more interested in the notebooks, varying in size, covers faded. One, announced on its first page as Nicholas's journal for 1866, he thrust aside after flicking through and glancing at a few more pages. The second, dated two years later, was only partly full and was also quickly dismissed. Other than the first pages, Florence had read neither. It would seem a breach of privacy. Nicholas had been on the Pacific Station in 1866 and in Abyssinia two years after that, a junior lieutenant.

"This one might be important." She handed the third notebook to Topcliffe. "It's different from the others."

It was a personal journal too, dated 1870, more expensive than the others, leather covered, though scuffed. An inscription on the flyleaf told that it had been a gift from his sister Susan. The records of his daily doings were brief enough for the first twenty or thirty pages to bring him to mid-year. But thereafter the records were longer, interspersed with jotted geometric pattens, their lines identified with a's and b's and x's and y's and what looked like Greek letters. There were sketches too of what looked like the innards of a clock. There were what must be calculations in algebra. Florence had never learned it, but she knew what it was. And hand-drawn tables too, pages of them, columns headed with dates and times and filled with annotations below. An unlikely name appeared again and again. *Oberon*. The pages thereafter, a third of the notebook, were wholly blank. He must have continued in some more confidential record.

Topcliffe was smiling as he flicked through the pages.

"He saw the significance even then, Mrs. Dawlish. A clever man, but you know that already. He was already thinking of refinements. It all seems so primitive now, but there must be a start to everything."

"What is it about?"

"Torpedo tests, Mrs. Dawlish, the first. Conducted by a vessel called the *Oberon*. Young though he was, your husband was assigned as an observer because most other officers saw things mechanical beneath them."

"Did all this lead to the Dawlish Cam?"

"That came much later. Everything was more sophisticated by then anyway. There's nothing in this notebook but first faltering steps towards the cam concept."

"Is it of any value?"

"Not as it is. But it could be for another purpose. It would take a little work, two or three days. We might have something then that Mrs. Bellamy would like and that we'd be happy to let her have."

"And I'd deliver it, Sir Richard?"

"In your own best interest, Mrs. Dawlish. In your husband's also."

It's not enough that Nicholas is risking his life in some God-forsaken place in the Sudan. Not enough that he might be dead already. Nothing he'll have done there will matter if I don't do this man's biding.

"Would you have her arrested then for possessing it?"

"Do you think that would save you, Mrs Dawlish, even if we could bring a case? Your word against hers?" His smile was condescending, his tone patient, as if explaining to a child. "Her defence counsel, and she can afford the best, would shred your reputation."

Her fear was back, mixed with anger she dared not show.

It's not going to end here. He'll use me like he uses Nicholas, threatening and rewarding to achieve his ends.

"You know about Mrs. Bellamy already, don't you, sir?" What she had suspected when he had listened, what she was sure of now.

"She's not unknown to me, Mrs. Dawlish. She's been useful once or twice. People like her are always useful. Other parties find that too. But she hasn't dabbled in anything as serious as this before that I know of."

He must have sensed her fear for he said, "There'll be nothing more difficult for you than in that affair two years ago. You handled that well."

Well perhaps, but not without danger. Memory of the acid meant for her that had splashed on Mabel still haunted her. There had been a woman as clever and as ruthless as Mrs. Bellamy then also.

"What am I to do now, sir?"

"Leave these papers with me. Mr. Raymond will take you to lunch and bring you back here later this afternoon. I've a few arrangements to make. I'll know by then what I want you to do."

No option.

*

Her train pulled back into Portsmouth just after ten o'clock. She had travelled back third-class, in her char's costume again, though Raymond's clarence had carried her to Wimbledon, blinds pulled down. It was better to board there, rather than at Clapham or Waterloo, he said, lest she was being trailed. Telegrams had been despatched and measures were already in hand to get her safely home. The Albert Grove villa would be watched from six this evening by Raymond's own people and she did not need to worry about burglaries. A man in workman's clothes greeted her as his sister on the Portsmouth station platform, ushered her into a decrepit cab behind the station and deposited her close to, but not at, the villa. She saw nobody else in the street and entered through the lane at the rear. It was overcautious perhaps, but awareness that Raymond and Topcliffe were now involved eased her mind, if even only a little.

The next two days were difficult, for she could only wait. She considered going to the Seaman's Rest, decided it was better not to, took walks along the Esplanade, wondered if one of Raymond's people, or even one of Mrs Bellamy's was following. A telegram arrived from Mabel in New York, bewildered but acquiescing in suspension of her Temple articles. Nothing would appear in print without Florence's approval. She thought of writing a letter of explanation to Mabel but held back.

Topcliffe would not approve. Her relationship with him was all but official now, for he had given her twenty-five pounds for expenses. She would have demurred but practicality overcame pride, she had to watch her outgoings. She should not feel uneasy about accepting, he'd said. There was a fund that covered these sorts of activities. He had asked her to sign a receipt, and she did.

On the evening of the second night, Thursday, she was in her study, at half-past ten, sitting so as to let the gaslight throw her shadow on the blind. Five minutes later a few pebbles rattled on the window. She had been expecting it and had specified a time when the cook and maid would already be in bed. She left the gaslight burning in the study but found her way to the kitchen in darkness and opened the door leading to the garden behind. A package lay on the doorstep. She picked it up, closed and bolted the door and went back the study to view the contents.

She must be familiar with them by tomorrow.

*

Her travel to London early next morning was in first-class. She was wearing her own best travelling clothes and carrying a large leather handbag.

A hansom carried her from Waterloo. Her knees were weak when she stood before the *Temple de la Beauté* and rang the bell. Mrs. Mobray looked surprised when an attendant showed her in.

"I want to speak to Mrs. Bellamy."

"There's no appointment for you today, Mrs. Lacy."

"Just tell her I'm here. She'll see me."

Ladies, middle-aged and old, were waiting for rejuvenation. She might have seen some of them before. Individuals might vary but the clientele always looked the same. No sign of Dear Clifford or his sister, but one distinguished-looking man of about sixty, possibly another actor, was talking to an even older lady.

Mrs. Mobray was back two minutes later, looking bemused. She might not have been as close a confidante of her mistress as Florence had assumed. Would Mrs. Lacy kindly follow her?

Again the office-boudoir. Mrs. Bellamy was behind her desk and didn't rise. Brisk good mornings, and Florence sat. Mrs. Mobray hovered by the door, was dismissed with curt thanks.

"You've brought me something, Mrs. Dawlish?"

"You're a bad hostess, Mrs. Bellamy. "I haven't been offered tea, coffee or elderflower."

"No need to play the fearless young heroine with me, ma'am." She pointed to Florence's bag. "You're not in a position to bargain for as much as a cup of tea. Show me what you've brought."

There's no point in a confrontation.

Florence took the package from her bag. It was wrapped in the oil-cloth in which she had brought the papers to Topcliffe. Mrs. Bellamy picked up a small scissors from her desk and cut away the fastening string. There was a slight whiff of some chemical when she laid the folded sheets on the chaise longue and opened them. Drawings, white on a blue background. An impression of Mrs. Bellamy's cautious satisfaction, so too when she leafed through the notebook.

"I can't judge if any of these have value, Mrs. Dawlish. Somebody must look at them for me." She looked towards the clock on the mantlepiece. "Be back here at four o'clock. If he's in London, he'll have seen them by then."

A tug on the bell-pull summoned an attendant.

"This woman is leaving. See her to the street."

Florence had spent less than fifteen minutes in the Temple.

But it was a start.

*

She went to a teashop nearby and sat there for a half-hour to recover her composure. Disgust as well as apprehension about the coming appointment troubled her. With five hours in hand, she walked up to the

236

British Museum. She loved the place. It had been part of her education, somewhere to go, and wonder, on her few free days. She had been a housemaid then in the Kegworth mansion on Piccadilly, hungry for knowledge. Agatha had not yet found her leafing through a book in the library that she should have been dusting. Her life had changed from that moment, from housemaid to lady's maid, to paid companion, to shared danger and to friendship, at last to sisters. And it had brought her Nicholas. The memories came back as she wandered through the vast halls, recognised again the relics of Babylonian and Egyptian and Greek and Roman greatness that had fascinated that fourteen-year old who seemed now a different person. And, even as she had then, she wondered if all she knew, this vast city, its glory and its wealth, its pride and reach of power, might also someday pass.

The thought depressed her as she walked the short distance to the Temple. Topcliffes and Raymonds, and Nicholas Dawlishs too, had striven in those vanished empires but, in the end, it had availed them nothing. And yet she felt her sense of resolution growing. All life, all endeavour, would end the same way. What was important was to ignore that fact, fight on, no matter what.

A shabby, nondescript man, maybe forty-five, balding and with a ragged grey moustache, was sitting with Mrs. Bellamy when Mrs. Mobray ushered Florence in again. He didn't rise.

"This is Mr. Brassard," Mrs. Bellamy said. "He's been looking at those items."

She pointed. A card table had been brought in and the sheets were spread on it and the notebook was open at a page. The magnifying glass normally employed for scrutinising skin lay on top.

Florence, uninvited, sat.

"Where did you get these papers?" Not just brutal directness, but something too that was not English in Brassard's tone. Not enough to place it.

"They're my husband's. I found them in an old sea-chest in the attic." She had prepared for this, but it still felt demeaning to answer this man. "There were pieces of old uniforms too, and odds and ends. Just crammed in anyhow, probably in a hurry when he once had to leave unexpectedly. He must have forgotten about them by the time he came back."

"Where's he now?"

"Serving Queen and Country." She said it with pride. "In Egypt or the Sudan."

"These things are dated '78 and '79. He was at HMS *Vernon* then, wasn't he?"

"Yes."

"And living with you in Albert Grove in Southsea?"

"Yes."

"Did you know what he was doing?"

"He was lecturing to other officers. But he was also conducting tests on torpedoes, firing them from boats. That occupied him most. And he must have been spending time in a workshop too. He often came home with oil stains on his clothes. And once he had cut his hand badly. When he was working on a lathe, he said."

He was well known for that proficiency. Something that I heard officers' wives sneering at and their husbands were often contemptuous too. Mechanic's work. But he was proud of it. The future of the navy, he often said.

"Did he ever talk about the Dawlish Cam?"

"I never heard of it until that woman mentioned it." She gestured towards Mrs. Bellamy. "If it's valuable enough for people like you to want it, then it was valuable enough for my husband not to talk about. He's a man of honour."

"When was that sudden departure you talked of?"

"Late in '79. November, I think."

Not just think, but know. When Topcliffe came to the villa one rainy night, when I first saw him, and Nicholas left so soon afterwards for South America. And whatever happened there was dreadful, something he'd never tell me of, something that haunts him still in nightmares.

"What would your husband say if he knew what you're doing now?"

"The shame would kill him."

238

"It's better that he'll never know then, isn't it?" Mrs. Bellamy said. "We'll see that he won't need to, won't we, Mrs. Dawlish?" She turned to Brassard. "Do you believe her?"

He shrugged. "It corresponds with what I know already."

"There'll be interest?"

"Certainly."

"We're finished with you for now, Mrs. Dawlish," Mrs. Bellamy said. "Don't come here again until you're invited."

A November fog was thickening in the dusk outside in Coptic Street. For all that it was acrid with coal smoke, it seemed somehow cleaner than the perfumed air within the Temple.

Chapter 23

Late as it was when Florence arrived back at the villa, she sat down to write a full account of her meetings with Bellamy and Brassard. It took four hours, including long periods lost in efforts to remember exact phrases, and it covered eight pages of foolscap. She slept with it beneath her pillow.

She walked to the Sailor's Rest after a late breakfast and posted the report in the pillar box outside. Raymond had specified the address, a number in an obscure suburban London street. The reply came next morning, unsigned. Expect Wilkinson at the Rest this afternoon at three. She was there a half-hour early, and was checking invoices and approving payments, when the superintendent, Mr Selby, knocked.

"There's a gentleman wants to see you ma'am. Well-established business in London, he says, cleaning materials, wholesale prices. He's opening a branch in Portsmouth soon and he's touting for customers. Here's his card."

Mr. George Wilkinson.

"Ask him to come in please."

Raymond, in a cheap check suit, billycock hat clutched in both hands as if in supplication, fawningly thankful when invited to sit before Mr. Selby was dismissed. He was a small tradesman personified, perfect even to the hint of Cockney accent.

He had not brought her report but he remembered every detail. Topcliffe had seen it too, and had been pleased. They were both of them especially interested in Brassard.

"We know of him," Raymond said. "He's a blackmailer. It's no surprise that he's an associate of Mrs. Bellamy. He probably tells himself he's a confidential agent because, when he can get it, he peddles information about foreign nationals, exiles and the like, to their embassies. And he jumps on any scrap that seems remotely political or military or naval in nature and sells it on. He's done no great harm and our friend the admiral has wanted him left alone because he might be useful someday."

"Which he now is?"

"Which he now is, Mrs. Dawlish. His background helps. French father, unknown but apparently distinguished. His mother English and unmarried. He was an army captain himself, captured by the Prussians in '70. He was involved with the Commune in Paris after that, some bad business then. He has preferred to live here ever since. With good reason. There's a warrant for a capital charge out against him in France."

"So what do I do now?"

"Just wait. You know how to contact me if you need to. And if it's an emergency, use this." He passed her a slip of paper.

And the waiting, Florence knew, would be hard to bear.

*

In mid-morning, three days later, Florence was practising piano when the housemaid entered. She looked embarrassed, hesitant.

"Is there some problem you want to tell me about, Susan?"

"It's about a young man, ma'am. I know I shouldn't have talked to him, ma'am. But I didn't see no harm in it."

"Did it stop at talking, Susan?"

The girl began to laugh, then supressed it. "Oh, it ain't nothing like that, ma'am. It was at the grocers in Albert Street just now when I was shopping for Cook, an' you'd told me never to talk to nobody I don't know. An' this young man, very smartly dressed too, he was, came up and asked me to give you this."

An envelope, addressed to Mrs. Nicholas Dawlish. Florence's hand trembled as she took it. Raymond would not have contacted her like this.

"Did you ever see this young man before?"

"No, ma'am. But he said he'd sailed with the captain, he'd been to Africa with him an' he just wanted you to let the captain know that he'd done well for hisself since he left the navy an' he's grateful."

"You're a very silly girl," Florence tried to sound stern but could think only of ripping the envelope open. "You should be careful of strangers who approach you like that, Susan. That's how girls can get

241

into serious trouble. You've learned your lesson, I hope, so we'll say no more about it for now. Go back to Cook."

A single sheet, an instruction, no signature.

Half-past seven that evening. Shoreham-on-Sea railway station, eastbound platform.

Bring fifty pounds in notes.

And clothes and other necessities for four days.

Not just travelling clothes, clothes for evening wear and dining.

She was frightened, very frightened now.

It had not ended.

*

No time for a letter, and the message was unsuited for a telegram. Florence had trusted for days past to Raymond's assurance that his people would be watching over her. If they were, she had seen no sign of them. Nor should she, she recognised. Their presence should not be obvious. But, even so, she felt unsafe after she had withdrawn the money from the bank in Victoria Road. It was a large sum, over a tenth of Nicholas's annual salary. Topcliffe would reimburse, she assumed, but it angered her that Mrs. Bellamy was forcing such expenditure on her.

She walked to the Queen's Hotel by a roundabout route and enquired at the reception if she might use the telephone machine there. It was in a separate room and it seemed an eternity before the pageboy visible in the glass-windowed booth in one corner managed to reach the number Raymond had given her. She waited until the boy had left before she spoke into one trumpet and held the other to her ear. First the agreed word of identification. *Tecumseh.* The crackling and distorted voice that answered might or might not be Raymond's but the reply was correct. *Santiago.* She had to assume it was him. It took her five minutes to convey the message. Noise like dry kindling taking flame forced her to repeat herself several times before no less distorted answers confirmed that she had been understood. That she would be on a station platform some forty miles from here that evening. And the inhuman metallic voice told her too to go ahead. She would be guarded from then on.

*

The rail line ran directly eastwards, parallel to the coast, and the journey took little over an hour. She carried a few requisites in a large leather handbag but all else she needed was enough to fill a small trunk that necessitated the services of a porter. The train deposited her at Shoreham, a small straight-through station, ten minutes before the appointed time. A misty, cold, drifting rain was falling but she sheltered under the canopy rather than in the waiting room. A time-table told that another train was due in fifteen minutes. Whoever was meeting her might come on that. The porter stood close by with her trunk on a trolly but the platform was otherwise deserted. A half-dozen passengers had alighted with her and she had assumed that one of Raymond's people might be among them. If so, there was no sign of them now, and it made her even more uneasy.

"Good evening, Mrs. Dawlish."

She had not heard him approach, but the accent identified him even before she turned. For all that an expensive astrakhan overcoat encased him, Brassard looked unclean. The smile was more than false, was a leer rather, with something even worse than lechery in it, delight in power over the helpless. She felt cold loathing and did not acknowledge his greeting.

"Go to the ticket office," he said. "Buy two tickets, first-class, to Newhaven Quayside. I'll watch this fellow." He gestured to the waiting porter.

The office was on the other platform and she had to toil up and across the cast-iron bridge above the tracks, hem dragging in the damp. She was very frightened now. Newhaven was a small port, she knew, but the station Brassard had specified indicated that it lay adjacent to a quay. That almost certainly implied boarding of a packet steamer to France. She had not expected this. The urge to lose herself in the darkness on

243

the far side was very strong but she resisted. There was no option but to play this out. Her hand moved up to her hat, touched the long pin fastening it to her hair. If all else failed, she had that.

She bought the tickets. The simple act of passing the money and taking the change disgusted her. She was expected to pay for betraying her country and herself. The train for Newhaven was due in twenty minutes but another came and stopped beneath her while she was returning on the bridge. Couples were alighting, some with children, disappearing from the platform towards warm domesticity. All were gone before she was down and she envied them. The train pulled away. It left the platform empty but for Brassard and the porter. He had given the man a cigarette, was smoking a cigar himself. Florence stood apart, unwilling to acknowledge him until she had to.

Long, desolate, minutes passed, an aeon, until at last the next train drew in. She did not turn but walked to the first-class carriage, saw a compartment that was already part-occupied by a gentleman and two ladies and she entered. Brassard had to follow and he directed the porter to load her trunk. It was a longer journey now, with several stops where the train collected more passengers than it lost. Florence sat in a corner seat and there was no place for Brassard to sit close or opposite. She took out a book and tried to read.

One change of train and then, at last, Newhaven. The station lay directly on the quayside. It was a terminus, had no other purpose but to serve the packet service. Beyond the glow of the line of lamps along the quay, Florence saw the profile of a steamer, what must be an overnight mail-service to France. She ignored Brassard but she heard him behind her calling for a porter to take her trunk. Then he came to her.

"Go over there, you see that ticket office? Buy yourself a passage to Dieppe. First class will look better."

"You're not coming with me?"

"No. Just buy your ticket and come back. I'll wait here."

It was essential to assume that one of Raymond's people was near and would follow. The fear nagged her that one would not, but she could only continue, trust to herself.

244

She paid for a single cabin. The passage would take little over four hours but she could sleep until six next morning before disembarking.

Two people, an air of shabby gentility about them, were moving away from Brassard as she came back. She had an impression, but could not be sure, that they had spoken to him. The man was thin and gangly, dark-bearded, the woman younger and fresh-faced. They joined an older man, prosperous, even distinguished-looking, with long white hair and the air of a patriarch. They shook his hand in respectful silence before disappearing into the ragged line of passengers moving towards the embarkation point.

"Over there." Brassard pointed to the shadowed angle between the ticket office and an adjoining wall.

He put his arms around her there and embraced her, like a loving husband taking leave of his wife, but she shrunk from him, from the smell of brandy on his breath, of sour sweat from his coat. Then he was pushing a package into her hands, telling her to put it in her bag. Beneath the brown paper she could feel the texture of the oil-cloth covering and she knew what was inside. It felt lighter than the package she had brought to Mrs. Bellamy but she could not be certain.

"What am I to do now?"

"When you get to Dieppe go to the Casino. It's a big hotel there. A room is booked in your name and you'll pay for it. You'll be contacted there."

"By whom?"

"He'll call himself Hugo. Just give him the package."

"When?"

He laughed. "At Hugo's convenience."

"Why can't you bring it to him?"

"Your name's Dawlish, isn't it? Like the thing itself. He'll trust the items all the more for that."

"There'll be customs examination at Dieppe." She remembered officials at Calais gleefully opening luggage, fingering through underwear, when she had crossed to France with Nicholas. "What if this is found?"

"It won't be. Hugo will have seen to that."

"What happens when I give him the package?"

"Whatever you want. Come back immediately to England if you like, or take a holiday if you've got the urge. It's your own affair. Not for longer than a week, though. You may be needed again."

He walked her towards the covered gangway, waited as she filed forward with the other passengers, subjected her to another rancid embrace before she handed over her ticket.

"And my compliments to dear Madame Hortense," he called after her as she mounted the steps.

She heard the mockery in his voice and hated him.

*

The stewardess who brought Florence to her berth was stout and kindly. It was comforting to talk to her as she turned down the bed, reassurance on this terrible night that there was still goodness in the world. She had held this position for nine years, she said, had supported four children by it after her husband had died, had made the crossing thousands of times, was proud of what she did.

The distant thrash of the paddle wheels and the vessel's gentle pitch and roll lulled Florence into sleep. She awoke with a start when stillness came and looked out through the scuttle to see that the packet had docked. Mailbags were being hoisted across to the quay. Closed carts waited for them there, the horses standing in patient misery in the lamplit drizzle. She returned to bed but fears assailed her now more than ever, not just for the present uncertainties, but for Nicholas. In daylight she could assure, and almost convince, herself that he would survive, prevail, no matter what the circumstances. In this lonely darkness, she could not. She lapsed at last into sleep again, troubled by dreams she could not remember when she woke, other than that they were miserable, devoid of hope.

She was already dressed when the stewardess brought her tea and toast and marmalade, as she had requested, at six o'clock. An hour later she joined a line of other passengers heading into the long reception hall. A cold wind was blowing through its open doors, baggage laid out in rows there, blue-bloused porters for hire. She engaged one, despite not having French, and he had enough English to understand her. They threaded through the other passengers seeking their baggage and she saw among them the couple she thought Brassard might have spoken to. She found her trunk and headed towards the tables behind which the customs officers were ranged. The porter followed. It was as she remembered from Calais, the same grubby officials, the same nervousness among even the most innocent-looking passengers. She was more than nervous herself. Her knees were weak, her heart thumping and she did not know how much credence Brassard's assurance merited. The package was in her handbag, not her trunk.

Her turn at the table. The porter swung the trunk up on to it.

"Votre nom, madame?" The moustachioed officer's tone indicated resentment that he should have to be here at this hour.

This must be it.

No identification had been requested at Calais. No papers were required to travel in Europe.

"Dawlish," she said.

The officer turned, caught the eye of another, more senior, standing behind, jerked his head towards her and received a slight nod in return.

"Ouvrir la malle, madame."

The key snuggled ready in the palm of her glove. She unlocked the trunk, opened it. Her clothes packed it to the brim. The official glanced in but touched nothing. He gestured what might be approval and, when she locked it again, scrawled a dash on the lid with chalk, and called the next passenger forward. He had ignored her handbag. The porter took the trunk again and they went first to the Bureau de Change, where she changed thirty pounds, and then out into the bleak morning.

Cabs waited for hire along the pavement. Several men in garish uniforms were standing beneath large umbrellas and holding placards with names of hotels. The Casino was among them. Within minutes her trunk had been loaded, the porter paid and a cab was carrying her there.

247

A wide beach and grey windswept sea lay to the right, an open park, criss-crossed with gravel pathways, to the left. It might be well-tended and attractive in summer, but it looked dreary now. The town lay beyond, an unbroken line of buildings facing seawards, many of them hotels. This was to Paris much as Brighton was to London, a seaside resort, less than two hours distant by train.

The Casino lay at the end of the park, a vast, rambling, ugly structure of no single style, its separate parts, mostly brick, jumbled around what looked like a medieval keep, twin minaret towers rising at one end. Long vaulted copper domes indicated large halls and salons and what must be the casino room itself. Florence had never seen a more unpleasing building anywhere. The ground rose beyond it, the ruins of a real castle on an eminence there, and white cliffs extended westwards along the sea shore.

The interior was vulgarly lavish. She approached the long reception desk across a huge chequered marble floor, dotted with potted palms. There must be steam heating here, for it was hot-house warm. She had expected it to be empty at this time of year but elegant women and smartly-dressed men were passing through this area to what must be late breakfasts.

It was no problem here that she spoke no French for she guessed that the suave young man who welcomed her could speak a half-dozen other languages. The look he gave her confirmed that it was not unusual for ladies to come here alone. She gave her name and, yes, Room 105 had been booked and was ready for her. Three restaurants offered lunch and dinner. Afternoon-tea – the English phrase was used – was served in the Palm Court. There were nightly concerts and if Madame would want to try her luck then ...

No, she said. She wouldn't.

I'm doing that already.

She asked if a message had been left for her. No, no message.

All she could do now was go to her room. It was more luxurious than most she had ever stayed in and there was a splendid view out on to the Channel. She bathed, changed into a day dress, rang for a maid and asked her to bring coffee. Then she tried to relax and read.

Waiting for Hugo.

*

She went down to a light lunch at what seemed the plainest of the three restaurants. Alone at a table, her handbag resting against her calf, she noticed the furtive glances of many of the men, of all ages, seated with their wives, and felt herself being assessed. Blackguards, Nicholas called such men who did not respect women. Now, however, she could not resist assessing them herself, looking quickly away whenever they returned her look. Any of them might be Hugo, and any might be one of Raymond's associates, sent to protect her.

Just before she finished, she saw the couple who had been on the steamer enter. Clothes plain, they looked out of place, and knew it, uncomfortable when a waiter seated them at the furthest corner table, confused by the menu. The man was upwards of thirty, she saw now, hair and beard beginning to grey, steel-rimmed pince-nez linked to his lapel by a black ribbon. They were too far off to hear but Florence had an impression of no great intimacy between them. Not spouses or lovers, but perhaps brother and sister, or business associates.

She waited until the restaurant was almost empty, lunch service over. Nobody, and certainly not Hugo, had approached her table with some excuse for making contact. She went back to the reception, found no message there, went back to her room, felt oppressed within it, for all its luxury. Better to go out. The rain had ceased, though it was threatening again, and she would walk through that bare park and back along the road beside the beach. She changed into her travelling clothes again, went down, with her handbag under her arm, and out into the chill damp breeze from the sea.

Others were walking on the gravel paths as well, couples in the main, some groups of three. The men as well as the women were fashionably dressed and she recognised several she had seen in the hotel. It felt uncomfortable to be the only woman walking here alone. Any one of them might be one of Raymond's people, sent to look over her, she told herself, but the hope might well be vain.

She had almost reached the port again before she turned back. The breeze was directly on her face now. She hastened her step, for the warmth of the room she had left was inviting.

Two men were coming towards her. She thought nothing of it. Others had passed, had tipped their hats, had given looks that might have been questioning but had made no attempt to speak to her. The small expectation that she'd had that Hugo might approach her in the open was gone by now.

The gravel path was narrow and one of the men had stepped off it to make way for her. He was wearing a long grey overcoat and his fur hat reminded her of the kalpak that Nicholas had worn in Thrace when he had come for her. She cast her eyes down and walked past.

And knew the voice.

"Florence Hanim, is it you?"

Fear coursed through her.

He had always addressed her like that, as he would a Turkish lady.

Count Sergei Ivanovich Livitski.

Chapter 24

He was dangerous.

Cultivated, charming, wealthy, educated partly in Oxford, a battle-hardened ex-officer of the Czar's Sumskoi Hussars, Livitski hadn't just been a diplomat when he'd been in London two years before. He had admitted that much to Florence when she had last seen him. That had been in the basement of the Russian embassy, after the brutal interrogation of the man who had thrown vitriol over Mabel Bushwick. *Vitriol meant for me.* Without Livitski's intervention, Mabel would have been scarred worse than she was. But that had been an incident in a much larger game, one that reached into the heart of British power to grasp secrets.

Livitski gestured to the man with him to walk on and leave them.

She had been taken aback by seeing him, was unsure what to say.

"You haven't forgotten me, Florence Hanim, have you?"

"No, Count," she said. "I haven't forgotten." Uncomfortable memories were flooding back. He had wanted her love before, and there had been nobility in the grace with which he had accepted her refusal.

"Are you surprised to see me?" he said.

"More than you me." She must be here at his request and she was waiting for him to say the name.

Hugo.

It would make sense. Russia was not Britain's friend. Its recent conquests in Central Asia made it a massive threat to India. Nicholas had told her that its navy, its greatest weakness in its war with Turkey eight years before, was expanding and modernising. It made sense to her that Russian admirals would hunger for an invention like the Dawlish Cam.

"Are you staying at the Casino?" Livitski said. "A short winter holiday perhaps?"

"Just a short holiday, Count."

"Accompanied by Captain Dawlish?"

"No." She would not expand. He had still not said the name.

"A short holiday for me too, Florence Hanim. Our ambassador, Baron Yahontov, asked me to join his party. A small one only. A little gambling – he loves the tables – and some good food and wine. Perhaps you might want to join us for an excursion if this weather clears."

Memories of herself and Agatha in his landau in Hyde Park, drawing admiring glances for the splendour of his matched pair and his Cossack-costumed coachman. She wondered if he had taken the horses with him when he left Britain.

"Are you at the embassy in Paris now, Count?"

"A brief visit only. I spend more time in Russia."

He must notice the handbag, she thought. It was larger than a lady would normally carry on a gentle stroll. But no, there were others walking on these paths and taking the package from her here would be too conspicuous. Hugo would not reveal himself here.

"Look there, Florence Hanim." He pointed seawards. A grey column of rain was drifting towards them. "This is no place to tarry. May I escort you back to the Casino?"

She pretended not to notice the offer of his arm and walked just a little apart from him.

"The American lady, Mrs. Bushwick," he said. "Did she recover?"

"The scars aren't visible. One would never guess. She's forever grateful for what you did. She regrets that she could not thank you personally but it took a long time for her to recover."

"And Lady Agatha? Well occupied as always?"

It was through Agatha that she had met him first, at the home of one of her learned friends, a philologist.

"She's read another paper to the Royal Society recently. I can't even begin to understand what it was about, but she was admired for it."

Clattering hooves to their right now, two landaus, hoods raised against the weather, two more humble cabs behind, four mounted gendarmes riding ahead and as many following.

"Monsieur Gauthier," Livitski said. "He's here as Baron Yahontov's guest. His train must have been delayed. He was expected an hour ago."

"Who is he?"

"Minister of Agriculture this week. Of Justice a month ago. Perhaps of the Colonies or of Finance or of Foreign Affairs another month from now." Tolerant contempt in his voice. "That's how it's here in France. It's difficult to keep pace with changes of ministries and governments. But Gauthier isn't a bad fellow in his way and Baron Yahontov finds him amusing. We're dining with him this evening."

"Who's paying?" She could not resist saying it.

He laughed. "You let little past you, do you, Florence Hanim?"

They had almost reached the Casino. The landaus had halted in front and staff had run out with umbrellas to usher the occupants inside. The gendarmes had posted in a cordon around the vehicles. Several other men, probably police in civilian clothes, detectives, were gesturing to onlookers to step back.

The vehicles were moving away, baggage unloaded. The gendarmes were cantering back to the town and the plain-clothes men had followed the visitors inside when Florence and Livitski arrived.

She expected that he would ask her for the package now but instead he said, "I can't invite you to join our party at dinner tonight, Florence Hanim. But you might find the sight of interest, an autocrat's ambassador dining like old friends with a republican politician. At *La Rotonde* at eight o'clock." He dropped his voice. "Don't let the expense concern you. It'll be covered."

It seemed a strange place for transfer of the package, but he must have his reasons. It would be good to have it over and done. She could leave here tomorrow morning, back to the modest comforts of Southsea, away from the possibility that he might renew the suit he had abandoned before.

She had feared that he might invite her to take coffee with him, as maintaining conversation was already awkward, but in the reception hall he apologised that he must leave her. A few official papers he had brought from Paris needed attention before dinner. Duty, like the poor, was always with us, he said in mock exasperation. She went to the reception desk and booked a table at *La Rotonde,* the most expensive of the Casino's restaurants. The clerk looked surprised that she would be alone but did not comment.

It would be difficult to bring the package into the restaurant this evening, for the handbag would look out of place. After some experiments, watching herself in a mirror, she found that she could carry the package in the crook of her left elbow, her silk evening-shawl draped over it as if casually. Not ideal, but the best she could manage.

She took out the evening dining gown she had brought, the only one she possessed. Shaken out, yet still creased, she recognised how modest and commonplace it would look beside the other dresses here. A pull on the bell brought a maid who would take it away and make it as presentable as possible. And yes, there was a coiffeuse on the premises who could attend to Madame's hair.

She would look the best she could.

Confidence must do the rest.

*

La Rotonde was a large salon, rich-curtained windows along one curved wall that faced the darkness of the sea, the ceiling domed and painted, groves of potted palms. It was perhaps a third-full when Florence entered. She saw no sign of Livitski but presumed that the tables separated from the others by a red rope must be reserved for the minister's and ambassador's parties. Electric lamps in chandeliers and wall lights, not gas jets, cast a harsh glare. A ladies' string-quartet was playing Offenbach's Barcarolle on a low platform to one side, a moustachioed pianist sitting at a grand piano below them, waiting his turn. She gave her name and a waiter, supercilious in English and probably unbearable in French, led her to a small table against a wall. She settled on her chair, the package on her lap, hidden by the table-cloth. She asked about the menu. It was fixed for everybody this evening, the waiter told her, six courses specified by the minister's aide.

The waiter returned two minutes later with a bottle of champagne in an ice-bucket.

"I didn't order this," she said.

"A gentleman wants you to enjoy it." He handed her a card.

Two words. *In admiration.* And the initials. *S.I.L.*

The same words that had twice accompanied gigantic bouquets delivered to the Southsea Villa two years before. They had elicited gasps of delight from Cook and Susan but Florence had been angered and embarrassed and had sent them to decorate the Sailor's Rest.

Livitski might still nurture hope.

The restaurant was filling now. A couple, a stout florid man with a much younger wife, prosperous bourgeois incarnate, took the table to Florence's left. Then, at the entrance, she saw the two young people she had last seen so uncomfortable at lunch, he now in formal dining attire that made him look scarecrow thin, she in an evening gown, in a fashion ten years out of date. They looked now as uncomfortable as before, unused to such surroundings. A waiter seated them at a table to her right. The man's coat was shiny with wear, the woman's dress faded and ill-suited to her figure. They sat down in silence, he toying with a glass, she sunk in what might be melancholy. The elaborate table setting, with its crystal glassware and silver cutlery, seemed to bemuse them. Florence felt a surge of pity They were shabby-genteel people in second or third-hand clothes, who had treated themselves to a luxury they could not afford and were already regretting it. On an impulse, Florence signalled to a waiter.

"This champagne," she said. "Bring it to those people. Tell them there's no need for thanks."

They were surprised by it, seemed to protest, fearful of the cost perhaps, but the waiter reassured them. They accepted and he poured for them. They looked towards Florence. There was what might be regret in the young woman's eyes and something of resentment in the man's. She smiled at them, then turned away, half-regretting what she had done. They might have thought it patronising.

Another group was entering, two officers in full-dress French Army uniforms, swords by their sides, the younger no more than twenty, the older twice that, at the least. Three of the plain-clothes detectives seen

255

earlier followed them in. They split, moving separately between the tables, casting only fleeting glances over most but stopping for silent scrutiny at some, then moving on, unsmiling. The older of the two officers, powerfully built, a half-dozen medals on his light-blue, gold-braid encrusted tunic, was approaching Florence. He came close, ignored the nearby bourgeois couple, paused at Florence's table, looked down at her. It lasted no more than ten seconds before he moved on again but she felt intense dislike of the oiled ginger hair, the moustache greased to extend like horizontal spikes, the fragrance, stronger than eau-de-cologne, that radiated from him, the diamonds glinting on his shirt-cuffs. There was lust as well as curiosity in his eyes. The sight of a woman alone always aroused that in such men and she despised him for it. Nicholas would have identified him as the type of blackguard who deserved a good horsewhipping. It was a remedy he often recommended for such men, but had never yet put into practice. It amused her and brought a flush of love by remembering it.

The officer moved on, took no notice of the impoverished couple at the next table, joined his colleagues and the detectives at the entrance. Heads together in a brief consultation, their conclusion obvious. No risks here for the illustrious guests. They stood back, the senior officer last of all, snapping his fingers to draw the quartet's attention.

Now the strings were flowing effortlessly from the Offenbach into the first bars of La Marseillaise. Everybody rose, Florence with them. A short, rotund cleanshaven man, a tricolour sash stretched diagonally across his torso, some order on his left breast, was entering, a blonde woman larger and younger than himself on his arm. He must be the minister. Behind him, in a plain dark uniform, a handsome bearded man, with a stately lady by his side, could only be the Russian ambassador. Another dozen followed, two by two, Livitski among them, some elegant, some vulgar in their ostentation. The quartet was playing what must be the Russian anthem now but it shifted into some lighter piece, Tchaikovsky maybe, as the newcomers took their places at the one large and two smaller tables reserved for them. Livitski and the senior French officer, and another gentlemen and lady, were sitting at the large table with the minister and ambassador and their wives. No speeches, for this was not a state occasion. The other diners were sitting down again and the maitre d'hotel was signalling to his staff to bring the first course.

Florence hardly noticed what she ate, though she was aware that it might be the best she had ever been served. She picked at the hors d'oeuvres and liked the soup, a lobster bisque, but her appetite was gone by the time the fish arrived. The party at the central table was lively now with frequent laughter. Educated Russians, Livitski had once explained to her, were as comfortable in French as in their own language and now his sallies seemed to be evoking especial merriment. The quartet was still playing, just loud enough not to drown the general hum of conversation at the tables. Only the incongruous couple were silent, going through the motions of eating, regretting what might be a month's salary or more – he could be a clerk or junior attorney – spent on this single meal.

It was uncomfortable for Florence too to sit here alone. She noticed several men eyeing her when the women with them were looking elsewhere and she didn't like it. She should not have come here this evening, she told herself, and even touching Livitski's card had felt like a small betrayal of Nicholas.

Somewhere in the Sudan.

The waiters, a small army of them, were bringing in the main course now, first to the minister's table, laying domed silver covers before each diner, standing back, waiting for the maitre's signal to step forward again to uncover. His hand was rising and the minister was half-turned toward him and calling some witticism that drew laughter from the others by him and –

The young woman at the next table was rising, had something in her hand, was reaching her arm back, was casting a black object the size of an orange towards the centre of the room. It arced above the diners – most hardly noticed, though one man seemed to think was a joke and cheered – and the quartet was playing on unaware. Florence saw it. Each second felt like a century and recognised immediately what it was. She threw herself to the floor, was aware that the man of the pair was on his feet too, a pistol in his hand, and she was pulling herself beneath her table when the bomb blasted.

Silence for an instant and then screaming, shouting, trampling feet. An internal voice told her to should stay under the table but curiosity overrode it. She half-rose to her knees, saw that yellow smoke was rolling in the centre of the room, that panicked diners were already stumbling towards any imagined haven, that others were paralysed with shock. The man with the pistol was darting forward between the tables towards the centre. Somebody, whose frantic wife was dragging him back, was trying to block him but his nerve failed and the gunman forged on past him towards the main table. The bomb had fallen well short of it, must have blasted glass or metal fragments into diners seated there, for blood was ghastly scarlet on shirt-fronts and dresses and faces.

The minister had risen, seemed frozen where he stood, face white, bewildered. The ambassador must have dived beneath the table and had dragged his wife with him. Livitski and the French officer were the only others on their feet there, resolute, waiting undaunted for the gunman to draw closer. The bomb-thrower was edging away to the right, closer to the entrance, her back against the wall, a small revolver in her right hand, what looked like another bomb in her left. She looked terrified herself but the diners at the nearest tables were shrinking back from her.

Livitski had drawn a revolver, had raised his left arm to rest the barrel on it, was sighting down it as calmly as if on a range. The senior French officer had whipped his sword from its scabbard, appeared to be about to mount the table. The minister was still standing. There was something magnificent about this portly little man at this moment, for Florence saw that hands were reaching up to pull him down and, though his face was ashen, dignity was preventing him from cowering.

The gunman had reached the table's edge, was swinging his weapon up towards the minister. Flame spat from Livitski's pistol and, though point-blank, its round must have shaved past its target and another report was almost simultaneous. The minister was collapsing backwards, eyes cast down and locked on the red blotch spreading on his white shirt-front. Even as he crashed down, the French officer was vaulting up on to the table, sword in hand. The attacker blasted up at him, and missed. He turned as the officer slashed at him and he began rushing for the entrance. A lane opened for him through the chaos. Livitski was pounding behind him now but holding his fire, for any miss would strike a panicked onlooker.

The young woman had all but reached the entrance, but she stopped short, switched the pistol to her left hand, the bomb to her right. She was trembling, but her nerve was holding. The gunman – brother, husband, lover? – was just ten paces distant but a plain-clothes detective was now emerging from the entrance and there must be more behind. He stood still for a moment, shocked by the chaos ahead, but she slipped behind him before throwing the bomb out into the hall beyond and drawing back into cover. Its detonation blasted a gale of smoke back into the restaurant salon, engulfed the dazed detective and rolled towards the fleeing gunman. He flinched for a moment, but Livitski did not for he charged on, smashed into him, threw him down. Florence was close enough to see the terror on the gunman's face as he tried to rise. Livitski's pistol was jammed against that face now, then blasting, not once, but twice.

Florence staggered back as a man and two screaming women came rushing from the direction of the entrance, was carried with them, urged on by a growing knot behind towards the now-deserted music stage. She tripped on the hem of her dress, went down, felt the trampling feet go past and leave her to struggle up. Detectives, their faces blackened, clothes shredded, pistols in hand, were emerging from the murk. The woman who had thrown the bomb was shrinking from them even as one's shot caught her on the right shoulder. She turned, came stumbling along the wall towards Florence, the shabby dress blood-soaked, one arm hanging limp, her face draining, eyes bulging in horror and despair. She was unarmed now, her pistol dropped.

A blow on her shoulder sent Florence tumbling to the floor. The senior French officer was barging past, the younger behind him, then halting before the wounded woman. She began to scream as she saw him sweep his sword back over his left shoulder, then arc it back again to bite into the side of her neck. Blood fountained as she tottered but he had caught her by the shoulder, held her, drew the weapon back, hilt level with his right hip, then drove it forward again into her breastbone. She didn't scream, must already have been dead when she slumped at his feet. He kicked her twice. No movement. Satisfied, he turned away, hurried back to where the dead minister's wife was shrieking over his body.

Florence stood transfixed by the butchery. Somebody had thrown doors open to the terraces outside and the salon was emptying. Livitski was hurrying the ambassador and his wife towards the entrance. She was shaking now, dazed. Her gown was torn and marked by feet and she realised that she was aching from the trampling. She did not notice the younger French officer come close until she felt, too late, his grip on her upper arm. She tried to wrench free but he was strong and he thrust her back against the wall.

"You, madame! You're one of them!" His English was scarcely accented. "The champagne, that was the signal, wasn't it?" He struck her backhanded across her right cheek. "You'll talk, madame! Believe me, you'll talk."

She was too taken aback to think or speak or see the second blow coming. It smashed against her eye.

He jerked his head to the detectives that were now turning over the mangled body. Two came forward, grabbed Florence, one to either side. He snarled an order and they began to drag her away. Just before they reached the entrance a woman, her dress torn, face grazed, hair in disarray, stood in their path and spat into Florence's face. Others, both men and women, heroism growing now that danger had past, were pressing close, shouting and gesticulating. Uniformed gendarmes had appeared and they forced the small mob back to make a lane through which they dragged Florence into the entrance hall.

Only when they flung her into a cab outside did the full horror of her situation dawn on her.

She had lost the package.

The package meant for Hugo.

Chapter 25

The cell was damp and marrow-freezing cold. The bed was of two planks, hanging from the wall by chains. The small window, barred and frost-glazed, with a glow of lamplight outside, was too high above to give any view. There was no light in the cell, but Florence felt lice crawling in the single filthy blanket and she threw it in the corner. Worse even than the cold was the stench, for there was no cover on the bucket in the corner.

Two detectives had held her down on the floor of the cab while it rushed her here, one grasping her hair and jerking her head each time she tried to protest.

"Tais-toi, salope!" he had snarled. "Cloue ton bec!"

Even without understanding French, the meaning was clear. There was more to their anger than the carnage, she thought. They had failed to prevent the murder of a government minister and they knew that they would suffer for it. Drumming hooves outside indicted an escort of mounted gendarmes and they formed a cordon when she was dragged out and hurried into a police station. Only when on her feet again did she realise how badly bruised she was. Ribs might have been broken and every breath and step were agony. Her head ached from the army officer's blows and she could hardly see through her swollen right eye.

Rough hands pushed her into a corner in the entrance hall and one of the detectives began to shout at the staff on duty. They must be normal municipal police and this arrival was a surprise. Tempers flared, others joined in the yelling. The most-senior seeming detective was gesticulating towards her and she heard the words repeated several times, *anarchiste, nihiliste, assassine,* and, most of all, *Russe.* The station's inspector appeared, calmed the situation, came up to her and judged her *une femme dangereuse.*

He snapped an order to his people.

Two grabbed her. One of them doubled her arm behind her back and the other forced her head down as she was bundled along a stone-floored corridor with cell doors on either side. The inspector and the detectives followed. They paused at the last door and tempers flared again. Nobody had thought to bring a key and an angry minute passed before a policeman came hurrying back with a bunch. The door swung open. Shouting came from within and two men entered to drag out a filthy wretch with matted hair who didn't want to come.

They threw Florence in. One detective held his foot out so that she tripped and landed on the slimy stone floor and hit her forehead on it. The door clanged shut and the voices moved away. She groped in the darkness, found the bed and dragged herself up to sit on it. Her hands were foul with the floor's filth. She ran them her down her dress. There were great rents in it and it had been made for evening fashion, not for warmth. Only now did she realise that nobody had asked her name and that questioning would be by somebody more senior than any of the detectives. She hoped it would not be by that older army officer. There had been cold deliberation, not wild fury, in his slaughtering. That woman had been unarmed by then, could have been as easily detained as she had been herself.

She was shaking now, and not with just cold only. Murder had been done, political murder, assassination and, from what she had picked up, suspicion was falling on Russian anarchists or nihilists. The ambassador, not the minister, must have been the target. She had been unlucky, and naïve, to have sent the champagne to that couple. It seemed obvious now that they must have been from the colonies of foreign political exiles resident in Britain. She could not be sure if indeed they had spoken to Brassard at Newhaven. She had been uncertain even at the time but now the possibility was frightening in its implications. Embarrassment for not preventing the incident would be massive in France. Those detectives were already frightened by the consequences for themselves. Guilty or innocent, somebody would be found and evidence distorted, even manufactured, to shift the blame away from those who had failed. And here they had the guillotine –

Stop!

She must not let fear override her. Nicholas had once endured captivity as squalid as this and she had helped rescue him from it. He

262

had endured, and so would she, even if she could not imagine how she might defend herself or explain her presence in Dieppe. If one of Raymond's people had perhaps been here and survived the carnage, if word could reach Topcliffe...

It was difficult to lie on the narrow bed without falling off but she rolled herself into a ball as best she could, drew up her knees, buried her hands under her armpits and accepted that she must suffer the cold. Ninety minutes before, she had been enjoying lobster bisque and hearing Offenbach. Now she was like a woman of the streets, brought in to the cells out of pity on a winter's night. She ached all over, found it hard to control her shivering.

But one thing beyond all kept sleep at bay.

She had lost the package. The police must surely find it.

And she could not think of an explanation.

*

She must have dozed off at last, for she was woken by the rattling of the cover on the door's spy hole. Coming off the bed revealed new aches. Pain stabbed with every move but, if somebody was coming for her, she would meet them on her feet. The cover had closed again but soon afterwards the door was unlocked, one policeman there with the keys, the other holding a tin mug and a piece of bread. He thrust them at her.

"Pas aussi savoureux qu'au casino, madame, mais c'est le meilleur que nous avons ici."

Even if she didn't understand the words, she recognised the voice of a petty, sarcastic tyrant who gloried in his power.

"Bon appétit," the other said and they both laughed.

The door clanged shut again. The coffee in the mug was weak and tepid, the bread stale, but she was grateful for them anyway though they did little to warm her. It must be about seven o'clock, for the lamp outside had been extinguished and cold winter daylight was brightening the glass above. She would not try to sleep again. Somebody must come to question her soon and she must be ready. Step-by-step, she went back over all had happened since she had first set foot in France. It made her feel no better. She would have to lie about the package, if it had been found. But that could only delay, give time for Topcliffe and Raymond to learn about her plight. She knew that this hope was desperate

Noise in the corridor outside now. Opening doors, shouts of protest suddenly cut off, a woman screaming, another sobbing, voices raised in abuse or pleading, rushing feet, doors slamming shut again. This must be the daily ritual of taking prisoners to court. The clamour died and the only sounds now were of quieter routines.

And the desolation of the cold cell again made worse by the dim daylight's revelation of just how tattered, how besmirched, how bruised she was.

Nothing to do now but endure.

*

At last, the moment came for which she had steeled herself. Voices outside the door, a key grating in the lock, light flooding in from the corridor. She saw a figure silhouetted there, half-turned away, waving for others to stand back.

"Florence Hanim!"

Livitski came to her, reached for her hands, held them. His were warm.

"This shouldn't have happened, Florence Hanim!" He must have felt how cold her hands were, for he was chafing them in his. "I only learned of it just now."

She heard no anger in his voice, was afraid that she might break down and weep, said nothing.

He dropped her hands, stood back, took in her state, looked shocked. Then he swept off the long fur-lined cloak he was wearing and wrapped it around her shoulders. He turned to the policemen. The inspector and one of the detectives from the night before were there too and he barked what seemed an order. They moved back down the corridor.

264

"Are you hurt badly?" he said. "I can carry you,"

"No."

Dignity demanded that she leave here on her own two feet but she accepted the offer of his arm and leaned on it. The inspector looked frightened and was obsequious in his willingness to assist as he led them to his office. A stove burned there and its warmth was an instant blessing. Livitski settled her in a chair close to it, gave the inspector curt instructions and sent him off.

"They think I'm Russian," she said. "An anarchist, a nihilist, God knows what. They think I was party to that outrage. You know me, Count, you know I couldn't be."

"There's no question of that. Your arrest was a stupid mistake. They know that now. I'd have prevented it if I'd known, but I was intent on saving Baron Yahontov. I didn't think of you, and I should have done. And Rivollet shouldn't have hit you. That wasn't necessary."

"Who is he?" She hated that brute, could never forgive the cowardly blow.

"He's a lieutenant, Fournier's aide."

"Who's Fournier?"

"Colonel Etienne Fournier. Who dealt with that assassin woman. He has some position on the army's General Staff."

"Will Rivollet apologise?"

"It's better not to press the matter, Florence Hanim, not in these circumstances. So much followed all night, diplomatic complications, accusations, the guarding failures, and this is just the start of it. That's why I only heard about you this morning. It makes it even worse that I had sent you that champagne, worse still that you gave it to those people."

"Who were they?"

"Russians, from some nihilist group, most likely. They weren't carrying papers but we'll find out who they were." Then sudden coldness in his voice "Why did you send the champagne to them, Florence Hanim?"

"I was sorry for them. They looked so out of place, so poor, so shabby. I thought they were spending money they couldn't miss, that perhaps he was trying to impress her, that –

He cut her off. "Had you seen them before?"

"No."

"Not anywhere? On the packet boat perhaps?"

She lied. "I didn't take much notice of the other passengers."

A knock on the door. The inspector was back and ushering in a waiter brought from a nearby hotel. He was carrying a basket and when he whipped the covering away, a rich smell of coffee and new-baked bread filled the room. He laid a white napkin on the table and, on it, china and silverware. He poured coffee, offered milk, butter and confitures, then left.

She ate and drank in silence, was grateful for the time to think. Livitski didn't press his questions but he said, "I can have a doctor come to see you here."

"No. But at the hotel, yes."

"It won't embarrass you to go back there?"

"I'm an innocent woman, am I not? Am I to sneak away because a cowardly beast mistook me and assaulted me? I'd be grateful if you can make it plain to the hotel management that I'm innocent. My clothes are there. I'll stay two nights more, to rest. After that, I'll be fit enough to travel home."

I need to stay. Even now, without the package, there might be some advantage in allowing Hugo to reveal himself.

"I thought you'd say that, Florence Hanim."

And, in his tone, she heard the same as he had written on that card. *In Admiration.*

*

Her face was even worse than she had thought, swollen, her right eye blackened, her body bruised in a half-dozen places. Pride had prevented her hiding her injuries when she limped through the Casino's reception

266

hall. Despite her pain, she had refused the support of Livitski's arm as he escorted her to the desk. There, he requested that a doctor be sent to her in an hour's time. She was determined not be examined until after she had bathed. The hotel was still ringed with gendarmes and thronged by police within. Nobody, staff and guests alike, was being allowed to leave before being questioned.

No ribs were broken, the doctor told her when he ran his hands over the silk chemise the nurse with him had brought for the examination. Madame had been lucky, he said. Others had been showered with fragments of glass or china but nobody other than the minister had been killed. It was only by the grace of le bon Dieu, he said, that the assassins had not filled their infernal machines with nails, as he understood had happened in an outrage in a Paris theatre.

She slept for several hours, woke in mid-afternoon, rang for coffee to be sent up, gave the maid who came fifty francs and asked her to buy a dark veil for her in the town and bring it next morning. In the cell, resisting the cold had dominated all other concerns. But now, in this luxurious room, looking out over a wave-tossed winter sea beneath dark clouds, another prospect depressed. She had to face the loss of the package. Somebody must have found it by now. Even if it was not traced back to her, the whole charade, Topcliffe's charade, of which she was a part, had now collapsed. She could bring nothing from the ruins but Hugo's identity, and that only if he was to reveal himself. That might not happen now.

The maid came back an hour later, carrying a large bouquet of hot-house flowers. The envelope with it was addressed to Mrs. Florence Dawlish and the handwriting was unmistakable. She tore it open while the girl arranged the flowers in a vase of water. No *In Admiration* this time. Livitski's message was brief. He had booked a private dining room for eight o'clock that evening. He hoped to see her there. There would be no impropriety. She could be assured that he intended nothing more than to discuss business.

Hugo!

267

*

Livitski offered her wine when she entered. She refused it. A small round dining table was laid out for two. A little beyond was another table, large enough for six or eight. Whatever was there was covered by a starched cloth that, under the harsh electric light, looked from its hummocks like a field of drifting snow.

Small talk, questions about how she now felt, if she was rested, if she had liked the bouquet. Baron Yahontov and his wife had left for Paris, Livitski said, and he had stayed to represent Russian interest in the investigation. The minister's widow was distraught, under sedation. France's Minister of the Interior was arriving from Paris tomorrow to see how investigations were progressing and he would visit the half-dozen casualties, none with permanent injuries, who had been kept in hospital. There would be a state funeral and Czar Alexander would be represented by a cousin, an archduke.

She listened with impatience, had heard enough, wanted no more beating about the bush.

"I won't dine with you, Count. You mentioned business. Now let's talk about that business, whatever it is."

"If you want it that way."

He moved to the covered table, drew back the cloth.

"This is what you came here about, isn't it, Florence Hanim?"

There was the notebook that Mrs. Bellamy had examined with such cautious satisfaction, its leather cover scuffed and stained. So too, spread out, the white-on-blue sheets of drawings, creased and faded, still giving off a slight chemical odour. The humble oilcloth from the Albert Grove kitchen lay folded to one side.

"You're Hugo, aren't you?"

He ignored her question. "Where did you find all this?" he said.

"Where did you find it, Count?"

"You didn't look after it very well when the chaos started, did you, Florence Hanim? I'm asking you again. Where did you find it?"

268

"In an old chest of my husband's. It had been in our attic for years with a lot of other junk."

He opened the notebook, the gift from Susan to her Dear Brother Nicholas at Christmas 1869 that had become his journal for 1870, with his calculations and sketches and records of the *Oberon* trials. Then, after them, a few blank pages before the additions began. Had she not known them to be forgeries, added in recent days, the work of some master craftsman known to Raymond, she would have taken them as Nicholas's own. Page upon page of scribbled notes. Many were in pencil, the hand shaky, as on a vessel in choppy waters, others in his normal script, recorded in ink ashore. Some pages were blurred as if by spray, others crossed out in frustration. The dates referred to '78 and '79 when he had indeed carried out endless torpedo firing trials on the Solent. There were references to numbered versions of the cam mechanism he had conceived, some dismissed as absolute failures, others suggesting promise if modified. Many pages were filled with sketches and calculations. They looked like notes for himself alone, brief reminders for use in preparation of official reports.

"You're sure that this is your husband's?"

She nodded. "I hadn't met him when he wrote the journal, but we were married, living in Southsea, when he made those notes in the back."

"Why in this book? He'd finished using it eight years before."

She had anticipated the question, had rehearsed the answer a dozen times. "For sentiment, I think. He'd attended the first torpedo trials in 1870 and he'd seen the promise. I think he was proud to be responsible later for perfecting the weapon. Maybe he wanted it all in the same notebook, one he could look over it with pride in his old age."

"And the blueprints. You found them too?"

"They were with it."

There are only five here, she saw. Raymond had delivered her eleven, created from scratch by his forger with the support of a Royal Navy torpedo expert. She had passed them all on to Mrs. Bellamy. She was not close enough now to read the title blocks on the bottom right-hand corners of the prints, but she knew that each carried the number of a version of the cam.

"It's a professional piece of work." Livitski was smiling. "But you don't expect me to believe any of it, do you? It's all a fake, isn't it?"

"No, it's —"

"If any of it's real, you wouldn't be here. Your sense of honour, your patriotism wouldn't let you. You don't have it in you to betray your country or your husband. You wouldn't do that, Florence, not at whatever cost to yourself."

No Hanim, just Florence, and there was respect in his voice. But she was trembling, sickened by realisation that all had turned to dust.

"It's one of Topcliffe's schemes, isn't it?" he said. "There's no need to deny that you know him. We do too. Britain's Fouché, one might say, and he's a master at it. And this time he's passing false information through that sordid little huckster Brassard, is he not? And I imagine that your complicity won't do any harm to your husband's career?"

She would not comment on any of it. "What are you going to do now?" she said.

"I'll hand these items to Hugo, neatly repacked."

"They're worthless, you've said that yourself."

"That won't matter to Hugo."

"Is Hugo Russian?" Doubt now rising in her mind.

"All you need to know, Florence Hanim, is that Hugo will be making the agreed payment to Brassard. He'll make no reference to the manner in which he received these items. He'll tell Brassard that you delivered them into his hands. I'll hold him to that. As far as Brassard is concerned, you've done what you came for and Hugo has the papers."

Further discussion would not help. She stood up to go. Her knees were weak but she forced calm into her voice.

"I'll be leaving tomorrow morning, Count. You seem to have influence here. I trust you'll see to it that the police don't inconvenience me any further when I go."

"You can be confident of that." He walked her to the door, then stopped. "You'll be reporting to Topcliffe. You saw the assassination, the carnage. We endure the same, dozens of times each year, in Russia, governors, judges, generals, bystanders."

"But this isn't Russia."

"It makes no difference to the nihilists. We know now that the two who were responsible for this outrage came from London. There are dozens, maybe hundreds, of others like them there. Tell Topcliffe that it's time to end toleration of so many Russian fanatics in Britain. Tell him he'll be welcome to our cooperation. By means, if necessary, of which Her Majesty's Government might not want to know the details, but will prove effective none the less."

She remembered such means in the basement of the embassy two years before. She had felt no more pity then than he had.

"I'll tell him, Count."

He reached for her hand, drew it to his lips and kissed it.

"Goodbye, Count."

"Goodbye, Florence Hanim."

Then she left.

And hoped she would never see him again.

Chapter 26

She arrived back at Newhaven at five the following afternoon, grateful that, before she had left, the Casino's maid had brought her the dark veil she had requested. Her face looked even worse now, the purple bruises fringed with a dirty yellow. She had taken headed stationery and an envelope with her from the hotel and, in the ladies' salon on board the packet steamer, she had written a note to Raymond. It contained nothing more than to expect her mid-morning on the morrow. Posted now, it would reach him by the day's first delivery. She always carried a few stamps in her purse and so, on arrival, she dropped it into a pillar-box at the Newhaven station. Due to her aches, the train journey back to Portsmouth was as comfortless as the Channel crossing had been. She reached Albert Grove just before eight.

"Don't be shocked, Susan," she said when she entered the villa, but the girl gasped anyway when she lifted the veil.

"Lord bless you, ma'am, that's –"

Florence cut her off. "I've tasks, very important and urgent ones, for you and for Cook. Please fetch her."

And Cook, Mrs. Singleton, was no less alarmed when she came, concern and anger on her great round kindly face.

"Who did this ma'am, who would do –"

"It's nothing," Florence said. "I walked into a door." She could see that neither believed her. "I need your help, Mrs. Singleton. Tonight, immediately. I want you to go to Clapham. There's a London train at twenty past nine. You'd have to stay the night, find a respectable lodging house near the station. Ask the station master if he can recommend somewhere. I'll give you the money for it. Could you do that for me?"

"Yes, ma'am." No hesitation. "If it would help you ma'am."

Florence reached out, took her hand and squeezed it. Moved by Cook's loyalty, she felt affection surge through her. "I'll tell you more presently, but first, you Susan, go to the cab rank in Albert Street and fetch a hansom."

A few instructions to Cook and then she went upstairs to pack a portmanteau with clothes. It was a lot to ask of an older woman but there was no option. She would make it up to her later. There was no guarantee that Raymond's people were still keeping watch on this house. She was convinced now, and angry, that none had followed her to Dieppe. The possibility that Mrs. Bellamy was having her observed could not be discounted. She had been bruised and beaten enough and would take no further chances.

Fifteen minutes later Cook was on her way to the station in the hansom, carrying not only her own bag but Florence's bulging portmanteau.

*

She started for the station at half-past four. She was a char again, and grateful for the protection of the old Turkish greatcoat against the light, cold, drifting rain. There was no need to make her plod look slow and painful. Her aches and bruises saw to that. She was once more invisible, one of the wretched who drew no attention from the few passers-by encountered. At the station she bought a third-class ticket and then went outside again to seek the warmth of coffee from the stall. She was not wearing a veil but her bruised face evoked no curiosity or comment from the cabmen and others clustered there. A woman such as she appeared to be must expect beating by her husband as her unquestioned lot. Memory of the pathetic gratitude of a derelict, for whom she bought a mug and slice of bread and dripping, haunted her on the train.

It was little after eight when Mrs. Singleton met her on the Clapham platform. The lodging house in which she had spent the night was close by, a well-kept decent place, owned by a sister of one of the station-porters. This landlady looked surprised by Florence's appearance, when she opened the door to them, but she did not deny her entrance. Mrs. Singleton asked for a ewer of warm water to be sent up to the room she had stayed in and then brought Florence there. Her portmanteau was waiting.

Fifteen minutes were enough for the transformation. Sponge-bathed, perfumed, hair arranged, clad now in her travelling dress and cloak, Florence was ready to enter through Raymond's front-door as a lady, not through the kitchen as a supplicant. Mrs. Singleton's brother, a printer, she said, lived in Clerkenwell and Florence gave her two sovereigns so she could visit him and his family. She could stay the night with them if she wished and she did not need to return to the Southsea villa until tomorrow evening. She could take the char's clothing with her. The lodging-house's maid could make a brown-paper parcel for it. Florence would keep the portmanteau with her, for it contained what she would need for an overnight stay in London. Then it was time to pay the landlady, who was surprised by Florence's metamorphosis, tip the maid and ask her to fetch a cab.

To Western Lodge, on Clapham Common.

Wearing her dark veil.

*

Raymond was at home. He came hurrying to the entrance hall behind the footman who had gone to announce her arrival.

"Thank God," he said "I thought that –"

"That I might be dead? It's no thanks to you that I'm not." She had intended to be calm but she could not keep the anger from her voice. "I trusted you, Mr. Raymond, I trusted you and you failed me."

He did not rise to it. "I can't excuse it. I'm not going to try. We can talk about it in my study."

"Nobody came to the Shoreham station, did they?" she said when she was seated. "Nobody to follow me at a distance, nobody to guard me, nobody who saw who met me there."

"The man I sent arrived late. It was as simple as that. He shouldn't have, and the train he took shouldn't have been delayed, but there it is. There was no sign of you when he reached there."

274

"I was well on my way to France by then. Do know where I've been? You've heard of the assassination of that French minister, have you? I was there when it happened."

She raised her veil, saw his horror and surprise.

"How did that —"

"I'm not telling the story twice. I'll tell it when we see Admiral Topcliffe. Wherever he is, bring me to him."

He didn't argue. After he left her, she could hear the telephone bell ringing, not once, but half-a-dozen times in the next twenty minutes. Topcliffe, once more, was not easy to reach. The footman brought her coffee and the *Times* and *Morning Post*. They were still warm from smoothing with a clothes-iron. She leafed through them as she waited. There was nothing new about the Nile campaign but endless speculation about the murder of the French minister. Civilisation itself was under attack, one editorial said. Nihilism threatened its foundations and recognised no borders.

Raymond came back. "He'll see us. I've ordered the clarence."

It proved an uncomfortable journey, for her anger had not faded, and she answered his attempts to make conversation with monosyllables. She had dropped her veil again, embarrassed for her face to be seen when she looked out the window. They bowled north across the river, through Chelsea and on to Kensington, and into a street of splendid houses there. She saw name at the corner, Queensberry Place, and they stopped half-way up it.

The same grizzled old seaman whom she had seen before opened the door. They were expected, he said. She had a sense that this house was occupied, used daily, guarded perhaps but not lived in, immaculately clean, no dustsheets, the smell of beeswax, closed doors, distant voices, the ringing of an unseen telephone machine and the faint tapping of a typewriter.

Topcliffe's office was at the rear, in what must once have been the dining room. Spacious and high-ceilinged, it looked out through bay windows to a courtyard garden. The room had a sense of impersonal order and neatness, huge framed maps on two walls, a row of cabinets on the third, a large conference table, Topcliffe's desk in one corner. He rose from it when they entered, did not shake hands, gestured to the chairs before him. He made no comment, expressed no sympathy, when she raised her veil.

"Tell me what happened," he said.

She took her time, left nothing out, was not interrupted, knew she would be brought back over it again and questioned, detail by detail. She thought that she saw Topcliffe show a flash of recognition when she mentioned Colonel Fournier, but he let it pass. When she finished, he said, "I fear we'll have to work through luncheon. You won't object, will you Mrs. Dawlish?" He pressed the button of electric bell and the old seaman appeared. "The usual," he said. "For three."

"Do you understand who this minister was?" he asked Florence, when the door was closed again.

"Monsieur Gauthier. Minister of Agriculture," she said. "Livitski didn't have a high opinion of him."

"Probably because he was trying to buy Gauthier, and the price was already high, and rising further. That was probably why Livitski had the ambassador invite him to Dieppe, away from Paris, to clinch the deal."

"What sort of deal?"

"Support of a Franco-Russian Alliance. It'll aim to contain Germany but no good will come of it for Britain either. We know that Gauthier had opposed it, not out of principle but out of greed. In the National Assembly he commanded support as corrupt as himself to block it until it was made worth their while. He wasn't a man to shed too many tears over, Mrs. Dawlish."

Yet at the last moment he had not flinched. He'd had that much good in him.

The old seaman was back with a large basket. He set out a starched white cloth at one end of the conference table, silverware, china, a cold buffet lunch, then left.

"You might give us the example, Mrs. Dawlish," Topcliffe gestured to it. "Would you lead the way, if you please?"

276

And afterwards the interrogation began, as she had expected. Both men asked questions but it was Topcliffe who asked about the white-haired patriarch at Newhaven.

"Would you recognise him if you saw him again, Mrs. Dawlish?"

She could not be certain. Topcliffe scribbled on a piece of paper, rang the bell. "Hand this to Mr. MacQuaid," he said, when the old man came.

"And the two others, the assassins, would you recognise them?" Topcliffe asked Florence.

"Probably. They were sitting close. And I won't forget the young woman's face when that French colonel killed her. It was as bad as anything I'd seen in Thrace."

Topcliffe shrugged. "A hazard of her profession. She knew what she was doing."

A knock on the door and a man of about forty entered. Civilian attire, but with the bearing of a military or naval officer. He was carrying an armful of large bound volumes. The hand on his right arm was covered with a black glove, the leather stretched smooth. From the stillness of the fingers as he laid the volumes down, Florence guessed that the hand was artificial.

"You asked for these, Sir."

"Leave them on the table, if you please, Mr. MacQuaid. That will be all for now."

He left.

"By the way, I'm pleased that Livitski thinks highly of me, Mrs. Dawlish," Topcliffe said. "The compliment's returned. Did you have an impression that he was surprised by the package's contents?"

"No." She paused. She had gone over this again and again in her mind. "And, though I can't be sure, I don't think he was surprised when he met me walking near the Casino either. He could not have been sure that what Brassard had offered for sale was genuine. I think he must have specified to Brassard that it had to be I who would bring them. Brassard would have liked the idea because he'd have thought it would

277

guarantee credibility. He didn't suspect that for Livitski it would prove the opposite."

"Livitski talked about Hugo as if he was somebody else. Did you believe him?"

"I can't be sure. But he promised that Hugo would tell Brassard that I had delivered the papers to him. Why would he promise that?"

"Maybe because you might suffer if Brassard wasn't convinced. Maybe because he was concerned for you, Mrs. Dawlish. He's due that much credit."

"You said that Livitski showed you only five blueprints," Raymond said. "You'd given eleven to Mrs. Bellamy. But he might have taken the other six from the package when he found it."

"No," Florence said. "They weren't in the package I carried. I'm sure of that. It was lighter than when I'd handed it to Mrs. Bellamy."

Raymond laughed. "Bellamy and Brassard are old hands at this sort of thing. They're holding the rest back, probably the later-dated ones, those that look like the final design. And if Hugo doesn't care whether they're genuine or not, they'll hear from him soon. They'll want a higher price."

Topcliffe gestured to the three volumes that MacQuaid had left on the table. "Let's see if you can identify some faces, Mrs. Dawlish."

They were folio-sized. He looked at the spines, chose the second.

"This is the important one," he said and flipped it open.

Florence saw that it was a photograph album. He turned pages over. Many were blank, others contained only one or two images, but a paper pasted beneath each identified a name and other details beside. The arrangement must be alphabetical. Many of the sepia photographs were faded to little more than mists but others looked sharper, more recent. In several, faces stared directly at the camera, boards with chalked numbers held beneath their chins.

"Who are these people?" She suspected that she already knew.

"Members of the exile community here. Nihilists and socialists – they're mainly Russian. Old Paris Communards who daren't go home. Irish Fenians who're keeping their heads down for now. Anarchists, usually from Spain and Italy. And a few like Brassard who'll undertake anything for anybody if the price is right and if he doesn't have to set foot in France."

"And maybe even an American gentleman who can make himself useful on occasion." Raymond was smiling.

Topcliffe glared at him, said nothing.

"If they're dangerous, why aren't they arrested?" Florence said.

"The majority are harmless. They eke out livings however they can, argue endlessly over abstract theories, fall out among themselves, break up into factions, print pamphlets to smuggle into Russia, talk and dream about revolutions they'll never do anything concrete to bring about. But a few are dangerous, very dangerous, and they're in this particular volume."

"The people that Livitski said that Britain should no longer tolerate? Whom he'd be willing to help you deal with?"

"We'll do that if and when it suits us, not before, and not at Russian convenience. Many of them can be useful in the meantime." Topcliffe was leafing forward, then stopped. "Do you recognise anybody on this page?"

A single photograph, taken in an expensive studio, perhaps even Locatelli's. Potted plants and a painted backdrop of an Arcadian scene. Seated in a carver chair, chin resting on one hand, a book open in the other, face tilted up as if in meditation. Benign dignity and wisdom, suited to a silver frame on an adoring son's or daughter's mantlepiece.

The patriarch.

"That man," Florence said. "He was at Newhaven. I've no doubt of it. Who is he?"

"Kniaz, that's Prince, Fyodor Pavlovich Obruchev," Topcliffe said. "Well-received here in high social circles, adored by some hostesses. They love and indulge him as a curiosity and he sponges off them. He translates Russian literature into English and he's reputed for decades now to be writing a magnum opus of his own. He hates what he comes from, one of the empire's greatest families, and he claims to have lived as a peasant for two years. That was before he found the joys of conspiracy and terror. Not that he ever pulled a trigger or threw a bomb himself, or ever will. He always has dupes to do it for him."

"Like that young pair in Dieppe?"

"Like them, like others before them. Mainly from a group called Narodnaya Volya. It means 'People's Will'. They murdered Czar Alexander and numerous officials besides. But Obruchev was gone from Russia by then, in comfortable exile here, and the assassins all hanged. While he's been here, there's never been evidence enough to arrest or deport him. Regrettable though it is, British Law is strict about things like that."

"And long may it continue!" Raymond said. "The respectable foreign resident deserves protection."

Topcliffe looked at his watch. "We need to make arrangements for tomorrow. Can you stay overnight in London, Mrs. Dawlish?"

"I assumed that you might suggest that I see Mrs. Bellamy."

He made no comment.

"I've brought a portmanteau," she said. "I can stay."

"Have you a preferred hotel?"

"The Charing Cross. They have a telephone there, and I heard one ringing here. May I have a room booked?"

Another scribble on a paper, the old seaman summoned again. A booking would be made.

"These two," Topcliffe indicated the other albums. "Those in them are lesser people, gullible and stupid. Just pawns. I'd appreciate it, Mrs. Dawlish, if you can go through the photographs to see if you can recognise the two assassins. The French don't seem to have identified them. Their press would have been full of it if they had."

She was given a small bare room to work in, bars across the window, a small table and four chairs, nothing else. It was easy to imagine interviews conducted there.

Most of the photographs were official, the notes below them indicating that they had been registered as aliens, but not detained. Some faces, both male and female, were haggard, old before their years, marked by suffering. The slums of London's East End, where so many were noted to be dwelling, might well seem a paradise compared with what they had endured in Czarist gaols or in Siberia. Others, younger, still had an air of arrogant confidence about them as they stared into the camera. Under a few of these, the notes recorded arrests. In fewer still, deportation. The affiliations most noted were Nihilist, Anarchist and Socialist. PW – People's Will – was rare, but always underlined for emphasis.

But a smaller proportion of the photographs were private, studio portraits like that of Prince Obruchev, or the obvious work of private amateurs, family groups among them. Florence wondered how they had come here, stolen perhaps, or traded by some false friend in need of money. A few looked comfortable, even affluent. Notes indicated employment of some as translators or language teachers. It was easy to imagine the ideals that had driven them fading over the years, a slow lapse into contented and harmless respectability, dreams of revolution long forgotten.

And then a face. Florence could not be sure, for the photograph was faded, but it could be that of the young woman who had thrown the bombs. She noted the name and moved on, found two other photographs of equally low quality that might be her either. A half-dozen young men looked like the gunman. Sunken cheeks, lank hair and wispy beards seemed almost like a uniform. She could not be sure of any of them either.

Almost at the end of last page of the first volume, Florence recognised her, had no doubt of it. She was in a white dress, holding a large-brimmed summer hat and sitting on a cast-iron bench in a well-tended garden, a handsome young man, not the gunman, standing behind, one hand on her shoulder. Both were smiling. The paper slip below identified her. Lebedeva, Yelena Ivanovna, born in Saratov, 1859. The letters PW, but with a question mark behind. A piano teacher, with an address in Battersea. Brother Oleg shown also, born 1862. Another hand had added to the note that he had been killed by his own bomb in a failed attempt to assassinate a judge in Minsk in October 1883.

Florence began on the next album, could be faster now that she had identified the bomb thrower. Several of the photographs could have been the gunman. Taken years before, the subjects would have aged by now and she had to make allowance for that. It was more than an hour before she saw him in a police photograph taken in London eighteen months before. Morozov, Yuri Grigorovich, born in Ryazan, 1853. PW with no question mark. Lodging in Whitechapel, undertakes translations. To be kept under observation, the note said.

If that was so, then somebody had failed, and failed badly.

She went back to Topcliffe's office and handed him the names. He thanked her, asked if she was sure, made no further comment. Raymond had already left, he said, had things to organise.

"Must I go to the *Temple de la Beauté* in the morning?"

"No. It's better you return home after you've helped with some other business tomorrow. Bellamy and Brassard will probably be hearing soon from Hugo about the missing drawings. Depending on what he may or may not mention about Livitski's involvement, they may want you to deliver them. We must wait until they contact you to do so."

The assumption that she would comply angered her.

"I could have been killed. Not just by the bombs, but by Hugo or anybody else," she said. "I'd assumed that I'd be followed and guarded. And I wasn't."

"It'll be arranged." Topcliffe's tone indicated no willingness to discuss it further. "Mr. MacQuaid, Major MacQuaid in fact, but it's preferable not to use his rank, will be handling this business. He'll have some measures put in hand before we meet tomorrow. You'll get a message at the hotel before you breakfast. And now, Mrs. Dawlish," he stood to walk her the door, "a cab is coming to bring you to your hotel."

282

Chapter 27

She woke in the early hours, troubled by the thought that she was in the same hotel where she had consented with so little thought, and such over-confidence, to help Agatha avenge Mrs. Chalmers-Bolger. It had been the first unthinking step into the ever-deepening morass in which Topcliffe found her useful – as useful as Mrs. Bellamy believed she was also – and from which he might never extract her.

In your own best interest, Mrs. Dawlish. She remembered his words and they haunted her. *In your husband's also.*

Sleep would not come now, she knew, and the fears would grow and gnaw. She turned up the gaslight, wrapped herself in her robe and sat in an armchair to read.

Just after five o'clock a slight sound alerted her to an envelope being pushed beneath the door.

The day's instructions.

*

She slipped a half-crown to a waiter, told him that for certain reasons – he must be a man of the world, she said, and he'd understand – she wanted to leave the hotel by a back entrance. He took her through the kitchen and a door opening on to Villiers Street. And there, as timed for five to ten, a clarence was waiting, blinds drawn. The door opened as she approached and she stepped inside.

"Good morning, Mrs. Dawlish." MacQuaid rose as she entered.

"Where are we going?"

"Hoxton. The address there will be used once only."

Conversation was artificial and formal, mainly observations about the weather which could not be drawn out for long. She knew he'd confide nothing about himself or what he did, and she would do the same. It would not have mattered anyway, she suspected. He probably knew as much about her already as he did of those in his albums and records.

283

It took some forty minutes, for traffic was heavy in mid-morning, but at last the carriage slowed, made a sharp turn that necessitated coming almost to a halt. The sound of a heavy gate being opened, then the vehicle moved forward and stopped again as the gates behind were closed.

MacQuaid handed her down. They were in a walled courtyard with stacks of bricks and timber, a dray standing idle, bulging sacks in an open fronted lean-to, stables in one corner. At the back of a three-storey house, it must be a building contractor's storage area. They passed in through a deserted kitchen, though cooking smells told that it been in recent use. The now-familiar old seaman was there to lead them to the floor above. The wallpaper, floor-druggets and framed lithographs indicated a family-home of modest affluence but there was no sign of any resident.

Topcliffe was waiting in what must be the parlour. He thanked Florence for coming and led her to the furthest left of the four armchairs arranged in a semi-circle before a welcome coal fire.

"I'll wait below," MacQuaid said, and left.

Topcliffe seated himself next to her and she took the opportunity she had hoped for.

"Where is my husband, Admiral?"

"I don't know, Mrs. Dawlish." The nearest she had ever seen of sympathy in his tone and eyes. "He's in the Sudan somewhere. He's doing his duty. If I could, I would tell you more. I wouldn't hesitate. I know that I can rely on you for confidentiality."

"It's about General Gordon, isn't it?"

"Yes. He's perhaps Gordon's last hope."

"I thought the expedition up the Nile was Gordon's last hope?"

"No. It started too late. There's a good chance that it will not reach Khartoum in time. But Captain Dawlish might."

"He's not with the expedition then, is he?" She was glad that she had not raised her veil. He couldn't see her welling tears, though he must hear the tremble in her voice.

"He's taking another route, with a small party. But –" He hesitated. "But I must tell you that nothing's been heard of him for two months."

The answer she had feared and had expected.

"There's still hope, Mrs. Dawlish. He's a resourceful man and –"

"I won't give up hope." A sudden memory of him arriving at the caravanserai in Thrace when all seemed lost. "I won't give up hope."

A knock on the door, MacQuaid's head appearing around it.

"The gentleman is here, sir."

"Bring him in please."

The patriarch.

I chose the correct photograph. This is the man I saw at Newhaven.

He moved with solemn dignity, as one used to respect and admiration, a topcoat with a velvet collar open to show a dark well-tailored suit, white shirt, grey silk Ascot secured with a golden pin. But for the flowing white locks, he might have been a successful banker. Topcliffe stood to meet him, hand extended.

"So good of you to meet at short notice, Prince," he said, his tone courteous. "I trust you weren't collected at an inconvenient hour?"

"No inconvenience, sir, no inconvenience." Obruchev's smile was tolerant and benign as he took Topcliffe's proffered hand. "I believe we may have dined together at Lady Penhallow's. A pleasure to meet you again, sir." His accent was that of a cultivated English gentleman. He inclined his head towards Florence "And the lady, sir, might I perhaps have the honour?"

"Let's say, Mrs. Smith."

Florence made no acknowledgement and did not rise. The carnage in the Casino was impossible to forgive.

MacQuaid helped him take off his topcoat and lay it aside. Topcliffe invited him to take the armchair to his right. MacQuaid, with a reporter's notebook and a pencil, took the fourth.

"A rather unpleasant business last week in Dieppe, Prince," Topcliffe said. "And tragic for Monsieur Gauthier."

Obruchev did not react.

"Tragic too for Mr. Yuri Morozov. A promising young man by all accounts. And for Miss Yelena Lebedeva. She was a talented musician, I understand, a good teacher of the piano."

Again, the Prince was silent, but the smile was gone, his jaws set.

"Protegees of yours, were they not, Prince?"

"The names mean nothing to me."

"No?" Florence ignored the glance from Topcliffe that told her to stay silent. "You're a cowardly liar, Prince." The dam that restrained the anger and bitterness she had felt for days was breaching. "I saw you give them your blessing in Newhaven. Poor dupes you sent to do murder, and to their own deaths. I saw you there, and that creature Brassard too, and I'll swear to it."

"I assure you, madam, that I was never in –"

"Let's be frank about all this, Prince." Topcliffe cut him off. "Let me mention three other names you know. Leonid Abramovich Kalganov, perhaps? A law student before he fled Russia in '81. A piano tuner now. You recommended his services as such, last year, to your friend Lady Shepstowe."

A shake of the head.

"Tatiana Constantinova Yaroslavskaya? A talented watercolourist who lives in Brixton and sells her work door to door?"

Blood draining for his face now.

"And Vladimir Mikhailovich Yurenev? An unpleasant young man, living off the immoral earnings of two women in Whitechapel so he can have the leisure to scribble pamphlets?"

"I regret that you are misinformed, sir." Obruchev's tongue was darting over his lips. "I don't recognise any of those names."

"Mr. MacQuaid?" Topcliffe glanced towards him.

"I had a chat with Mr. Kalganov last evening," MacQuaid said. "He knows you well, he said, Prince. There's a warrant outstanding against him in Russia – a bomb attack that failed to kill the governor of Tver province but blew off a policemen's legs. He's most unwilling to go back. We've enough to deport him and he'll swear to anything to avoid it."

"I believe you talked to Miss Yaroslavskaya last evening also," Topcliffe said.

"A rather sad young woman," MacQuaid leafed through his notebook and consulted a page. "She's concerned about her brother. He's in not-uncomfortable internal-exile in a village on the River Lena in Siberia, but he's consumptive. She's frightened that a word from us to the Russian Embassy about her activities here might lead to him being sent to hard labour. She knows that it would kill him."

"And Yurenev, Mr MacQuaid?" Topcliffe spoke as if he didn't know.

"He's in a cell in Bethnal Green police station since last evening. His two women have admitted that he was living off them and there are other witnesses. There's enough to have him deported immediately as an undesirable alien. I mentioned to him that the regular service from Tilbury to St. Petersburg will be departing tomorrow."

Then a long silence. Florence was pleased to see sweat on Obruchev's brow, his lower lip trembling, his pudgy hands gripping the arms of the chair. The embers in the grate rustled and settled. MacQuaid reached out for the tongs, used it to add a few lumps of coal from the brass scuttle and sat down again.

Obruchev spoke at last. "I know none of those people. I've told you that already." His voice was bordering on a croak.

"But they know you, Prince," Topcliffe said. "They've all agreed to swear to it. Don't despise them for it. They have good reasons. Mr. MacQuaid has statements from all three that you tried to commit them to what you call 'Propaganda of the Deed', and we call murder. They'll swear that Morozov and Lebedeva, who put your suggestion into action at Dieppe, were present too."

"I deny everything they say."

"Deny it as much as you like, Prince," Topcliffe said, "but if you do, I'll present these people's statements to the Home Secretary this afternoon, and one from Mrs. Smith also about what she saw at Newhaven. He'll sign the deportation order and you'll be departing from Tilbury tomorrow."

Florence saw a soul in terror and felt no pity.

"I suspect it'll be Sakhalin, Prince," Topcliffe said. "A dreadful place, I believe, worse than Siberia. Perhaps chained to a wheelbarrow and moving broken stone. But be consoled that it won't be for long. I don't imagine that you'll last more than a month."

"What do you want of me?" A whisper.

"A signed statement about your dealings with Mr. Brassard. Especially regarding what happened in Dieppe. Nothing more. Not for now, at least."

"I can assist you with the statement, Prince," MacQuaid said. "And an attorney's waiting in another room to see to attestation. It'll be a full affidavit."

"What happens if I sign?"

"Your admirers here won't know of it." Topcliffe was smiling. "They'll still vie for invitations to meet you at Lady Penhallow's soirees. They'll still flock to your lectures on the Russian Soul and they'll still subscribe towards a book you'll never complete and may not indeed have started. Lady Shepstowe won't evict you from those chambers in the Albany that she pays for. And you'll be welcome to keep contact with your revolutionary admirers. Just as long as you keep us informed of anything they have in mind."

Obruchev was weeping. A soft, snivelling, cowardly old man.

"I'll do it," he said

*

After Florence had completed her statement and had taken an oath on it, formally witnessed by the attorney whom MacQuaid had waiting, Topcliffe wanted to see her again.

"Bellamy will contact you," he said. "I've no doubt of it. I don't know when, but it'll be soon. She'll have instructions. Obey them to the letter."

"I was promised protection last time," she said. "I was let down."

He ignored her resentment. "Do you employ a gardener, Mrs. Dawlish?"

"A man comes in two days a week for gardening and odd jobs"

"Tell him he's not needed for the next three weeks. Pay him for it. You'll be reimbursed. You have a garden shed I presume?"

"Yes, a small one."

"You'll have a full-time gardener from tomorrow. He'll sleep in the shed. He's a professional, one of ours, and he's used to worse. If Bellamy gives you instructions, this man, not you, Mrs. Dawlish, will be the one to let us know. By telegram or telephone, he'll keep Mr. MacQuaid and Mr. Raymond informed."

He stood up and looked at his watch.

"You'll be taken to Waterloo station in time to catch the four fifty-five to Portsmouth. And thank you, Mrs. Dawlish. You've been most useful."

The word stayed with her in the train, and it smarted.

Useful.

*

Florence's regular gardener was grateful when she told him her concern about him working outside in the continuing bad weather. There had been rain most days, and sometimes sleet. He was elderly and had had pleurisy two years before. He was even more thankful when she paid him in advance for three weeks of rest at home.

It was raining again later that day when Cook came to see her.

"There's a man at the back door, ma'am," she said. "He says he's hungry and he has nowhere to go. He says you was kind to him once, and that you'll remember him."

When she saw him, she didn't, but she acted as if she did.

"You came up to my husband one day in Portsmouth, I think. I was with him," she said. "You had served under him. Your name is –"

"Dawson, ma'am, Sim Dawson. With the captain in Ashanti, ma'am, ten years since."

289

The agreed identification.

"I was down on me luck, ma'am, you gave me a shilling, never forgot it ma'am." Voice whining. "And times is still hard ma'am, even if I did give up the drink long since, God's holy word, I did."

Water was dripping from his rags on to the kitchen flags and he had edged so close to the range that steam was rising from him. He was fifty at least, worn, grey, unshaven and filthy, but perhaps still too well-fed for the role he played. A worn carpet bag lay at is feet.

Florence turned to Cook. "Give this poor man something to warm him up. And then a good hot meal. It's what the captain would want."

"God bless you, ma'am."

"Where have you been sleeping?"

"In a doorway last night, ma'am, but a constable moved me on. An' then I thought of you ma'am, how folk talk well about you an' –"

She turned again to Cook. "We can't leave this unfortunate man out in this weather. It'll kill him. Perhaps he could stay a few nights in the shed until it gets better."

"But, ma'am –"

"No buts, Cook. It's our Christian duty."

Susan, the maid, had appeared, was regarding the saturated wretch with alarm.

"There's an old mattress in the lumber room, I think," Florence said to her. "Let's put it in the shed, and a few old blankets too."

"God bless you, ma'am," Dawson said, "an' the captain too."

"You'll stay in the shed, Sim. Not in the house, mind, and only for a few days. Keep the outside privy decent and no bothering Cook or Susan either You know what I mean, don't you? They'll see you're fed and there'll be some jobs to do in the garden."

The back garden only, walled, screened from the street.

She left Dawson stammering thanks, Cook far from happy and Susan frightened.

It didn't matter.

She had her line of contact to MacQuaid and to Raymond.

*

She passed the next nine days in uneasy wait for a summons that might never come. The bruises on her face faded enough for her to venture, still veiled, to the Seaman's Rest and to immerse herself in administrative details there. They might have seemed onerous at any other time but now provided welcome diversion. She declined several invitations to tea but did walk almost daily on the Esplanade, and once to Mudie's Circulating Library in Albert Road to change her books. Her concern for Nicholas was greater since Topcliffe had indicated, with apparent truthfulness, that his present whereabouts were unknown. She spent several afternoons in second-hand bookshops, seeking out items he would enjoy, history especially. When he returned, she would have a box of them that he could bring when he next went to sea. She had to believe that he would.

It was early December now. That the weather did not improve made it easier to justify Sim Dawson's presence in the shed. He was no bother, Cook said after the second day, and he was always thankful, always willing to undertake chores. She wondered if there were any of the captain's old-clothes that he wouldn't miss and Florence said yes, there were things that should have been given away years before. When she brought them out to the shed herself, she was surprised just how comfortable he had made himself. Cook had found an unused kerosene lamp for him and a pile of old newspapers and magazines which he sat reading in the evenings.

Other than his initial words of identification, he made no reference to his duty and he knuckled his forehead in gratitude whenever he saw Florence. And yet, however unobtrusive, however almost-invisible, he might be, his presence was a reminder that the nightmare was not yet over and, worse still, that she was just a pawn in it.

The days passed until at last the summons came. Susan, was leaving a grocer's with purchases, early on a Tuesday afternoon, when an unknown woman handed her an envelope. The message was similar to that before. Money, clothes and necessities for four days. A station

291

platform at nine o'clock that evening, the only difference being that it was at Lewes, not Shoreham. Brassard was lazy, she realised. Lewes was on a direct line from London and only a few miles from Newhaven. He was not inconveniencing himself by meeting her at some station such as Shoreham that would necessitate him changing trains. She did not doubt that she would be on a night packet to Dieppe. Hugo, she suspected, had a liking for the Casino, might use it often for such meetings.

She had expected this call, had stiffened her resolve to meet it with courage when it came, but fear still washed through her, would not go away, now that it had. She had been hurt badly last time. Now, it might be as bad again, or worse.

Her portmanteau had been packed for days. All that remained was for Sim Dawson to earn his pay, to slip out through the back lane to telegraph or telephone MacQuaid and Raymond that she was on her way.

Chapter 28

Florence stepped on to the station platform at Lewes at half-past eight. Sleet was drumming on the canopy above and, knowing that she would find a coal fire there, she headed for the first-class waiting room. So too did a half-dozen other arrivals, likely as herself, she thought, to be bound for Dieppe. The train from London to Newhaven, with mail and passengers for the night crossing, was due in just under an hour. She scanned the faces, mainly of businessmen, for few travelled for pleasure at this season. She wondered if the guard she had been promised was among them. It was possible that protection had followed her from Portsmouth. If not, there must surely be somebody coming to watch her. The assurance of safety had been hollow before and fear that it might be so again nagged her.

She went outside again just before nine, the appointed meeting time. The wind was icy, knifing beneath the canopy and along the deserted platform. Feigning interest in the posters there, she walked back and forth to stay warm. Ten minutes passed. A local service was due soon.

Now an office door was opening, a figure emerging.

"It's better that you stay inside, ma'am, on a night like this."

His uniform identified him as the station master. She heard the mix of urgency and concern in his voice, and saw it on his face. Somebody, somebody like her perhaps, a veiled woman, troubled, might well have thrown herself beneath a train here and he would never forget it.

"First Class, isn't it, ma'am?" He had taken in her clothing. "Just let me show you the waiting room, ma'am, it's just this way."

"Florence! I'm so sorry to be late!"

She turned, saw Brassard hurrying towards her. He was carrying a travelling bag.

"My sister always frets so," he said to the official, his words a little slurred. "She worships punctuality." He reached for her elbow, nodded towards the waiting room. "We'll be warm there, my dear."

Even before they entered, she could smell the drink. He guided her towards a padded bench where there were several empty places. They sat. Nobody took any notice of them.

"It's Dieppe, isn't it?" She kept her voice low, could not disguise her loathing. "Something for Hugo again, I presume? Whatever you've got for him, give it to me now and then get out of my sight."

"It's Dieppe." A quaver in his tone. He passed her a train ticket. First class from here to Newhaven, one and threepence. "It's Dieppe. I'm coming with you."

"Why?" She had not expected this, felt sick.

"Hugo wants to see me. Not just you alone." He glanced around to see if anybody was looking at them. Satisfied that none was, he reached to his bag and fumbled with the clasps. His hands were trembling. "It's better that you carry this." A large, thick brown envelope.

"Is it too heavy for you, Mr. Brassard?"

"Keep your voice down." His eyes were flitting around, searching for listeners. "It's better that you carry it."

"I thought that Hugo had some influence with the French customs?"

"Be quiet, woman! Just take it." He thrust it towards her.

She took it, slipped it in her bag.

"You're frightened," she said. "Why's that, Mr. Brassard?"

His jaw clenched and he said nothing but she sensed that he would have struck her if he could. Her hand rose almost involuntarily to touch her hat-pin. To a woman, even a coward could be dangerous.

They sat in silence until the train arrived. When it did, she found a place apart from him.

*

She stalked away from him when he approached her at the Newhaven Quayside station. She purchased a ticket for a first-class single cabin. Brassard was still waiting to do so also, a half-dozen others in line ahead of him. She did not look back and went on alone up the gangway, felt

294

that the wind, blasting from the north east, held the promise of snow. It pleased her that the stewardess she had met before was on duty. It would be a rough crossing tonight, the good woman told her, but there'd be nothing to worry about, she'd seen worse before. She remembered that Florence liked marmalade with her toast and she would put two extra blankets on her bed.

The pitch and roll were powerful through the night, the paddles' thrash uneven as they lifted from the water, then plunged again to send shudders rippling through the hull. Florence slept only fitfully, was thankful that she was not prone to sea-sickness and hoped that Brassard was. If so, he deserved it. She sought reasons why he too should be crossing. There must be more to it than a simple delivery of the envelope. From its size and weight, it was likely to contain the drawings held back before. She could have brought it alone. Her name would have been a guarantee that the plans of the Dawlish cam were genuine, to Hugo at least, if not to Livitski, if he was involved. But Hugo, whoever he was, wanted Brassard to be there too…

It was after ten in the morning, hours late, when the packet docked at Dieppe, running in between the harbour's protective piers after standing off, bow-on to the waves, until the wind had abated somewhat. Florence only came on deck when the vessel was secured and saw that the sky was leaden grey and that light snow was falling. She did not look for Brassard and engaged a porter, glad to pass into the chill protection of the customs hall. This time the officer did not ask her name or order her to open her portmanteau. He scribbled on it with chalk and motioned her through. There was no option now but to wait for Brassard. She looked back, saw him still in line, looking pale and ill and frightened. The customs officers were only going through the motions of inspection, spending little more time on other passengers than they had spent on her. On this cold morning, their only thought must be of escaping back to a warm office.

Brassard reached the inspection table. She could not hear him but he looked obsequious as he replied to some question from the official. He was no less fawning in his thanks when he was waved forward without further examination. He saw her standing by the exit, came towards her.

"What now?" she said.

"Just wait. We'll be collected." He still looked frightened.

Other passengers were moving past them to the line of cabs outside. The snow was falling more heavily now. Two or three inches lay on the ground already and was casting white cloaks over the tarpaulins on the horses' backs. There were fewer hotel employees holding placards than previously, none from the Casino. Loaded, the cabs rolled away one by one. A small crowd of passengers was still gathered in the shelter of the hall's exit. One or more of Raymond's people must be among them, Florence thought. She could not allow herself to think otherwise. It was impossible to guess if any were. All were as well muffled as herself, even the scattering of women.

A thickset man entered, beating snow off his topcoat, all but his eyes hidden by a scarf. He stopped, looked at those still waiting, his glance sweeping past Florence and Brassard, then returning to them again. He came over.

"L'ami de Monsieur Hugo?" he said to Brassard.

"Oui."

"Suivez-moi."

He led them out, past the cabs, around a corner, down an alleyway. Florence's porter was expostulating. It was too far, he wanted more money, she guessed. The Frenchman snarled at him, shoved a few coins in his hand, took Florence's portmanteau and sent him off.

A four-wheeler, a single wretched snow-cloaked horse between its shafts, waited in a courtyard behind a house. The driver stepped out and helped Florence enter. Brassard and their guide followed. The driver mounted the box and the vehicle lurched into motion.

She sat in a corner, facing forward, keeping her distance from Brassard on her left. The Frenchman pulled the blinds down, sat facing them, and showed no inclination to talk. The coach was moving at a walk, snow deadening the rumble on the cobbles. It turned, once sharply, then more gently. Sounds from without, fewer than in more clement weather, indicated that they were passing through town streets. Florence was alarmed. The route to the Casino had run along a park, which must be deserted now. This was not it. She released the blind. It rolled up to show shops and a few muffled figures toiling along snow-covered pavements, heads bent against the white swirl that was even thicker now.

"Ferme-le!" The Frenchman was on his feet, leaning across her, pulling down the blind. "Ne touchez plus!"

Her alarm was fright now, but she knew she must not show it. She turned to Brassard, saw that he was looking away, feigning not to have noticed.

"Will you allow that man to speak to me like this?"

He shrugged, said nothing.

They lapsed into silence, the Frenchman seemingly as much a stranger to Brassard as he was to her.

The horse's plod slowed, for the snow was deepening. The town's sounds died away. They must be out in the countryside now, no cobbles beneath the wheels, and the vehicle slowed further, and stopped once. Snow must be drifting across the road and the driver could be heard getting down to lead the horse through.

Over an hour passed before halting again. The driver was calling, somebody was answering, followed by the noise of a gate opening. In now, cobbles again. The driver descended, opened the door and helped Florence to step out.

It was an ugly two-storey red-brick villa that stood in a garden separated by iron railings from the road running past. What looked like a small stables and coach-house structure lay at the end of the short driveway along the side. Flanked by similar dwellings, and with others like it across the road, the villa could be the residence of some solid citizen, a doctor or lawyer or a local functionary. This must be a village, close enough to Dieppe to serve as a distant suburb for the affluent, or the summer residence of rich bourgeois Parisians.

The stocky Frenchman led them to the front door through six inches of snow. The man who admitted them, and took their outer garments, could have been his twin. Both gave the same impression of solidity, of strength, of indeterminate age, that Florence associated with naval petty-officers or sergeants of marines.

Brassard spoke to them in fluent French. The fear which had been evident before was gone now and he spoke with a degree of authority that they seemed to accept. He had once been an army officer, Raymond had told Florence. Degraded as he now was, something of the confidence of command still remained.

He turned to Florence.

"Hugo isn't here yet. His train has probably been delayed by the snow. They say there's a room prepared upstairs for you."

"Is there a maid here to help me unpack?" The request was a trivial one but the presence of another woman would be reassuring.

"No maid. And don't leave the room. One of these gentlemen will bring you food on a tray."

The room was sparsely furnished and there were horizontal bars across the single large window. That was usual in nurseries, but Florence felt allocation of this room to her disquieting. There was a fire in the grate however, coal in the scuttle by it and a wing-chair and a comfortable-looking bed. There was little movement on the road outside. Only a few unwilling figures trudging past on essential tasks, children playing with snowballs until dragged away by mothers, an occasional farm cart. Smoke drifting from chimneys told of families confined indoors. The white blanket was deepening over everything. It was impossible to imagine that any of Raymond's people could know that she was here. She felt a surge of panic but fought it down. She went to her door, opened it, saw that the man who had brought her was sitting at the landing and reading a newspaper. He looked up, saw her, said nothing, continued reading, already a bored gaoler. There were bolts on the inside of the door and she closed them. The possibility of Brassard intruding repelled her. Voices outside drew her to the window. The coach was driving out again, turning left towards Dieppe.

Now tired, she lay on the bed. Drifting into sleep, she told herself that conditions here were better than at the police station in the town. She would endure.

Knocking on the door awoke her. She took a poker from the fire-irons, refused to open until she was sure that it was not Brassard there.

"Votre déjeuner, madame."

The man who had opened the hall door was there with bread, cheese, hot coffee and milk on a tray. He seemed not unfriendly and she felt a little foolish to be holding the poker behind her back as he laid it down, then left. The food was welcome and afterwards she sat before the fire. She tried to read the novel she had brought but her mind kept returning to her present situation. There could be no advantage to Hugo to detain or harm her once he had the drawings, she told herself. She would return to England tomorrow. There was nothing to fear. And yet she did.

Soon after four o'clock she heard the carriage return. It halted at the side of the house, so she could not see it, or who left it, but soon after she heard the hall door open, the sound of stamping feet, indistinct voices. Hugo must have arrived. She prepared herself for the inevitable meeting and she would look her best, even if she had not changed from her travelling dress. She tended her hair, decided not to veil. She would wear her fading bruises as notice that she was not cowed. No need for a bag. She would carry the envelope with the plans in her hand.

The summons came a half-hour later, the man who had brought her lunch asking her to follow him downstairs. Then along a short corridor, French voices sounding though an open door. Even before she reached it, the smell of cigars was strong. It was a dining room with sideboards, heavy curtains, paintings, a long table.

Brassard was sitting, facing her, and he half-rose as he saw her. The other man's back was towards her but the oiled ginger hair told her who it was even before he turned.

Colonel Etienne Fournier.

Not in uniform this time.

Hugo.

The butcher.

He drew on his cigar as he looked at her as he might regard a horse or a harlot. His smirk told that he recognised her, that the sight of the bruises pleased him. He bowed in mocking courtesy.

"A pleasure to meet you again, Mrs Dawlish. Your servant madam." His English was only lightly French-accented. "Monsieur Brassard tells me that you've something for me."

"Take it!" She threw the envelope on the table, outside his reach.

His fist clenched but he did not strike.

It was hard to restrain the loathing she had felt ever since that night at the Casino but she would play on as if she had not encountered him previously.

Brassard was showing no surprise.

Livitski has been true to his word. Fournier must have indeed told Brassard that I handed the first package over as agreed. And Brassard probably knows nothing of my meetings with Livitski either.

"Show me the drawings," Fournier said to Brassard. "You've held them back long enough."

"You'd better sit by me, Mrs. Dawlish," Brassard had taken the envelope, was already tearing it open. "The good colonel will have only a few questions for you."

Distasteful as it was, sitting with Brassard put the width of the table between herself and Fournier. At the far end she saw a stack of folded drawings, the notebook with the scuffed leather cover on top, the contents of the first package she had brought across. Livitski had passed everything to Fournier.

Brassard was extracting the blueprints from the envelope, unfolding them, smoothing the creases and laying them on the table, all six, side by side, turned towards Fournier so he could read the title blocks in the bottom right-hand corners. All faded, some frayed at the edges, several stained as if something had been spilled over them, every appearance of intensive past use, no hint that they had been created just weeks before.

"Are there more?" Fournier said to Florence, when he had examined the last. He might have spoken to a scullery maid like this. "Are you holding any more back?"

"They're all I found. I gave everything to Mrs. Bellamy, Mr. Brassard's friend. I swear there are no more."

"You'll swear to somebody else tonight, madame."

"Who?"

It can't be Livitski then. He knows the truth already.

"Who? A gentleman who wants to know that they're genuine." Fournier said. "He'll want to know how I've come by them. How Brassard came by them. How you came by them. Why you've been prepared to trade them." He paused. "And why you're willing to betray your country and your husband."

"You want to humiliate me, don't you?" Anger, not wholly feigned, in her voice. "You know it all already. There's no need to degrade me more, make me confess the shame of it to some other stranger."

"Do you think that I want to be here either? Mrs. Dawlish," Brassard, wheedling. "But it's business, business only. The gentleman will question me no less thoroughly than you. It's normal in such dealings, it's not unreasonable. Nobody wants to pay for something they can't trust." He spoke as if convincing a reluctant child. "You'll never see the gentleman again. Just a few questions. That'll be the end of it. We'll be on the packet to Newhaven in the morning."

"We're wasting time," Fournier said. "You must both be prepared. I know the questions that I'd ask if I were in his place. I'll ask them now. I'll hear your answers. I'll ask them again and I'll keep asking until you reply the way I want."

"And if I don't want?" Florence said.

"Believe me, Mrs. Dawlish," Fournier had raised his hand, was stroking his right cheek, nodding towards the yellowing bruises on hers. "You'll want."

301

Chapter 29

Darkness had fallen by the time she returned to her room. She looked out before lighting the kerosine lamp there. The road outside was unlit, but lights burned in the windows of several houses on the far side, enough to show that the wind had not abated and still carried snow in swirling flurries. Had the window not been barred she would have lowered herself to flee to one of those houses, and beg shelter and protection, for she was badly frightened now. That Fournier was Hugo had changed everything. If it suited him, or whatever he was involved with, he would not shrink from stopping her leaving alive.

A tray with bread, soup and cold meat arrived, but she had little appetite. A miserable hour passed until she heard movement outside. She looked out. A closed carriage, drawn by a pair, was at the gate. Fournier's two helpers were opening it. The vehicle entered, was lost to her sight along the side of these house, then shortly afterwards came sounds from the entrance hall below. Fournier must be welcoming his visitor.

Ten long minutes passed before she was told to come down. While on the stairs, she could smell cigars, hear male voices, forced bonhomie in one of them, Fournier's.

To the dining room. Fournier was bent over the table, pointing out some detail on a blueprint to the man standing next to him. Both with cigars, glasses in hand, the aroma of cognac almost drowned by tobacco smoke. An immediate impression of Fournier desperate to be agreeable, the other aloof. They looked up as she entered. The newcomer was perhaps forty, light-haired, moustache as fiercely spiked as Fournier's, wearing an immaculate tweed suit. What struck her most were the scars, long-healed slashes, on both cheeks. This was no Frenchman. He jerked upright when he saw her. He bowed abruptly, little more than a fast, stiff inclination.

"So, you are Mrs. Dawlish?" Unmistakable German intonation in his English.

"Yes. And you, sir? Whom have I the pleasure of addressing?"

302

"Mr. Robinson will do." He smiled, proud, she saw, of his wit. He turned to Fournier. "Why is this woman's face bruised? Have you forced her to —"

Florence cut him off. "An accident in England. I slipped on ice."

Brassard arrived. He reached out his hand but Robinson ignored it. "I know who you are," he said. "Another fine French patriot."

"Sit there," Fournier said to Florence, and to Brassard, "You there, next to her." He invited Robinson to sit by him, across the table from them, offered him more brandy, was refused.

"Are you not ashamed to be here, Mrs. Dawlish?" Savage contempt in Robinson's voice. "An officer's wife. An honourable man, from all I hear of him." He pointed to the blueprints. "And this is his work, the Dawlish Cam? Work of which he is no doubt proud?"

She was here on pretence, was forced to play a role, but the accusation still hurt. Her own folly and overconfidence had brought her to this.

"I'm being blackmailed." She cast her eyes down as if in embarrassment. "By a friend of this creature Brassard. She discovered that I'd done something very foolish." Her voice dropped to a whisper. "I regretted it immediately but it was too late."

Fournier laughed, nudged Robinson, who shrank ever so slightly from him. "The old story. She doesn't want her husband to know."

Brassard was nodding beside her, sniggering. She was convinced that he did not know the hold that Mrs. Bellamy had over her, that he assumed that it was just about some squalid infidelity. That appalling woman was using him as ruthlessly as Topcliffe was using her.

"Tell Mr. Robinson where you husband is now." Fournier said.

She could see that he enjoyed her humiliation.

This was how the woman taken in adultery must have felt. And nobody is hesitating to cast the first stone.

"My husband's in Egypt."

"And when the cat's away the mice will play. That's the English expression, isn't it, madame?" Fournier said.

She could sense Robinson's distaste, even if Fournier didn't. Head bowed, she dabbed her eyes. "I love my husband." Voice even lower now. "It was only a foolishness. It shouldn't have happened... but... but it would break his heart if he knew."

"But you don't think it will break his heart when he comes home and finds all these papers gone, do you, Mrs. Dawlish?" Robinson said.

"I was hoping that... hoping that whoever bought them might be merciful. That they might have them copied and then give them back to me. Nicholas would never know. It might be years before he opened that old chest again and he'd never suspect that..."

"I regret that cannot be." Something akin to pity in Robinson's tone. He looked at Brassard. "You must be proud of how you make your living."

Brassard tried to laugh. "But you're buying anyway, aren't you?"

"How did you find them, Mrs. Dawlish?" Robinson said.

The same story she had told Topcliffe and Raymond without reserve, and Mrs. Bellamy, Brassard, Livitski and Fournier, with only small adjustments. The forgotten chest in the attic, the old items of uniform, the saved bundles of personal letters, the journal, the drawings. It sounded all the more convincing since most of it was true.

"Previously did you know of the Dawlish Cam?" Robinson said.

"I never heard of it until Mrs. Bellamy mentioned it to me and said it was important. My husband would never talk to me about anything confidential."

"He was testing torpedoes. That you knew?"

"Yes."

She did not have to lie, just told him of Nicholas's days and nights in the Solent in '78 and '79. The sob she choked back was genuine. It touched her to recall how he had so often returned saturated and half-frozen, changing, eating, going to his study afterwards, until the small hours, to write reports. But he had never mentioned details to her. They had married earlier that year and had been so happy together.

"His rough records of the tests are there," Fournier pointed to the notebook lying before Robinson. It was open at one of the pages of recently-forged material towards the back. "You can see her husband's notes, his corrections, his ideas about redesign. The first seven blueprints here are for the earlier versions that didn't work, but the last four are final. Hand them to an expert machinist with a well-equipped workshop and you'll have a working Dawlish Cam within a fortnight"

"You've had one built and tested yourself, have you?" Robinson didn't hide his scorn. "Is it that I must believe?"

"No, but one of our own experts examined everything here," Fournier said. "He's confident about the design."

"An expert? Another traitor like yourself?"

"Does that make him any the less one of the French Navy's torpedo specialists?" Fournier shrugged. "You'll never worry again about your torpedoes maintaining constant running depth, he says. And your navy will have the Dawlish Cam. France's won't."

"And there'll be more," Brassard, ingratiating. "Not as significant as all this perhaps, but maybe other useful information this woman may come by. Her husband will let something drop now and then. She'll be keeping us informed for years to come." He nudged Florence. "You'll be glad to, won't you Mrs. D?"

She sprang to her feet.

"I've had enough!" Her indignation and disgust were unfeigned. "You, Mr. Robinson, or whoever you really are, will you allow a helpless woman to be subjected to more of this? Have you a wife? A mother, sisters, daughters? Are you any better than these two creatures?"

Robinson didn't meet her eyes but he said to Fournier, "All I need to know from this woman, I have heard. She can go. But for him I've some questions." He pointed to Brassard.

Florence moved towards the door and neither of the men standing just outside made any move to stop her. She turned back just before she left.

"I was blackmailed, Mr. Robinson. What else could I do?"

"You could have shot or drowned yourself." All trace of sympathy gone. "That is what an honourable woman, an officer's wife, would do."

She clapped her handkerchief to her eyes and made herself to sob. But, on the stairs back to her room, her heart soared. A foreign power had lusted after Britain's secret, Nicholas's achievement. It was paying a high price for a design that had been so subtly modified that any torpedo guided by it would jump from the water and beat itself to fragments in a succession of dolphin-leaps.

But the highest price of all must be paid by Fournier and Brassard and Mrs. Bellamy.

That was what mattered now.

*

Florence bolted herself into her room again and found that she was less frightened now. She had held her own, and Fournier had not disputed Brassard's suggestion that she could be a source for years to come. The dishonoured Mrs. Dawlish was valuable, a goose who might lay yet more golden eggs. Her life was not in danger and she would be on the steamer to Newhaven tomorrow.

Unless…

The fear was back.

She knew too much now of Fournier. He was a traitor to his country, a man who traded its secrets, who would stand before a firing squad if it were revealed. He would not hesitate …

I placed too much trust in Raymond.

She looked out. Snow was still falling outside, the faintest light cast on the road from the few illuminated windows opposite. A door opened at one house, a man and woman emerging, putting up umbrellas, thanking their hosts, passing out through the gate arm-in-arm, walking slowly to a villa a little beyond, shaking snow from their coats as a housemaid opened its door to them. Florence fancied that they were laughing, and she envied them. She stayed at the window, saw a single carriage toiling past towards Dieppe, carrying local post perhaps. And then, one by one, the lights in the houses were extinguished.

While Robinson was still here, she was still safe, she told herself. But the discussions could not last longer. His loathing for Fournier and Brassard would send him away as soon as the deal was completed. She must be ready. She took the long pin from her hat and thrust it through her piled-up hair, put on her outer coat, drew on her gloves. If she could somehow fight her way outside, cold would also be an enemy and...

Voices from below, from the hallway and even, faintly, from outside. She went to the window, saw that the coach and pair with which Robinson had arrived standing just behind the gates, ready to depart. Looking down, she could see light flooding from the open hall door. Three figures emerged. One was Robinson in a heavy topcoat. He called the driver and handled him a bag and gestured to him to put it inside. Fournier and Brassard extended their hands but Robinson affected not to see them. The driver helped him into the coach and mounted the box. Fournier's two men had difficulty pulling the gates open, for the snow had accumulated beneath them. The driver cracked his whip, the horses strained forward and the coach passed on to the road, turned towards Dieppe and was lost in the falling snow.

The light cast from the hall died as the door was closed. The two men dragging the gates back again were just dark shapes, intent only on getting back quickly to warmth.

They had no awareness of the two figures coming up behind them from the corner of the garden, what looked like bed-sheets thrown over their outer clothing. The gates had been drawn to and Fournier's stooping men were rising after dropping the securing pins. Then the newcomers were on them, arms locking around their necks, pressing something against their faces until they slumped, dragging their limp bodies into the shadows. Fournier's two helpers would have left a side door, maybe the kitchen's, unlocked. Now a sheet-draped figure was pulling one side of the gate partly open, was on the road outside, was beckoning.

Raymond hasn't failed me!

She went to her door, placed her ear against it, could hear muffled voices. They could only be Fournier's and Brassard's for there were no others in the house. She detected no sense of alarm. A peal of laughter now, brutal and triumphant. They must be pouring cognac, lighting cigars, toasting themselves, must have no inkling of what was happening without. She went back to the window. Two men, darkly clad, passing through the gate, into the shadows where the bodies had been dragged. She thought that one was Raymond himself. The urge to call to them was strong but instead, when she opened the window, she remained silent. She thrust her arm out between the bars, held the lit lamp to illuminate her face.

Raymond – she was sure it was he – emerged from the shadows and gestured, his message clear.

We know where you are. Go back. Be quiet. Be ready.

He stepped back from sight. She returned to the door and laid her ear against it again. More laughter from downstairs. It gave her a savage delight that they were oblivious of what was to come.

It was brief when it did. Just a single startled cry, instantly cut off, a sound of scuffling, a glass breaking, a chair overturned, resistance ended in under twenty seconds.

Then steps on the stairs, a knock on the door, a familiar voice.

"Mrs. Dawlish?"

Raymond.

*

Fournier and Brassard lay face-down on the dining room floor, mouths gagged with handkerchiefs, hands bound behind their backs and tied to their feet.

"Hog tied," Raymond said. "Uncomfortable and undignified, but it won't kill them."

Hatred blazed in Fournier's bulging eyes, terror in Brassard's. Florence felt no mercy.

"What's going to happen to them?" she said.

"They're coming with us."

She recognised the voice, turned and saw MacQuaid.

308

"I trust you weren't harmed, ma'am," he said.

"No time for explanations," Raymond said. "We must finish here and go. We can talk in the coach."

The two men who had overcome Fournier's helpers were dragging them into the room. Florence caught the smell of ether.

"Give them another dose before we go," Raymond told his people. They were English, built like prize-fighters. "Take off their boots and trousers. You can dump them in a drift later. Coats and jackets too. When they come to, they won't be eager to go out in this snow."

A search now of the house, top to bottom, Florence helping. It was clear that it was not a family residence, rather a villa furnished for summer rental, most likely taken now for a week or a month by Fournier. Cupboards, drawers and desks yielded no papers, nor Brassard's baggage either, but MacQuaid smiled when he looked in Fournier's attaché-case. He took it with him.

It was time to go. Out through the kitchen. A coach, with a pair of large, powerful beasts, was waiting outside, one of the two that had brought Raymond's group. Fournier and Brassard would lie on its floor, guarded by the prize-fighters. The driver was ready, whip in hand.

Raymond and MacQuaid led Florence out and down the road for two hundred yards, away from Dieppe, steadying her as her hem dragged through the ankle-deep snow. Another villa there, no lights, clearly unoccupied, gates open, and another coach and pair waiting in the darkness to the side, driver ready. They helped her in and Raymond called up "Nous sommes prêts! Allons-y maintenant!"

Past the darkened houses now, towards Dieppe, snow crunching beneath the wheels. As it passed the villa where Fournier's helpers lay drugged, the second coach, with the captives, pulled out to follow behind. The village was left behind, progress slow but steady, the horses surefooted, snow still carried on the wind.

"How did you find me?" Florence asked.

Raymond's lookout had been on the packet, had lost track of her when she left the customs shed with Brassard. That must have been when they turned down the alleyway at the side. He had been distraught when he arrived at Raymond's yacht.

"The *Shamrock*?" Florence had never seen the steam-yacht in daylight, only remembered its masthead and green starboard lanterns as they disappeared towards France with Agatha's fugitive brother. "How did she get to Dieppe?"

"We arrived in her two hours after your packet-steamer docked," Raymond said. "Sim Dawson's telegram told me that you were on your way to Lewes, but I didn't yet know which port you would go to. It could have been Folkestone or Dover either, besides Newhaven, so I sent people to all three. I'd kept the *Shamrock* at Folkestone for the last two weeks to cover all eventualities. I telegraphed ahead to her captain to raise steam and MacQuaid and I headed there by train directly after. We were already there when a telegram arrived from your guard at Newhaven to say that you were there with Brassard."

"It was a rough crossing in the *Shamrock*," MacQuaid said. "Longer than yours too, Mrs. Dawlish. We had to stand off until a pilot was available to take us in. When we came ashore, we found that your guard had lost you. That was a bad moment."

"We could only hope then that Hugo would come by rail, be delayed by the snow," Raymond said. "We thought it likely he'd be either Livitski or Fournier, so we went to watch the station. We were too late. The Paris train had already arrived and whoever was on it was long gone."

"It seemed hopeless," MacQuaid said, "but we waited for the next train, just in case. And we were lucky. We recognised Brandt. That was a surprise. Topcliffe's been concerned about him for some time and –"

"Who's Brandt?" Florence said.

"The man who came to buy the papers."

"He called himself Robinson."

"He's Korvettenkapitän Heinrich Brandt. Deputy Head of Intelligence of the Imperial German Naval Staff. We guessed immediately why he'd come, so we followed him. We had the coaches standing ready. The snow was a Godsend for masking us."

310

"He's an honourable man," Florence said. "Not much pity in him, but honourable." She laughed. "He went away thinking that I'm a scarlet woman. He also went away happy with his purchase."

The coaches had sheltered at the unoccupied villa and Raymond's men had kept watch on the house until Brandt had left. In a day or two he would be spreading the blueprints on a table in Wilhelmshaven, basking in the congratulations of superiors and peers alike. Their reaction would be different when the device underwent its first testing.

"Did you know that the Germans wanted the Dawlish Cam?" Florence asked.

"Topcliffe though they might," MacQuaid said. "He was suspicious after you told him that Livitski had said that Hugo wasn't concerned whether the documents were fakes or not. He thought that there must be more to it than that."

"We still have questions we want answered." Raymond said. "That's why Fournier and Brassard are coming with us."

*

The coaches trundled through snow-blanketed Dieppe just after three o'clock. The streets were deserted, only a few lamps casting isolated pools of light. They turned down a lane, halted before a double wooden-gate and MacQuaid dropped down and knocked. It swung open and the coaches entered, then closed again behind them. Somebody came forward with a lantern.

"All ready?" Raymond asked.

"All ready, sir. The pilot's squared and he's on board. Steam's up. We'll be gone within the half-hour."

It seemed to be the yard of a factory or mill.

"Be careful, Mrs. Dawlish." MacQuaid was handing her down and leading her to what proved to be a quayside. Black water, clustered barges, inland, not sea-going, shipping. A dog barked on one, grew tired of it, fell silent. This was a canal basin that must be linked to the main harbour. Florence was helped down the steps and into what must be one

311

of the *Shamrock's* lifeboats. The others followed. Raymond's prize-fighters escorted Fournier and Brassard, still gagged and bound, but loosened enough to walk.

The oars bit and the boat glided across the calm basin, through another channel and then, ahead, were bright lights along a quayside, a paddle-steamer moored alongside. The night's Newhaven packet had arrived and the mail she carried was being swung to shore.

And a little further on, a dark shape that showed its trim, elegant lines as they approached, smoke drifting from her funnel.

Raymond's *Shamrock*.

Chapter 30

They gathered at noon in the steam-yacht's small salon. Florence was well rested, for Raymond had insisted that she take his cabin. Both he and MacQuaid looked no less fresh, in contrast to Fournier and Brassard, who had been confined, unbound, in the paint locker.

Florence had been out on the bridge. The sky had cleared, but the sea was still rough. *Shamrock* was pitching as she steamed slowly north-east up the English Channel and into the dying wind. Florence had stood for long minutes, cold spray on her face, feeling cleansed and liberated for the first time in weeks.

"What do you want of me?" Fournier was trying to look defiant but his eyes betrayed fear.

Brassard, with traces of sea-sickness streaking his front, had begun stammering excuses when he was brought in. Told to hold his tongue, he was now slumped in shameless self-pity on a chair.

"What do we want of you, Colonel Fournier?" MacQuaid said. "Everything."

Raymond was nodding agreement. Florence saw that he deferred to MacQuaid, Topcliffe's man. Rich as Raymond was, he was here because he too was being used by the old Lucifer.

"Let's talk about Count Livitski," MacQuaid said.

"That Russian?" Fournier shrugged. "A good man with a pistol. That woman can tell you that." He jerked his head towards Florence. "I never saw him before that night at the Dieppe Casino."

"Not during the negotiations for a Franco-Russian military alliance? Not when you took money from him for yourself?"

No answer. No need. His paled face was answer enough.

"The formal treaty was near to signature, was it not?"

"I wouldn't know. I'm a simple soldier."

"But Minister Gauthier was greedy, wasn't he? He was holding out in the French cabinet against the deal. He wanted too large a Russian bribe before he'd support it. He went too far though, didn't he?"

"I told you. I'm a soldier. Nothing more."

313

"Livitski asked you to sort the matter out. Cleverly, two birds with one stone. Not just get rid of Gauthier, but oblige Her Majesty's Government to take stern measures against Russian nihilist and socialist exiles in Britain. And he knew enough about you that he was sure that you'd cooperate."

"This is all fantasy." Fournier was shaking his head, clasping his hands, knuckles white.

"Perhaps Mr. Brassard has something to say," Raymond said.

"I never saw the colonel before last night," Brassard was sweating, eyes bulging. "I never –"

"Never met Prince Obruchev either?" Florence said. "Maybe I mistook the nice old man you were talking to at Newhaven for him."

Blood drained from Brassard's face. "I don't know who you're speaking of."

"Maybe Prince Obruchev was lying then?" MacQuaid held up a document, six pages clipped together. He leafed through them, showed signatures scrawled at the bottom of each. "It's an affidavit, Mr. Brassard, duly witnessed. Obruchev was only too willing to sign."

Silence, while Brassard suffered. At last, voice hoarse and trembling. he said, "What do you want?"

"A full confession here and now. Your affidavit can wait until we get back to Britain."

"Say nothing, Brassard!" Fournier shouted.

"We'll land at Folkestone tonight, Brassard," MacQuaid said. "It'll be better if we've draw up the confession document by then and if you've signed. You wouldn't be prosecuted. You might even want to help us now and again in the future."

"You can't trust them," Fournier bellowed. "Don't do it!"

"If you don't cooperate, Brassard, we'll have a choice to make," MacQuaid said. "You can be charged in Britain for passage of secret documents to a foreign power. A trial in camera for treason, evidence from Mrs. Dawlish, sentence a foregone conclusion. Not death, mind you, but two decades at the least, hard labour, Dartmoor or Portland. The Portland quarries are particularly hard, I believe." He paused, let the words sink in. "Or the alternative. Formal deportation to France as a *persona non grata*. Police escort, official hand-over to the French authorities, no sneaking through as you did at Dieppe. We know that you have some serious charges to face there."

"The thought of the guillotine has always chilled me," Raymond said. "I've heard that if they hold up the head and shout the name, the eyes blink."

"It was the colonel's idea," Brassard's words came in a rush. "I never heard of this Russian count you've mentioned. I swear I didn't."

"But you had approached the Russian embassy in London and you offered to sell the documents," MacQuaid said. "The embassy must have passed on the word to Livitski. He guessed that you'd probably offered them to the French too. And you had, hadn't you?"

Brassard nodded.

"So Livitski contacted you, Colonel Fournier. He suggested that the plans would be of value to both France and Russia. That they'd be shared, a symbol of mutual confidence in a Franco-German alliance. And that would be signed in a month once Minister Gauthier had been removed."

"Was it Livitski who demanded that I bring the papers?" Florence felt cold fury. The betrayals were not only Fournier's and Brassard's. "Did he want me to see the assassination, want me to carry word back to London that measures must be taken about the Russian exiles there?"

Fournier shrugged. "You can't prove any of this."

"But Livitski had told you about Obruchev, hadn't he colonel?" MacQuaid said. "That he was a vain old man who didn't hesitate to let others suffer to further his ideals and who wanted money to pay for his comforts. So you asked Brassard to contact him."

Fournier looked away, didn't speak.

"You, Brassard," MacQuaid said, "you spoke to Obruchev. What did you tell him?"

"What the colonel told me. That two Russian nihilists would have been reprieved if Gauthier hadn't blocked it. He'd been Minister of Justice then. There'd been a bombing in a theatre in Paris and there was doubt if the two who were convicted were those actually responsible. But Gauthier didn't care. Guilty or innocent, they lost their heads. Any nihilists would have done as examples."

Brassard was voluble now. He held nothing back, confirmed what the white-haired patriarch had confessed in London. That he had convinced a foolish young man, and a foolish young woman, that killing Gauthier would be Propaganda of the Deed, justice no less than retribution. That he had money to fund it, though he did not say that it was coming through Brassard from Fournier. That nihilist sympathisers in France would meet them at Dieppe and hand over a pistol and two bombs. That there'd be others present at the Casino who would cover their escape.

"The bombs were for blast only, weren't they, Fournier?" MacQuaid said. "No nails, no buckshot. You saw to that. You didn't want to run the risk of yourself or Livitski being hit. Though it would hardly have mattered. You knew you'd both be under the table before the detonation, and Livitski would have dragged his ambassador down with him. You were both armed and ready, and determined that Obruchev's two dupes wouldn't live to be interrogated."

"I could have been killed!" Florence could not hold back her anger. It hurt her most that Livitski had wanted her there, had used her. She had been indebted to him before, had felt flattered that he had admired her, respected him for accepting with grace her rejection of his advances.

She turned to Fournier. "Livitski gave you the package that I was to give you. Did he mention me? Did he tell you how he had come by it?"

"He told me he'd found the package on the floor after the bombing," Fournier said. "Livitski said he was surprised when he opened it and saw what it was. He never mentioned you."

Raymond began to laugh. "But you didn't want them for France, did you, colonel? It would be for a private deal. You'd be selling them on to the Germans. As you did last night."

"That German, that man Brandt," Florence said. "He had your measure, hadn't he? He despised you as a traitor and knew that he couldn't trust you. That was why he wanted me, Mrs. Nicholas Dawlish,

316

wife of the Cam's inventor, to vouch for them. He despised me too, by the end of it, but he believed me."

She could see it all now. Livitski too had Fournier's measure, had guessed that the plans would never reach the French Navy, that he'd sell them on to France's and Russia's enemy. Her involvement had convinced Livitski that the plans were fakes just as it convinced Brandt that they were not. Livitski and his masters would be content. The expanding German Navy would waste money and effort that could otherwise be better spent. Topcliffe would have preferred it to have been the French but he'd settle for impedance of German ambitions.

"I don't think we need to fall out about this, Colonel Fournier," MacQuaid said. "No need for hints to the French press that there's an active traitor in the Army General Staff. No dropping of names. No extracts from Prince Obruchev's confession reaching certain members of the National Assembly and indicating that the late-lamented Minister Gauthier was the actual target in the outrage that killed him. No need for any of that, colonel, none at all."

"What's your price?"

"Just some information now and then. Some insights from French General Staff thinking. And maybe material that we'll supply you with to pass on to other parties we'll nominate. You'll hear from us in a month or two and now and again after that."

And Florence saw that something of the old brutal swagger was creeping back. Fournier had thrived in the world of deceit and betrayal before. He knew that he would again.

Worse than a blackguard, something far lower still.

"He can wait in the paint locker again until we can get rid of him," MacQuaid said to Raymond. "We've a little more to discuss with this fellow." He gestured to Brassard. "And I think Mrs. Dawlish will have more still."

She had.

*

317

The French fishing boat was a chasse-marée, *Shamrock's* captain told Florence as she watched Fournier leap across. It was one of a half-dozen that had been driven up the Channel by the recent weather and were now crawling back to their home port of Ouistreham on the Normandy coast. Its skipper was glad to accept Raymond's assurances that the French gentleman would pay generously for his passage and he had deftly caught the Gold Napoleon tossed across as a first instalment.

The boat fell away. *Shamrock* surged ahead and her bows swung around.

Towards Britain.

*

Shamrock docked at Folkestone late in the evening and Raymond wouldn't hear of Florence travelling onwards. He saw her settled in a hotel near the station, then followed MacQuaid and Brassard on to London by a late train. She wouldn't be needed there for two days at least. There were arrangements to be made before then. She would be informed when she was needed.

She slept well, breakfasted late, left for Portsmouth before noon, was back in the Southsea villa by three o'clock. Domesticity enveloped her like a warm, comforting blanket. There was pleasure in changing clothes, in ordering tea brought to her study, in avoiding the artless probes from Cook and Susan about where she had been, in opening letters, in reviewing grocer's and butcher's bills, in writing a cheque. Sim Dawson, still resident in the garden shed, was proving more useful than ever for odd jobs and Cook was hoping that he'd stay longer. Sleep would be sound in the knowledge that he was there.

This evening she would allow herself to forget what had passed in the last two days, would settle herself before the fire with a novel and go to bed with no fear other than for Nicholas. She would spend most of tomorrow attending to administration at the Seaman's Rest, would walk in the Esplanade regardless of weather, would visit Mudie's Library for new books.

And savour what was to come.

*

The telegram she awaited called her to London on the following Monday. A room was booked for her at the Charing Cross Hotel and she would be collected at ten next morning. Should she wish to stay longer, the cost of three further nights would be covered. She arrived in late-afternoon, resisted the urge to contact her father, or Agatha, even though the Piccadilly mansion was less than a mile distant.

No need now for a furtive morning exit through the kitchens to meet MacQuaid's clarence in Villiers Street. It stood waiting on the forecourt and he hurried towards her when she emerged from the front entrance. Pleasantries exchanged, he handed her into the vehicle and joined her.

"Where are we going?" she asked.

"A little surprise, Mrs. Dawlish. The admiral's suggestion. He thought it would give you satisfaction."

The driver knew his London thoroughfares. He was avoiding the main arteries, traffic-clogged at this hour, was weaving through a labyrinth of narrow, less frequently streets, and always northwards. Florence had guessed the destination now, was not surprised when they emerged on the broad thoroughfare of New Oxford Street and turned westwards along it.

Two police vans, drawn by a pair, were waiting close to the corner with Coptic Street. One was large but the smaller had barred windows high in its sides. No sign of constables but, as the clarence passed, MacQuaid leaned from the window and waved to a burly check-suited man standing near.

"Twenty minutes past ten, Mrs. Dawlish." He had flicked his watch open as the clarence turned the corner. "The Temple must be thronged with its devotees by now."

A turn now into Coptic Street, past the wine merchant's offices, the shop selling prints, the expensive stationer. A four-wheeler had halted

319

outside the familiar door. It was open and Mrs. Mobray had come out to help an old lady descend and enter the Temple.

"Wait!" MacQuaid called to the driver. The clarence pulled in to the pavement twenty yards from the door of Number 9. It had closed again and the four-wheeler moved away. It disappeared around the corner at the far end of the street just before a police van entered and halted, blocking access to other traffic. Florence looked back. At the New Oxford Street end, the larger police van she had seen there had sealed off entry there also. At both ends, uniformed constables were emerging from the vehicles. The small van with the barred windows was moving up the street. It halted directly outside the *Temple de la Beauté*. A dozen uniformed policemen came up from the corner, led by the man in the check suit.

"Superintendent Chatterton," MacQuaid said. "An efficient man."

He was ringing the doorbell now, his men ranked behind him. Florence recognised the attendant who opened, the surprise on her face, then shock, as Chatterton and the constables pushed past her and disappeared inside.

"Are we going in too?" Florence wanted to be there. This was better than she had ever hoped.

"No. Just wait. Watch."

The door opened again. Mrs. Bellamy emerged, constables flanking her, Chatterton following. She held her head high, moved with dignity, showed no fear. It was impossible not to admire her at this moment. She refused assistance to mount the steps into the closed van and entered without hesitation. The door closed behind her. The superintendent, standing on the pavement, waved to the driver and the vehicle pulled away.

"We'll follow," MacQuaid said.

"Shall I see her?"

I want her humiliation. Not for myself, but for Margaret Chalmers-Bolger, for God-knows how many more. She despised others, destroyed lives. It's her turn now.

"We need you to see her, Mrs. Dawlish."

320

"What about the customers?" There must a dozen at the least inside at this hour, waiting or undergoing treatment.

"They'll be allowed to leave once they've given their names. They won't like it, but that's all to the good."

"And the staff?"

"That'll take longer. Some will be glad to talk, even cooperate. Some won't. That's how it goes in such cases."

The clarence had left the street now, was heading eastwards past the British Museum, following close behind the police van. Its barred windows were too high for Mrs. Bellamy to see from, but that would not matter to her. Even now, her cold, cruel, calculating intellect would be focussed on possible trades, on evading justice.

*

It was another of the unoccupied houses beloved of Topcliffe, this time in a decaying street in Smithfield. The closed yard in the rear allowed the police van and MacQuaid's clarence to park unseen. Musty and unkempt, Florence sensed that it must have been empty for months, that someone might have died there, that relatives might still be feuding over a will. Topcliffe had been waiting in the drawing room at the front and Mrs. Bellamy was already seated opposite him when Florence and MacQuaid entered. He motioned to them to sit on a worn settee. No constables present, but two posted outside the door.

"I believe you've met Mrs. Dawlish previously, ma'am," Topcliffe said to Mrs. Bellamy.

She didn't look at Florence.

"I won't detain you long," he said. "You'll have a train to catch at three o'clock, ma'am. Or should I say Madame Hortense?"

"Mrs. Bellamy will do." She paused. "A train you said, sir?" There might have been something of hope in her tone.

"We'll come to that later," Topcliffe said. He withdrew papers from the briefcase by his side. "Your friend Mr. Brassard has been most

321

talkative. You're welcome to read his affidavit. It will take a few minutes, but we'll be patient."

She shook her head. "Just tell me what he said."

"Collusion in blackmail of a naval officer's wife. Sale of official secrets to a foreign power. He turned to Florence. "You'll testify to that, won't you, Mrs. Dawlish?"

"Yes, without hesitation."

"You fool," Mrs. Bellamy was looking at her now, hatred in her eyes. "Even if you do, your reputation will be destroyed in court, you'll —"

"There's more than that, of course," Topcliffe said. "All that's minor compared with assassination of a French minister in Dieppe. There's another affidavit here." He held it up. "From Kniaz Obruchev. It confirms what Brassard says in his. Two naïve Russian dupes whose travel and whose weapons were funded with money passed to the Prince by your associate Brassard."

"I don't know —" Mrs. Bellamy had paled. "I know nothing of this, Nothing. Brassard's lying."

Topcliffe held up his hands. "He may well be. It hardly matters, does it? And even if there was none of this, the game's up anyway. There's nothing here for you anymore."

"How?"

"In so many ways, Mrs. Bellamy," MacQuaid was speaking now. "Your files and documents are being gathered up this moment in your Temple. All the blackmail, all the exploitation, all the evidence that compromises so many people whom we'll be glad to know about. And not just in Coptic Street. That house you rent in St. John's Wood is being raided at this moment. You don't own any properties, do you? You're always ready for a quick departure, aren't you? Your business is gone as of this morning. Mrs. Dawlish will be sending a telegram across the Atlantic as soon as we leave here."

"To Mrs. Emily Daley of Indianapolis," Florence said. "And her friend Mrs. Mabel Bushwick will be arranging publication of articles in the *Columbia Home Gazette*. All the Nubian Balms and Empyrean Baths and Lotions of Samarra, all the lies and greed and bleeding gullible women dry. The Temple will be named, and you too, with all the nonsense about Madame Hortense and her *Woman's Mystery, Woman's Heritage.* Six articles, and maybe more, and all to be seized on by the *Fortnightly Review,* and others like, it for republication here."

"I'd suggest another name next time," Topcliffe said. "Not Hortense. Roxane perhaps, or Anouk, or Eloise. Something that'll sound exotic in Buenos Aires."

"Buenos Aires?" The words chilled Florence. "Do you mean that she's to walk free?" She saw a smirk on Mrs. Bellamy's face as understanding dawned upon her.

"Not quite free," Topcliffe said. He turned to Mrs. Bellamy. "The only account of yours we can trace, Mrs. Bellamy, is with the Capital and Counties Bank. Three hundred and seventy-three pounds, eight shillings and tuppence three-farthings at close of business yesterday. You'll give us a cheque for it. It'll cover your travel expenses."

Mrs. Bellamy shrugged. "I'll sign. What then?"

"To Liverpool today. A few nights in custody there. You'll be watched well, depend upon it. And a second-class ticket on the monthly service to the Argentine. A country with boundless opportunities, and thriving, I understand. You'll do well there. Better than anywhere in Europe after a word about you has been passed to certain people in France and Germany and Russia and a few more places besides."

Florence felt anger surging through her, made no attempt to supress it. She owed that much to the wretched woman who had died in a pond at Hampstead. "She's worth more than three hundred pounds!" she said. "Thousands more! In accounts you haven't traced." She wanted to see her beggared, broken, in despair, sewing mailbags with bleeding fingers in a filthy cell for twenty, thirty, forty years to come.

Mrs. Bellamy pointed at Topcliffe. "If he can locate whatever money's in England, then he's welcome to it. He knows that I'd have been a fool to keep it here."

Florence saw the faintest smile on Topcliffe's lips. Of admiration, even of respect perhaps. Himself and Bellamy, two of a kind.

"You're a busy lady, Mrs. Dawlish," he said. "We won't detain you longer."

She stood, shaking, but said nothing.

"Your Mrs. Chalmers-Bolger, was a very stupid woman," Mrs. Bellamy said, amusement and triumph in her tone. "Just remember that, Mrs. Dawlish. Or should I say, Mrs. Lacy? Of Bentley, Hampshire?"

Florence felt, as she had once before, the urge to launch herself on her and rake her fingernails across her face.

But she's her own punishment, a small internal voice reminded her. *What she is, degrades her, mutilates her spirit, lessens her. She carries her Hell within her.*

Florence moved to the door, stalked out, found the entrance hall, left through there rather than from the yard where the clarence that had brought her waited. She would find her own transport.

MacQuaid caught up with her.

"It had to be like this," he said. "You must understand that."

"*Raison d'etat?*"

She had once heard those words from Topcliffe. And some concerns were even stronger than justice, he'd also said.

"Nobody could gain anything from a prosecution," MacQuaid said. "There are too many ramifications. The woman's ruined. You must be content with that."

But Florence wouldn't be. Not ever.

"You're bothering me, Mr. MacQuaid," she said. "Let me pass."

For she had a telegram to send.

The End

Bonus short story *Britannia's Collector* follows, with a Historical Note thereafter

Britannia's Collector

7th February, 1866

Nazareno, Pacific Coast of Bolivia

It was an almost perfect natural harbour, protected from Pacific storms by the low island of Rafaela that was joined to the town by a stone causeway. The port was deserted now. The shipping that had packed it when HMS *Sprightly* had arrived two days before had been towed out, either by their own crews straining in pulling boats or by the port's four small steam tugs. Now everything from small brigs to huge four-masted barques, all here to load sodium nitrate, lay at anchor outside, waiting.

The chutes along the wharves, through which the fertiliser was shovelled into vessels moored alongside, were standing idle. The huge greyish-white heaps behind them looked forlorn. What could be seen from *Sprightly's* maintop of the town's streets inland from the harbour showed little movement. Word had spread quickly that the powerful British gunvessel was here to enforce payment of a debt. Moored by a bow anchor and by a kedge astern, she lay beam-on to the customs-house, range all but point blank.

"I'm damned if I'm waiting more than another day for the *Adour*," Commander Frederick Weatherby said. "You can never rely on the bloody French."

Sprightly's captain was sitting in the sternsheets of the gig stroking towards the landing steps before the port's customs-house. That would be the target – if it came to that – but this visit was to the British consul's office further along the harbour front.

"Do you think they'll agree to pay up, sir?"

The gunvessel's third officer, Sub-Lieutenant Nicholas Dawlish, rather hoped they wouldn't. The prospect of brief action was attractive. Ambitious young officers could get noticed on such occasions.

"Pay up? Of course they'll pay up," Weatherby said. "His Excellency just needs encouragement. There's no shortage of money – mining

325

licences, royalties on every ton dug, levies on every one exported. This place is as good as a gold mine."

The dust that covered every surface here, that dulled even the calm surface of the harbour, and cast a grey film on *Sprightly's* holystoned decks, attested that. The nitrate dug from the all but limitless accumulations in the Atacama Desert that stretched away behind the town was the most effective, and valuable, fertiliser on earth. Crop yields across Europe depended on it. Bolivia's economy was largely built on it. The country's short strip of Pacific coast, lying between the borders with Peru to the north and Chile to the south, gave access to the vast nitrate reserves. All three nations prospered from their own portions of the Atacama.

Successive governors of this coastal province had been intent on grandiose transformation of the town. The incumbent had outdone his predecessors by deciding that it needed a theatre, and now it had a large and very ornate one. It complemented the new street lightening, the new governor's palace – with an equestrian bronze stature of Simón Bolivar himself in front – and a new ayuntamiento, seat of the municipal government. Both buildings, unpleasing, if opulent, mixes of European and Spanish colonial architecture, fronted on to the bay. All was paid for by the loans that British and French banks had made to the provincial and municipality governments, with nitrate revenues as collateral. What interest had been paid so far had been financed by further loans, and now even those payments had stopped. Patience had run out in London and Paris and powerful men had brought influence to bear. That was why *Sprightly* now lay in the harbour and why her French counterpart should have been here by now also.

And the gunvessel was a brave sight, Dawlish thought, as she lay at anchor. The gentlest of onshore breezes carried light drifting smoke from the ochre funnel that rose above the white hull's bulwarks. None of the hinged sections that sheltered her guns had been dropped. There was nothing here to endanger her except whatever few antiques remained in the old Spanish star-shaped fort on Rafaela Island. There was a small garrison there but it had done nothing since firing a feeble salute when *Sprightly* had arrived.

The Bolivian guard drawn up at the top of the steps went through the motions of saluting. Their uniforms were gaudy, though threadbare, and even the officer looked slovenly. And no, Dawlish told them on Weatherby's behalf, no escort was needed for their short walk along the front towards the consulate, identifiable by a Union flag drooping on a flagstaff above. They had not brought seamen or marines ashore to protect them, a silent statement that the persons of Royal Navy officers, Britain incarnate, should be inviolate. Or else.

The consulate was in a large building in Spanish style, offices at street level, two residential floors above. The consul was honorary, a nitrate-shipper himself, established here for years, an Englishman married to a Bolivian, by all accounts a lady with powerful family connections. The consular office was located within his larger business premises.

"I'm not sure I can trust the fellow," Weatherby had told Dawlish after he had first met Henderson. "That's why I want you present when we speak to the governor."

The smattering of Spanish that Dawlish had picked up in the Caribbean had improved on this station and had made him valuable to his captain. The French he spoke with fluency – dating from a boyhood stay at the spa town of Pau – would be valuable when the French gunvessel finally arrived. He sensed that Ashton, *Sprightly's* first lieutenant, and Sanderton, her second, felt affronted by his aptitude for languages. Like many officers posted to the backwater that was the Pacific Station, both lived in a state of general resentment, even at the best of times.

Weatherby brushed away Henderson's offer of coffee and cigars after they were seated in his office.

"Has the governor answered?" he said.

"No, not yet. But His Excellency will. In due course. It's how things are here. They take time and he has many groups to keep contented." Henderson pointed to the two newspapers laid on his desk. "*La Gaceta*, has always supported him, and it's got the business community behind it. *El Libertador's* been undermining him for years. But now they're both calling for damn nearly the same thing. No repayments, no caving in to

327

foreign pressure, national sovereignty, Bolivar's heritage, liberty or death. His Excellency can never be president – and that's his goal – if he's seen to yield too easily on this."

"He promised us a reply by noon," Weatherby said. "It's one o'clock now."

"We must be patient. We can't hurry these fellows. It's not like Britain, captain. Not like France either. Monsieur Charpentier understands that."

"I don't give a tuppenny damn what the French consul understands. Weren't we clear enough when we met the governor yesterday? And on the day before?"

They had been clear enough only because Dawlish had been able to alert his captain to the Henderson's conciliatory weakening of the message when he translated it. Weatherby had insisted on its unambiguous restatement.

"We shouldn't sour relations. We don't want trade to be harmed," Henderson said. "There are big investments here. Not just my own firm, other British companies too. You can sail away after this business but we must stay afterwards. We need to be on good terms with them here."

"So we're to wait another day?"

"We could request another meeting with His Excellency tomorrow, captain. And if that French ship's here by then also it'll –"

"She should have been here by now," Weatherby said. "She was to leave Callao no later than a day after us. That was the agreement. It's just three days' steaming. We can't wait forever."

"If we were to telegraph Sir James in Lima." Henderson said. "Ask his advice. He's been ambassador for three years. He knows the country well and –"

"And Sir James damn-well requested action himself," Weatherby said. "He'll hear nothing more from us until the job's done."

It had been fortuitous that *Sprightly* was coaling at Callao, Lima's port, when Britain's and France's ambassadors – both of them accredited to Bolivia as well as Peru – had received instructions from their governments that resolute action was needed. Joint action. Another day and the gunvessel would have been heading back to the Royal Navy base at Esquimalt, on Vancouver Island. It would be completion of the long patrol that had brought her into every major port along the Americas' western coasts where there were British commercial interests. Vessels on the Pacific Station had little more to do than show the flag.

"But there's nothing can be done without the French," Henderson began again. "There's no sense antagonising His Excellency before they get here. He'll take it more seriously then. He will, I guarantee it."

"He'll take it more seriously then, but it might be too damn late," Weatherby said. "The French's last resort is usually their first resort. They'll open fire even if we won't. The customs-house, the ayuntamiento, maybe the governor's palace. And His Excellency will like it even less if they land, which they will. Bloody savages, the French, when they take it in their heads." He turned to Dawlish. "You've seen it too, haven't you? In China, wasn't it?"

"I won't forget it, sir."

He remembered the French as magnificent at the second, successful, storming of the Taku forts and at the Palikao Bridge six years before. But how they had behaved afterwards at Pekin – rapine, looting, slaughter of innocents, abuse of women – scarred his memory. Many British and Indian troops had been little better, but at least their officers had not turned a blind eye.

The French gunvessel *Adour's* presence at Callao also had been fortuitous and her captain had received similar instructions to Weatherby's. To present a demand at Nazareno, secure initial payment – nominal sums, twenty-thousand pounds in sterling-equivalent to the British creditors, as much again to the French. Sums to be lodged at the consulates in specie, not in paper. The remainder to be paid, with specified interest, in nine instalments in the next eighteen months. Appropriate measures to follow if agreement was not forthcoming.

"Beware of that bloody word 'appropriate'," Weatherby had told Dawlish. "There's nothing that can end your prospects faster. It means the decisions are yours. There'll be scant thanks if you're successful but you'll be disowned if you're not."

The meeting of *Sprightly's* and *Adour's* captains at Callao had not gone well. Dawlish had been the interpreter, first of formal expressions of mutual esteem, then for what should have been detailed planning. He had tried, without success, to smooth the distrust and frustration of each side with the other. Little concrete had been decided and he was not surprised that the French gunvessel had still not arrived. Perhaps her captain also knew about the word 'appropriate'.

Weatherby was standing up to go.

"Have you a larger Union flag, Henderson? Bigger than you have at present?"

"No."

"I'll send a larger one ashore for you," Weatherby said. "A few smaller ones too. Hang them from the windows here. Better the French have no doubt that this building's British. They won't bombard it. But if they land and their blood's up and their officers lose control then –"

"Should I move my family?" A tremor in the consul's voice.

"Have you daughters?"

"Three."

"If it were my family, I'd move them today, Mr. Henderson. I wouldn't wait. Let them stay with relations outside the town. Overcautious maybe, but in such matters –"

"It's sound advice," the consul looked alarmed. "Yes, yes, it's sound advice."

Dawlish guessed that the daughters and their mother would be packing within the hour.

"Maybe you've got a brother-in-law, Henderson?" Weatherby said.

The consul had no less than four.

"Perhaps one of them's a friend of His Excellency?"

They all were. The Lopez-Contreras were a respected family.

"Useful things, brothers-in-law."

"Do you want –"

"No, not at all. Just curiosity, nothing more. Let's just wait to see if there's a reply tomorrow. I'll wish you good day then, Mr. Henderson."

And Weatherby was smiling as the cutter pulled back to *Sprightly*.

*

330

Dawlish was touched that Weatherby suggested that Grove, *Sprightly's* marine lieutenant, and a half-dozen of his men, might escort him when he went ashore at eight o'clock next morning. Hostile feeling in the town about the gunvessel's presence was probably growing and might get out of hand.

"We managed well enough yesterday, sir," Dawlish said. "I'll be fine on my own today. I don't need an escort." He knew that young officers got remembered for statements like this.

"Good fellow," Wetherby said.

Sprightly's daily routine – holystoning, painting, hanging washing, airing hammocks – was in full swing, unaltered, as on the previous days, when the captain's gig brought Dawlish ashore.

The Bolivian lieutenant commanding the guard at the landing steps was one whom Dawlish had not seen before. He was his own age, more smartly turned out than the others, and he proved officious.

"Your business, señor?" He was blocking his path.

"I'm going to the British consulate, teniente. Other than that, it's none of your business."

"You're on Bolivia's soil, señor. That makes it my business."

Dawlish turned slightly, nodded towards the empty harbour, *Sprightly* there alone. And a mile beyond, in the open roadstead, a forest of masts, ships awaiting cargos.

"None of us want this," he said. "Not you, not me, teniente. And I'd take no offence if you saw fit to have me escorted to the consulate."

No answer, but the lieutenant turned, barked an order. Two slovenly soldiers fell out and stood behind Dawlish. He took no notice of them as he set out on the four-hundred yard walk towards the consulate. Four Union flags landed from *Sprightly* the previous afternoon had been strung from its window ledges. The larger flag that also came with them flapped weakly from the staff on the roof. Two bullock carts were being laden with furniture, carpets and paintings outside. Henderson's valuables were following his wife and family, who had been seen departing in a landau the previous afternoon. Damn good-looking women too, Weatherby had commented as he studied them through his telescope.

"Is there any word from His Excellency?" Dawlish asked.

He was seated now in the consul's office, pleasantries of greeting over. The clerks' desks in the large room outside, the centre of Henderson's business activities, were all but deserted.

"No word."

A pause. Dawlish felt himself being evaluated. The consul was wondering how much to confide, how much to say to him. But the fact that Weatherby had sent a junior officer in his place was confirmation of time indeed running out.

"If you'll excuse me, sir." Dawlish stood. "I must return to *Sprightly*. I'm instructed to report directly."

He had reached the door before Henderson said, "Wait."

Dawlish sat again.

"They take honour very seriously here," Henderson said. "Pride's important to them."

Maybe they should think of paying their debts then, Dawlish thought. The need to live within one's means had been drummed into him from childhood. But he didn't say it.

"His Excellency wouldn't want bloodshed," Henderson said. "I've heard that from a good source. Not from him, mind you, but from somebody who knows him well."

"He sounds like a decent man," Dawlish hadn't been authorised to give an opinion but this could do no harm.

"Decent and honourable," Henderson said "A man with the good of the population at heart. Not just at heart, but in fact. Foremost at all times. You can see that from what's been spent on this town to make life better. And friendly to business. Endlessly cooperative."

"I'll report that to Commander Weatherby," Dawlish said.

"And proud. A proud man also. Very proud."

"I'll report that too, sir."

"It's hard for a man like that to submit to threats. Not if he's to hold his head high. Dignity matters here."

"I'll tell Commander Weatherby that, sir."

Dawlish saw that the consul must think him endlessly obtuse, incapable of rising to hints. So he kept silent.

And the silence continued. It seemed like centuries. Dawlish was looking past Henderson now, out through the window to the harbour, empty but for *Sprightly*, and to the distant forest of bare yards of the nitrate-hungry ships moored beyond.

"It's not just the money," Henderson said at last. "It's there, I've heard. There's willingness. But there's pride at stake."

"Flesh and blood also," Dawlish looked back at the consul. "It's a pity there's not more time for negotiation, sir. Commander Wetherby feels that also." He was exceeding orders now. "But with the French on the way —" He forced regret into his voice, didn't finish the sentence.

"His Excellency's a humane man." Henderson paused, looked straight at him, held his gaze. "He cares about the poor especially. Like those packed into the narrow streets behind the ayuntamiento."

"Behind the customs-house also, sir?"

"No. Not behind the customs-house. There's just commercial property there. No lives at stake there."

"I understand, Mr. Henderson," Dawlish said. He looked to the clock on the wall. "It's nearly noon, sir. I'm to report by then. I must leave now, if you'll excuse me."

And Mr. Henderson, Her Majesty's consul, doyen of the British community and major nitrate exporter, made no attempt to detain him.

*

Sprightly's boiler had been maintained at harbour pressure, not enough to take her to sea, but sufficient to allow her to manoeuvre within the anchorage. Despite that, Weatherby ordered it stoked. Over-stoked. Black smoke spilled from the funnel as the new coal, too much of it added too soon, half-smothering the glowing embers in the furnace before taking light itself. The dark cloud drifted shorewards across the calm waters, urged by only the lightest of airs. Dawlish, waiting at the bow with the capstan party he commanded, saw the weakening billow dammed briefly against the façade of the customs-house before weaving past it in long, acrid tendrils. Several figures emerged, seemed bewildered, retreated inside, alarmed that something was afoot but not sure what. Two men, clerks perhaps, for they wore dark coats and white shirts, came out soon after and settled into clumsy half-runs towards the ayuntamiento. One disappeared inside and the other continued on to the governor's palace, two hundred yards beyond.

Dawlish looked back. Weatherby was on the bridge wing, scanning the buildings through his glass. A smile was hovering on his lips. A cluster had appeared on the steps before the ayuntamiento. There was movement too on the balcony that ran along the front of the governor's palace's entire first floor. A flash of light indicated the sun catching a telescope lens there. Somebody was looking back, was studying *Sprightly*. They must see that she had dropped her cutter and that it was already busy in the slow process of raising the kedge astern.

It took a half-hour before the smoke thinned and a faint glow shimmered above the funnel. Knots of spectators had gathered along the harbour frontage. Time now to move. The kedge had been recovered and the gunvessel had swung bow-on into the faint breeze from the ocean. Now the screw churned, a few revolutions only, but enough to urge *Sprightly* ahead, over her anchor. Dawlish acknowledged Weatherby's shouted command, gave the word to the capstan party. A dozen men threw their weight on the radial bars, took up the slack, pressed on. The pawls clicked faster as bare feet settled into a steady tread. In less than three minutes the anchor broke surface and hung suspended, ready for fast release.

Foam boiled beneath the counter as the screw bit and settled into quarter revolutions. The cutter lay unrecovered astern, oars shipped. It would shortly have more work to do. Up on *Sprightly's* open bridge, Weatherby and his first officer, Ashton, were flanking the quartermaster at the wheel. It was spinning over now, edging the bows to port, straightening again to head southwards, parallel to the harbour frontage at walking pace, past the deserted chutes and the nitrate heaps and toward the causeway linking town and fortified island. Small groups stood watching all along the shoreline, half in curiosity perhaps and half in dread. Now the bows were swinging over to starboard, carrying *Sprightly* into a long curve back towards the harbour centre. As she turned, Weatherby ordered a long blast on the steam-whistle. All

Nazareno must know that something was intended. Something unwelcome.

Sprightly was under the guns of the old fort on the island now. Ancient as they were, even muzzleloaders firing plunging solid shot could inflict serious damage on planked, unarmoured decks, had the will been there. And Weatherby, confident that there was no such will, not even token, had not unmasked or manned the weapons lying behind the hinged bulwark sections.

The gunvessel was at the harbour mouth now, straightening out, running northwards parallel to the inner shore, the customs-house passing first on the starboard beam and then the ayuntamiento and the palace. At a word from Weatherby, his first officer was reaching for the handle of the brass telegraph next to the wheel and ringing to the engine room for dead-slow ahead.

Dawlish, still at the bows with his capstan party, saw sunlight flash again on the palace's balcony, two locations, two persons at the least focussed on the now crawling gunvessel. The building was falling away on the starboard quarter and the town's northern fringe was straggling into a scattering of huts along a beach, fishing craft drawn up on it. Speed had died to a creep as the helm went over again, swinging the ship into a broad sixteen-point, half-circle, turn before straightening again. She passed southwards again parallel to the shore, a cable's length from it, her speed so low that a young child could have kept pace with her.

Past the palace now, Weatherby's gaze fixed dead ahead, ignoring the figures on the balcony. On then towards the ayuntamiento, and it too slipped past on the port beam until, just beyond it, the command rang out to release the anchor. A half-dozen slow revolutions astern killed the vessel's forward motion. Dawlish's party, familiar with the drill, performed with clockwork precision. The anchor splashed, the cable ran out, was then secured. It was good holding ground here and *Sprightly* weathercocked into the breeze, presenting her stern to the shore. The cutter stroked up under the counter, her pulling crew holding her stationary there as the kedge was lowered to her bow.

It took ten minutes to drop the kedge, draw in its cable, hold *Sprightly* moored fore and aft directly in front of the ayuntamiento. The crowd that had assembled there was thinning. Even at this distance, Dawlish saw that as well as the dark-clad municipal clerks there were women and children and old people also, many ragged and barefoot. Curiosity had drawn the residents of the narrow streets behind the building, the poor about whom His Excellency cared so much. Now fear was trumping that curiosity and dispersing them.

Dawlish could relax now – his party had done well. The demand for action was passing now to Sanderton, the second lieutenant, responsible for *Sprightly's* guns. Deckhands stood by the hinged bulwark forward that masked the single pivot-mounted sixty-eight pounder, ready to knock the securing pins away. Others, closer to the stern stood ready too, waiting to reveal the two broadside-mounted thirty-twos there. Sanderson's face was lifted towards the bridge, saw Weatherby nod to him, and he gave the order. The hammers pounded, the pins fell away and the tackles that held the bulwark sections from crashing down against the vessel's flanks were eased. Hinged along the deck-edge, the sections arced over slowly to lie flat against the plating below.

Now revealed to the watchers onshore, the sixty-eight pounder still lay locked fore and aft, but it was manned. At Sanderson's command, its crew strained on its tackles and pulled it over with deliberate slowness – it must look all the more menacing for that – until it bore directly on the ayuntamiento's facade. The thirty-two pounders aft were similarly exposed. Nobody watching from shore could know whether or not they were loaded.

Then nothing, nothing but the gunvessel's crew resuming normal duties, thin grey smoke drifting from the funnel, gun crews stood down, men not on watch dismissed, a lookout sent to the maintop with a telescope and night glass to scan the western horizon as the sun dropped. A relay of sharp-eyed young seamen would succeed him through the night.

Soft darkness engulfed *Sprightly,* her presence revealed only by her lanterns.

Waiting.

*

336

Dawlish was officer of the middle watch, and two hours into it, when a call from the darkness announced a boat approaching. He recognised Henderson's voice and directed hands to draw the craft alongside and assist him on board. The consul smelled of drink but there was a hint of elation about him when he asked to be brought to Weatherby. He waited with Dawlish in the cramped salon aft after the captain's steward was sent to his cabin to rouse him. Five minutes passed. When Weatherby arrived, he was in full uniform.

"His Excellency has bitten, has he?" Satisfaction in his voice.

"He wants to see us.," Henderson said. "You captain, me, the French consul. Now, as soon as possible."

"No French consul," Weatherby said. "He'll be told afterwards. He can sign whatever's put if front of him if it's needed."

"But His Excellency wanted him present and –"

"His Excellency can want what he damn well likes. That doesn't mean he'll get it."

Weatherby turned to Dawlish, took in his working rig. "You'd better change, best bib and tucker. You'll translate for me."

"I can translate," Henderson began. "I know these people and –"

Weatherby ignored him. "I'll see you at the entry port in five minutes," he said to Dawlish. "And have my gig ready. Mr. Henderson will be joining us."

The same Bolivian lieutenant who had challenged Dawlish the previous day was waiting at the landing steps. Illuminated by street lamps bought by a portion of the loans now at issue, his men were drawn up as an honour guard. They made a fair hand of swinging their rifles into a salute. Formalities over, the lieutenant was courtesy incarnate, pleased to welcome *el capitán ingles* on behalf of His Excellency and to escort him to the palace.

They entered through an arched gateway set in the frontage and passed into the central courtyard – the palace was a hollow square. A half-dozen donkeys stood tethered there. Soldiers, supervised by their officers and sergeants, and watched by ledger-ticking clerks, were loading small sacks into the wicker paniers. Through lit windows at ground level,

Dawlish glimpsed two manual printing press in use. There was a frantic air about the operators as they swept inked poster-sized sheets from the beds and replaced them with blanks. Drying copies hung like washing on lines stretched across the back of the room.

A grandiose white marble staircase, wide enough for a dozen men to climb abreast, led up to the governor's own offices. A flunky in livery waited there and conducted them to him. He was sitting at a huge desk, bare but for two ormolu lamps and a small copy of the Bolivar statue outside, the whole room lit up by kerosene, the night air heavy warm and here despite the open windows and high ceiling. White haired, goatee-bearded, watery eyes behind thick-lensed spectacles, linen immaculate, he could pass in London as a superannuated-banker or university don. A younger man, no less perfectly dressed despite the hour, and probably a secretary, stood to one side behind him, holding a portfolio.

Once the greetings and formalities and apologies for a summons at such short notice were past – with exquisite courtesy on both sides – the business itself was completed in ten minutes. There had been a procedural delay, His Excellency said, but now it had been resolved. Señor Henderson, as a man of business, and Commander Weatherby, as a man of action, would understand. The necessary papers discussed at previous meetings could be signed directly and the funds in question transferred before sunrise. For security, it was better to move such large sums in darkness, even when escorted.

The secretary coughed, the governor inclined his head and listened to a whisper from him, turned again to the visitors. Would Señor Charpentier be joining them?

Weatherby listened to Dawlish's translation, then said "Tell him that we're also representing Monsieur Charpentier. Tell him that everything on those donkeys, British or French payment, it makes no difference, goes to Henderson's office." He noticed that the consul was about to protest but he stopped him with a gesture of his hand. "Tell His Excellency that Henderson will settle matters with that Frenchman afterwards. And another thing, tell him we'll need an armed guard of his own people placed on the British consulate. If he isn't willing, tell him I'll land bluejackets and marines to do the job for him."

Dawlish translated in more diplomatic terms and His Excellency had no objection to the proposal. He had one request however. Could the English warship re-anchor further out in the harbour? Clear of the entrance? And ideally at eight o'clock? Weatherby was glad to agree and hoped that he'd see vessels loading nitrate at the chutes before *Sprightly* departed.

At a word from the governor, the secretary stepped forward, opened the portfolio, laid the documents inside it on the desk. They were the same as had been presented previously and they had been disputed then. No objections now, no request for revision.

His Excellency passed the consul a silver inkwell and a gold pen and invited him to sign. He asked if there was a consular seal and Henderson had indeed brought one with him. He pressed it into red sealing-wax dribbled beneath the signature by the secretary. The same process followed for a second copy.

"Pass me the pen," Weatherby said. He saw Henderson hesitate but he took it from him anyway. He signed with a flourish, then paused before he put the letters RN behind his name. "Better than any bloody seal," he said to Dawlish in an undertone. "Always remember that."

The secretary lifted the papers, turned them towards the governor, dipped the pen in ink and handed it to him. His Excellency made to sign but, at the last moment, nib hovering above the paper, he asked Dawlish, "Your capitán understands eight o'clock? Not before, not later."

And Weatherby confirmed it. Eight o'clock to the second.

Now His Excellency's signature, twice the size of Weatherby's, followed by his seal. Then handshakes, thanks, mutual appreciation, assurance that Henderson would secure Monsieur Charpentier's signature later in the day. The secretary produced a large cardboard tube and rolled the British copy into it for the consul.

As they passed down the steps to the courtyard, two gentlemen were being escorted up them. Both looked bleary eyed, and hastily dressed. One nodded to Henderson as he passed but the other stood for a moment and bowed before going on. Neither acknowledged Weatherby and no words were exchanged.

"Uribes of *El Libertador* and Escrivá of *La Gaceta*," Henderson said when they were gone.

The donkeys were gone from the courtyard but the printers were still busy. Workmen, some barefoot, were scurrying out with armfuls of printed sheets and disappearing out through the courtyard entrance.

The officious lieutenant was waiting for them. His men stamped into a salute and formed again into an escort.

"I told you they had the money," Henderson said to Weatherby as they passed along the seafront. "It's how things go here. It just takes patience."

"And the later instalments? D'you think you'll see them?"

Henderson laughed. "You might be coming back. You or someone like you. And not just once either. It's a game. That's what it is, a game, and they play it well."

They were level with the ayuntamiento now. A dozen identical posters lined the front, huge black letters at the top, smaller print below At the end of the façade, a man was up a ladder steadied by a companion and busy sticking more. Down the street running along the side, Dawlish saw similar pairs. The walls of every next building passed were also in the process of being plastered. The men were mostly ragged and barefoot, stevedores and labourers perhaps, wageless since suspension of the nitrate loading, grateful to be roused from sleep to earn a few centavos. By sunrise half the town would be covered by posters.

"Find out what they say, Dawlish," Wetherby said. "I'll continue to *Sprightly*. I'll send the gig back for you."

The lieutenant did not protest, but he ordered two soldiers to follow Dawlish. He took no notice of them and walked up to the nearest poster. The paste that held it to the wall had soaked through and the ink was blotched, running in places. The word *Proclamación* at the top, in font large enough to span the sheet, followed by smaller letters below to confirm that it was *a todos los ciudadanos de Nazareno*. At the bottom the governor's name and, in between, two dozen lines of text. Agents of foreign usurers had threatened merciless bombardment, slaughter of mothers and fathers, children, infants at the breast, the old and the infirm. With a heavy heart, but with love for his fellow heirs of Bolivar

340

exceeding all else, His Excellency had authorised an unreasonable payment to stay the tyrants' hands. If some might see shame in this, then it was a cross that he would be content, and proud, to bear alone.

Dawlish read it through twice, then transcribed in pencil in the notebook he carried. Weatherby would be pleased to see it.

And His Excellency might be one step closer to the presidency of the republic.

*

Small groups began to assemble on the seafront wharves soon after sunrise. By seven o'clock they had fused into a single crowd. It was especially thick before the palace, waving flags and cheering each time His Excellency appeared on the balcony, a coloured sash across his torso, his hand raised as if in benediction. Good to his word, a full platoon of soldiers was standing guard on Henderson's office and the wealth lodged in the safe inside. An irate Monsieur Charpentier might have arrived there by now to negotiate sharing. Two bands arrived and began to blare in competition what were probably patriotic airs. Newspaper vendors moved through the throng. One of the more enterprising had himself rowed out to *Sprightly* to sell the special editions of *El Libertador* and *La Gaceta*. Even less prestigious publications, one of them just a single double-sided sheet, had rushed out something to honour this day of deliverance. Dawlish, like the other officers, bought copies of them all as souvenirs. Regardless of affiliation – and enmities were bitter between parties here, he understood – all hailed His Excellency as the hero of the hour, a man of honour, a man of humanity, a patriot on whom Bolivar himself would have smiled.

Sprightly waited. The kedge had been recovered in the last hour of darkness and she was held now by the bow anchor only. The boiler fires had been stoked with care – no need for black smoke now, nor for full pressure. The bulwark sections had been raised to mask the guns. Weatherby, still in full uniform, was consulting his watch on the bridge and counting the last minutes to eight o'clock and Dawlish, in working rig again, was with the capstan party at the bows.

Fresh cheering now as a small tug puffed from a wharf and out across the mirror-calm waters of the bay towards the moored shipping outside. Two more followed, and then a fourth strained in their wake. Well before noon the first of the waiting vessels would be manoeuvred beneath the chutes to be obscured by clouds of billowing dust.

Now Weatherby was snapping his watch closed, nodding towards Dawlish. The bridge telegraph was ringing the signal down to the engine room for a brief churn of dead-slow ahead and the men at the capstan bars took up the cable slack. The anchor-raising went like clockwork, as well it should in this dead calm. The cheering from the shore swelled and drowned the bands as *Sprightly* crawled ahead, built speed, and headed at quarter revolutions towards the broad harbour mouth. She anchored just outside. The clamour from the town faded and a large barquentine, the first of the waiting vessels to have engaged a tug, was already under tow toward the chutes.

Weatherby called Dawlish to the bridge. He was in the wing, a telescope in the crook of his arm.

"Not a bad days' work, Mr. Dawlish," he said. "Not a bad night's either, eh? And everybody happy."

"Not bad at all, sir."

"And something there to warm your heart, Mr. Dawlish." Weatherby handed him the telescope, pointed to the north-west. "Here. Take a look."

A smudge of smoke and a vessel just hull-up on the horizon. Dawlish adjusted the eye-piece, sharpened the image.

It might have been *Sprightly's* sister. But then all gunvessels, regardless of nationality, looked much the same.

"The *Adour*, sir."

"Too late to do any damn good."

And then *Sprightly's* captain laughed.

"It's always good to get one over on the bloody French," he said.

The End

342

A message from Antoine Vanner and a Historical Note

If you've enjoyed this book, I'd be most grateful if you were to submit a brief review to Amazon.com or Amazon.co.uk. If you're reading on Kindle you'll be asked after this to rate the book by clicking on up to five stars. Such feedback is of incalculable importance to independent authors and will encourage me to keep chronicling the lives of Nicholas and Florence Dawlish.

If you'd like to leave a review, whether reading in Hard Copy or in Kindle, then please go to the *"Britannia's Morass"* page on Amazon. Scroll down from the top and under the heading of "Customer Reviews" you'll see a big button that says "Write a customer review" – click that and you're ready to get into action. A sentence or two is enough, essentially what you'd tell a friend or family member about the book, but you may of course want to write more (and I'd be happy if you did!).

You can learn more about Nicholas Dawlish and his world on my website www.dawlishchronicles.com. You can read about his life, and how the individual books relate to events and actions during it, via www.dawlishchronicles.com/dawlish/

You may like to follow my weekly (sometimes twice-weekly) blog on www.dawlishchronicles.com/dawlish-blog in which articles appear that are based on my researches, but not used directly in my books. They range through the 1700 to 1930 period.

By subscribing to my mailing list, you will receive updates on my continuing writing as well as occasional free short-stories about the life of Nicholas Dawlish. Click on: www.bit.ly/2iaLzL7

Historical Note

In the Victorian Era, luxury beauty parlours, in addition to selling exotically named and outrageously overpriced treatments and cosmetics, could provide cover for very sophisticated blackmail activities. The most notorious of such operators was "Madame Rachel" Leverson, whose establishment in New Bond Street, London, like her pamphlet that publicised it, was named "Beautiful for Ever." She enjoyed considerable success until her exploitation, and beggaring, of a middle-aged widow led to her prosecution in 1868. This lady, recipient of love-letters allegedly sent by a prominent nobleman, finally appealed to the authorities. She was however ridiculed in court as "a senescent Sappho" during Madame Rachel's subsequent trial. Lord Ranelagh, the actual nobleman whose name had been used, without his knowing, attended the trial. The judge invited him to sit on the bench next to him. The noble lord joined in the laugher at the widow's gullibility when the letters were read out. The jury was unable to reach a verdict but, after a second trial. Madame Rachel received a brief prison sentence. On release she was soon back in business and was successful for several years more. One wonders how many unfortunate women in total were victimised but who kept silent for fear of humiliation in open court should they or their families press charges. At last, convicted of fraud again, Madame Rachel died in prison in 1880.

Henry Jackson (1855 – 1929), a real-life character who appears in *Britannia's Morass* when a lieutenant in HMS *Vernon*, was to have a stellar career. He joined the navy in 1868 and his service included action ashore in the Zulu War in 1879. He was appointed First Sea Lord – professional head of the Royal Navy – following resignation of Admiral Lord "Jacky" Fisher over the failure of the Gallipoli Campaign in 1915. Jackson's greatest contribution may however have been his pioneering in radio technology. He was the first person to achieve ship-to-ship wireless communication over a distance of three miles and his cooperation with Guglielmo Marconi led to development of a fleet wireless communication system in the early 1900s. His scientific achievements were recognised by election as a Fellow of the Royal Society in 1901 and he achieved the highest naval rank, Admiral of the Fleet.

Adam Worth (1844 – 1902), alias Henry Judson Raymond, also existed in real-life and featured previously in both *Britannia's Shark* and *Britannia's Amazon*. He was to continue his successful criminal career – and double life as a respected socialite in Britain – until 1892, when he was convicted in Belgium for an uncharacteristically bungled robbery of a major cash transfer. He served four years and on release promptly stole £4000 worth of diamonds in London to finance his new operations. He returned thereafter to the United States and negotiated a deal with the Pinkerton

Detective Agency. This involved return of the Gainsborough portrait of The Duchess of Devonshire, which Worth had stolen in 1876, against a payment to him of $25,000. He returned to London and died there. He was buried, under the name of Raymond, in Highgate Cemetery, not far from Karl Marx. In his own lifetime he was referred to by senior Scotland Yard officers as "The Napoleon of Crime" and is believed to have been the inspiration for Sir Arthur Conan Doyle's Professor Moriarty, whom Sherlock Holmes described by the same title.

The Casino at Dieppe was indeed as vast and ugly as Florence found it in 1884. It was to play its part in history some six decades later, at the time of the disastrous Anglo-Canadian "reconnaissance in force", Operation Jubilee, of 19th August 1942. This landed a force of some 6000 troops, supported by 58 tanks, mainly along the beach and between the harbour and the Casino. This latter had been heavily fortified by the Germans. Few of the troops, and none of the tanks, got off the beach. The park where Florence met Livitski was lashed by fire from the Casino, making it impossible maintain an advance into the town. The British and Canadian survivors were evacuated after ten hours, having suffered some 3600 killed, wounded or captured. 106 RAF aircraft were lost as well as 33 landing craft and a destroyer. The lessons learned so expensively in this ill-conceived operation were to prove of significant value when Allied Forces invaded France in June 1944.

Readers of *Britannia's Collector* will probably have noted that Bolivia does not have a sea-coast today. It did indeed have one in 1866 however but it was to lose it after the War of the Pacific 1879 – 1884. In it, Chile fought the combined forces of Peru and Bolivia to extend its hold over the Atacama Desert's nitrate accumulations. This vicious conflict was fought at sea, in the Atacama and in the Andes mountains. Chilean forces ultimately proved victorious. Bolivia was forced to cede its coastal regions, and its share of the Atacama, in the peace settlement. From that time, Bolivia has been a landlocked country and its lack of access to the Pacific still rankles.

Old Salt Press is an independent press catering to those who love books about ships and the sea. We are an association of writers working together to produce the very best of nautical and maritime fiction and non-fiction. We invite you to join us as we go down to the sea in books.

Our writers are Rick Spillman, Joan Druett, Linda Collison, V. E. Ulett, Alaric Bond, Seymour Hamilton and Antoine Vanner, all of whom write fiction. Joan Druett, in addition to her novels, also writes meticulously researched maritime history.

Visit: oldsaltpress.com/about-old-salt-press

Made in the USA
Middletown, DE
14 January 2021

30051719R00192